THE TOLLS must GO

Also by Scott Burgess

Once to Die

THE TOLLS must GO

A Novel by

Scott Burgess

PUBLISHING

First Edition
Printed in the United States of America

Library of Congress Catalog Number: 2007941630
ISBN-13: 978-0-9667246-9-1

Cover photo: Jennifer Casto

Disclaimer:
This is a work of fiction.

Wythe-North Publishing
P.O. Box 1208
Proctorville, OH 45669

www.wythe-north.com

Acknowledgements

Thanks to Annette for the brainstorming sessions that directly led to this book. Thanks to Tammy for her enthusiastic review of the semi-finished product. Thanks to Mrs. Duty (who recently passed on into that good night) for her instruction in literature and English. Thanks to Mr. Davis for providing the typing skills that, without which, neither this book nor *Once to Die* would have happened. Thanks to Marshall University for stoking the coals. Thanks to Drema for introducing me to Beckley and her citizenry. And thanks to Mark for giving *Once to Die* and this book the 'winning' look...

A special second thanks to Bill and Cheryl for taking the chance in the first place...

Dedication

Dedicated again to Hannah and Katie.

Read this at night.

Golf with me in the daylight...

I would also like to dedicate this book to my sister-in-law Mary Lynn.
She was an avid reader and a really good friend.
She was looking forward to this publication.
We miss her laughter the most...

1

Annie Wolf could feel the sweat run down her back as Robert C. Byrd, senior senator from West Virginia, regaled the Beckley crowd outside the courthouse with stories of his youth not too far from this 'stoic, historic setting.' This Fourth of July was an unusually hot one. Annie scanned the crowd, seeing the assessor, the sheriff, a couple of magistrates, the county clerk, and a multitude of faces that even God himself might not recognize on a busy street. A slight breeze brought a moment's relief then died as soon as it had begun. Annie shifted on the chair and could feel her sweaty legs sticking to the metal through the fabric of her pants.

"It was in 1932, or was it '33..." Byrd continued, hesitated, then continued again, "that on the steps of this courthouse that I first received what could only be called a vision, a vision of public service to the good people of this community."

Annie fanned herself with her reporter's notebook. Being the 'cub' reporter for the Beckley Register-Herald, she had to cover countless boring speeches this day while her colleagues were at home grilling hamburgers. And she had heard this particular speech, or a version of it, several times before. The white-haired, fiddle-playing Byrd rarely, before the home folks, prepared a stately oratory. Rather, he simply spun his folk wisdom in lieu of hard-hitting issues like global warming, which was definitely in full force on this day.

"In '56, during the Eisenhower years..." Annie stood and slowly made her way out of the grassy aisle and to the back of the crowd. She could feel the sweat momentarily cooling her legs as the fabric separated from skin. While Byrd droned on, she scanned the crowd again for faces she might have missed while seated earlier. A wave caught her eye. It was a county deputy that she had been working with on a homicide case in Shady Spring. She smiled and made her way to his perch near the fountain. He stepped down from the knee-high wall and shook her hand.

"Did the family talk with you last night?" Eddy Thompson asked eagerly. This particular murder had vexed the local police since its occurrence three weeks ago.

Annie shook her head. "No, we talked for maybe a half hour, but they were very cautious about everything they said. It was like they were being coached by Johnny Cochran."

Eddy laughed. "I don't think these people could afford the deceased Mr. Cochran. I'm not even sure they could afford Taylor there." Eddy nodded his head in the direction of the town drunk, Jimmy Taylor, asleep on a bench twenty feet away. "Can you imagine, sleeping through one of Byrd's speeches?"

Now it was Annie's turn to laugh. Thirty-four, never been married, the dark-haired reporter motioned for her photographer to get a picture of the sleeping drunk. Her pointing told the photographer to angle the photo so that Byrd's image was beyond the unconscious, alcoholic mass of flesh.

"EDDDDDDDDDDDDDDDDYYYYYYYYYYYY!!!" the voice called out from across the courtyard. The entire gathering stopped, including Byrd, to watch the young cousin of Eddy Thompson trot through the crowd to where Eddy and Annie stood. 'EDDY!' the voice called out again, this time close enough to leave powder burns. Byrd's speech was still on hold while the youth reunited with his long lost cousin.

"Ralphie," Eddy hissed, "would you quieten down, Byrd's in the middle of his speech."

Ralphie Johnson turned and now realized that the gathering was indeed, collectively, staring at him. He threw up his hand in Byrd's direction and called out, "Sorry Bob, go ahead!" Byrd smiled weakly as the crowd turned to face him. His train of thought was entirely lost. With hands in pockets, he tried to pick up where he left off.

"In 1946, just after the war..."

Ralphie slapped his older cousin on the back quite hard and asked, again way too loudly, "How the heck have you been Eddy?"

"Shhhhhhhhhh, you wanna keep your voice down? I've been fine. How's Aunt Minnie?" Eddy's embarrassment was apparent as he nervously glanced around to see the chief of police looking his way.

Ralph had finally brought his voice down to a decibel level that was acceptable, given the nature of gathering. "She's fine, her arthritis ain't near as bad in the summer as it is in the fall and winter." Ralph paused for just a second before continuing. "Did you know Aunt Bertie wrecked her Escort last week with Mom going to the store?"

Eddy shook his head. "Yeah, I saw the report. She ok?"

"Yeah," Ralphie replied matter-of-factly, "the car and the telephone pole are totaled though."

It was Annie who spoke up. "Did that happen out on 3, there close to the Go Mart?"

"Yeah," Ralphie nodded his head, for the first time noticing the raven-haired lady, "last Thursday."

Annie's eyes showed recognition. "I covered that. She said a moving truck ran her off the road? I can't remember."

Ralph shook his head no. "She said it was a horse van."

"That's right," said Annie, "she even gave a very detailed description of the van. Didn't she cut her head on the dashboard?"

"It bled a lot worse than it was," Ralph explained, "they didn't even have to put stitches in her head, just some of that skin tape they use nowadays."

An awkward silence passed between the three as Annie looked over the crowd to Byrd who now seemed to be up to 1964 for what she believed to be the second time. She could feel Ralph looking her up and down, and could also feel Eddy's distaste at Ralphie's actions. Eddy broke the silence.

"Listen Ralph, we were talking official business here, could you..." Eddy nodded his head back toward the gathered throng, causing Ralph's head to nod off in the same direction.

"Oh, ok," Ralphie finally agreed as the light went on inside his head, "sure, right. Listen..." he paused, offering his hand to the lady, "it was nice meeting you. I didn't catch your name."

"Annie," she smiled politely with a nod of her head, "Annie Wolf."

"Well it was sure nice meeting you Annie," Ralphie gushed, his pleasure obvious. He shook her hand for a long time then released it, disappearing back into the crowd. Eddy exhaled a good bit of air.

"Sorry about that," he apologized, running his fingers through his thick dark hair, "you've heard the expression 'that boy just ain't right'? Ralphie was who they said that about first."

Annie laughed and said that's ok. She recounted her conversation with the family of the victim from last evening and Eddy could not believe their lack of cooperation. It just didn't make sense. Their son gets whacked, execution style, and the family clams up. The obvious answer was that they had been threatened by the murderer or someone close to the murderer, but still this was their son. Annie promised to share any news with him, and Eddy would do the same. A nice round of applause echoed off the downtown buildings as Byrd concluded his remarks and waved to the crowd. Governor Manchin retook the podium and lavished praise on the man who brought highways, federal courthouses, and the FBI to 'almost heaven' West Virginia.

Annie eased her way up Main Street in the back of the crowd as Manchin was preparing to introduce another public servant of considerable national renown, Senator Jay Rockefeller. She was sure she'd already heard a version of his yet-to-be-given speech too. So, with stomach growling, she ducked into the courthouse to get a snack at the vending machine. She was digging through her purse for change as she approached the windowed vendor, sensing someone else was making their final selection. The gum pack cascaded and landed softly in the tray below just as she had rustled up fifty-five cents for her Snickers Crunch. The person in front of her turned abruptly and the two crashed together, her purse dumping out on the floor and the change rolling in wide arcs across the broad, marbled hallway.

"Ralphie!" Annie cried in anguish, the contents of her purse littered at her feet. Ralph was beside himself in embarrassment.

"I am SO sorry," he said earnestly, "I was daydreaming." Just as he bent to retrieve her purse items Annie did the same, their foreheads thudding soundly together. 'Ouch' they both said in unison, standing and backing away in some pain. Exasperated Annie bent down again and on her hands and knees approached her purse trove. Ralphie began scanning the floor for change he had knocked out of her hand. Finally, they were both on their feet again, none too much the worse for the encounter.

"I am so sorry," Ralphie repeated himself, handing her the errant change, "can you forgive me purty lady?"

Annie's head drew back at this forward pronouncement. "Yeah sure, no problem," she muttered in her flattest tone, recounting the money in her hand. Ralphie stepped out of the way as she approached the vending machine with which she should have completed her transaction several minutes earlier. The coins filtered into their designated slots, a credit of fifty-five cents showing on the digital screen. Pressing B-53, her Snickers Crunch lolled to the front then got hung on the silver spiral just as it was about to drop. She sighed and thumped her already bruised forehead onto the clear glass.

"Here, I can get that." Ralphie gently pushed her aside and stood before the shiny, sweet-filled monolith. He blew into each hand then, with more deliberation than was truly needed, he placed a hand on each side and began shaking the machine violently, the sounds echoing up and down the hallowed, empty halls. The Snickers Crunch had long fell, as had a bag of chips and a Nestle Crunch, before Ralphie let go of the machine. All Annie could think about was the amount of law enforcement in the general vicinity, along with dignitaries from Washington and Charleston who would see her led away in cuffs over a fifty-five cent candy bar.

"Here you go," Ralphie said with a smile that stretched from ear to ear, obviously sure that she was pleased with his wiry strength. "You cain't let these machines cheat you, they ain't no way of getting your money back. Believe me, I've tried."

Annie smiled weakly and accepted the candy bar she had originally intended to purchase but not the chips or second candy bar. "You keep those," she instructed, "you're the one who EARNED them." Her excessive emphasis on the word 'earned' went unnoticed by Ralph, who had already broke open the bag and was enjoying his just reward.

"You know," he said, flecks of chips spraying between his lips, "this woulda never happened if you hadn't been so purty." Adding more chips to his mouth, his cheeks now looked like a chipmunk's preparing for a long winter. At this moment, his good-natured innocence shone through more so than his oafish clumsiness or his over-the-top enthusiasm. With more compassion, Annie looked at the young man—mid-twenties she guessed, and saw a good heart—a bull in a china shop—but good nonetheless. She smiled her first sincere smile to him since their initial meeting a half-hour earlier.

"Now why would you say something like that?"

"Like what?" he questioned.

"Like I'm purty," she deadpanned, using his pronunciation rather than 'pretty'.

Ralphie nearly choked on a mouthful of chips, the bag now empty and wadded up in his hand. Catching his breath, he swallowed deeply a couple of times then looked down to his feet, somewhat embarrassed. "You ARE purty," he said, gulping, "you're about the purtiest thing I've ever seen. You remind me of Tom Cruise's wife. Ex-wife." He looked back up to her and their eyes met. It was Annie who looked away, embarrassed by his earnest compliment.

"Sheesh," she muttered, trying to break the awkward moment in half, "hasn't this been a hot summer already?"

"Yeah," Ralphie agreed wholeheartedly, "our garden's done plumb cracked and dried up." Annie smiled at his use of the local vernacular, a talent she had never developed, even though she grew up in neighboring Princeton. Ralph continued, eyeing the notebook in her hand. "Do you work for the TV station?"

"No," Annie confessed, "newspaper. Register-Herald."

Ralphie nodded his head in approval. "How come y'all got rid of Garfield?"

"Pardon?" Annie asked.

"Garfield, the comic strip. Y'all dropped it last month."

She now understood. The paper had received hundreds of letters and emails protesting the change on the funny pages. "The editors saw a way to save a buck. They can get that new strip Shadowlife a lot cheaper than they can Garfield. It's pretty tight down at the paper right now."

"So what do you do?"

"I cover the courthouse and downtown. So," she said, sensing an opportunity to make her escape, "I'd better get back out there and see what Rockefeller has to say." She was easing her way around the young man when he asked yet another question.

"This is kind of a dead town ain't it? I mean, for a newspaper reporter of your caliber."

Right, thought Annie, you don't know me from Adam but you're putting me on a Bob Woodward pedestal. "Yeah," she admitted, "it has been kinda dull around here, particularly since the New Year. There's nothing going on that's really newsworthy. I interviewed a couple of twins down at Shoney's the other day, just because they're twins, and that made the front page."

"Jeez Louise," exhaled Ralph, "must be kinda boring just sitting around all day."

Again, Annie was touched by just a hint of compassion. She made a confession to him that she had shared with no one else, not even her parents. "I'm seriously considering moving to Charleston, if I can get a promise of a job with the Gazette or Daily Mail. At least the legislature comes to town once a year."

Annie was startled by Ralphie's wide-eyed surprise, bordering on shock. "Nooooo," he pleaded, "you cain't leave Beckley." His ardent cry again caught Annie off guard, left her hanging.

"And why not?" she honestly demanded, gently backing away from this strange, transparent young man.

Again he smiled from ear to ear. "'Cause we just met, Anita."

Annie groaned, forced a smile, and turned down the corridor to the exit. The least you could do, she muttered under her breath, is get my name right.

2

Annie had just eased into a scalding hot bubble bath when the phone rang. Fortunately she had brought the cordless into the bathroom with her. It was her editor, his voice frantic.

"I hate to bother you this late but could you run down to city hall?

Betty just heard on the scanner that a brick was thrown through the window of the prosecutor's office."

Annie was somewhat dismayed by the request. This didn't seem like an emergency that would preclude an already drawn bubble bath. "Can't this wait until in the morning?" she pleaded. "After all, the window won't be replaced until tomorrow."

"No, you don't understand," he breathed into the phone. "There was a note attached. Threatening. I'm not sure who or when, but the police are concerned, have cordoned off the entire block. I need somebody down there."

Annie let her sigh go directly into the mouthpiece. "Alright," she said, rubbing her forehead, "I'll get right on it." She was about to hang up the phone, then added, "Hey, I get comp time for this later, right?" The phone was dead, he had probably anticipated her question. Without letting the water out of the tub...this shouldn't take long she hoped...she stood and toweled off. Putting on the same clothes she had worn all day, she eased out of the house and pulled the door to, locked. Her pickup reluctantly started, thinking it too was in for the night.

As soon as she approached downtown she could see the flashing emergency lights reflecting off the sides of the taller buildings. Hmmm, she thought, this appears to be quite a crowd for this time at night. The courthouse clock tolled eleven times as she eased her car into a parking spot just before the yellow caution tape blocked off the street.

Ducking beneath the tape, she had walked a half block before she caught the attention of one of the patrolmen. "Hey," he called out, "this IS a police matter. I need to ask you to..." It was then he recognized Annie and her already held up press ID. "Hey Annie," officer Legg smiled broadly, "what's a nice girl like you doing in a place like this?"

Annie slid her ID back into her purse but did not smile back. Officer Legg was one of several on the Beckley police force—all married— that had hit on her, more than once. Sometimes she wasn't sure who she feared the most, the hard-core criminal element present in every community, or some of the lechers on the local detachment.

"Hey Jim," she acknowledged, "what's going on that's got my editor all tied up in knots?"

"You ever see the Andy Griffith show?"

"Sure," she responded, "my dad's favorite show."

Jim Legg scratched his ample forehead beneath his official hat. "Remember that nut who came to town occasionally who threw rocks through the courthouse windows?"

Annie nodded her head. "Ernest T. Bass."

"That's it, hold on a minute." Legg walked down the street maybe twenty steps, Annie not far behind. "Hey chief," he called out, getting his super's attention, "it's Ernest T. Bass." The chief immediately recognized the name and the gathered officers began to chatter all at once. Legg turned back to the reporter. "Thanks. Wasn't a one of us that could remember his name."

"No problem. You're telling me Ernest T. Bass did this?"

Legg pulled out a handkerchief from his back pocket and wiped his brow. The heat of the day was not in any hurry to vacate the heart of Appalachia. "Nah, but it's a rock, with a note attached. Only this note ain't wanting a uniform, it's threatening to blow up downtown."

Annie's eyes widened appreciably. "Blow up downtown? Why, did it say?"

Again Legg's look showed tired resignation. "No, short note. We've all read it, so I don't think fingerprints are going to do much good." At this Annie had to chuckle, imagining the entire force scanning the note and passing it back and forth before someone thought to fingerprint it. It wouldn't be the first case in which the force contaminated evidence.

"Was the note handwritten, or typed?" she asked.

"That's the funny thing," Legg responded, "in this day of computers and laser printers, the thing was handwritten. Not very bright if you ask me." He paused. "Definitely not the Unabomber, he's already in jail."

"Can I see the note?" Legg nodded his head and approached his boss.

"Hey hoss, can the lady here see the note, she might be able to help us track down the handwriting." The chief drew the note out from his breast pocket and handed it to Legg who handed it to Annie. It read simply:

This brick is just a warning. The entire downtown may be next.

The handwriting was clearly legible, but not neat, like someone had struggled to make it readable. It appeared as though they had even written the note on the brick, given the uneven hand.

"It's not Ernest T.," Annie said loud enough for all to hear. Several questioning looks later Annie shared her theory. "It's not a poem, his threats usually rhymed." Again the collective group began chattering at once. She rolled her eyes as she walked away from the scene, noticing for the first time the busted window that now only partially read Prosecuting Attorney. Much ado about nothing, she decided, heading back to a now cooling, devoid of bubbles, bubble bath.

3

Those in attendance quaked in fear as their boss paced back and forth the next morning, holding the day's front page in hand, already delivered to most of the county. It wasn't often that the veins in his forehead popped out like they were now, and whatever hung heavily in the air was about to hit the fan.

"I can't believe this," he screamed, running his hands through his thinning hair. "Dave," he turned suddenly, questioning the on-call photographer from the night before, "you're sure Annie didn't call you to come down for a picture?" Dave simply nodded his head toward the front page that his editor had nearly worn out from worry. "Of course not," he muttered. "No story, no pictures." He raised his voice and looked out over the newsroom. "Annie show up yet?"

The receptionist turned back into the room shaking her head no. With great exaggeration, he wadded up section A of the morning paper and slammed dunked it into the nearest trash can, his tie fluttering up then back down toward the floor.

"Ok, listen up people," he said, his voice straining against the stress he had imposed on himself, "if I call you after hours, no matter what time it is," he paused for effect as he visually scanned the room 360 degrees, "and ASK that you go cover a story, I darn well EXPECT a story the next morning. You got that?"

As everyone nodded and the editor turned toward his office, the receptionist saw Annie bouncing up the steps, reaching for the door. She began making a shushing noise and motioning Annie down. Not understanding, Annie approached the front desk as she did everyday, only this time with confusion etched on her facial features.

Whispering, Carla said quickly, "Howard's on the warpath, and you're the paleface." Annie understood the words, but didn't understand their meaning. She looked up across the newsroom just as her editor turned in his office to sit. He saw her and rose as quickly as he went down, making the door in three giant steps.

"ANNIE!" he screamed, "get in here RIGHT now!"

Annie winced and looked down to Carla, who shrugged and said, "Sorry, I tried to warn you." Still confused, Annie walked through the staring, compassionate eyes and through the door Howard framed with his seething energy. She walked straight to the desk and took the single seat without looking back. In her mind she was now sure her faux pas involved last night's phone call, but she was equally sure she was justified in disregarding it.

Howard fell back into his chair and leaned back, arms locked behind his head, his growing stomach unattractively held in by a couple of fragile buttons. After several heavy sighs, he finally chose his opening salvo.

"Do you think I picked up the phone and called last night just for the RUSH of hearing my voice?" Before Annie could answer the rhetorical question, Howard continued. "Do you think we keep the scanner on JUST because we're a bored, middle-aged couple with nothing better to do?" This time Annie knew the question to be rhetorical, and remained silent. She knew Howard well enough that he always strung three rhetorical questions together when he was mad. This was no exception.

"Do you think you've got a better SENSE of this business than I do? How long have you worked here?"

Uh oh, Annie groaned, he had her personnel file out. AND that was his fourth rhetorical question - he knew darn well that she'd been with the paper just over a year, he personally hired her. Again she took the low, silent road of confrontation.

"One year," he said, nodding his head mockingly. "One freaking year." He stood and turned, pointing to a plaque on the wall. "You see that," he pointed toward his award from the West Virginia Press Association, "you see that?" His hand pointed to the certificate that he had won for investigative reporting regarding the coal industry's poor safety record prior to 1980 in the southern coalfields, but his eyes held Annie's hard and fast. "Do you think I got that because I walked away from a nothing story that was going nowhere? No," he said resoundingly, "I took what seemed to be a nothing story and developed it. I could have sat on it, let someone else pick it up, let it die. But I didn't. I climbed on top of it and rode it until THAT came out of it," still pointing toward the plaque on the wall. Annie was glad that he'd only won the one.

Howard sat back down and placed his head in his hands, staring down at his desk. Those in the newsroom with either sensitive ears or quick eyes were aware that, after ten minutes, Annie was yet to speak. That was to end, but not loud enough to satisfy the curious beyond the glass.

"Howard," she started, a matter-of-fact tone to a voice quite nervous, "it was a rock...with a note attached."

"The note," Howard interrupted, "threatened the entire downtown."

"Howard," Annie started again, the same tone to her voice, only a half octave higher, "I read the note. It said something like...this brick is a warning, the downtown is next. He wasn't threatening to blow up downtown, he could have easily been threatening to rock every window. Granted, that would be news worthy, but only because we're sitting in Beckley." Annie winced as the words came out of her mouth. Howard, a lifelong resident of Beckley save for his college days at Marshall, resented the implication that she had clearly made. She opened her mouth to apologize when Howard spoke up.

"Did you know there was a witness?" Annie did not, and her expression revealed it. Howard pursed his lips in a thinking manner. "What time did you leave last night?"

"I don't know," Annie lied slightly, knowing very well she had left at 11:15, "maybe 11:30, maybe midnight."

Howard stood again and walked around his desk, opening the door. "The witness is at the precinct right now working with a sketch artist." Annie quickly stood to avoid the final bullet in the mental chamber. She wasn't quick enough.

"If you have the time," Howard said condescendingly, "could you mosey on down and work something up for, say, tomorrow's paper," he paused as Annie passed through the door and had traversed halfway across the still silent newsroom, "BEFORE THE GAZETTE AN HOUR AWAY GETS THE STORY!!!" The glass literally shattered to pieces as he slammed the door behind him. He stopped, his back to the door, and called out for Carla.

"On it," she yelled back, picking up the phone to order a replacement window.

4

Annie drove the half-mile to the Beckley Police Department seething inside, nearly blind from the rage that consumed her. How dare he question my reporter's instincts, she said to the dead air in her Ford 4x4. Parking one block beyond the main entrance, she bumped both the car behind her and the car in front of her as she parked, not even noticing. Mumbling as she exited the truck, foregoing the usual meter feed, she stormed into the new facility like a June tornado in Kansas. The receptionist, recognizing the usually friendly reporter, just stared as she icily walked by without a word.

She pushed through the glass door labeled 'Detectives' and faced an officer behind the counter a head shorter than she, one she did not recognize. Her attitude still unsettled, at best, she glared down and growled, "I understand someone saw Ernest T. Bass heave the rock through the prosecutor's office last night."

The rookie, new to the Beckley area, stared up incredulous at the news that Ernest T. Bass was indeed alive and well in Beckley, West Virginia. "Uh..." he stammered, uncertain, "I don't know, lemme check." As he turned to seek help, the chief himself stepped out of his office and recognized the usually more-than-fair and cooperative reporter. And, he thought to himself with a smile growing, not hard on the eyes.

"Annie!" he boomed, striding across the office, shaking her small hand. "Glad you're here. Can you come in for a moment?"

Annie passed through the recently installed metal detector successfully and strode into the chief's office, taking a seat. Chief Lester Hall could sense her foul mood.

"You want some coffee or something? Maybe a donut?"

Annie shook her head, still unable to talk without anger in her voice. She was about to cry she was so mad. The chief waited a moment, then got down to business.

"Listen, we got a witness last night who SAYS he saw who threw the brick through the window. Now if you ask me," he paused, glancing up to the ceiling quickly, "I'd bet my next paycheck that it was THIS kid who did the damage."

Annie's reporter's instincts kicked in, against her will. "Did you get a handwriting sample?"

The chief frowned. "Yeah. And no, not even close, but somebody else coulda wrote the note for him." Each mulled this notion over with no clue as to its validity.

"If he came forward," Annie asked the other obvious question, "as a witness, why would he do that if HE broke out the window?"

Again the chief frowned, burped silently, and shook his head. "It don't make any sense, but he didn't exactly come forward. We spotted him down the street just after you left. I called your boss this morning to ask if maybe you had seen him when you came up."

Annie now had enough pieces of the puzzle as to why her job was on the line. What she didn't have was a clear picture of this witness. "Who is he?"

Chief Hall picked at his fingernails, wondering if this information should be made public at this time. It shouldn't, he knew, but maybe the lady had some insight into this particular young lad. Besides, he was enjoying the conversation.

"Twelve year old boy named..." he looked through the papers on his desk, "Michael Oather Justice. Goes by Michael."

"Not surprised," Annie mumbled, unfamiliar with the name Oather, surname or otherwise. "Where is he?"

"Down in the conference room. Eddy's trying his hand at drawing the description. I believe that boy's got a future in the sketch business."

Enough cat and mouse, thought Annie, they want something from her and she needed to find that out. "So," she deadpanned, "why are you telling me all this?"

Again Hall picked at his fingernails. "We were wondering if you might talk to him, off the record of course. He don't seem to...relate well to our manly methods. A feminine touch might get him to open up a little bit."

Already burned by the non-story once, Annie was reluctant to help. But there was the matter of Howard, she thought, and agreed to do what she could. The ride down the elevator to the next level was made in silence, and Hall knocked twice before entering the conference room. Eddy stood to greet Annie while the young boy kept his head down.

"Mike," Chief Hall said softly, "we got a lady reporter here who helps us out from time to time. We've got a meeting to go to in about two minutes," Hall winked at Eddy, "would you mind if we left her to talk to you for just a minute?" The boy shrugged, never looking up. He was a street rat that Annie recognized from his many visits to the courthouse sidewalks with his skateboard, with which he was quite adept. Eddy handed her his sketchbook with apologies.

"Sorry, this ain't quite right, but it's not too far off either." Both stared down at the strangely familiar face, but neither could quite tighten the image down to a recognizable face. She nodded to Eddy, who left with Hall. She pulled out the seat that Eddy had been using and sat down. Michael Oather Justice was yet to look up.

"Michael," she began hesitantly, seeing the smudge on his right cheek, "you ever win that state championship in skateboarding?" This caught the boy's attention and he looked up to his new visitor. Not a single inquisitor had known he was an avid skateboarder.

"Not yet," he smiled for the first time, a pretty smile, "maybe next year." He rubbed his nose and dropped his head back down.

Well, thought Annie, contact had been made but lost. She thought of NASA and their occasional, brief contacts with satellites that had long ago passed beyond their useful and productive lives...and range. But there, occasionally, startlingly, a blip on the recorder indicated that satellite X had communicated again, well beyond the orbit of Pluto. Annie stared at the top of the head before her, wondering if communication had been irrevocably lost. In the next room, watching through a two-way mirror, Eddy feared that she had lost him. Chief Hall simply enjoyed looking at the attractive reporter.

Annie thought about walking out, dropping the ball, letting someone else get the nothing story, but the image of Howard kept flashing in her mind. Finally she tried another, more direct tact.

"What were you doing downtown last night?" The boy remained motionless, staring down at his feet. She tried again. "What did you see?" This time Michael smiled, his body moved slightly from the tiny bit of air that escaped his mouth.

"I saw that guy," he pointed at the sketch, "well, not really that guy but not, say, you..." he paused for effect, "walk up, toss the rock through the window, then take off - toward Neville."

"That's it?" Annie asked, sure that there was more, but unsure how to extract it.

"Pretty much," Michael responded, making eye contact for the second time. "What else was there to see?"

Annie shrugged. "Why were you down there? That's kinda late for a 12 year old boy."

"Thirteen," he interrupted with conviction, contrary to the chief's report.

"Thirteen," Annie repeated. "How do they..." she nodded toward the two-way mirror, bringing a grimace from both officers in waiting, "know that you didn't throw the rock?"

Michael looked toward the two-way mirror then back at the reporter, smirking. "They think they're pretty smart don't they?" Annie smiled and looked directly toward the mirror.

"Eddy, Chief, could you leave us alone for a minute or two?" She and the boy listened closely for a door to close, then the door to the conference room opened up and a red-faced Chief Hall mentioned that they'd be upstairs if needed. Annie smiled and nodded her approval.

"So," she asked again, "what are you NOT telling me?"

"Can you keep a secret?" he asked. Annie nodded her head convincingly. "That does look a lot like the guy, seems the nose might be a little bigger, and the hair was messier, ears bigger, but he looked a lot like that."

"That's not a secret," Annie observed.

To this Michael Oather Justice smiled broadly. "You're right. The secret is..." Michael's eyes scanned the room, looking for some clarity in his mind, "the guy was totally cool. He wasn't mad, he wasn't stressed, he was WHISTLING," he said with emphasis. "I seen a lot of weird dudes downtown in daylight and in dark who was up to no good, but this guy was out for a Sunday walk. I don't care what no note said, he ain't got it in him to destroy downtown. This is, as my momma would say, a mountain out of a molehill. Can you get me outa here?"

For the second time this morning Annie was furious as she successfully extracted Michael from the building. Both Chief Hall and

Eddy protested, but Annie's demeanor convinced them that she was in no mood to be messed with.

Michael thanked her and made his way toward the north end of town, presumably toward home Annie hoped. Annie headed straight for the office, banged noisily on her keyboard, producing a scathing story of incompetence at the newspaper. After that ended up in her trash can, face up, she carefully constructed a dull, lifeless report of an equally dull, lifeless story. Howard was not amused.

5

Governor Manchin approached the bottom floor of the rotunda of the state capitol building flanked on each side by state troopers. He patted his breast pocket, reassuring himself that he had picked up his speech. The din grew even louder upon his approach, then applause erupted as he passed through a narrow opening into the center circle. Giving speeches in the round was a challenge, but he liked the informality it bred and the acoustical boost of having a wall of people around him. The applause died down as he smiled to the grade-schoolers.

"Greetings," he said smiling broadly, swiping the hair from his expanding forehead, Kennedyesque. The group, not all in unison, mumbled greetings back. With speech on the podium, he took a deep breath and launched into his discussion on the importance of education and his commitment to fund it adequately, while exploring the possibility of expanding table games, which excited the younger children who thought he was talking about Chutes and Ladders.

After twenty minutes and a half dozen questions about his lifestyle as governor, Manchin thanked the group for coming and invited them back anytime. He shook each of their hands then exited the circle, the two state troopers falling in beside the elected official.

"John," he said, turning to the trooper on the right, "get maintenance up ASAP to get that graffiti off the marble. That looked hideous. I can imagine what the kids must have thought."

John Gray looked to the governor then to his partner who shared his look of concern. "Sure thing governor." After a few additional clicking steps on the marble floors, John asked, "What graffiti, governor?"

Manchin looked to his bodyguard like he was stupid, or on drugs. "Right there on the upper level, opposite of where I stood. You didn't see it?" he asked incredulously. John shook his head no. So did Kevin, with the governor looking on. "It was right there," he pointed upward, his voice becoming shrill. Still walking he continued, "On the north side, said 'the tolls must go'—kinda in italics. I can't believe you didn't see it."

John and Kevin made eye contact again, still unsure if perhaps the governor was making a joke. His sense of humor, while healthy, wasn't always clear. But even this seemed out of character for the man. "What tolls?" Kevin asked.

"I don't know," the governor shrugged. "Turnpike maybe?"

The three entered the reception area of the governor's office while the two state troopers stopped to stand sentinel at the door. Manchin quickly made his way back into his office. After a momentary pause, John Gray broached the subject. "You see any graffiti?"

Kevin Lampley shook his head. "I didn't see nothing. You want me to go back and take a look?"

"Sure," said the slightly older Gray.

Kevin turned on his heels and walked quickly back to the now empty rotunda. He stood in the center, precisely where the governor had stood, and turned 360 degrees. He looked up, he looked down. He looked way up, he looked way down. He ascended the marble staircase to the second floor, this time looking down on the area in general. He slowly made his way around the circle, his hand following as it lay on top of the cool marble. Nothing.

John was just dialing maintenance when Kevin returned. He covered the mouthpiece to receive Kevin's report. "Nothing John, nothing. Not even a scratch. You can call maintenance if you want, but there's nothing there to clean."

John returned his attention to the phone and reported the incident to the head of maintenance as if he hadn't personally been there, just 'a report' of graffiti somewhere around the rotunda area. He hung up the phone and smiled at Kevin. "The tolls must go," he repeated, chuckling. "I think the press is getting to him."

6

A week had passed uneventful since the rock was thrown through the prosecutor's window when a similar sized rock with a similar note shattered the plate-glass window of a lawyer's office on Neville. This incident occurred in the early morning hours, just before what little rush hour Beckley would expect, according to the security report. Annie saw the police cars and one lane of traffic across from the courthouse and quickly parked in an open space. Hoping for more, she groaned upon learning Ernest T. Bass was up to his tricks again.

"Same note?" she asked the nearest cop, surveying the damage.

He nodded. "About the same content, same handwriting. We'll catch him sooner or later."

Later, thought Annie as she crossed the street to the courthouse. She was just about to dash up the steps when a familiar voice called loudly from across the street.

"Anita!"

Annie groaned, recognizing Ralphie's voice, knowing she didn't have time to talk to him before the nine o'clock hearing in the magistrates' office that she was to cover. She turned to wave, only to see Ralphie leap through and between cars gazelle-like, heading straight toward her.

"Anita!" he said again, just as loud, although he was now on the same side of the street. "Glad I caught up with you," he huffed, somewhat winded from his jaunt. Annie was about to excuse herself when Ralphie pulled a copy of the paper from his back pocket. "Great story last week," he said excitedly, pointing to her lifeless report of the rock through the prosecutor's office. "You've got a knack for writing a good story."

Annie was in no mood, as she found herself more and more these days. God, she groaned to herself, I've got to get a resume out to Charleston. Again she was about to back away when Ralphie plunged forward.

"They said there was a witness huh?" His eyes searched Annie's, and again she saw the good heart through the layers of abject goofiness. She glanced at her watch.

"Yeah, young kid. Gave the police a pretty good description, they've got a sketch artist working on it."

"Really?" Ralphie asked, "they've got a sketch artist on force?" Didn't make sense for small time Beckley.

Annie shook her head. "Nobody full time. As a matter-of-fact, it's your cousin Eddy. He does a real good job."

Ralphie's eyes widened. "Eddy can draw that good?" He gulped, his ample Adam's apple bobbing up and down.

"Well, the guy ain't been caught yet," Annie confessed the obvious, "so he must not be that good." It then occurred to her, now that there was a second window broken—they hadn't run the sketch in the paper. "Hey Ralph, listen, I've got a hearing that started two minutes ago," she said, glancing at her watch for effect, "I'll catch up with you later."

Ralphie smiled broadly, reading much more into her parting words than she meant. As she entered the courthouse he muttered to himself, "I can only hope that you catch me purty lady." He sauntered back across the street, eyeing the police who were gathering what they hoped would be evidence for this latest crime. He turned down a side street and disappeared into the alley.

7

The following morning's paper this time carried a livelier story, WITH the latest version of Eddy's handiwork accompanying the story. Front page. It landed on every stoop and inside every paper box for miles around. In the article the police were requesting any assistance from the public with either the picture or any other information that they might have. Even Howard was pleased with the coverage, and expressed as much at their morning meeting as they explored the ground they were covering.

"Annie, this could be big," Howard said, half jokingly, "could be that Pulitzer you've been wanting."

Annie smiled but said nothing, still seeing it as 'small town, big story'. Oscar Davitz, one of the copy editors, known to all as Oscar the Grouch, offered his two-cents worth.

"I seen the kid that broke out those windows," he said authoritatively, as if by saying it the issue would be resolved. When no one offered a counter, praise or otherwise, he continued. "I can't put my finger on where I seen the kid, but I seen him alright." With a nod of the head he was done, and silence followed for several seconds.

"Ok," continued Howard, "what about the rumored strike up at Glade Springs, Donna?" Donna was just about to respond when Carla knocked and quickly entered the conference room.

"Got another Bass report, this time out on Harper Road. The Holiday Inn, right through their front window."

Howard said thanks and nodded to Annie. She gathered her notebook and few notes and purse, slipped her shoes back on, and headed out the door. The day shift photographer was waiting outside, drawing the last few puffs on a Camel filtered. The two climbed into her truck and made their way south to the Holiday Inn.

The usual gang was gathered at the front of the building. There were three or four police, all city. A few employees of the establishment stood back, shaking their heads at who would do such a thing. A couple of onlookers always found their way to such events. And, of course, Annie with a photographer. While he walked around and snapped pictures from both inside and out, Annie began questioning the nearest cop.

"Ernest T?" she asked, somewhat bored. The officer never said a word, just nodded his head in the affirmative. "Note?" Again he was speechless, just nodding his head.

"Same content, handwritten?" She was surprised when this question brought a different response.

"Same handwriting," he said, his voice gravelly from too many years of cigarettes, "but different content this time." Annie waited through several coughs that came from deep within. "This note threatens the ENTIRE county."

Annie looked toward the shattered glass then back. "In what way?"

He shrugged his heavy shoulders. "Rocks through our windows I guess." With a smirk he tipped his hat and rejoined his fellow officers.

8

The head of the state police detachment responsible for the governor's security had been on staff since Arch Moore took office for the first of three terms in 1974. Marshall Williamson had seen them come and go, with little substantial changes in either the work force of the state or general health and well being of its citizenry. The small state tended to ebb and flow with the tide of the national economy, but usually lagging several months if not years behind. The tide raises all ships, someone once said. But, unlike the tide, the national economy's good news took longer to filter into the heart of Appalachia than it did into other parts of the country. West Virginia, with its mountainous backbone and history of isolation, was a slow study in the ways of the new, global economy.

Marshall looked down the table at his twelve-member force, absent one due to illness. He had been having these staff meetings every other week at the behest of then governor Caperton, who was big on staff meetings. Rarely did anything substantial come from such gatherings, but he stayed on course and continued with Caperton's wishes through another couple of governors. He was seriously considering abolishing, or scaling back, the meetings, when Officer John Gray changed everything.

"Oh yeah," Gray said as an afterthought. He looked around the room, a little sheepish at what he was about to reveal. Marshall told him to go on, and John continued. "Last Thursday at thirteen hundred hours Governor Manchin was giving a speech to some grade schoolers in the rotunda, level one. As we left the area—Kevin Lampley and I— the governor was all worked up about graffiti on the upper level. Kevin and I did not see the graffiti and Kev immediately afterward went back to check and again did not see any desecration of the area. We reported it to maintenance, as per the governor's orders, who also reported back that nothing was out of order. Just a head's up in case the good Governor tries to pull your leg too."

Marshall leaned forward in his seat at the head of the massive, wooden table, placing his hands before him on each side of his appointment book. "Did he say what the graffiti said by any chance, John?"

John nodded his head and looked around at the faces that stared his way. "Yeah, said something about the tolls." He laughed out loud then repeated his suggestion that the press was finally getting to the governor. The light chuckling that filled the room quickly abated when Marshall asked if there was anything else. Some shook their heads, most just stared blankly.

"Dismissed." As chairs were pushed back Marshall caught John's eye and asked him to stay for a moment. As the room emptied Marshall motioned for John to sit back down. "The tolls?" Marshall asked with a cock of his head. "Can you remember precisely what it said?"

"Uh…" John began, looking up to the muraled ceiling. In his mind he returned to the previous week and his conversation with the governor. "Yeah," he concluded, "it was 'the tolls must go'." He looked back to his boss of twelve years. "Why?"

Marshall pushed his chair back and stood. "Nothing," he said unconvincingly, his thumb and forefinger pinching his bottom lip. "Nothing," he repeated, motioning John to leave with a wave of his hand. Once alone he returned to his office, moving straight to a metal filing cabinet in the corner. Retrieving his keys from his belt, he finally found the correct key and unlocked the cabinet. The bottom drawer slid out noisily, not seeing much action over the years. To the back Marshall flipped through the aging manila folders until he came upon the one he sought marked simply 'Tolls'. He withdrew it, left the drawer open, and settled into his desk, turning on his reading lamp. Very solemnly he opened the file, mentally preparing to make another addition to the file that, with the passing of his former boss and friend of 30 years last fall, only he knew about. He carefully considered to whom, if anyone, he should now pass the file along.

9

Annie woke from a fitful sleep as the distant sirens coursed through the heart of the city of Beckley. After clearing her head of the stupor that the sleep had left her with, she listened carefully. She now recognized the distinct whine of fire, police, and ambulance sirens. Her feet hit the floor, noting the time at 2:15am, and threw on some jeans and blouse and headed out the door.

Downtown looked like a carnival with the lights of the different emergency vehicles reflecting off the three and four story buildings. Neville Street was blocked off as soon as downtown proper began. Annie whipped her truck into a vacant handicap space, hopped out of the truck and bounded down the street. Sliding between two cones that didn't quite come together, she marched up Neville with pen and pad in hand. It wasn't long before her obvious presence was known.

"Hey Annie," one of the officers called out as she approached Main Street, "can you come here a minute?" It was Chief Hall, wearing his robe over his pajamas. Annie had to laugh.

"Can I get a picture Chief?" she joked, smilingly broadly. The Chief acknowledged her joke but quickly shook it off. Something was wrong—as was evidenced by the show of force on hand. "What's up?" she asked somberly.

Turning, he barked an order into his walkie-talkie, then turned back. "I think it's your friend again."

Annie blinked. "My friend?"

Chief Hall nodded. "Ernest T. Bass."

Annie resented the implication. "Hey," she exclaimed, "he's not my friend. Just because I was the only one who could remember his name..." She let her voice trail off in obvious disdain, which Hall detected.

"Of course not, it's just that it's been your story since the first incident." A garbled request came over the walkie-talkie as the Chief turned and took a couple of steps away. He listened carefully then said 'well...be careful' and 'rogered' out.

Annie had been scanning the visible area and, aside from the presence of an abundance of law enforcement, nothing else seemed out of place. "What's going on Chief?"

He let out a huge amount of air. "He called me." He let that sink in as Annie looked at him stunned.

"He called you?" she repeated his statement.

"Yes," he paused, the gravity of the situation weighing heavily for the first time since taking the head position on the force. "Bomb threat. Said there was enough TNT to blow up the entire downtown. We're scanning the area, looking for packages, bags, whatever. But none of us have training in explosives. If the guy has one of those triggered to go off with movement, we could all die."

Sheesh, Annie muttered, looking around again with more appreciation of the moment. "Is that all he said?"

The Chief indicated no with a shake of his head. "Nine o'clock. Just when everybody's downtown for work." He cursed and looked down at his watch, just after three. "We'll have to shut the town down unless we either find it or..." he paused, wincing, not finishing the sentence.

The cool, dead air, coupled with the seriousness of the threat, gave Annie chill bumps. "Can I help?" she asked sincerely.

"Sure," the chief responded, handing her a whistle from around his neck. "Look where we're not. If you see anything suspicious, anything, you blow in that and we'll come running. Don't be a hero. The clock is ticking," he said more to himself than Annie, scanning the downtown that had been his since birth. Losing it to an act of terrorism, particularly on his watch, was more than he could take.

Annie walked slowly as she approached the heart of downtown, the new federal building, the old courthouse, the businesses, both vacant and bustling during daylight hours. She thought of Oklahoma and the Murrah Building. September 11th. The key difference between those acts of terrorism and the prospect of this act was that the former occurrences had no warning. The good people of Oklahoma City and New York had no clue that one minute they would be alive and the next dead. In this case, thought Annie, Ernest T - as she and the county had come to know him—seemed to be toying with them. She thought of Mike's assessment—a man on a Sunday stroll, no anger, no issues. She thought of the sketch Eddy had done—how it seemed somewhat familiar.

Lost deep in thought, Annie found herself nearing the courthouse entrance on the east side. She walked up the steps and checked the door. Locked, just as it should be. Turning to scan the area, she seemed to have the courthouse grounds to herself. She could see the men with flashlights scanning the periphery of the federal building. Obviously terrorism wasn't on her mind alone. She went back down the steps, turned to her right and cut through the grass to check out ground level of the courthouse more thoroughly.

With the streetlights that lined the downtown streets, she could see pretty well as she cautiously made her away along side the building. Nothing. No packages, bags, even beer bottles in places where they usually were. She was almost to the far, western side of the building when something caught her eye.

That's strange, she thought, turning back and looking into the basement window that led into the map room of the assessor's office. She had worked a brief stint across the hall in real estate two years earlier. The window was up about four inches and she could have sworn she saw movement within. She touched the whistle that she now wore around her neck, then dropped it, easing down to her knees at the window. Very gently she raised the heavy, metal-framed window that surprisingly slid up with no noise. Looking back to the federal building and seeing no one approaching, she entered the courthouse feet first, quietly stepping on the mapper's desk then down onto the floor. She considered closing the window, but decided against it in case she needed to make a quick exit.

The lights of the city only penetrated the courthouse where windows were present. The inner offices and halls were dark, save the glowing red signs hanging from the ceiling that indicated 'Exit'. Annie was sweating, even in the cool night air, as her heart raced from both the mild exertion and the dark corridors. She was now in the main hall in the basement. She looked to the left and saw the stairs leading to the western exit of the building, supposedly locked, and the first level. She looked to the right, which dead-ended maybe seventy-five feet away. The second door on the right had an exit sign—the exit that fed out of the middle of the building on the first floor and toward the federal courthouse.

She softly padded the few feet to the yawning door and peeked around—her breath immediately caught in her throat. There, looking up to the windowed outer door, was a man—average build, average height. His body posture suggested someone in hiding, someone being sought, not wanting to be caught. Again Annie fingered the whistle around her neck, wanting so desperately to sound the alarm, yet realizing that she would be, at best, his hostage. Breathing shallow, she ducked back to where just her left eye peered around the corner. She was on the verge of backing to the mapper's room and climbing out the window when she heard someone rattle hard the door behind her at the western exit of the building. She turned and saw a cop, his flashlight now peering up the stairs to the main level. She had to get his attention, she realized, just as a hand cupped her mouth and dragged her, trying to scream through the rough fingers, into the small hallway leading up to the center exit.

It was then that Annie came to recognize first the cologne, then the tone of the voice softly cooing her to be quiet. And his use of the words 'purty lady'.

Just as he let her ago she spun around and hissed into the half-light, "Ralphie, what are you doing?" She glanced back out into the hallway when Ralphie pulled her back into the small passageway.

"Shhhhh," he whispered again, his finger to his lips. "We gotta be quiet or they'll find us."

Annie blinked away her dumbfound expression. "Why are we hiding, Ralphie?" Her tone, as had been her life the last few weeks, was on edge.

Ralphie moved around her and peaked back up to the doorway where the cop had been rattling the door. No one. He looked back to the exit near where they stood. No one. He smiled, a knowing grin if Annie ever saw one.

"Things been hopping around here lately huh, purty lady." Annie stared at the youngish face, looking for some clue as to what the heck he was talking about. It was his next words that brought the fuzzy picture into horrifying focus. "You ain't gonna up and go and move to Charleston now, are you?"

With wide eyes Annie gulped down the realization. "YOU'RE the one whose been throwing these rocks through the windows?"

Again Ralphie smiled, pleased as pudding at her recognition of his unselfish deeds. "Yep," he drawled, "it was me. Had 'em going there for a while, didn't I?"

Annie's skin crawled at the implications. SHE was, in a way, responsible for her own series on the rock thrower that the town had come to know as Ernest T. Bass. SHE was standing, trespassing really, in the courthouse with the very perpetrator. SHE, she quickly realized, was in big, big trouble.

"Ralphie, you idiot," she hissed, "every cop in this town is within a football field of this building and WE'RE in it!" She considered flailing him with her tightly clutched reporter's notebook.

With that pronouncement Ralphie smiled and leaned against the nearest wall. "Annie, the building is locked, they ain't going to open it up when they're looking for a..." His words were cut off as they heard a distant shout, one indicating that a window was open. Ralphie's eyes widened as he peered around Annie to the dark hallway.

They unmistakably heard the sound of a body, or several, climbing through the same window Annie had recently entered. The voices were whispered, but the orders filtered through the empty corridors and indicated for everyone to 'spread out'. Annie looked back to Ralphie who now had a sick look on his face. He turned partially around and drove his fist into the wall.

10

The five officers just beginning to fan out into the courthouse from the map room heard the swoosh followed by a loud clap, then followed by what sounded like the closing of a heavy stone door. Each crouched as the noises occurred and grabbed the butt of their guns still holstered.

As the silence quickly returned each man bolted out into the hall and fanned different directions, guns drawn, flashlights bouncing their beams in all directions.

As these men made quick work of the basement and first floors, additional officers were let in who, with the same air of readiness, searched every nook and cranny and unlocked door on the third and fourth floors. After a half hour the entire force regathered in the main hallway on the first floor to reconnoiter. Rick was the senior officer of this particular group of men.

"Anything?" he asked, his eyes scanning around him at the panting, mostly middle-aged men around him. All responses were in the negative, whether verbal, a shake of the head, or a simple grunt. Rick crossed his arms then rubbed his face vigorously beneath his cap with his right hand.

"I'm sure what I heard when we first came in was downstairs." Rick raised his eyes in thought toward the ceiling for a moment as he came up with a plan. "You five go to the basement from the far end," he said, pointing that direction, "you two take these stairs," again pointing at the staircase in the middle of the building, "and you three come with me. Let's check every door, every hallway, every possible hiding place we can find. I assume Jimmy's still got the window covered outside?" A couple of uncertain shoulders were raised. "Let's assume he does," Rick replied with little confidence, "and hey, let's be careful down there. I KNOW someone was in here."

The small groups made their ways to and down the assigned staircases. In the basement the beams of the flashlights began to intertwine as the three groups slowly converged to the middle. Nothing. Rick made his way into the mapper's room and found, to his surprise, that Jimmy was still standing guard outside the window.

"Anybody come out this window, Jimmy?" Jimmy Atkins knelt down and peered inside, shaking his head no. Rick returned to the hallway where the group stood quietly, listening for any sign of life. He shined his light to the ceiling and the mass of pipes and wires that coursed overhead, glad it wasn't alien life forms for which they were looking. Hollywood had made that prospect too grisly.

"Ok," he sighed, resignation in his voice. He hated to leave the first real sign of life this case had, but there was no way nearly a dozen men were going to overlook another human being in this building. "Dave, you and Mark stay inside, keep a sharp ear, and look for any sign of a bomb while you're at it. The rest of you exit toward South Fayette, the direction we were headed anyway. I'll report in to the chief."

With that, the courthouse was secured and the manhunt continued its way north. The chief received Rick's report with interest but had nothing to share himself. Aside from the possible breach of the courthouse, they hadn't found anything that would indicate something was amiss in the downtown area. With the first rays of the sun now peeking over the eastern hills, a decision had to be made: close downtown for the morning, or assume Ernest T. is indeed a big bluff and go about business as usual. Chief Hall looked to the morning sky for some sign, some show of the course of action he could take. The morning sky, as always, was deadly silent.

11

Ralphie immediately knew something was wrong as his fist did not intersect the hardness of white-painted stone, but instead was met with a softness, a rubbery substance that allowed his clenched fist to land without the knuckle-cracking pain that he fully anticipated. Beyond this softness came a thud, his hand finally intersected something solid and a distinct, single click occurred. It was then, with no warning, that the floor dropped beneath them and the two fell feet first, their screams piercing the darkness as the slight light from above disappeared as quickly as it had opened up. They screamed and screamed as they fell, arms flailing, grasping for something, anything, to hold onto, finding nothing.

Suddenly they landed on a steep incline, so steep that it didn't break their fall at all, just began to direct the course of their free fall. Even though they had not landed with a splat, their lives at an end, it did not quell their violent cries into the night. This incline did not deviate to the left or the right for some time, but then gently it grew less steep. Both now had the sensation, what little sensation they could muster above their cries for mercy, that they were on a slide—a very smooth, stone slide with a rounded out bottom. In the suffocating darkness the turns, growing sharper, finally made them stop screaming, to be replaced with gasps as the g-forces began to lessen but their speed had hardly abated. A couple of loop-d-loops in the darkness brought back their screams, but only for a moment. At times Annie's feet touched Ralphie's head or shoulders as their descent slowed around winding bends or sharper curves. Ralph only knew he was being touched from above, and guessed it was the lady reporter.

A faint light, coming from below, made their interior roller coaster somewhat visible—not necessarily a good thing. Ralph could see first, then Annie, seemingly the end of the world when the slide would drop out of sight, only to catch them as their speed increased with the near vertical drop. Then they would slow down just a bit before Ralphie would see an upcoming loop-d-loop, or an apparent gap in the slide where it appeared that they would be required to sail through the air to the other side of the abyss. Sure enough, such gaps were real, and their screams echoed in every direction when their backsides left the comfort of touch to be greeted with the uncertainty of dead air. But time and time again they landed surprisingly unharmed, only to continue the downward spiral to the bowels of the earth. Both felt the strain of neck muscles kept taut while trying to see what lay ahead. The soft light and the tunnel vision did little in showing the way. But they both were now silent as they sensed a slowing, arms now to their sides, looking every bit like riders on water tubes that were ubiquitous throughout the southern tourist states. And while this wild ride was not on water, neither could feel the burns one would expect from the constant friction their backs and butts were subjected to. Annie even relaxed somewhat and laid her head on the cool, solid surface, giving her neck muscles a much needed rest.

All at once their speeding course to the center of the earth slowed appreciably. They eased to a stop in what appeared to be an oversized spoon. Both groaned in some pain as their minds came to rest inside bodies that had endured the equivalence of a three round amateur boxing match. Annie sat up first and blinked into the faint light. Nothing was visible beyond the smooth depression in which she sat on her haunches. Ralphie popped up, talking, as he was prone to do most of his waking hours.

"What in the world was that!" he exclaimed, his voice echoing both upwards and below. His head turned from side to side, trying to see where they might be. Annie shushed him, hearing the faintest creaking. Ralphie leaned to one side, as if by doing so it would sharpen his hearing. He nodded his head.

"It sounds like this cave is creaking right below us," he whispered, getting up on his knees and gently easing forward, the direction they were headed before the sudden stop.

"Be careful Ralphie, you don't know where this thing is going," Annie whispered back. Ralphie had only gone two or three feet when he announced that the chute or slide or whatever it was just seemed to end. He laid his body down and eased his head over the precipice trying to see below, as there was nothing to see around or above them. Annie was just getting ready to warn him again when an audible crack right beneath them echoed through the chamber. Very slowly the slight depression dipped forward, the heavy sound of rock grinding on rock filling their ears. Annie immediately tried to back up but found the surface too slick. As Ralph got to his hands and knees the angle of their perch dipped dramatically, in the direction they were formerly heading, serving to pitch them headlong into the darkness again.

"Yaaaaaaaaaahhhhhhhhhhhhhhhhh!" Ralphie screamed into the silent well, arms and legs flailing about trying to replicate a flying motion to no avail. Annie managed to yell, "Ralphie you idiot!" as her free fall began, then joined in the incredibly loud, incredibly futile scream.

As their initial fall from the courthouse had directed them to the chute they'd spent the last twenty minutes on, this fall too ended on, or in, a slide that was precisely vertical at first but soon had cradled their bodies in something of a controlled fall. Realizing once again their free fall had been broken and they were now coursing through the bowels of the earth on somewhat of a roller coaster ride, both shut up and turned what senses they had left on red alert for any change—hoping of course for a sensation of slowing down. This sensation came, but after another twenty or so minute slide which included additional loop-d-loops and jumps over what appeared to be nothingness.

But they hadn't slowed much and Ralphie, now on his belly, had a bird's eye view of the road that lay ahead, at least what little they could see. When he screamed Annie screamed, she knowing that her reaction would no doubt mirror his. It was now noticeably warmer—to the point of hot. But the sweat that oozed out of their bodies did little to slow their descent.

It was Ralphie's loudest scream in a while that drew Annie's head erect again, and her scream followed immediately. The bottom dropped out of the slide and they were now free falling again, arms and legs flailing desperately trying to slow their fall. Peripherally each could sense below a whiteness, both realizing that this was indeed the end. They screamed and pleaded with their respective heavens far, far above for mercy as the whiteness quickly engulfed them, surrounded them, consumed them entirely. It was as if they were falling into a cloud. Their free fall soon stopped, both spitting and puffing and climbing as if their lives depended on it.

After an exhausting climb through...nothing, sometimes stepping on each other, they finally emerged to the top of what appeared to be a huge vat whose top was level with the ground—a vat filled to overflowing with feathers. Wee little feathers still swirled around in the half-light—now a little bit lighter than their journey down. The sweat on their bodies made feathers cling to their faces, arms, backs, and necks. Both continued to spit puffs of air, trying to relieve their mouths and throats of the tickling feathers. They looked like chickens, and it would have been funny had the situation been different. Ralph began picking feathers out of Annie's hair, thinking incorrectly he had extricated all from his body. Annie was in no mood for his courteous action.

"YOU," she mouthed, half whispering, "just HAD to lean over and see what was on the other side back there!" She continued to pull feathers from her arm and face as Ralphie backed away and did the same.

"So," he shrugged, somewhat resigned to their fate, "I'd rather be here where it's a little more roomy than up there in the middle of nowhere. At least here we're at the end."

Annie asked, enunciating each word slowly and clearly, "The end of what?" Her pupils slowly grew in the half-light. "At least up there we were halfway home. Down here," she continued, looking around at the cavern they now seemed to be in, "we don't have a chinaman's chance of ..." She stopped in mid-sentence, shushed Ralph as he began to speak, and listened intently. "You hear that?" she whispered, straining to focus her hearing on the faintest of sounds. From Ralph's expression it seemed as though he didn't hear.

Annie moved closer to the vat, looking first down into the millions of feathers, then up, deciding the sound was coming from above them. Ralphie joined her, now picking up the growing sound of something. All at once what appeared to be a bird exploded before them in a shower of wings and activity, causing both to scream and cover their heads. As soon as the startling event occurred it was over, the object clapping to the ground between them. Ralph leaned over and picked it up as Annie uncovered her head.

"It's your notebook," he said emotionless, remembering it in her hand as he drug her into the hallway up in the basement of the courthouse. Annie snatched it out of his hand and patted her pants pocket, thankfully finding the pen that might facilitate their escape back to the surface if they could somehow manage to get a note up to the top.

12

The barricades turned away everyone from downtown Beckley. Half of them were happy to get a paid day off, the other half had either too much work to do or needed to check their email and complained until it was obvious that they weren't getting through.

The newsroom at the paper, just outside the cordoned-off downtown, was abuzz with conversation about the downtown ban and corresponding bomb threat. Howard watched nervously for Annie's arrival. This was her story and, he hoped, she had gotten some good coverage for tomorrow's paper.

Annie's absence from the nine o'clock staff meeting caused concern. Howard had Carla call Annie's house, her contacts at the courthouse, anywhere she might be in hopes of locating her. Sometimes stories took reporters to the very edge of the county and beyond, but Annie had not missed a staff meeting since she had started. At ten Howard sent his staff on their way and returned to his office, spinning his Rolodex.

It was several minutes before Chief Hall came on the line and acknowledged his old friend and, sometimes, adversary at the paper. He filled Howard in with the 'official' line, then grew silent when asked about Annie Wolf.

"Yeah, I saw her," he said after considerable thought, "before dawn, way before daybreak." His tired mind perused the events of the previous night in which he was deprived sleep. He remembered her offer of help, him handing her the whistle in case she spotted trouble. What he didn't remember was seeing her again the rest of the ordeal.

"Howard," he said, after explaining her abbreviated role earlier in the morning, "I think we've got a problem. She never did show back up, and I totally forgot about her until this very moment." Again his mind raced through the night's events. He wondered if he should reveal the one thing that was somewhat unusual. He decided to, off the record.

"That's it?" replied Howard, drumming his fingers on his oversized, cluttered desk, "a noise in the courthouse?"

"Yep," the chief drawled, pulling out his top desk drawer and extracting a mint, "only thing is, that's the direction Annie headed. Now you're telling me she's missing."

Howard sighed into the phone, unsure of what to do. "I'm not saying she's missing for sure, I'm just saying it's uncharacteristic of her to not show up for a staff meeting. Can you send a couple men over to her house to check it out?"

"Sure thing." The chief sucked hard on the mint, wishing for a cigarette. He had given them up over the holidays. "I sure hope nothing's happened to her," he said sincerely. Howard was nodding his head in agreement when the chief continued his thought, "'cause she's awful easy on the eyes."

13

Their eyes had adjusted quite well to the light and they could now see the cavern around them. It was conical with a chute coming right out of the center, seemingly the only portal in or out of the place. There was always the bottom of the vat, but neither wanted to try that again without exhausting all other options. Slowly they made their way around the feathered pit, a good twenty feet in diameter, scanning the wall for any signs of a break. It was Ralphie who saw it first.

"Look over there," he said, pointing just ahead about a quarter turn in the cavern. There was a faint light down low at the base of the wall—the source of the light seemed to be coming from outside the shell they were in. They cautiously approached the half glow in total silence, Ralphie leading the way.

"It's an opening," he whispered, pretty quietly for Ralph. They stopped just short of the faint rays with tiny, dancing feathers visible in their light. The hole was small, neither was sure they would even fit through, assuming they decided to try. With an exaggerated motion Ralphie stepped over the dim glow and stood on the other side—both now looking like cats waiting for the mouse to poke his head out.

"What do you think?" Annie asked quietly after several minutes. There had been neither sound nor apparent movement on the other side of the opening since they had seen it. Ralph's eyes met hers and he shrugged his shoulders.

"I'll go first," he sighed, dropping to his knees and for the first time peering into opening. "I swear I don't know if we'll fit through. They's not a cop on the force upstairs that would fit through here."

Annie had to smile at that. Many of the officers, up to the state police level, were heavier than you'd like your police force to be. Might be a good story, she thought, a study of law enforcement's weight problem in Raleigh County.

Ralphie sat down on the dark, stone ring around the vat and eased his legs into the opening. Annie kneeled beside him and took his arm. He smiled up at her. "Hey, thanks."

Annie didn't like either the smile or the implication that they were getting 'chummy' all of a sudden. She still blamed Ralph for their current dilemma and their future dilemma if they ever got out of Hades central. Ralph was now to his hips—small—but still the biggest part of his lithe body. He completely blocked out the visible light and seemed to be momentarily stuck until, continuing to wiggle his legs, he eased through. His chest, shoulders and head squeezed through and he disappeared to the other side.

"Jeeeeeeeeeezzzzzzzzzzzzz," Ralph said loud enough for Annie to hear.

"What is it?" she asked, not knowing if they were in mortal danger or if he'd maybe found others who had been unfortunate enough to make the same downward plunge they had.

"You gotta see this," he said, poking his head back into the hole, "you ain't gonna believe it."

Annie hunkered down and, like Ralphie, approached the opening feet first. Her hips, somewhat bigger than Ralph's, were quite stuck until Ralph grabbed her by the legs and helped wiggle her through. "Close your eyes," Ralph whispered as she started to stand. Sheesh, she muttered to herself, but closed them anyway. Now standing, she was waiting for Ralph to let her open them. "You afraid of heights?" he tried to ask casually, and Annie immediately knew she was in trouble.

"Yes," she said, squinting her eyes closed now harder, all of sudden not wanting to open them. Gently Ralph eased her back until she was half sitting in the opening they had just come through. He shushed as he moved to the side, the light now visible through her eyelids.

"Ok." Annie said a real quick prayer then opened her eyes. Her head instinctively leaned backward against the rock wall as she gasped for breath. The chamber they were in now, near the top, was huge—as tall as any major league domed stadium but only as wide as maybe the field itself. It was like they were inside a huge, hollow beehive. Her heart raced from fear as she pressed her head into the wall behind her. She closed her eyes again and wondered how they were going to get back through the hole, and then what. But she certainly wasn't going to navigate on the narrow ledge on which she now found herself.

About to cry, Annie dropped her notebook, grabbing her companion's arm. "Oh God, Ralphie, what are we going to do? I can't do this, I'm going to have a heart attack!"

Ralph shushed her again and stroked her arm, looking around the ledge to see how it spiraled—Guggenheim-like—gently to the bottom. He knew he could make it, as it would only get better, not worse, as they descended. He had his doubts about Annie, but he certainly wasn't going to leave her either there on the ledge to faint and fall to her death or to crawl back into the tomb-like catacomb.

14

The Boyd Church of God was gathering solemnly for an unusual Tuesday evening service. This was Annie's church, and word passed through the community like wildfire when her truck was found parked on Neville, near the blocked perimeter during the downtown bomb search which, thankfully, never materialized. That was the good news. The bad news was Annie hadn't been seen since, and a search of her home yielded no clues that might pan out as to her disappearance.

Some cried as they entered wood-frame structure, fearing the worst. Others prayed. Howard, not a church going man, parked tentatively toward the street and awkwardly got out his car. He adjusted his tie as he saw 'the family of God' moving into the church arm in arm. He checked his watch, five minutes till. Swallowing hard and lost in thought, he took his first step toward the door but was nearly run over by the patrol car that cut him off.

"Sheesh!" he cried aloud, jumping back in true fear. He relaxed when he saw it was Chief Hall, realizing he too was parking and joining the service.

Hall, also not an avid church attendee, got out of his car just as awkwardly as did Howard. And his uniform made him stand out even more. The bell in the steeple began to ring as the two gangly troubadours entered the foyer. Reverend Brown, a heavy set man, short in stature and balding of palette, greeted them. Brown closed the outside door behind them and the inner doors as they took seats in the very back pew.

The man of God slowly walked down the center aisle and occasionally touched the shoulder of a brother or sister sitting near the center. He ascended the carpeted stage and took his position behind the pulpit. On his belt he turned on his mike and coughed softly, checking that it was on.

"Good evening," he intoned softly. Reverend Brown could rock and roll with the best of them in the Pentecostal world, but he could be solemn and sober when the situation called for it. A few parishioners repeated his good evening and fell silent again.

Without prepared remarks, he stared out at the gathered family and friends of Annie. Not knowing her fate made it all the worse. If they had known, if there was a body, if there was some finality, he had a litany of remarks that would do in that situation. But they didn't know—there was no evidence of foul play. Likewise, there was no evidence that she was alive and well either. He feared his congregation was in for a long, tough fight in this instance.

"We come out this lovely Tuesday evening with a single purpose in mind—to pray for our beloved sister whose whereabouts, whose very fate, is unknown at this time. But I've got good news..." The entire congregation looked up to him in anticipation. His pause was uncomfortably long. With a nod of his head he pronounced the good news. "God knows." As the congregation took in his meaning they collectively felt that, indeed, it was in God's hands.

Howard leaned over to Chief Hall and whispered, "I wish he'd give us a call." Hall lightly chuckled then stared back down at his hands. Both felt a measure of responsibility for this gathering—for Annie's very life—both had put her in harms way in one capacity or another. The choir entered the chapel from the back and took their places behind Reverend Brown and the pulpit. A feeble lady softly tickled the keys as they opened their hymnals to the same page. Once everyone was set, the pianist paused briefly then tore into a rousing version of 'What a Friend We Have in Jesus' as Reverend Brown shouted 'glory hallelujah.' Hall looked over to Howard who returned the look. A nod of the head and both quietly exited the back of the church, the sun still quite high in the early evening sky. They walked in silence to their respective cars. It was Howard that spoke first.

"Man, I hope she's ok."

Hall nodded in agreement, unwrapping a piece of candy and popping it into his mouth. "Me too," he agreed, continuing to nod, looking toward downtown and seeing Annie walking away from him less than twenty-four hours ago. Of the two, Hall was the less optimistic. He had seen a lot of things over the years as an officer of the law—horrible things that happened to people just as nice as Annie. In his mind he knew she was dead—and dreaded receiving the call of confirmation. Would she be...no, he stopped his mind from thinking the worst.

"Wanna get a cup of coffee?" he asked Howard. The newspaperman nodded as Hall mentioned Cracker Barrel. They drove off as the choir inside was on their third song of heavenly hope and prayer.

15

Annie sat with her eyes closed listening to Ralphie's logic and pleadings regarding their necessary journey downward. She couldn't keep her head from shaking side to side in an emphatic display of 'no'. But she knew in her heart that going back—assuming that she could—would lead to nowhere. Her breathing finally regulated, her courage just a tad past the proverbial cowardly lion, she finally said she'd try and Ralph said 'thatagirl.'

"What time do you have?" he asked, trying to distract her from her fear of heights. Annie held her left arm all the way up near her eyes before opening them. The light was dim but with the press of a button the dial lit up.

"It's 9:40," she replied drolly, her mind not distracted from the five-hundred foot plunge straight down. She was still not sure if she could do it, even though she had agreed to try.

Ralph shook his head. "No it's not, it's ten o'clock."

Annie shook her head. "No, it's 9:40."

Ralph stared at her like she was from another planet. "I saw your watch, it said precisely ten o'clock." His head continued to shake in disbelief.

Annie clutched her stomach with her 'watched' hand and managed a peak down—she shuddered and closed her eyes again wanting more than anything else to not have to confront her fear of heights. She swallowed hard, her throat dry and tight. "I keep my watch twenty minutes fast," she said quickly.

Ralph heard the words but didn't believe them. He shook his head as if trying to clear it of water in his inner ear. "You're telling me you set your watch twenty minutes faster than the real time?" Annie nodded. "Why?" he asked, the question so obvious he didn't feel as though he needed to ask it.

Annie rolled her head, keeping contact with the stone behind her, and looked at Ralph somewhat askew. "Gives me some leeway if I'm running late. My clocks at the house are twenty minutes fast too."

Again Ralph shook his head hard. "It doesn't change the time," he said knowingly, "the time is still whatever it is."

With both hands at her side, Annie slowly pushed herself to a standing position—still leaning somewhat backwards, but only her feet and hands touching in an uneven tripod. "C'mon," she said, grabbing his left arm with her right hand, "let's start down."

Very easily Ralph began sliding to his right, keeping as far back as possible from the precipitous drop. Annie followed his lead, staring into his shoulder that was at eye level. Her left hand trailed behind her, feeling the smooth but uneven rock behind them. Ten minutes passed and sweat poured from Annie's scalp down her forehead and into her eyes.

"Stop," she'd say, then lean to the right and wipe her eyes on Ralphie's shirt, clutching his arm, still steadying herself with her left hand. "Ok." They would go another few minutes and she'd say stop again, again needing to remove the stinging sweat from her eyes. Patiently Ralph surveyed the spiral below and estimated their time of descent at about four days. He rolled his eyes to the ceiling as the running of what was left of Annie's make-up gave her an eerie, Halloween look. They were about a third of the way down when Ralphie noticed that both of Annie's hands were relatively empty.

"Where's your notebook?" he asked with dread. Their eyes met and he knew the answer. He looked around her then up, shaking his head. "I can always climb back up if we need to write anything." Annie didn't argue as she didn't want to be left alone on the precipice to forever.

They began to make a little better time near what Ralphie estimated to be the halfway point. Annie's confidence seemed to grow even though her legs were tiring considerably given the constant side-to-side movement. She still held on tightly to Ralphie's arm—but most of her make-up was now on his sleeve. Her unadorned face, Ralphie noticed, was even prettier than when a full makeover had been applied. But, Ralphie thought to himself, this light had fooled him before with women. He turned his attention to the remaining journey to what they both hoped would truly be the bottom.

About four spirals from the bottom, now only about fifty feet up, there was a slight alcove with what looked to be a bench carved out of the stone. Ralph eased into the opening and sat down, Annie following. Both took a deep breath. Annie finally leaned forward to peer over the edge—now not near as daunting as it had been over an hour ago. With legs crossed and arms resting on them, Ralph made a casual observation.

"So," he baited her, eyes forward, "what time is it now?"

Before she realized her chain was being pulled she turned on the little light on her dial and announced 11:05. After a moment's pause Ralph again asked the obvious.

"Now is that 11:05, or 11:25, or 10:45?"

Annie's head whipped around, fury apparent in her face. "What in tarnation does it matter if it's 11:05 in the day or night down here..." Her voice trailed off as her gaze moved to the left beyond Ralph's wide-eyed expression to the wall behind him. "Would you look at that..."

Ralph turned his head to match her gaze and found what had caught her attention, and perhaps saved his life from her growing wrath. Graffiti. Looked to be chalk on stone. Ralph approached it with his index finger when Annie slapped his hand.

"Hey, what was that for?" he drew back quickly, holding his hand as if it were seriously injured.

"Don't touch that—we have no idea what primitive culture left those drawings." Her eyes drew closer as she looked to the contact between the stone and the chalk. "Or for that matter, if it was humans at all."

Ralph stood and backed up two steps, taking the entire drawing in. He cocked his head to the left and the right, his eyes questioning if the top was truly the top or if the top was really the bottom of the drawing. In the very center appeared to be a very smooth, black shiny stone. Small—looked like obsidian. Ralph began to reach his hand toward it when he thought better of it.

"Can I touch the stone in the middle?" he pleaded with Annie. After a heavy sigh and closer inspection, she said to go ahead.

Very gingerly Ralph extended his hand, index finger leading, and touched the smooth, cold surface. He lowered his hand so that his fingertip was now gently massaging the glass-like stone. He continued to rub, neither he nor Annie noticing the faint glow that had started behind them down at the bottom of the cavern.

The glow rose quickly, starting at their feet and in no time had encompassed their entire bodies. Both turned and stared the fifty or so feet down to what used to be the cavern floor. The swirl of colors and light took their breath away. It reminded Annie of her visit to Yellowstone a second time and the many and varied hot springs that she had seen. This pool lacked the definition of those in Yellowstone—and the accompanying steam—but was no less beautiful. Without thinking Ralph let his finger slip off the stone. As quickly as the whirlpool had appeared it disappeared. Annie looked to Ralphie with wonder in her eyes.

"What the heck was that?" she asked of her solitary companion.

"I don't know," Ralphie replied, looking back to the drawing and the stone in the center, "but it seems to have started when I rubbed this stone." He paused for just a minute. "Want me to rub it again?"

Annie pursed her lips, thinking of the possible risks. Finally she looked to Ralph and nodded her head.

Again Ralph gently touched the stone, both fixing their eyes on the cavern floor—which looked to be nothing more than a gray, stone surface. As Ralph began to massage the stone the floor began to take on colors of the most vibrant hues—blues, greens, yellows, purples— all beginning to swirl in a clockwise direction. Soon the floor was no longer visible as the spinning whirlpool grew faster and faster. Again the glow crept up and danced along the walls and paths until it had bathed Ralph and Annie from head to toe. Now they looked up and watched the swirl of colors as it climbed the catacomb toward the top. Just ten feet remained when Annie lightly took hold of Ralphie's arm.

Both tensed as light now filled the cavern. They gasped as they were hit by a wave of water that nearly knocked them off their feet.

"WHOA!" screamed Ralphie as his hands grabbed onto the stone seat on which they had rested. Annie too fell to her knees and grabbed on, the growing vortex of the whirlpool behind sucked at them, trying to pull them to the depths that now appeared to be endless. Their bodies lifted from the stone path and were horizontally flapping in the vortex. "Hold on!" Ralphie screamed over the din created by splashing waves. Annie didn't respond but did hold on tight. They were both soaked from the virtual storm that had erupted in the cavern.

As soon as it had started, it ended. They fell to their knees, their knuckles still white from holding onto the stone seat with all their might. Very reluctantly each released their grips on the stone that saved them from obvious doom and destruction. Climbing back to their feet, Ralphie touched Annie's arm and pointed below. The last remnants of the whirlpool of water disappeared and the floor again became dull, dry stone. With her fist Annie drilled Ralph in the right arm.

"Ow!" he cried, "what are you hitting me for?"

"If you so much as touch one more thing I WILL kill you, do you understand?" She was serious, and Ralph nodded his head in agreement—wanting to make the point that she said he could rub the stone—but not wanting to incite her more than she already was. He asked the only question he could think of.

"What time is it?"

Annie glared at him and, with only fifty feet to fall, began walking quickly on down the spiral toward the bottom, her hand sliding over the smooth, wet wall for balance. Ralph chuckled silently and followed.

16

The first story about the missing reporter with the Register-Herald appeared two days later. Howard himself penned the piece. It was short, provided her official bio and a pic that accompanied her many stories—one in which the community at large was very familiar. Front page, bottom right. A brief mention of her coverage of the bomb threat that had closed the downtown area for half a day in conjunction with her disappearance. People all over the county stared at the lovely reporter's picture and knew in their hearts, collectively, that the worst had happened.

Howard too sat in his office staring at Annie's picture, wondering what had happened to her, hoping against hope that his worst fears wouldn't be realized. In a daze he scanned the remaining stories on the front page, finding nothing of interest to take his mind off of his lost compatriot. Page two was even less compelling. Page three contained world and national news of no interest. Page four was the editorial page, again a virtual desert of banality. He finally closed the paper and had laid it down on his desk when Dave the photographer knocked and stuck his head in the door.

"Hey boss," he called out, trying to convey a lightness to his voice, "going out to Taco Bell for lunch, you want me to bring you anything back?"

Howard shook his head no. His appetite had been lost since Annie's disappearance. Dave stood awkwardly at the door for a moment then completely entered, shutting the door behind him.

"Listen Howard," he began tentatively, "Annie's a big girl, she can take care of herself."

Howard exhaled heavily and looked out the glass window behind his photographer, hoping to again see Annie bouncing across the newsroom with a fax or photo in hand. He looked back to Dave with a totally blank expression.

"You believe she's alright?" he asked flatly.

Dave shrugged his shoulders. "I hope so," he said, resignation now in his voice too. "She's quite a lady, I think she'll be ok." Dave paused for a moment, chewing on his bottom lip. "Have we considered that maybe she's just run off to get married or something like that?"

Howard stared at Dave with a slight measure of contempt. "That's why you're a photographer," he said, uncharacteristically cutting down one of his better employees. "Why would she leave her truck on the street, a half mile from home, to get repeated tickets and ultimately be towed?" The question was obviously rhetorical and Howard continued. "Why would we not in some way know she was dating the love of her life? And she was..." Howard winced at his use of the past tense... "is...very dependable. She would have never jeopardized her job by not acquiring the proper approval for leave. No," Howard summed up his strong opinion, "she's not out gallivanting around on some Roman holiday."

Dave again shrugged his shoulders, uncertain what exactly a Roman holiday was. "I guess you're right. Want me to make up some banners and begin to post them around town?"

Howard nodded his head disinterestedly. "And thanks for the offer, but I'm not hungry."

Dave stood to leave, then pointed down to the back page of the newspaper. "I'd have loved to have gotten a shot of that."

Howard glanced down to the page, saw nothing worthy of Dave's photographic talents. "What?" he asked, looking up.

Dave touched the story mid-way in the page. "The waterspout. Came out of the Kanawha River right outside the Capitol building. Hundreds saw it. Just lasted about a minute but soaked some cars and one security guard on the capitol grounds. Bent right over the boulevard and touched down there behind Lincoln's statue. Some who saw it said it was like a water-filled rainbow rose up out of the river and leaned over to kiss the earth, then disappeared. Man, I'd have loved to have photographed that."

Howard was now reading the story with interest, half hearing what his photojournalist was saying. Might have been a water main rupture, but the water company reported no water loss of that magnitude. Could have been a mini tsunami—had there been a minor quake, explained one geologist. But no sensors in the area picked up any seismic recordings. Upon completion Howard muttered, "Well I'll be darned," looking up just as Dave was shutting the door behind him.

17

Michael Oather Justice settled into the metallic seat next to his best friend Gary. Having been on tours of the Beckley Exhibition Coal mine numerous times, with it practically right in his back door, he was fairly bored with the annual field trip. While it was his heritage and while it was the occupation of his father and while his grandfather had died in a similar mine not too far from this one, mining just didn't interest Michael. Now had they took up the rails and paved the fairly narrow mine passages and put up some black lights and posters, maybe then Michael would have been a regular, enthusiastic tourist/skateboarder.

But those changes hadn't been made and the black tour guide and former miner droned on about safety while a couple of his stock jokes fell flat on the wooden ties to which the steel rails were anchored. A whistle blew and the tram lurched forward, the mountain quickly swallowing up the seventh grade class from Park Junior High.

The tram rumbled along and made its usual right at the first intersection. In all the tours Michael had been on, he had never been taken to the left, it had always been to the right. Sitting in the very back of the nearly full car, Michael revealed his plan to Gary in a whisper.

"When he turns off the light, I'm heading back. I'll catch up with you outside."

Gary's eyes widened. "You can't do that!" he said way too loud.

"Shhhhhhhh," Michael shushed him, "I can too, and intend to. What if Tom Sawyer never went in that cave with Becky? What if Huck had never gone to that island with Jim?"

"That's fiction," Gary intoned, again too loudly.

Michael nodded his head. "I know it's fiction, but Mark Twain had to have done something like that himself to have written about it."

"And you wanna be a writer?" Gary mocked his friend, knowing full well that what Michael wanted was to be mischievous. He finally sighed and held up his hands. "All right man, but I ain't covering for you if you get caught."

Michael looked to the front of the car at his teacher and the tour guide. "You can come with me if you want."

"Yeah, like they ain't going to notice BOTH of us gone."

The stop finally came. The retired miner ambled out of the car and talked about black damp and carbide lamps and a nickel per ton coal. With a big smile he said he was going to turn off the lights now, so all could see just how dark it was without artificial lighting. Michael patted Gary's leg and eyed the track and the roof that lay behind them. The light went off and he stepped out of the car. Gary scooted slightly over to take up part of the absence for when the light came back on.

As the guide droned on about methane gas and canaries, Gary could hear the soft padding of Michael's tennis shoes heading away. The light came on and Gary saw Michael in the distance quickly duck against the rib and remain still. The guide retook his seat on the tram and fired it up. As they drove away Gary watched Michael hug the wall and make his way back toward the entrance.

18

Annie and Ralphie stood at the bottom of the humongous cavern and looked up, nearly tipping backwards to see the very top of the beehive-shaped cathedral. The narrow opening near the top from which they had entered was no longer visible. Even the winding trail from which they had made their way to the bottom couldn't be seen in spots. Ralph looked down to the nearly dry floor and wondered how the wall of water had so quickly appeared then disappeared.

Annie rubbed the side of her neck as the tension in her muscles was reluctant to subside. Ralph squeezed the back of her neck in a massaging motion as Annie began lolling her head from side to side. She suppressed the moan that wanted to come, but did mutter that that felt good. Ralph smiled and now, with both hands, massaged her shoulders and drove his thumbs into her shoulder blades. Annie finally said stop and quickly recomposed herself, reestablishing the invisible cocoon between she and her companion. Both began to look around for an exit. Finding none, Ralph hoped aloud that nobody came down and rubbed that button, or they'd be goners for sure. Annie's eyes widened in the realization that he was exactly right, yet neither were sure that it was rubbing that stone that brought in the torrent of water. Their pace around the circle quickened as they desperately began to seek a way out.

They were approximately half way around the cavern when Ralph grabbed Annie's arm and stopped her forward progress. He was looking back in the direction they had came, then Annie saw it. Something about the wall wasn't right. They approached it cautiously.

"This is a labyrinth," Ralph whispered, as their eyes now recognized clearly the exit—and the probable source of the water's exit—from the vast chamber. This time Annie let Ralph take the lead as they slowly approached the narrow slice through the solid rock wall. Ralph intentionally passed the opening to see it again from the other side. "Would you look at that," he said in astonishment, shaking his head.

Annie joined him on the far side as she too studied the unbelievable optical illusion that masked the crevice. It was totally hidden from view—only by walking in a clockwise direction was it visible—even then you had to be really paying attention. Yet the spiral down from the top brought them in a counter-clockwise direction, naturally feeding them in the same direction along the bottom. After a couple minutes spent ogling the opening, Ralphie nodded his head in a forward direction.

"Let's roll," he said, his eyes now set to the passageway. Annie gulped and fell in line right behind him, now sure that death, doom and destruction must lie on the other side of this wall.

19

Michael's heavy breathing wasn't from exhaustion—he was in good shape from his hours and hours of skateboarding in and around town—it was from nerves. While he was admittedly quite mischievous, he realized this could have been his most brazen, foolhardy act to date regarding a school function. It took him less than ten minutes to get back to the fork in the tracks where he stood for a moment catching his breath. He could either leave by the way they came in, or he could continue on the left track and see where it went. After a moment's hesitation, he continued with his original plan and headed left. While not as well lit as the right track, there was still ample light—at least to the first right turn a football field away.

With hands in pockets he walked between the steel rails as he had done so many times on the outside with the several tracks that coursed through Beckley. Usually he whistled and/or threw rocks, but this time he was as quiet as he could be, knowing there were two, maybe three other conductors that sometimes spent time inside this mine refilling lamps, checking switching stations, etc. He came to the gentle right turn and found a straight stretch of track for what looked to be a half-mile, then a left bend. Again the light was sufficient to proceed and he did so.

It was in the next turn that he got the fright of his life. The turn was gentle enough, the lights were still on, but in the distance he could hear a slight rumble. His first thought was maybe there was an earthquake and his slight claustrophobia kicked in. If this mine were to collapse AND he survives, he would be trapped, only to die of starvation and lack of oxygen. While these thoughts danced in and occupied his mind, it took him a moment to recognize the dual lights that approached far down the tracks. As his mind did begin to focus on the lights, he recognized them as being on the very tram he had hopped off of less than twenty minutes ago! Holy smokes, his mind cried out as the tram barreled his way. He quickly looked to the left and right searching for a place to hide. Then he spotted it—just behind and to the right was a dark, untracked area that seemed to be a spur off of the main line. He quickly darted back and eased into the darkness, peeking around and seeing the tram amble closer and closer.

Man, what an idiot I am, Michael thought to himself. Of course this is the return route, he realized. Now the light of the tram actually shown on the left side of his hiding place and the reflection made him quite visible. He eased deeper into the spur where the darkness began to consume him, even with the radiated light from the train. His left foot touched something hard and metallic and he nearly tripped, his right foot quickly came around to catch his balance, also hitting the same piece of metal. He fell face first, dust lifting off the floor and swirling around him. He pushed himself up with his arms and looked back to the opening just as the tram conductor passed by, his back to this particular opening. Michael didn't move a muscle, knowing that his classmates on two cars would be passing by next. There they were, all riding mindlessly along. Michael watched closely for Gary and caught just a glimpse of his as the car passed by. He wasn't sure but he felt as though Gary had seen him too for the brief window of time that the car passed by.

Carefully Michael stood up and held onto the closest wall while his eyes adjusted to the darkness. This spur was very narrow with crag-like corners—very different from anything else he had seen in his many 'supervised' trips into the mine. As much as he knew he needed to leave and join his class, as a headcount was inevitable, he was drawn deeper into the maze. His eyes had adjusted nicely to the darkness and he could make out the walls but nothing on the floor. Slowly he slid each foot forward, careful not to trip and lose his balance again. The floor was surprisingly smooth and without texture—he was thinking this was skate-boardable, except for the sharp twists and turns it took to the left and to the right.

He was maybe fifty feet deep into the narrow passageway when he detected a faint glow ahead. He continued to ease his way along, pretty sure that this passage led from where he had just been to the other side somewhere near where he had hopped off. When he got there, he would hotfoot it back to the entrance and hopefully join everyone in the gift shop. The light grew brighter and Michael knew the tracks had to be right around the corner. Sure enough, he came into the source of the light, but discovered that it wasn't from the right-hand tracks where he jumped off, but instead the light came from above—a narrow hole in the ceiling that seemed to go all the way to surface of the hill that covered this mine. He first looked at it from the obtuse angle with which he approached, then stood directly beneath it and looked heavenward. His eyes had just focused on the light above when the floor beneath him dropped open. His scream was quickly swallowed up by both the earth and the closing of the portal—from above. From below, however, his scream carried well into both space and time.

20

Annie touched Ralphie's arm as they began to enter the passage to God-knows-where. "Ralph, you think we'd be better off going back?"

Ralph joined her gaze backward into the vast cavern and up the daunting distance to the portal in. He shook his head. "Nah, if we go back we just end up in the feather room with no way back onto the slide that brought us in. Even if we could get up to it, there's no way we could climb that thing. It was straight up and down most of the time, very slick, and sometimes we flew over nothing. Not sure how we'd manage that going back up." With that, he turned back toward the only exit they had found when Annie again touched Ralphie's arm.

"Listen," she said in a whisper, listening carefully, "do you hear something?"

Ralph strained his ears but could hear nothing. He turned to continue when Annie again pulled on his arm. This time he heard it.

It was faint, distant, but was the unmistakable sound of someone screaming. And it seemed to be growing in clarity, if not volume. Ralph and Annie gently eased out of the opening of the passage and back into the voluminous cavern. A pause came in the plaintive cry. Ralph and Annie looked at each other with some concern in their countenance. A minute or two passed of total silence. They were about to turn, disheartened further, back to their only reasonable way out when they heard it again. This time they could make out screams punctuated with 'whoa's' and curse words that—in a weird kinda way—made them even more homesick. The volume increased again and actually began to echo in the vast chamber in which they stood, giving the moment a surreal texture that frightened them more than they had been on their entire journey. It reached a fevered, wailing pitch then stopped—stopped dead—as if the life in the tortured soul had been extinguished.

The hair on the back of their necks rose as the echoes died and the silence grew. Annie pushed Ralph forward and said let's get out of here. Ralph needed no encouragement and eased back into the passageway, both afraid of the uncertainty in either direction.

They found themselves in a narrow tunnel that seemed to be winding slightly downward, continuing for all practical intents and purposes in exactly the wrong direction from the surface for which they longed. The walls and roof was featureless, lacking any primitive artwork that might give them some direction. But there were no choices, no forks in the road, no hidden passageways.

"Where do you think the light comes from?" Annie asked quietly, her voice echoing off the tunnel walls then coming back to them moments later. Ralph shushed her, then whispered in her ear.

"I think it's coming from up ahead." Annie noticed how warm his breath felt in her ear. She remembered hot baths and warm beds in the not-too-distant past—then remembered that were it not for her present company, she wouldn't be in the current predicament she found herself. Her eyes tightened as she watched him cautiously move ahead. On the one hand, she was grateful that she wasn't experiencing this alone. On the other hand, were it not for the idiot in front of her, she'd probably be at work—she glanced at her watch—no, lunch, right now. Thinking of lunch made her realize just how hungry she was.

Around a bend to the right they found a second sitting area carved out of the stone walls—this one without primitive engravings or the bath-time button they had found on the trip down. Annie sighed then gave out the slightest giggle.

"What," said Ralphie, looking to his companion.

Annie smiled. "I'd take that bag of chips you wrestled from the machine the first time we met." Without looking at him, Annie could feel Ralphie's big, dumb grin beside her.

"You cain't let those machines rip you off," Ralph said again, as if this were his mantra at this point in his life. Just as he was about to speak again his stomach gave out a long, low growl. Ralph and Annie looked at each other and burst out laughing, both so hungry they could eat a horse.

Their laughter echoed up and down the chamber and came back to them not unlike the screams they had just heard inside the chamber. Their smiles vanished and Ralph nodded his head in the direction they were going and whispered, "Let's go." Annie stood and joined his quiet progress.

21

Michael Oather Justice scrambled up like a madman out of the huge vat of feathers in which he had landed. Spitting and hacking and flailing, he finally reached the top and pulled himself out, lying on the cool stone as tiny feathers and feather-parts swirled around him. His heavy breathing captured more than one stray feather causing him to cough violently until he had cleared his throat. He finally sat up and looked around at his surroundings, blinking away the darkness as his eyes adjusted to the half-light. His eyes focused on the shoe-horn-of-a-thing that threw him into the vat of feathers. It reminded him of water parks where chutes dropped you straight into pools of water. He next looked to the vat of feathers, full to the brim, giving the appearance that one could simply 'walk across' to the other side. He knew better.

Standing, he surveyed the rest of the room, which was nothing.

Featureless. What the heck am I supposed to do now, he thought to himself. He wondered about Gary and the rest of his classmates, they were probably having lunch now. At what point would they miss him, or would they miss him at all? And would Gary confess that his friend had jumped ship—or, more appropriately, railcar—halfway through the tour? And, more importantly, would a search party be formed and how in the world would they ever find the tunnel he had fell through and into this dark underworld.

His breathing now normal, he began to walk around the small room. He looked high and low for some hint of an exit. Finally he found it, right at the base of the room, about halfway around. A faint light glowed from the other side. Cautiously he approached, continuing to scan the room for a second or maybe third exit. Seeing none, he eased down to his knees and peeked through the opening. The hole was fairly deep and he could see nothing. He lay on his belly and gently began inching through the crevice which was quite big enough to allow his slender body through. With legs still in the feather room, his head now poked out the other side. A wide-eyed look of fright took over his countenance as his mouth uttered a low-pitched Jeeeeeeezzzzzzzzzzzzzzzzzzzzzzzzz.

He quickly backed out stood again in the feather room. His breathing was labored again as he walked the periphery looking for a second exit. None. He looked back up to the chute—no chance of getting to it, much less getting up it. Michael went back to the opening and sat down, letting his legs dangle into the crevice.

"This ain't good," he spoke aloud to no one, continuing to stare into the faint light of the other room. He weighed his options. He could stay where he was, hoping against hope for a search team to find him. Or he could go through this hole and plunge a thousand feet to his death. Picking a feather off of his right shoulder, he gently began to ease through the opening.

With his head about halfway through his feet touched the spiral stairway on the other side. He paused as his feet rested on terra firma, wondering if he should continue on or push back up and into the feather room. That didn't seem to hold any options, so he eased on out of the hole. Using the end of the opening as a seat, Michael steadied himself with his eyes closed, his knuckles showing white on either side of his legs.

"C'mon," he encouraged himself, "you can do this." With that said he opened his eyes and again laid his head back to the cool wall behind him. "Whoooooooooaaaaaaaaaaaaaaa," he said, his head now turning to the left attempting to get even closer to the wall behind him. "This is

NOT good," he repeated into the vacant air, knowing his short life was about to come to an end. It was then that he distinctly felt his right foot was on something that wasn't exactly stone floor. He wiggled his foot slightly and, sure enough, the floor moved with him. Very cautiously he leaned his head forward and peered down to his foot. It was a notebook of some sort. He lifted his right foot and carefully scooted the notebook between his feet, then placed his right foot back on solid earth. Squatting, with his head as far back as he could keep it and still see the pad, he eased down and grabbed it with his right hand. A little quicker he stood back up and sat again in the mouth of the crevice.

A little more comfortable than before, he began to leaf through the notebook, noting the feminine hand that had composed every entry. The notes weren't shorthand, but the text was. Cochran @ 8. Photo shoot 9:30. Don't forget lunch OTD Thursday. He looked at the front of the book and again at the back—no identifying signature. He started to toss the thing into the abyss, but quickly came to realize that he might very well need a pad of paper if he were to find help. Tearing out the top page full of notes that meant nothing to him, he wadded it up and tossed it back just inside the crevice but not into the feathers. He nodded his head. A paper trail, he imagined. He'd leave paper for as long as it lasted. Very carefully he began to ease his way down the spiral.

22

The staff meeting that Howard called was unusual in that it was on Wednesday, and included the chief of police and one of his several deputies—Eddy Thompson, who did the artist's sketch based on the description given by Mike Justice. Howard cleared his throat as the last reporter ambled in with a full cup of coffee.

"Ok, listen, heads up guys." Howard looked at each person in the room as his notes lay on the table. "We're going on the offensive regarding Annie's disappearance. The reason I've asked Chief Hall and Eddy to come by is that we think—well, we pretty much know for sure—that Annie's disappearance and the window buster downtown are related. Eddy talked to the kid who saw the incident and rendered this sketch..." Howard held up a copy of the sketch and turned it for all to see. "We're going to run both Annie's picture and this sketch on the front page of tomorrow's paper. Any suggestions, or reasons that we should not run this tomorrow?"

A moment of silence passed before one of the photographers spoke up. "Any kind of reward going to be offered?"

Howard nodded approvingly. "Yes, I've personally pledged $5,000 for her safe return, and the city has offered twenty grand. Double if Annie is returned safely AND this punk is convicted of the crimes he committed."

This time it was Oscar the Grouch who spoke up. "Crimes—you mean busting out windows?" He glanced around the room with a smirk on his face. "That oughta land him in the slammer for life."

Howard's glare was menacing, but it was Chief Hall who explained the severity of the situation. "By crimes," he interjected, "I think Howard means the threats attached to the rock—which we know of— and the possible abduction and transport of one of our better citizens— of which we're pretty sure." Oscar's smirk vanished as he began to look at his fingernails as if they could use a good trimming.

"What would be a good headline?" asked one of the copy editors.

Howard pursed his lips, pinching them between his thumb and index finger. "Hall, what do you think?"

"Hey hoss," Chief Hall quickly responded, "this is your business."

Again Oscar spoke up. "You know what I think?" With no pause for a possible quip from those gathered, he continued. "We oughta run a big headline—something like 'Register-Herald Reporter Abducted'— you know, covering the entire width in 36 point type. Then...then," he repeated, looking around the room like a scientist on the verge of discovery, "then you run a story about Annie down the left side of the page with a subtitle and a story about Alfred E. Newman here with his own subtitle down the right side of the page—single headline, dual pictures, dual story." Oscar nodded his head once as if to seal the deal.

Howard continued pinching his bottom lip, then spoke softly. "Oscar, you old fool, I like it. But tell me, what makes you think this guy is Albert Newman?"

Oscar chuckled as several nodded their heads smiling. "ALFRED E. Newman...you know, the guy on Mad Magazine. I knowed I seen the little fellow before when I first saw his picture. He just needs some freckles." His glee was obvious as he looked around the room.

Howard erupted again. "This does NOT look like Alfred E. Newman!" His glare turned compassionately to Eddy Thompson who had drawn the sketch. "This man looks like the abductor of one of our own— now I suggest we take this a little more seriously." Howard was hot under the collar. "And," he dug at Oscar, "there is no such word as 'knowed'." With that he began barking orders as to who would do what in preparing for the morning addition. When everyone related to the paper had left the room, Howard looked again to Eddy whose face was slightly red.

"Eddy, it don't look like Alfred E. Newman, or whoever. That's a good sketch if you ask me."

Eddy didn't respond but looked deep in thought. Chief Hall thought his silence was rude and nudged him with his elbow. "Eddy, Howard's talking to you."

Eddy startled as if from a fitful sleep. "Oh...what?" he asked, blinking rapidly.

"I was just saying that it don't look like the Mad Magazine guy."

Eddy stood, he eyes set, and asked if he could use the phone. Howard said sure and glanced to Chief Hall, who shared his quizzical look with a shrug of the shoulders.

Eddy stepped out of the office and to the nearest cubical, dialed 9 for an outside line, then dialed the local number. Howard and Hall were out of earshot, but remained silent while Eddy carried on the brief conversation. He hung up and returned to the conference room, but did not sit down.

"I think I know who this is," he said with a certainty that defied comment. After a momentary pause he made his pronouncement. "This," he said, holding up the original sketch, "is my cousin Ralphie Johnson."

Both Howard and Chief Hall looked at him dumbfounded. "What makes you think that's Ralphie?" asked Chief Hall. Deep in his cerebral cortex Hall seemed to recall Ralph had once applied for a job on the force.

Eddy stared up at the ceiling, wishing that it wasn't true, but now sure that it was. And he also quickly realized the gravity of the charges that would be leveled against his good-natured cousin. "Two things. First, I introduced him to Annie on July the 4th, when Byrd and Jay were here." Chief Hall nodded his head, recalling how Ralphie had shut the gathering down cold by yelling across the courtyard at Eddy. "He was quite taken with Annie, I could tell."

Howard stood and moved to the window looking out at the reporter's cubes that went to the far wall. "So," he said, "go on."

"Second, I just called my Aunt Minnie—his mom. He ain't been home since the night of the threat downtown. The very night Annie disappears, so does he. Ain't it obvious?" Eddy looked from Howard to his chief and back to Howard. It was Hall who spoke.

"It does fit, Eddy, but that's pretty circumstantial. Is Ralph prone to disappearing from time to time?"

Eddy sighed. "Yeah, and Minnie hadn't thought nothing about it. I didn't mention my suspicions, didn't want to worry her to death. He'll run off to Charleston or sometimes to Charlotte or Darlington without telling nobody—he's a big NASCAR fan."

"Are there any races going on?" Howard asked.

Eddy again sighed and nodded. "There are races every weekend somewhere, once Daytona kicks off the season you can count on it. And Ralphie has been known to hitchhike as far as Florida."

The three men sat in silence, contemplating their next course of action. Howard sat back down heavily and pulled the rolling chair up under the table. "Ok, let's still run the sketch, as we have no evidence to suggest that it's actually your cousin. We'll not even mention it to James out there who is writing that particular story—don't want to prejudice him in anyway. Maybe somebody out there will recognize the sketch as somebody else, and Ralphie shows up tomorrow with a tan and a ball cap from Talladega."

Both Hall and Eddy looked at the editor quizzically. "Hey," Howard said, holding his hands palm up, "don't they race there too?"

23

Ralph and Annie slowly crept along the passage as it turned ever so slightly to the right and downward. A hint of a breeze seemed to wind its way up from the depths and felt cool on their skin. With Ralph leading the way and Annie lightly touching his sleeve from behind, they came upon a long, straight passageway with what appeared to be both shorter and taller tunnels that intersected the main one at ninety degree angles. The arched exits seemed to be in total darkness, and Ralph and Annie stood silently while surveying the situation.

"What do we do now?" Annie whispered into Ralphie's ear. Ralph shrugged.

"I suggest we stay on the main path," he whispered back. "Number one, at least we can see. Number two, we can always come back." With that said they gingerly inched forward, all too soon coming to the first archway, this one leading to the right and quickly down. It was totally dark beyond the faint light that peered in from the main hallway. And ominous. They hesitated only a moment then proceeded on. The next archway was about twenty feet beyond and exited to the left. Annie's eyes widened.

"Ralphie, this one goes up!" Ralph too had noticed the sharp incline just inside the half-lit portal. But he shook his head and suggested they stay the course. Annie turned several times before the next exit and looked longingly back to the one path they had found that led in a direction other than the center of the earth. From that point on they passed no less than fifty alternate passages, with only a few headed in an upward direction. Some actually seemed to stay on the same level as opposed to heading up or down.

"Oh no," groaned Ralphie, half turning toward Annie.

"What is it?" she asked tentatively, fear coursing through her already tense body.

With a heavy sigh Ralph said, "Dead end." Annie peered around him and could see the tunnel ended twenty feet or so ahead. She looked behind them, certain that she was only choosing a passageway that led up. They were at the conclusion of the tunnel and Ralph turned to her, disappointment on his face. "I cain't believe it," he drawled, leaning against the solid wall at the end.

Or at least he thought he was leaning against a solid wall, but quickly fell to the floor through the wall. He scrambled to his feet as Annie turned to see only wall.

"Ralph!" she called loudly, scanning the solid wall into which he seemed to disappear. Then his head—only his head—poked through the wall causing a slight scream to escape from Annie's lips.

"It's ok," he said calmly, "it's just a hologram." His hand came through the wall and she took it. Gently Ralph pulled her to and through the wall. As she passed through the very real hologram, every nerve ending seemed to pulse with excitement as if it had been lightly touched. On the other side Annie turned to look at, again, a solid wall. She slowly raised her hand and watched it and her arm disappear through the image.

"Wow," she said, impressed with the illusion.

"You think that's something," Ralph intoned, "you gotta see this."

Annie turned and looked into a round chamber twice the size of the original chamber in which they had entered. The light was barely sufficient to take it in. But this one was different. While the other had little more than the spiral walkway to the bottom, this chamber was filled with what looked to be rows of desks, amphitheater-like, all facing a center stage on which stood a circular podium into which a speaker would enter from the far side.

And the desks weren't desks per se, but were desk-like spaces that appeared to be hewn from the very floor. Behind each was not a chair but a single bench seat, also carved from the stone. Ralph and Annie surveyed the room from their vantage point and estimated the desks at about fifty. They found themselves at the top of a stairway feeding down to the center and outward in rows to the immovable workstations. Ralph took the first step gingerly, making sure that the steps weren't as convincing a hologram as was the wall immediately behind them. The steps were real and solid and quiet to walk on. Annie followed closely behind as they made their way down towards the center of the room, their eyes trying to take it all in while still focusing on the narrow steps before them.

"What do you think this is?" Annie whispered to Ralphie, her arms filled with chill bumps in the cool air of the chamber.

She saw Ralph shrug as he slowly continued downward. "I ain't got a clue," he said honestly, now head-high with the center podium that was a bit raised from the floor around it. They were close enough to touch the podium but did not. Ralph looked all around the room and Annie mimicked his actions. After a considerable pause Ralph began to walk around the raised dais, his hand lightly skimming the cool, gray stone.

On the backside they came upon three large steps leading upward to the podium. Ralph looked to Annie for encouragement but she simply shrugged her shoulders, keeping a keen eye out for movement in the amphitheater. Ralph took the first step tentatively, the second step with more confidence, and the third step as a politician making a victory speech just beyond the midnight hour.

"Let's get ready to rrrruuuummmbbbllle!" His voice boomed then echoed in the hollowed-out chamber, Annie covered her ears with her hands as the sounds bounced and re-bounced from left to right and from top to bottom. It was a full minute before the chamber was silent again and a faint hello was heard in the distance.

Annie looked to Ralph as he looked to her. He shushed her and motioned for her to duck with him behind the podium. The only entrance that they were aware of—not visible because of the hologram—was the one in which they had entered. They peeked out from each side as they listened carefully for additional sounds.

"Hellllooooooo," the voice intoned again, a little louder this time, with slightly audible footsteps. It definitely came from behind the hologram, as Ralph scanned the podium unsuccessfully for a loose rock to throw, if needed. Several anxious moments passed before they heard the voice grow more distant with another tentative hello. Quickly Ralph bounced up from behind the podium and jogged down then up the steps to the hologram as quietly as he could. Annie came up behind him as he cautiously poked his head through the hologram. He quickly drew it back in and made the surprise announcement.

"It's a kid," he said, incredulity in his voice.

Annie also eased her head through the hologram and quickly withdrew. "It is just a kid," she said, equally surprised even though Ralph had just made the announcement. This time Ralph did find a loose stone and tossed it through the hologram, hearing it rattle around in the tunnel beyond. They heard the footsteps stop, they imagined his turn, they heard his faint hello course toward them again.

"Shhhhh," Ralph shushed, then whispered, "we'll let him get back up to here then catch him, see what he knows. I think we can overpower him." Ralph made every effort to poke just one eye through the wall and was largely successful, seeing the youth about halfway up the corridor and gingerly making his way back. Ralph held up his hand to convey silence as the footsteps came closer and closer. Finally he mouthed the words, "When I count three."

The footsteps were now very close, they could even hear light—perhaps heavy—breathing. Ralph's upheld arm closed into a fist then he mouthed the word 'one' as his index finger shot out. 'Two' followed, his middle finger shooting out, then with 'three' and the ring finger they burst through the hologram and inadvertently knocked the young man down to the ground who was just turning at the dead end. Michael Other Justice scrambled to his feet and faced his attackers with fists drawn.

"MICHAEL!" Annie cried out, recognizing the young man from the police department interview. He recognized her too, but began stuttering as he also recognized Ralphie as the rock thrower of downtown.

"He...he...he's..." His wide-eyed gaze moved from Annie to Ralph and back to Annie, his index finger pointing to the man he saw toss the brick through the prosecuting attorney's office and walk away with a lilt to his step and a whistle on his lips.

"I know, I know," Annie cut him off, nodding knowingly. "He's Ernest T. Bass." Ralph looked to Annie, his face a mask of confusion. She nodded her head toward Michael. "He's the witness who saw you brick the PA office."

"Ohhhhhhhhh," said Ralph, now understanding the union between the two. He looked to Michael. "Where were you? I looked around all over before I busted it out."

Michael shrugged. "I was in the doorway of the print shop. I saw you carrying the brick and hid once you threw it. Why'd you do it man?"

An awkward silence passed as Ralph looked around searching for some reasonable explanation while Annie rolled her eyes toward the cave ceiling. "Uh...well" Ralph stammered, "uh, it was a mistake," he lied, "I thought the prosecutor had done something he didn't do."

Michael, generally a good read of character, knew that Ralph was lying and also knew that Annie knew that he was lying too. He sensed their strained relationship, then asked the only question he could think of, "Where did you guys come from?"

Ralph smiled and stood next to what he knew to be a hologram and raised his right fist and drove it—without consequence—through the false wall. Michael said 'whoa' and approached it himself, his hands held out in front of him. His hands simultaneously disappeared into the wall, then his elbows, and finally the entire front of his body was gone but the back of his body was still visible. Ralph and Annie heard him clearly say, "Whoa, this is TOO cool."

After a minute of passing into and out of the great hall, Michael finally returned. "Where are we?"

Ralph shrugged his shoulders. "Be danged if I know," he admitted, "but I'd guess we're pert near about twenty mile into the belly of the earth." After a pause and a quick look from Annie, Ralph asked, "How'd you get in here?"

Michael half-blushed and shook his head, embarrassed to say. "I was where I shouldn't have been." After a momentary pause in which neither Ralph nor Annie took their eyes off the youth, he went on. "Tour of the mine, I hopped off when they turned off the lights and somehow fell into this hole trying to hide."

"Did you come down a real long roller coaster?" Annie asked.

"Yeah, without a car though."

"That's good news," Ralphie announced confidently. Annie and Michael both stared at him until he explained. "Two portals—at LEAST two portals. The more ways outa here the better chance we got."

The three stood in silence as they surveyed the great hall again. The slight light that made the room visible just seemed to be there—had no apparent source. They were about to approach the podium again when they heard—and felt—the slightest rumble behind them and the hologram. They momentarily froze until they realized the noise was growing in intensity and headed straight toward them down the hidden corridor. Ralph grabbed both by the arms and pulled them around to the right—then crouched low behind one of the stone desks. Annie and Michael did the same.

The roar of what sounded like an engine grew deafening in literally seconds. All three covered their ears to filter out both the high-pitched whine and the low rumble of what sounded like the baddest, meanest Harley ever made. And their mouths flew open as the hologram was shattered into a spray of dancing rainbows as the rushing entity burst into and crossed the room, banking off the far wall and roaring directly over their heads only to spiral forward and return again in no time. Even though they remained crouched low to the floor they still ducked as the madman buzzed directly overhead.

After maybe ten or so tours of the outer wall, the big bike spun down and now rolled from desk to desk, starting with the back row and making it's way down. Its one pass directly on the stone desk that the three hid behind was equally deafening and frightening. You could see the underside of the massive wheels as it lightly skimmed from desk to desk. They peered farther out from behind their hiding place to see the thing slow considerably. It was now more than a blur and a noise to be deadened. It was a bike. Not just any bike, but a Harley—the biggest and shiniest Harley that Ralphie had ever seen, and he'd been to both Daytona and Sturgis in the last two years. The saddlebags were as big as sidecars. The seat was nearly the size of a full seat in the cab of a truck. Even the kickstand was as big as a small tree.

"Holy smokes," Ralph whispered, so appreciating the thing of beauty before him. Now he noticed for the first time the rider—a petite man— or so it seemed so on the massive bike. With helmet and back to them, the rider eased to a stop beneath the podium, dismounted, throwing his right leg back and over the leather seat. His right hand struggled to loosen the chinstrap, then he lifted the helmet off revealing his graying hair. All three gasped.

"That's Jimmy Taylor!" Ralph exclaimed in a whisper, with Annie and Michael nodding their heads in agreement but not taking their eyes off one of the few homeless people in Beckley. "Jimmy Taylor," Ralph repeated, his voice lower and saddened as he looked back to the killer bike. "Wow."

The man they called Jimmy Taylor laid his black helmet with no shield on the seat of his bike and began unsnapping the clasps to the left saddlebag. As the last clasp was released, the three heard the muffled yelps of a dog. And not just any dog. This was a Pomeranian, a fur ball if nothing else. For all the size of the bike that the duo came in on, this dog was about the size of one of the spark plugs. Taylor was nuzzling the dog with his nose and talking baby talk to the pet that stared directly at the body parts that weren't hidden by the desk on the back row.

24

Minnie Johnson poured the darkest tea her nephew Eddy had ever seen. It almost looked like coffee. "Sugar?" she asked, and Eddy said yes, a lot.

"What kind of tea is that, Aunt Minnie?"

The heavyset, short woman, who looked like a female, squat Ralphie, smiled graciously. "Got that down at the health food store at the mall. It's herbal—part ginseng, part quinine, part May apple."

Eddy gulped down the drink he had in his mouth. "Ain't quinine poison?"

"Nah," Minnie replied, "that's strychnine you're thinking of."

With very slight but overly noisy sips Eddy continued pretending to enjoy the worst cup of tea he'd ever tasted. He finally sat it down on the coffee table.

"Aunt Minnie, when precisely was the last time you heard from Ralphie?"

Minnie just shook her head, a hint of sadness in her look. "I guess he's done gone off to Charlotte for the race this weekend. I'll tell you that boy worries me to death." She rubbed her forehead lightly and Eddy noticed where she had an injury from the accident late last week.

"How's your head doing?"

"It's fine," taking her hand away and showing the healing contusion. "That would have been fifteen stitches a couple years ago the doctor told me," she said proudly, leaning her ample forehead toward Eddy, who nodded appreciatively. "No, Ralphie left the house...let's see," her eyes looked to the ceiling as her mouth dropped open, her best thinking position, "it was Tuesday I believe it was. Never said one word about where he was going, I looked for him all night. He'll have kids someday and I hope they do him the very same way."

Eddy's mind was reconstructing the events as they had unfolded, particularly since the disappearance of the reporter. That had happened in the wee hours of Tuesday.

"Are you sure it wasn't Monday," he asked her, giving her a moment to think without possibly putting the suggestion in her head that it was indeed Monday. With eyes recast to the ceiling, but this time with her mouth closed, she didn't seem to be able to correct what Eddy was sure was a chronological mistake.

"If you remember," Eddy prodded, "they closed downtown on Tuesday—because of the bomb threat. Are you sure you saw him that day, or was it the previous evening?"

Now Minnie lowered her big head and looked to the floor beyond her folded arms and crossed legs and bare feet. She sucked her lower lip way into her mouth, exacerbating the slightly visible mustache her hormones had pushed out in the last few years. Finally she let out with a snort not at all unlike a pig and said, "I don't remember, it could have been on Monday."

Eddy looked around the room at the unique decorations his mother's sister had chosen to highlight her living room. There was the Elvis picture, varnished on wood. Several rain lamps and a few lava lamps, big digital clocks—ten of them—with the big red letters. No two carried the same time. Carved away from this house and put somewhere in Graceland, the room would seem to fit the now-taped tours of the stately mansion.

"Can I look at his room?" Eddy finally asked, not wanting to arouse Minnie's fears even further but wanting to find some clue as to the nature of this disappearance. Sure she said, nodding her head to the left doorway at the far end of the living room. Eddy had been in Ralphie's room many times, even spent the night a half dozen times or more when they were kids. The door was closed but opened easily with a slight turn of the knob.

While it was a mess, it wasn't awful. Didn't have half-uneaten food lying around, no overly soiled clothes in the floor. Eddy picked up the bed sheet and shook it out, nothing—tossed it back on the bed. On the headboard was a NASCAR schedule, with Daytona circled but this weekend's event at Charlotte not. The mirrored dresser top was full of junk, including NASCAR and movie tickets torn in half. There were drywall screws, two basketball needles, a small hand pump, coins of every denomination including a few No Cash Value gold colored coins that belonged in an amusement hall somewhere. A poker chip from The Sands in Nevada. His unused driver's license lay under a road map of West Virginia with Arch Moore's picture on the back—a governor of at least two decades back. Eddy heard the footsteps and turned to see Minnie joining him, picking up lint and fuzz off the carpet as she came.

"What's up Eddy," she asked, "is Ralphie in some kind of trouble? You know he's a good boy at heart and wouldn't hurt nobody."

Eddy knew precisely that, but he also knew—at least in his mind— that her son and his cousin was the prime suspect in the disappearance of the lady reporter and perhaps the bomb threats that had half-paralyzed the community of late.

"No, he ain't in trouble. It's just that since everything's been going on with the rocks through the windows and that news lady disappearing..."

Minnie cut him off with a concerned, "Well I'll be darned." Eddy turned to see her thumbing through something of a scrapbook. He joined her side.

"What is it Minnie?"

She turned page after page. "Every article in here is by that Wolf woman that disappeared."

25

Jimmy Taylor sat his tiny dog on the seat of the bike after loving on it for a minute or two. The dog never took his eyes away from the desk behind which the three intruders hid and occasionally peeked around. As Taylor walked around his bike checking this and that, the dog danced around him to retain his view of the out-of-sorts desk.

"That dog is going to give us away," Ralph whispered low, never taking his one eye peeking around the corner off of the dog that stared back with two. Annie, who was looking over Michael's shoulder, groaned knowing it to be true. "Anybody got a gun?"

After Taylor had his bike sufficiently shut down to suit him, he hopped on the center podium like a man much younger than his appearance would belie. He called to the dog to join him, never noticing the dog's rapt attention to the back of the room.

"Come on Matika, we got work to do." As Taylor ducked behind the podium looking for something Matika hopped down off the bike to the floor, around to the back of the podium, and up the three steps. He disappeared briefly behind the podium which gave the three a moment to relax and adjust their posture and tired muscles, then quickly reappeared on top of the podium as if he were the featured speaker. His eyes were again trained on the desk, but this time with a far better vantage point. The three froze again and met the dog's two eyes with one each. Sweat beaded on every forehead as the cat and mouse, or in this case, cat and dog, game continued.

"Now where is that agenda," they heard Taylor mutter as he continued to rummage behind the podium out of sight. Ralph and Annie revisited the podium in their minds and neither saw a hint of a paper or notepad or file from which the man might find an agenda. Taylor stood up and surveyed the room quickly, his keen eyes briefly sweeping their portion of the room.

"SMOKEY!" he called aloud, his voice echoing around the empty chamber as had Ralph's when he announced the WWF wrestling match NOT to be held. For the briefest moment Matika's eyes left the desk and glanced toward the hologram entrance, only to return back to the three who had not yet—as had Matika—heard the approach of another visitor.

Matika's gaze for the first time shifted from desk to the hologram from which they had entered. Each relaxed momentarily until the dog's eyes shifted back to them, sensing movement, but then were recast back to the false doorway.

It was Ralph who heard the faintest whine of...something otherworldly. Its piercing wail seemed to be echoing before it got into the room and again once it entered, rendering it totally unintelligible/non-musical. Annie and Michael now heard it as a sense of dread began to fill each of them. The more people that entered this room the more likely they were to be discovered, particularly if that dog had anything to do with it.

But it was then that the dog did something very strange. She began to howl, her head thrown back, her tiny mouth forming an 'O', and a wail not unlike the sounds now filling the hall cascaded upward to the ceiling. Ralph ducked back behind the desk, hiding his movements by the cacophony of sound and whispered, "It sounds like something died."

Annie groaned as Michael slumped behind the desk, attempting to cover his ears from the deafening wail of sirens and fingernails on chalkboard. Ralphie peered back around the desk to see Matika standing on her back legs, hopping in place to the growing, echoing din.

Just as the sounds were about to become unbearable, a solitary form in some sort of uniform emerged solemnly through the hologram and, with slow, deliberate steps, began to descend toward the podium. The only uniform Ralph had ever seen before that resembled this one was the one always worn by Moammar Khadafi of Libya. And, as Ralph had come to surmise, his instrument of choice was bagpipes. This must be Smokey.

Matika stood on her back legs from the time the journeyman had entered the room until he made his way up to the podium and joined the man they new as Taylor. Holding one note for seemingly an inhuman length of time, the man nodded to Matika then released the bagpipe as the music—new music—stopped suddenly. But the old music, the music still echoing from down the hall and in the room, continued on for several minutes—if not in actuality, in the ears of those who had heard it. Finally Taylor nodded approvingly and smiled.

"That will do nicely, Smokey," he said as if this was just a warm-up to some later engagement. "Now cut the crap," he said sharply and, starting to examine again the empty podium, "where the devil have I put that agenda?"

With a slight smile Smokey reached into the breast of his uniform and laid a document on top of the podium while Taylor looked beneath it. With a heavy sigh Taylor stood again and, with no more surprise than a chicken who's laid it's umpteenth egg, said, "Oh there it is," and began rifling through the multiple pages. His inaudible mumbling seemed to indicate he was looking for a time or date. Ralphie noticed Matika had again settled her anxious gaze back in their direction while Smokey stroked her small back.

26

At Shoney's with the Chief and Howard, Eddy leafed through the scrapbook of recent articles by Annie Wolf. All the articles had been subsequent to her first coverage of the villain known as Ernest T. Bass, with the exception of one—the story on the twins that worked at this very Shoney's. That article had appeared several weeks before the Bass incidents, and seemed out of place with the puzzle they were putting together.

"Ok," breathed Chief Hall, weary with the burden he felt from the case. "Eddy, would Ralph hurt the girl in any way do you think?"

Eddy shook his head emphatically. "Absolutely not. But I can't believe he'd abduct her either, and it appears he did."

A long silence followed. It was Howard who broke it. "Maybe if we publicly state that we know it's Ralph Johnson and plead for her safe return. Promise a lighter sentence."

Eddy sighed. "It might not hurt, but this is so out of character for Ralphie, I don't know what to do. But THAT will kill Aunt Minnie—she only has a slight suspicion that Ralph's involved in this. I'd have to prepare her first."

Hall sipped his coffee. "You'd better do it then, Eddy. I think it's our only hope."

The waitress came around with a fresh pot of decaf, noticing the scrapbook article. "Hey, that's me and my sister," she said cautiously, noting the two uniforms that sat on each side of the table.

Hall's eyes widened. "That's you?" he asked, now recognizing both the face and the background.

"Yeah," she said, still a proverbial foot in the bucket. "Why do you have a copy?"

"Did you know that Annie has disappeared?" asked Howard, some compassion in his voice.

The girl with the nametag that said Jan winced. "Yes, I saw that. Joanna and I both hated it, she was so nice and wrote such a good article. Didn't make us out to be freaks like stories in the past have."

"Did," Chief Hall queried, "she interview the two of you here?" Jan said yes. "Did she by any chance have anyone with her?"

"Yeah," Jan said, looking back toward the kitchen, having heard her name in the distance. All three men sitting at the table sat up. "Photographer," she said, turning back toward them. "You guys need anything else besides the check?"

The three slumped back down, what little wind in their sails knocked out. Eddy dejectedly announced he'd resign his position as a deputy if the Chief wanted him to.

"What in tarnation are you talking about?" Hall responded.

"It's all my fault," Eddy nearly cried, "he's my cousin, I'm the one that introduced him to her."

Hall bristled. "Listen Eddy, first of all I don't hold any of my employees responsible for acts committed by their relatives. Second, the only way we know, or suspect, that it's Ralphie is through you. If anything the city, and the paper, needs to thank you for your courage to come forward with the information. Nine out of ten would have clammed up and not said a thing."

"Besides," interjected Howard, "you know your cousin better than anybody. You need to get off your pity wagon and start thinking how Ralphie might be thinking. And, if anybody put Annie in harms way, it was me for sending her down there and Chief for letting her participate in the search." The Chief winced at a truth he had long known and felt deep within.

27

"It's tomorrow night!" cried Taylor, obviously flabbergasted. Smokey smiled politely as if he very well knew that, and Matika never blinked as she stood on tiptoes looking in the direction of the three wayward souls.

"It's always on July 6th," Smokey said in a droll voice, "always." He stroked Matika and noticed her intent gaze toward the podium in the back. The three gently eased back and wondered if they had managed to elude the gaze of the bagpipe playing Smokey. Each looked at the other and, through silent talking, agreed Ralph should be the one to see if they'd been spotted.

With every ounce of stealth that he had, Ralphie turned back and slid his right eye outside the edge of the desk that had hid the three of them this long. Smokey's back was to them now, gazing up to the high ceiling in exactly the opposite direction. Matika, on the other hand, clearly saw the eyeballed greeting and howled as his little front feet danced up and down on the center podium.

"Now, now, Tiki," Taylor said stroking the thin fur as Ralph eased back behind the desk, his head shaking from side to side.

"That dog is going to be the death of us yet," he mouthed, both Annie and Michael comprehending his meaning and in agreement. Finally Michael motioned for them to watch his lips.

"What if we just introduce ourselves, what harm could they do to us?" Annie looked to Ralphie who was shaking his head vigorously.

"What if they're hungry?" Ralph asked silently. Both Annie and Michael shrugged their shoulders, both confused by the non-sequiter. Ralph gave them a knowing, condescending look. "Have you seen one lick of food since we've been down here?" he asked.

"Ohhhhhhhhh," Michael and Annie both mouthed, retracing their many steps since they had arrived in this underworld. None. Not even a refrigerator. Nothing. All three stared straight ahead until they heard something of a slap down at the podium.

"Well, Smokey," Taylor drawled, "I'm gonna go up and get some rest for the big day. Can we count on you to welcome us tomorrow?"

Smokey half smiled and nodded, turned abruptly as would a soldier minus the salute, and placed the mouthpiece to his mouth and took a deep breath. Starting slowly, the wail became louder and louder until finally something of a song emerged and Smokey began to ascend the stairs toward the hologram. The three crouched tighter behind the desk so as to avoid notice as he exited. Two kick-starts later the huge bike roared to life, Taylor racing the engine so loudly the three had to cover their ears. If the bagpipes could be heard now they were at a decibel range that mortal humans rarely enjoyed. The throbbing of the Harley engine engulfed the meeting hall as only a Harley could. They heard the tire screech and just caught a glimpse of it as it burst through the hologram. Not three seconds on the other side they heard Taylor yell out 'Sorry Smokey' and the noise drifted away quickly. Smokey could be heard picking himself up while mumbling. The bagpipes again whined to life and Ralph eased out behind the desk and peered through the hologram as the man marched without stopping until he disappeared around the distant corner. It was several minutes later before the bagpipes, or the sound waves of the bagpipes, completely died. Annie and Michael joined Ralph at the door.

"What's tomorrow night?" asked Annie, her face pale and drawn. Both looked to Ralphie for answers he didn't have.

"I don't know," he finally said, "but I am plumb starved to death."

28

The headline the next morning was the width of the paper and, as Oscar had suggested, carried two separate stories—one of the missing reporter, the other of the rock thrower and their possible connection. The sketch rendered by Eddy Thompson was included, as was the possibility that it represented Ralphie Johnson of Bienvenue Circle.

"I can't believe Ralphie would do such a thing," his mother Minnie, who he lived with, was quoted as saying. "He's a good boy, never been in anymore trouble than just a few fights, typical boy stuff." The extended community read with interest Ralphie's occasional disappearances—usually to NASCAR or other sporting events. Always hitchhiked, never drove even though he had a license. Those who new Ralphie were in agreement, he'd never do anything like that. Those who had from time to time picked him up along the highway also felt it wasn't in him. For the public that didn't know the boy personally, he was guilty as sin. While the article was fairly objective without slant, the circumstantial evidence painted a pretty clear picture—from the scrapbook he kept to the sketch which now did resemble him considerably to the disappearance of both at about the same time. Minnie was heart broken, as was Eddy. While more often than not he saw his cousin as a goofball, Eddy loved Ralphie and felt as though he'd been betrayed.

Howard sat quietly in his office rereading for the umpteenth time the dual stories, his eyes moving from Annie's photo to the sketch that Eddy was now was sure was his cousin Ralph. And, Howard noticed without any humor, the sketch did resemble the Mad guy a good bit. And the Mad guy, Howard noted, didn't look that much different than Ernest T. Bass in his younger days. His door opened. It was Davitz.

"Hey hoss," he called, sliding the door to and taking a seat uninvited. "I been thinking," he said, scratching his five o'clock shadow and looking down to the desk, "I picked up Ralphie a time or two within the last year, once I took him out to the high school for a basketball game—he found his own way home I assume—and the other time he said he was going to work."

"Work?" Howard asked, sitting up in his chair. In all of his discussions with Eddy, he didn't recall Ralph ever having a steady job.

"Yeah, out at the Exhibition Coal mine, he just did general stuff, took out the trash, swept the parking lot, polished the windows and such. I don't think it was long term—particularly in light of their closing every winter."

Howard stared at one of his least favorite employees, somewhat confused. "Oscar, you got a point to this?"

Oscar chuckled a little, then sat back in the seat. "Kid came up missing out at the mine day before yesterday. Was on a tour of the mine with his class—never came out. One of his classmates finally broke down and said he left the tram when they turned out the lights, but said he assumed he was headed back out. Just wondering if, maybe, there might be a third connection to this puzzlement."

"What was the kids' name?" asked Howard.

"Dunno. Just saw Benny putting the story together a few minutes ago for tomorrow's paper. I just think it's curious that Ralphie, then Annie, then this kid disappear, two out of three with a connection to the coal mine." Oscar paused for the briefest of moments, then quipped, "You know what they say hoss, a mine is a terrible thing to waste."

Howard shook his head in disbelief as the hobbit-like man made his way out of his office. He was on the phone to Chief Hall immediately. While Oscar was annoying, occasionally he came up with a pretty good idea. This one was worth checking out.

"Hall," he barked into the phone, "Howard here over at the paper. You got any leads on the boy who is missing over at the exhibition coal mine?"

Chief Hall nodded for Eddy to get on the extension. After Eddy picked up he spoke. "Funny you should call about that," he said, adjusting the air conditioner vent more toward his reddened face. "Eddy here was the officer who went out on that case and learned...well here, let Eddy tell you." Again he nodded to Eddy, who looked pretty nervous.

"In the course of my investigation," Eddy began, "I remembered that my cousin Ralphie worked out there part time last summer. He even worked back in the mines, doing some track maintenance and general stuff like that. And here's the clincher," he said, his voice as somber as death, "the boy that disappeared—he was the witness to the first window busted out at the prosecutor's office. It was from his description that I drew that sketch that kinda looks like Ralphie."

A silence filled the line for several seconds while Howard took in this new information. "So," he began, then paused. "This brings the three together. The boy saw Ralphie rock John's office, Annie interviews the boy as you're doing a sketch of Ralphie, then all three disappear within 24 hours of each other." He paused, waiting for confirmation. It was Chief Hall who provided it.

"That's the connection - as good a boy as Ralphie seems," Hall glanced to Eddy with some measure of compassion, "the evidence is mounting that he's become unstable in some way. Now we've not informed the family of the boy of our suspicions, but if we're going to go public with this we need to. Why don't we get together, say, at five down at the Dunkin' Donuts, and 'choose' a direction we want to go with this...officially."

29

The three sojourners made their way back out of the meeting hall and up the gentle incline that led to it. They were in search of food. Ralph and Annie were starved, Michael was just hungry, having missed only one meal. They peered into each portal leading away from the main corridor—each darker than they were comfortable with tackling. But they also knew around the next bend they would find the water chamber, and knew they hadn't seen a McDonald's in there either. Finally one led up and was a little bit lighter than the many they had previously passed. The two looked to Ralphie who had become their unofficial leader in this deep underworld.

"Why not," he said, his eyes surveying the opening and the narrow passageway that quickly turned to the left. "You'd think we'd see an occasional rat or something."

Annie and Michael looked at each other, their faces indicating that they weren't THAT hungry yet. Slowly Ralphie eased through the portal, his hands touching each wall as he completely entered. Michael followed, then Annie. The turn was upon them. Gently Ralph eased around the corner, Michael and Annie practically his shadow. The turn ended, and they stood staring at a set of stone stairs that went almost directly up with no end in sight. Annie groaned as Ralphie stood transfixed by the passageway up.

"You wanted a way out," he deadpanned, turning to his companions, "this looks to be straight up."

The three turned and exited the portal and Ralph made a mental note of a slight marking on the stoned archway. No sense in going in there again in the foreseeable future, he mused to himself, unless he smelled chicken. They chose the doorway almost directly across the corridor. This one was darker but, as stomachs growled, no one was content standing still. Shuffling his feet along Ralphie noted how the path would dip down for a bit, level off, then go up a bit. After fifteen minutes or so of absolutely nothing, they came to a very small room with a couple of benches along the sides. Michael and Annie sat on one side of the path, Ralphie on the other.

"You say you came in through the coal mine?" Ralphie asked of Michael.

"Yeah," he shrugged, "shoulda stayed on the thing."

"Where did you come through at?" Annie shuddered at Ralph's conclusion of a sentence with a preposition, but quickly realized that, outside of her newspaper world, it didn't really matter much.

"You know on the left hand track going in?" With his hands Michael indicated a fork in the passage and Ralph nodded his head. "When I jumped off I came back to the fork—and shoulda come on outa there, but didn't. I went on back in the left-hand side..."

Ralph interrupted with, "The tram comes back thataway."

Michael nodded his head. "Yeah, tell me about it. I was maybe a couple hundred feet in when I saw the headlights. I ducked back into an opening, tripped over something, then found that it went a good way back in. I finally came into a little opening, not too unlike this," he said, looking around them, "and this weird glow came from an opening in the ceiling. When I stepped right under it to get a better look, I fell and...well...here I am."

Ralph pondered those directions a bit. Of all the times he'd been in that mine, he couldn't remember the opening that Michael described. He stood and continued along the tunnel, Michael and Annie dutifully following. They walked at least two miles with seemingly no progress— they hadn't descended any, nor had they ascended any. This path seemed to lead to nowhere. Annie finally spoke up.

"Maybe we should go back."

"To what?" Ralphie asked. He let the question hang in the air a bit before answering himself. "We know what's back there, nothing. We cain't afford to run into anymore of those people because—if they're cannibals—and they must be, they might be as hungry as we. We gotta press on. If we go back and try another passageway, we lose the time and distance we've made in this one."

His logic was irrefutable, and Annie's stomach growled in agreement. She couldn't imagine street person Jimmy Taylor being a cannibal, eating the very flesh off of fellow humans, but had seen him digging through the courthouse garbage on more than one occasion. On they pressed.

"Where does this light come from?" Ralph asked of no one, looking forward and backward. He'd been in the exhibition mine several times when the power went out, and it was pitch black WITH exits at both ends. This made no sense to him at all. The few odd jobs he'd had in the mines, even the drift mouth operations got completely dark a thousand feet or so from the portal, depending on how quickly the passageway turned. Ralph shook his head as he continued walking.

30

The city police, county sheriff, and local detachment of the state police converged on the Beckley Exhibition Coal Mine with warrant in hand to search the premises. Nothing out of the ordinary, Chief Hall assured the lady behind the counter at the gift shop, just a routine look-see as the investigation of the missing boy continued. The clerk, as with the handful of tourists who had shown up hoping to get a tour of the mine, was in awe at the sheer number of officers wearing different uniforms. Even a couple of fire trucks had wheeled into the parking lot and backed—beeping all the way—as close to the portal as they could get.

The retired miners who normally led the tours were quarantined in the shop where the trams were stored, repaired and maintained. A couple officers from the state police detachment quizzed the men about the boy, particularly the one named Chuck who was leading the tour the day Michael Oather Justice disappeared. The three were questioned extensively about Ralph Johnson, part-time employee and occasional tour guide when one of the regulars called in sick.

Led by Hall, about forty officers from different detachments entered the mine wearing hardhats that they had managed to scrounge on short notice. None were equipped with headlights, as these were not designed for underground, dark conditions. All carried a flashlight in lieu of the usual light attached to the hardhat. While these men began their journey into the exhibition mine, another ten or so began searching the grounds—the houses, the museum, the church—looking for any sign of evidence that might explain the whereabouts, or disappearance of, the three in question.

At the first fork in the track, Hall turned to the largest contingency of law enforcement he had ever had the privilege to lead and requested their silence. The men stood still and those of military background actually snapped to some semblance of attention.

"Gentlemen, I'll be honest with you. I have no earthly clue if there's anything in here to find, but let's be diligent." A handful of flashlights shown in his face and nearly blinded him as he talked. His head-turning squint clued the men in to shine the lights lower, and he continued. "You were given the fact sheet, but let me summarize once again. Two days ago the boy disappears after entering this mine with his classmates. You have the photo. Now this is the same boy that witnessed the first rock throwing that's had this city on edge for the past month, and it was his description that led us to the sketch and the concern that the perpetrator is one Ralph—goes by Ralphie—Johnson—you have his photo and the sketch also. While in custody the boy was interviewed by Annie Wolf, the lady reporter whose photo you also have. Ralph, it would appear, has something of a crush on the unmarried Ms. Wolf based on his scrapbook of her stories since they met on July 4th. And the final piece of the still emerging puzzle is that Ralph has worked out here at this tourist facility on and off for the past couple years. The evidence is entirely circumstantial at this time that the three are even connected, but they all seem to have this coalmine in common. We're not looking for bodies—hopefully—we're looking for clues, anything, that might shed some light on what's going on. Any questions?"

A voice from the back piped up. "Can we get on with it? I'm a little claustrophobic." The group gave out a collective, nervous laugh—he wasn't alone—and Hall smiled appreciably.

"Right. Ok, you have your assignments. Those of you assigned to me, let's go to the right, leaving no stone or passageway unturned. If you're assigned to Eddy Thompson, who knows or has met all three of these individuals very recently, go to the left. We'll meet out the other end and see what we've come up with. Regardless, we'll be coming back through. Let's give this old cave a once-over like it's never had."

With that, Hall turned to the right and his bevy of men followed. Eddy led the other twenty or so men to the left. About fifty feet in Hall and his crew came to a set of tracks that went back to the left toward the other crew. Hall called out to Eddy, knowing their paths hadn't diverged enough to be out of earshot yet. Eddy called back.

"You send two men this direction and I'll send two that direction. When they meet in the middle they can turn and come back. Ok?" Eddy responded ok and Hall motioned for two of his closest men to follow the track. "Look for anything, anything, that might be a clue, no matter how slight it seems." The two men nodded and headed left. The flashlight beams of Eddy's men were already visible, so the spur wasn't long at all. Hall went on.

His group came to one of the first stops on a typical tour—a cut out section on the left where a car full of coal and a couple pieces of old machinery stood. The face—where the men would work to hand-dig or dynamite then dig the coal—was recessed back in fifteen or so feet but ended. The men looked high and low, in front of and behind, every nook and cranny and piece of machinery to find nothing. Hall grunted and moved on.

The next stop on the tour focused largely to the right of the tracks and again featured some older equipment, a birdcage for the days when canaries were used to check oxygen levels, and the main light switch. On a regular tour the guide would warn the group then turn out the lights, demonstrating how dark it got without artificial lighting. Hall fingered the switch but didn't shut it off. That action was planned for the return trip if nothing else was found.

Again the men moved on, eventually coming to another spur that went off to the left, toward Eddy's group. Hall yelled into the opening, yelled again, before Eddy yelled back faintly. "Send in three men," Hall said as loud as he could without actually screaming. A faint 'ok' came back shortly and Hall pointed at three men and told them to be careful. The three headed left, lights dancing off the ribs and ceiling. After they turned the corner Hall turned and headed on. The partially lit mine began to reveal the beginnings of daylight and Hall let out a sigh— partly because he too was a bit claustrophobic, and partly because they hadn't—at least his group hadn't—found anything horrendous. They emerged out into the daylight just ahead of Eddy's group. The six men who had searched the last spur came out a couple minutes later, shaking their heads no.

Hall moved away from the growing throng and got their attention again. "Anything?" he asked, looking around and through the men to a chorus of no's and shaking heads. "Alright, in a way that's good news. Eddy, you take your men back through the way we came, and we'll go back your way. Never know when we may have missed something, or maybe something will be visible from this angle that we hadn't noticed coming through. Again, let's be careful, and diligent. We're talking three people here, remember that." Hall started to lead his men to the other side when he stopped abruptly. "Eddy, don't forget to give a warning on your whistle then turn off the lights. When you hear the whistle men, turn off your lights and Eddy will shut down the main power. Be very quiet and listen for 2 minutes. If there's nothing out of the ordinary Eddy you turn the power back on and we'll continue back toward the entrance."

Eddy nodded and led his men back into the left opening while Hall and his men headed back down the right entrance. Intuitively both leaders sent three down the first connector, knowing they would meet in the middle and return back to the group. After ten minutes Eddy came to the area with the main power switch, told his men to turn off their lights, and gave a blast on his whistle. After a few seconds passed he hit the switch and, unlike the gasps given by many tour groups, silence was immediate and the darkness overwhelming.

Almost the full two minutes had passed when one of the deputies on Chief Hall's side had noticed a faint, unnatural glow ahead—toward the original entrance. He called out to Hall who shouted as loud as he could to Eddy, who didn't hear and switched the lights back on. One of Hall's men trotted down the tracks to the nearest spur and yelled through for Eddy to turn the lights back off. A moment passed and it went dark again.

"What did you see, Robert?" Hall asked of one of his newer deputies, and distant cousin. A moment of silence passed before the officer responded.

"I...I'm not sure, there was this purple glow, real faint, right along this wall." In the complete and utter darkness nobody could see but everybody could sense that Robert was standing near where he saw the light. "It ain't there now," he said in disbelief, "have him cut the lights back on." The request was made through the spur and the lights came back on. Everybody's eyes focused in the direction from which Robert had spoken. He was standing near the wall, rubbing his hand along it.

"So weird," he said, his eyes nearly crossed he was so close to the solid rock wall. Everybody had slowly gathered around and could now see what it was that had caught his attention. Every light now focused on the ancient looking hieroglyphics.

31

It was hard to tell if it was daylight or dark. Annie's watch was of the dial variety, only kept twelve-hour cycles—and was twenty minutes fast. They had been in the bowels of the earth so long they were clueless of the time that had passed. They weren't even sure, at this depth, if a twenty-four hour period constituted a day. With no sunrise or sunset, just a constant, eerie glow, they had lost all track of time. All they knew was that they were starving, their energy level weakened to the point of hallucination.

They had walked for hours since Annie had originally questioned whether they should continue on this particular path. Even Ralph was beginning to have his doubts when they turned another corner to find nothing new—just the same old path going on and on. He sighed and leaned back against the left side of the passageway.

"Ok," he sighed, resignation in his voice and posture, "I'm open to suggestion." It was Michael that responded.

"We can't go back, we're looking at seven or eight hours just to get back to nothing. I say we press on. Surely this comes out somewheres."

"Somewhere," Annie corrected the young boy. When he looked up at her with confusion on his face she spelled it out for him. "Somewhere. There is no such word as 'somewheres,' you'll never get anywhere in life if you don't use words correctly." She paused for a moment then added, "County commission maybe."

Ralph pushed himself away from the wall and began lumbering forward, his legs balking at going any further. Annie could hardly go on, while the younger Michael, used to skateboarding several hours a day and having eaten breakfast before going to the exhibition mine, was still on his first wind.

It was an hour later when Ralph turned a corner and stopped dead, frightening both Annie and Michael with his sudden hesitation. "Shhhhhhhh," he whispered, beginning to tiptoe toward what Annie and Michael now recognized as an opening into another hall—the first such intersection since they had chosen this particular passageway. Within a few feet Ralph held his arm out indicating to his companions to wait for a moment. Stealthily he eased out to the opening and stuck his head out, peering both left and right. He looked back to Annie and Michael, pain on his face. Once again he leaned forward and took in the perpendicular tunnel. He stepped out into the passage and disappeared to the right. Annie and Michael quickly followed.

Ralph groaned an 'oh no' as he leaned his head into the meeting room—his upper body disappearing into the hologram where they had first came across Michael hours and hours ago. He pulled back through the hologram and leaned against the wall, sliding down until he was sitting on the cavern floor. Michael and Annie followed suit.

"I'd eat that little dog raw right now if it came through here," Ralph said with no hint of mirth in his voice. Annie's stomach was beyond growling—she had actually reached a point where she wasn't hungry anymore, but knew that it wasn't from lack of hunger, but the contraction of her stomach from not eating. The three looked at each other with a measure of sadness.

"What now?" asked the younger Michael. His taste for adventure in the exhibition mine had been more than sated since his fall into this underworld nightmare seemingly a day ago.

Ralph shrugged his shoulders. He looked to Annie who did the same. Each had just dropped their heads—tired and resigned to a death by starvation—when they heard a faint noise way off in the distance.

32

Officer Hall resented being made a second-class citizen in his own station, but the new FBI liaison seemed power hungry and driven. He was barking out orders to HIS men left and right. Mostly they were pouring over the blown-up digital photos of the hieroglyphics found on the wall of the exhibition mine. Agent Jack Dare had designated the workroom as their 'command center' until the case was closed. Hall retreated to his office and called the newspaper.

"Howard, Hall here." Chief Hall was overwhelmed by conversation on the other end and had to catch his breath. "Yeah, yeah, I know, sorry about that. I wanted to involve the press but the state police rep was strictly against it. How'd you find out about it?"

"Let's just say," Howard replied smugly, "I have my sources. Found some cave markings or something?"

Hall drew in a breath. "Looks like some sort of intelligent form of communication—you can quote me on that—but it doesn't look ancient or anything like that. Could just be kids with a can of spray paint." A commotion in the 'command center' drew his attention away. "Hold on Howard, something's going on. I'll call you right back."

Hall pushed back his chair and moved out into his new command center. Several were hustling about, copying things, while Agent Dare was at the white board scribbling furiously. Hall watched in amazement as the cryptoquip above was being translated below. He read aloud as Dare wrote as fast as he could translate.

"To all ye who enter these premises, to all ye who so desire, to all ye who regard life, be prepared...for...the...fire."

Jack Dare stood back and admired his handiwork. For ten minutes he explained how he broke the code and the more interesting aspects of the code itself. That was it? thought Hall. He finally interrupted. "What fire, Jack?"

Agent Dare stopped in mid-sentence and looked to the portly Chief of Police with the disdain many in federal agencies looked upon those in county and local offices. He finally smiled and stepped back from the white board.

"You're more familiar with coal mining and the many deadly accidents that occur—you tell me what kind of fire we might be looking at." Jack held Hall's baby blues, demanding a contribution to the effort already expended.

Hall was completely at a loss and felt every pair of eyes upon him.

Were it not for his own men looking to their chief for an answer he'd have told them where to go. That thought gave him a response.

"Maybe, just maybe," he drawled, gaining momentum as he thought on his feet, "it ain't referring to fires brought on by coal mining. Maybe it's referring to the fires down below—the hell fires we hear about every Sunday. After all, it does seem to indicate something more than just a mine fire."

All eyes now shifted back to Dare, who was somewhat reeling by the semi-intelligent gibberish this donut-eating, elected official spouted. The collective crowd sensed the momentum change with most smiling inwardly at the federal agent's sudden unease.

"Ok," he finally said, looking back to the translated message. He pinched his bottom lip as he scrutinized it word for word. He looked back down to the photos—all close-ups, none showing the circumstances of the message within the mine. "Pick five of your men, let's go back out there and look over the situation."

Hall rolled his eyes after the agent had looked away and said he'd be right there. He called the newspaper and 'leaked' the information to Howard as he gathered up his keys and flashlight.

33

The noise had grown louder and Ralph was certain it was Smokey on his way, bagpipes echoing off of every wall to the point of being merely white noise with no discernable tune. "C'mon," he said, passing through the hologram, "we gotta find a safer place to hide."

Annie and Michael began scanning the top rows while Ralph went down and circled the podium. It was Michael who called out, his voice echoing in the hollow chamber.

"Hey guys, check this out." Ralph took giant strides up the amphitheater while Annie shuffled quickly from around the other side. "Look," he said, passing his hand through the wall. "Another hologram."

Ralph's eyes widened at the find while the arrival of Smokey seemed imminent. He stuck his head through the hologram. It was a single, shallow room with a stone bench, capable of seating three, maybe four medium sized individuals. The cacophony of bagpipes now swirled, almost visible, in the empty, open chamber. "Get in," Ralph demanded and followed the two inside. They took seats and found they had a bird's eye view of the chamber. Smokey burst through the hologram, his cheeks ballooned out and red from the exertion of playing the ancient, Celtic instrument.

"Shhhhh," Ralph whispered, "let's not move just in case we can be seen in here."

"What do you think is going on?" whispered Annie, her eyes wide with fright. All three forgot their hunger for the moment.

Ralph merely shook his head from side to side, then nodded toward Smokey who seemed to be circling the room, starting with the highest level. "He seems to be dressed fancier than he was before."

He was indeed. And he was about to pass on the top level right in front of them. He'd disappeared from sight around the right edge and was coming closer and closer to their hologram. His black-booted feet appeared first, then his hairy legs and skirt, then his full body supporting the heavy-looking bagpipes. As he passed he took a deep breath and again blew into the mouthpiece. It was a surreal scene to be sure.

Once he had finished with the top row, he moved down to the next row and repeated the trip, never changing the tune or looking away from his predetermined journey. Three more rows remained, and the three sojourners wondered if they could take it. Finally he circled the raised dais, began to ascend the four stone steps, and stood before the stone tablet and completed the song he'd started seemingly an hour ago. He danced a quick jig, then stood as still as a statue. Ralph gave an uneasy glance to his companions as someone's stomach gave off an audible growl. They were ill prepared for what happened next.

All around the chamber people emerged from the very walls, talking, arguing, laughing, slapping each other on the back. Some smoked cigarettes, some smoked pipes, a few did neither. And they were the strangest grouping of people the three had ever seen.

34

Howard crouched in the nearest spur, hopefully hidden in the darkness and by the rib of coal left when this mine closed in the early part of the last century. His photographer nervously fingered the buttons and lenses of his high-tech, high-dollar camera. He was very claustrophobic, and told his boss so before leaving the paper. Neither had been able to spot the hieroglyphics that Hall had described, but knew they were in the general vicinity of the now approaching crew. The voices echoed up and down the one-hundred year old corridor. Howard leaned back against the rib, one eye peeking around the corner.

The mixed bag of law enforcement approached, their flashlight beams dancing in the semi-darkness. Just before the spur Chief Hall stopped them and pointed his flashlight at the far wall.

"Well I'll be darned," he muttered, hardly audible.

Agent Dare stared at the featureless wall for several moments, thinking he just wasn't seeing what was readily visible to everyone else. He imagined the many 3-D images he'd been shown in the course of his lifetime—most he saw immediately in visual stereo, but a few required some time before he could extract out the 3-D image. He was still drawing a blank when Eddy cleared up the confusion.

"It's gone, Chief."

Hall stepped over the right track to run his hand over the smooth, featureless surface, stunned at the absence of hieroglyphics.

"You're telling me it's gone?" Jack Dare asked condescendingly. The momentum was beginning to shift again. Everyone but Dare had seen the images that were copiously photographed just this very morning. Howard felt sorry for his friend who was clearly flummoxed.

Hall stepped back over and between the tracks to get his bearings. There was the shovel he had carefully laid beneath the carvings. He began to scan left and right with his flashlight, thinking someone had maybe moved the shovel as a joke. But he was sure this was where they had found the writings before. And he knew the Beckley Register-Herald editor was just around the corner, prohibiting another full search of the exhibition mine.

"Eddy, it was right here wasn't it?" Eddy replied with an emphatic nod of his head. "Then where in tarnation has it gotten off to?"

Hall moseyed on down the corridor just far enough to peer into the spur where he knew Howard to be hiding. His flashlight never illuminated them directly, but he could detect the editor's shadow against the wall. He walked the few steps back to the confused group.

"Get some pictures Ronnie, maybe when we develop them the images will re-emerge. And maybe we can find other common features to determine that this was indeed where the images were. I can't believe it," he said exasperated.

"Amateurs," Agent Dare muttered under his breath as he turned and stalked out of the mine. Eddy and Chief Hall gave each other a pained glance and quickly followed.

Howard and his photographer let the noises completely die down before emerging from their secret lair. He was more disappointed for his friend and sometimes moral and mental combatant than he was for the hour he had wasted. The two stretched their taut muscles after remaining perfectly still for so long. The photographer expressed an interest in getting out as soon as possible. Howard let out a slight chuckle and began the half-mile journey to the exit, hoping—and pretty sure—the merry band of law enforcement weren't hanging around to talk.

"Holy smokes," his photographer muttered behind him, "I don't believe it."

Howard turned quickly, chill bumps making the cool, damp air even cooler. The photographer's flashlight was trained on the wall precisely above the shovel, where a half dozen flashlights were trained only moments ago. Howard's gaze and flashlight joined in on the viewing. There, above the shovel and right where Chief Hall said they would be, were the haunting inscriptions that warned any who passed through of the dangers of hell fire. The photographer, no longer aware of his intense claustrophobia, was setting up his tripod and lighting to capture the images that seemed to have a life all their own.

35

The doorbell startled Minnie Johnson from a nap on the couch as Vanna White spun the wheel of a small fortune once again. She groggily sat up and ran her fingers through her sparse hair and made her way to the door. There, on the other side of the screen door, was a man she recognized but did not know by name.

"May I help you?" she politely asked, trying to place the familiar face. The middle-aged man bowed slightly at the hips, his hat off and in his hand to his chest, then nodded.

"My name," he said with some deliberation, "is Jimmy Taylor. I have temporary employment with the Fuller Brush Company. I was wondering," he said with a look of wistfulness in his eye as he glanced up to Minnie's disheveled hair, "if I might show you a sampling of our products."

Minnie and the man stared at each other for quite some time. Fuller Brush salesmen were largely a thing of the past, the distant past - at least door to door. But she was lonely and could use the company, and he seemed harmless enough.

"Yes, come in Mr. Taylor," she said, unlatching the screen door and backing away as he made his way in carrying a briefcase. "Would you like some coffee or tea? I have some special tea that's supposed to be real good for your heart."

"That, my dear, would be lovely if it would be no trouble."

"Oh no," Minnie assured the man, passing him and headed to the kitchen, "no trouble at all. You wait right there. Feel free to use the remote and find something that interests you." She passed into the kitchen and turned on the burner. From her tea and spice cabinet she chose the new box she had recently bought down at the health food store and pulled out two bags. On a tray she put the tea, a cup of milk - in case he was British, he didn't sound like he was from around here - two cups and two spoons with a third in the nearly full sugar bowl. When she re-entered the living room she found that Jimmy had indeed used the remote - the television was off. The quiet was unsettling.

"I hope you don't mind," Jimmy Taylor said apologetically, seeing her obvious disdain at the silenced TV. "I don't own one myself and with my hearing loss from the war...you understand."

"Of course," exclaimed Minnie, setting the tray down on the coffee table before her guest. "Not at all. My Carl was in the war too, are you talking the big one, World War II?"

Jimmy shook his head, partially recoiling from his first taste of the special brew tea, and partially acknowledging that his war, as he coughed it out, "was Korea."

"Oh..." said Minnie, her voice trailing off, somewhat disappointed. On occasion she ran across a vet of her Carl's war and it was always a treat. Not a single time had any of them known her Carl, but just the chance that they had crossed his path somewhere 'on the continent' as she liked to say was special. Her Carl had been dead nearly twenty years, and those had been the twenty loneliest years of her life. Of course, Ralphie had come along at an awkward time when a family should be planning retirement, not diaper schedules. But still, her Carl left a void in her life that no child could ever fill.

"But," Taylor continued, "there were quite a few in my platoon that had served in the big one." At this Minnie smiled, maybe indirectly her Mr. Taylor had indeed crossed her Carl's path. She also noted, with glee, that Mr. Taylor seemed to be enjoying the tea she had spent nearly a fortune on that was good for the heart. Something about triglycerides the clerk had told her. She eyed the briefcase standing beside his right leg.

"Fuller Brushes you say, Mr. Taylor?"

At this Taylor smiled and placed the cup of tea on the tray and laid the briefcase on his lap. With two snaps the case lid opened, he pulled out a comb and a brush, and closed it back. Minnie couldn't believe her eyes. These were Fuller Brushes, he was a Fuller Brush salesman. She nearly clutched her heart at the revelation. Maybe, she thought, when I go to the store tomorrow, bread will be twenty-nine cents a loaf and a candy bar will be a nickel.

"My goodness," she finally said, taking the brush from the smiling man. "May I?" she asked, pointing toward her hair.

"Be my guest," Taylor nodded approvingly, "that's what they're for."

The brush seemed to massage her scalp as no brush had in years. The yellowed bristles were just the right firmness, the curved handle fit in the palm of her hand perfectly. She reached for the comb and again Taylor nodded.

"Ah, these are wonderful," she said smiling, pulling the comb through her fine hair. "How much are they, Mr. Taylor?"

Taylor smiled sweetly and pulled a notepad out from his vest pocket, put on a pair of half-moon glasses, and scanned down the sheet. "Those two go for..." he scanned further, flipping the page, "a dollar and a quarter each, or both for two dollars." Pleased with himself, he placed the notepad back into his breast pocket and smiled broadly at Minnie.

"I'll take them both," Minnie said, having to fight back the tears at both the price and the incredible feel of the hair care products. She dug into her dress pocket and found two rolled up dollars inside what looked to be a lottery ticket. Taylor took the money graciously.

"Oh, before I go, is there anyone else in the house who might be interested in a nice comb or brush?" He raised his eyebrows and let the word 'brush' dangle slightly before closing his lips. "Anyone at all?"

Minnie shook her recently combed head from side to side. "No, it's just me. My boy ain't been home in close to a week and from what I can tell he could be in a lot of trouble. They said he might have kidnapped a lady reporter and maybe a young boy. I cain't believe it myself, Ralphie would never do a trick like that, but my sister Lilly's Eddy is a deputy downtown and he'ns said it don't look good."

"Ralphie, you say," Taylor held her stare for some time. "Good boy?"

Minnie nodded. "As good as could be expected. Me and Carl were in our forties when Ralphie caught us off guard, then Carl up and died when he was just a boy, so I've practically raised him all by myself. He's spent a lot of time at cousins' and such, but he ain't never got in any real trouble before now. You think he's guilty?"

"I don't know the boy," Taylor stood, placing his hat on his head, "nor do I know his circumstance." He shuffled his way around the coffee table and headed for the door, turning just as he reached it. "But if you tell me he's a good boy, I believe he's a good boy. You don't worry about Ralphie, it sounds like he'll do the right thing."

Minnie smiled weakly as the Fuller Brush salesman made his way off her porch and down the sidewalk. She looked down to the brush and comb set in her hands, her smile gaining in confidence as she replayed in her mind the words Taylor had spoken. "He will do the right thing," she said out loud.

36

Ralph, Annie and Michael sat perfectly still as the growing gathering began to make their way around and take their seats. It reminded Michael of his visit last year to the House chamber when his class visited the state capitol in Charleston. He recalled sneaking away from the group and touring the rotunda area alone. He hadn't gotten into trouble that time for his indiscretion. This time his number seemed to be up.

"Greetings!" a beaming Jimmy Taylor said as the last seat was filled and the noise died down to near silence. He repeated the word greetings and a few 'howdy do's' echoed throughout the chamber.

"Welcome back," he said throatily with great joy and pride. Ralph could imagine he saw a tear welling up in each eye, even from his considerable distance to the podium. Peripherally he scanned his two companions for movement but saw none. Jimmy Taylor continued.

"It is with great pleasure that I welcome you to this, the 141st annual convention." A general murmuring and slight applause attempted to fill the vacuum but fell short.

Ralph whispered in Annie's direction, "Convention of WHAT?"

Jimmy held his hands up indicating for the gathered throng to quiet down. As their silence grew, Jimmy took in a deep breath and tore into a not-too-bad version of the Elvis standard, It's Now or Never. To this the group began to clap and hoot and holler and stomp and actually throw wads of paper toward the podium.

"Jez," muttered Annie, not concealing her voice at all, "surely this isn't an Elvis impersonation convention." Surely not, she thought without saying, not a jumpsuit in the place. Taylor nailed the final high note and the place erupted like the British Parliament on steroids— whistling, caterwauling, slingshots were being fired—it was truly a sight to behold as Ralph, Annie and Michael finally looked to each other with sincere concern. Their hunger pangs were temporarily forgotten.

Taylor finally got the riot under control with a few wolf-whistles of his own. A dull grumble finally washed back into silence. With a gleam in his eye Taylor smiled, nodded his head, and said in a distinctly British accent, "I suppose any of you could have done better." The question appeared rhetorical and drew no response from the eclectic madhouse.

Rifling through his papers he came upon the next item on the agenda.

"Bill," Taylor said aloud, looking around the room searching for the one he called Bill, "ahhhh, there you are. Can you give us a report on the last election?"

The one called Bill stood up and adjusted his glasses, ahemmed, and looked down his copious notes. He was a short, hobbit-like man with gray, wispy sideburns that were quite long. He snorted, spat to his left—causing the occupant in that seat to quickly move his foot then look back up with disdain—and began a dissertation that was utterly foreign to the three unseen guests.

"The DEMOcrats," he looked around the room with some glee making eye contact with several, "got elected a northerner from the county of Marion by the name of Joe Manchin—I think I'm pronouncing that right. This would mean, then," Bill was having a hard time controlling his upwelling glee, "that Governor Manchin lives in the Governor's Mansion!" With that he burst into laughter and actually collapsed back into his seat in convulsions. Few joined in his frivolity, just some polite laughs, mainly by those sitting next to him. It was then that Annie noticed it.

"There's not a woman in the place," she said incredulous, scanning the room.

"Yeah there is," responded Michael, leaning out a little and pointing to the left, past Annie and into the highest row of seats. Ralph and Annie both leaned out and caught sight of to whom Michael was pointing.

"THAT'S a woman?" Ralph asked too loud, causing Annie to shush him. She was indeed unattractive, to say the least. And big. Bill was back on his feet wiping his ample forehead with a handkerchief, about to regain his composure. After another snort and spit, he continued.

"Now then, the RePUBlicans—if you can call them that—did gain a few seats in the Legislature," Annie's eyebrows rose at the news that she was viewing the oratory of a supposed colleague, "none of which seem overly qualified or competent."

"Great," said Taylor, looking around the room. "Discussion?" With that he raised his eyebrows and pushed his lower lip up above his upper lip and scanned the room. His perusal was greeted with silence and headshakes. "Fine then. Arnold, can you give us an update on the power plants along our western flank?" Jimmy turned completely around, scanning the room in vain for the one he called Arnold. Someone from the top yelled 'he ain't here yet.'

"Now where in tarnation is that boy," said Taylor with some consternation. "ARRRNNNOOLLLLDDDD!" he cried aloud. The room fell silent in anticipation of who-knew-what. Heads turned to the left and the right, scanning mostly the upper tier. One of the attendees actually lifted his notepad and looked under it. Ralph and his companions leaned forward a little to take in as much of the upper tier as they could. Ralph nudged Annie as he saw Taylor pull something from his breast pocket. It looked to be a shiny, metal whistle.

Taylor put the whistle to his lips as his cheeks puffed out and his face turned beet red. But no sound came out. Ralph whispered, "Dog whistle. Hope it's not that mutt."

Silence enveloped the hall as all heads now turned to and fro. The anticipation was building as, from directly behind the three sojourners, a figure flew by so fast and furious that wisps of Annie's hair actually blew forward and through the hologram in which they sat behind. Ralph said 'golly' while Michael cursed. Their comments were drowned out by the cheers that erupted from every desk. Even Jimmy at the podium seemed pleased with their new guest.

But who was their new guest? The thing—Arnold—flew around the very top of the chamber with such speed that he/she/it was just a blur. Someone would throw a wadded up piece of paper at it and it would literally change directions on a dime and bat the paper out of the air— resulting in additional applause and jubilation. This went on for nearly ten minutes before the thing began slowing down, high-fiving some as he came down, teasing, speeding back up. Finally he came to a full stop on the dais, in front of the podium, and raised his arms high above his head, looking for all the world like a newly crowned heavyweight boxer.

"Jez," said Ralph as he stared in disbelief.

"Holy smokes," whispered Annie, stunned beyond belief.

"Who is it?" asked Michael innocently. "WHAT is it?"

It was Ralph who answered. He actually had to speak up a little to be heard over the din. "You never heard of Mothman?" Michael had, but knew little about the creature other than his name. "Don't look into his eyes," Ralphie warned both, "they'll burn you."

"What eyes?" Michael questioned.

It was then that the creature turned around and was really visible for the first time, seemingly enjoying the accolades he was receiving. His bright red eyes—embedded in his chest—glowed with energy as Ralph, Annie and Michael covered their own and peaked through cracks in their fingers. With his arms waving Taylor indicated for the crowd to shut up and slowly the silence returned.

From a mouth that hadn't been visible until he spoke—located between his eyes and just below—'Arnold' said his first words heard by human ears.

With a sing-songy, childlike voice he asked, "Now what was it you wanted to see me about?" He drummed his fingers on the podium as he waited for an answer.

Taylor reached up and patted him just below the shoulders—as high as he could reach. "It's our annual meeting," he said softly, "didn't you get the memo?"

Mothman shrugged as he shook his upper body from side to side. He seemed to be checking pockets that weren't visible. His impressive shoulders drooped. "Nope. Didn't get it."

"No big deal," replied Jimmy, "we just needed an update on the power grid up your way."

To this Mothman turned and, if he had a chin, stuck it out. Or it might have been his chest. His great red eyes glowed even brighter and seemed to double in size.

"The power grid," he said enunciating clearly, "is safe and efficient. Plenty of coal is stockpiled for the winter, prices are moderate, and upgrades are being implemented where and when needed." With that statement he gave a wink of his big right eye as he turned around to address all that were in attendance. "Of course the damage to the environment continues as the fossil fuels are being burned. Global warming and all."

There were general catcalls and harrumphs and one called out 'pollution smollution.' Mothman merely stood still as a statue as the room grew silent. He then leaned over to Taylor. "By the way," he said in a lower voice, pointing, "who are those people in my cubby hole?"

With that every eye in the chamber turned in the direction of the three lost souls. Ralph reached out and put a hand on the nearest knee of each of his companions, prepared to defend them to the death if necessary. The hologram that they thought were protecting them seemed now to have vanished.

"Yes," said Taylor, his smile fading a bit, "let's greet our visitors."

37

It was early afternoon when Howard left the office uncharacteristically early and headed home. The coffee he got at the Shell station was bland. The beef jerky was full of taste, and added to his already cholesterol-soaked arteries and veins. His wife was startled when the front door opened and her husband entered.

"Is everything ok?" she asked, real concern in her voice.

Howard tossed the paper on the coffee table and flopped down onto the couch, looking ten years older than a week ago. He shook his head.

"No." He placed his face in his hands and rubbed vigorously, as if trying to wake up from a bad dream. "I have no idea what is going on, but I've got this weird, sixth sense if you will, that Annie's in trouble—needs help." He looked up to his wife of 14 years. "I'm going to take a leave of absence, go look for her."

"Howard," she said, exasperated, "the police are doing everything they can. Let them do their work. Where would you go?"

Good question, thought Howard. What little he knew of Ralphie, he could be in any city hosting a NASCAR event. But he had this nagging suspicion that they were still around, still local somewhere. His efforts would focus on Raleigh County.

"I don't think he's taken her away from here. Call it intuition, gut feeling, whatever, I just feel in my bones they're still here, in the county." On impulse, he picked up the paper and rifled through to the want ads. He scanned Special Notices, scanned the Personals, briefly glanced at the Help Wanteds. Nothing.

"Howard," his wife said again, resigned, "talk to your publisher, tell him you'd like to organize a search party of available newspaper staff. And family. I'll join in the search."

He smiled at his loving wife. "That's not a bad idea. We could include members of her church and the food bank where she volunteers. We could get quite a group together and blanket the county." The wheels were turning now. "We'll need a recent photo of Ralph—we've got one of Annie. We'll go door-to-door, turn over every stone. Yeah…we can do this." He grabbed the paper up again and headed out the door.

"Thanks, honey. That's a great idea."

38

Ralph, Annie and Michael were each trembling as every eye in the chamber now held theirs. It didn't seem as though they were prepared to attack, but their demeanor wasn't friendly either. After a period of silence Jimmy spoke again.

"Ralphie, Annie, Michael, won't you come in and join us?" With that said he beckoned with his hand, coaxing them out of their hiding place.

Ralph groaned and whispered, "We had to hide in Mothman's cave.

Sheesh." Ralph stood and was joined by Annie and Michael. With chest stuck out he took the step through where there used to be a hologram and into the chamber. While the silence was deafening, Annie felt sure everyone could hear her heart pounding inside her chest.

Michael, thinking of Ralph's cannibalistic concerns, whispered, "Think we can take them?"

Ralph wasn't sure if he was joking or not, but he gave a quick shake of the head. For once in his life, Ralphie was literally speechless.

It was then that Matika, from out of nowhere, hopped up on the podium, eyes wide and body shaking, and lifted his head toward the ceiling and let out a long, mournful wail that gave the three chill bumps. Had a rock been laying around, Ralph would have drilled the little fur ball back into Neverland.

"Matika," Jimmy cooed, stroking the little dogs' back while maintaining eye contact with the visiting delegation of three, "let's not be rash, let's wait and see what they have to say for themselves."

While Ralph and Michael were on-edge, Annie was about to hyperventilate. Had she had the opportunity she would have gladly taken on the spiral and the dizzying heights to get away from the scrutiny they were now getting. It seemed obvious—they were indeed unwelcome and just might be the main courses at the next dinner. Her legs were shaking so bad she could hardly stand.

"Motion!" The voice came from the upper tier, behind Jimmy.

"So noted," replied Taylor, turning to acknowledge the speaker. It was another short, squat, balding man with wire-rimmed glasses.

"I move..." he said with a hint of malice in his voice, "that we string 'em up and dangle 'em over the Pit." A hearty chorus of 'here here's' followed, with a few seconds. As the quiet died down most eyes were now on Jimmy, the ball in his court with a motion made.

"Discussion?" Taylor cocked his eyebrow as he continued to pet Matika.

Silence. Ralph finally raised his hand. Jimmy, as did most, eyed him suspiciously. Even Mothman seemed to be wearing a frown, if such a look could be discerned from a faceless creature.

"Yesssssssssssssssssss?" Jimmy nodded, extending the word out cautiously.

Ralph lowered his hand, knowing he now had the floor without a clue as to what he should say. He cleared his throat. "Pardon the three of us, your honor." Annie rolled her eyes at Ralph calling a homeless person in Beckley 'your honor.' "But we're here entirely by accident and we have no intention of harming you in any way."

Jimmy nodded with condescension in his posture. "That's comforting," he said, looking around the room at the fifty or so drawing a slight chortle from some.

"What I mean is," Ralphie stammered, recognizing his slight gaffe, "that we didn't mean to come here in the first place. We got here by accident, and we're more than willing to just return to where we came and forget about all this."

"All what?" asked Mothman, folding his arms almost across his red eyes.

Ralph stared in disbelief. "All this," he said pointing around the room, "all of you."

Mothman's upper body turned to Taylor as if to say 'see I told you so.' Jimmy nodded and took a step forward.

"Ralphie, you're honestly telling me you could forget all this?"

Ralph shrugged his shoulders. "No. But I wouldn't say anything, honest to God." He looked to his two accidental tourist companions. "None of us would, would we?" He turned to Annie and Michael who both shook their heads vigorously.

Taylor took another step to the edge of the raised dais and jumped down, his stocky body jiggling from the impact. Matika danced excitedly on the podium as Taylor made his way up the aisle toward the three. He stopped two steps down and looked up at them.

"What about missy there? She's a reporter, she gets paid for a lot more boring stories than this one." His eyes now fixed on the lady reporter.

Annie drew her head back at the attention. "Hey," she said defensively, "they'd never believe this in a million years—up there." She pointed toward the ceiling, the surface. "Never."

Jimmy squinted as he took in her words. "You don't think it would be a BIG story." His eyebrows rose with the word 'big.'

He had her there. It certainly would be a big story—much bigger, now that she thought about it, than the Ernest T. Bass story she'd been covering that got her here in the first place. Her glazed-over eyes spoke volumes to Taylor.

"It would be a big story, wouldn't it Miss Wolf." Again Annie was shocked that he knew her occupation AND her name. Taylor turned to young Michael.

"What about you there, skater boy—think you could forget all this?" Taylor swept his arm out wide behind him, indicating the gathered throng. "Well?"

"Sure," Michael said nervously, "sure."

Taylor harrumphed and turned, made his way slowly back to and upon the dais. He stoked the preening Matika as he turned back around.

"Further discussion?"

A mumbling erupted immediately with an occasional, high pitched 'string 'em up' coming from the one who had made the original motion. Ralph decided on one last tactic.

"What about you, Taylor?" he asked, some defiance in his voice.

At the sound of his name Taylor stopped stroking the dog and gave Ralph his full attention. "What do you mean, what about me?"

Annie and Michael both looked up to Ralph wondering where he was going and the wisdom of his argumentative tone. "You're up there a lot—but you don't tell nobody about what goes on down here." Good point thought Annie, turning to gauge the reaction of Taylor. "And what about you Mothman, you're up there quite a bit." Very quietly Ralph whispered, "At least you were."

An audible gasp erupted from the room at this accusation. Even Taylor stared up to his unlikely companion. Mothman's arms dropped to his side as his hands clenched in fists.

"What did you call me?" he asked in that high pitched, near-hair lip drone of his.

Ralph, now wondering himself about the wisdom of his tact as the beast seemed to be getting angrier by the minute, quietly repeated the moniker as all ears listened intently. "Mothman."

At this Mothman again turned toward Jimmy, anger seeming to seep out of his every pore. "Did you hear what he called me?" he said, now a bottom lip visible and sticking out. "Did you hear what he called me?" he repeated louder, his right arm darting out with his index finger pointing at Ralph.

Taylor patted his arm in a calming manner as he leveled his gaze at Ralph. Matika gave a low, menacing growl. "I don't think name calling is exactly what you ought to be doing right now young man."

"I didn't call him that." Ralph held his gaze and continued. "The newspapers did." Another audible gasp erupted from the gathering as Mothman turned this way and that, shaking his upper body as if to deny what Ralph had said. He lifted his palms skyward—or rather ceilingward—and shrugged his shoulders—child-like - as if to say 'it wasn't me.'

"The newspapers?" asked Taylor, disbelieving. Mothman recognized Jimmy's doubtful tone and nodded his head—or shoulders—in agreement.

It was Annie who chimed in. "He was big news back in the late 60's, maybe 70's. National. Maybe even international." Taylor looked up to the towering creature beside him with a hard glance. Annie continued with, "They've just erected a statue in his honor in Pt. Pleasant."

This news brought the house down. About half of the gathered throng gasped in horror while the other half hooted and congratulated 'Arnold' on his new-found notoriety. Taylor raised his arms to command silence. The room grew quiet, sensing a showdown about to emerge.

"Statue?"

Ralph answered. "Yeah, you know, a sculpture of a person's likeness…"

Taylor interrupted him. "I know what a statue is," he said briskly. "A statue of our Arnold here?" Annie nodded her head. She hadn't seen it in person, but had seen the photo in the Charleston Gazette that a friend had emailed her. Now that she recalled the image, it looked nothing like the real thing. She hoped that this group wouldn't require an actual photo of the stainless steel monster, but had no idea the capabilities of the group with which she met.

"Where is it?" Taylor barked out the question, irritated.

Ralphie shrugged his shoulders. "Never been there, but it's somewhere downtown. I saw the pictures on the internet."

With that bit of news Taylor took charge, pointing to the ceiling with his right hand while his left rested on Matika's soft, small back. He seemed to be drawing energy from the little dog, as right before their eyes downtown Pt. Pleasant began to materialize in a haze of smoke, light and shadow. Like playing a video game, the image quickly changed as each street was viewed—the image abandoned as no sign of a statue was visible. Finally the visual swung to the left and there it was, the image in question, glistening under a bright and sunny sky. The collective group took in a breath as the image grew nearer. Annie and Ralph both groaned as the amber-eyed creature seemed to growl back at them.

"Hah!" exclaimed Mothman in apparent victory, "you see, it looks nothing like me." The image shifted and slowly began to move around the sculpture, stood at the back, as catcalls filled the room with things like, "Nice butt," and "What a crack," were shouted. The visual continued on around until it was back to the front again, and Mothman himself began to levitate up and stand beside the image of the steel statue. The REAL Mothman stood beside a stainless steel, androgynous creature WITH a head full of hair going down into cornrows. The few chest hairs looked like worms, and the statue had an impressive six pack for a stomach. Four sharp, pointy fingers matched the number of fang-like teeth just below the birdlike nose. The only resemblance, really, was the amber eyes.

"I ask you," he said, his confidence overflowing, "is this the image of moi, a sophisticated, urbane gentleman such as myself?"

Michael knew little of the Mothman legend, but did know now that their goose was cooked. As the general din of the gathering grew, he leaned in and whispered to Ralph, "Wanna make a run for it?"

Ralph was considering that option when Annie spoke again. "Look at the plaque down at the bottom, see what it says." She was pointing to the base of the statue where indeed a plaque rested. The visual scanned down and left the real Mothman standing not beside the false image of himself but beside words, words that the entire gathering began to read in unison, their voices growing louder with each spoken word.

Legend of the Mothman. On a chilly fall night in November, 1966 two young couples drove into the TNT area north of Point Pleasant, West Virginia when they realized they were not alone. What they saw that night has evolved into one of the great mysteries of all time; hence the Mothman legacy began. It has grown into a curious phenomenon known all over the world by millions of curious people asking questions. What really happened? What did these people see? Has it been seen since? It still sparks the world's curiosity, the mystery behind Point Pleasant, West Virginia's Mothman.

With the last word spoken the room grew silent, as all eyes now shifted back to the slowly sinking Mothman as he settled back down on the podium. The gig was up. His red eyes paled, grew more pinkish than red, seemed to fill with water. After stammering several times he looked back to Taylor and said, "I was just getting some books."

Taylor averted his eyes away from Arnold. A sniff emanated from the monster-like creature. Taylor looked up to the three, pain in his eyes. He almost seemed to be searching, looking for a way out of what they didn't know. Mothman's shoulders completely drooped.

"Motion." The voice came from high up and to he right of Michael.

With no enthusiasm Taylor responded with, "So noted."

"I move that we banish Arnold the Youngest from the Society for the Prevention of the Proliferation of Corruption of Elected Officials Above." Taylor didn't call for discussion—he didn't have time. Immediately every voice began to express an opinion, some angry, some beseeching, all drowned out by the fervor of the others.

Ralph said to his companions, "Society for the Prevention of what?" Annie wished more than anything she had her notepad and pen.

Taylor raised his hands for silence. Begrudgingly the group obeyed.

"We'll begin our discussion with Ulysses the Elder." He half turned to his left and looked down to the front row. A very old man sat quietly, didn't seem to hear the invitation to weigh-in on the apparent breach of policy. "Ulysses?" Taylor looked down, coaxing his old friend to speak.

Finally the old man stood, he looked to be the oldest man the three had ever seen. He was slightly bent, long gray hair hung straight toward the ground. He slowly turned to look up at Ralph, then Annie, then Michael. You could hear a wisp of wind the underground room had grown so quiet.

39

His voice, it turned out, wasn't as fragile as his body appeared to be. It was steady, baritone, full of authority. As he spoke, he never looked up to the podium but surveyed his compatriots at every level.

"As you know," he began, trying to straighten up to his full height, which might have been six foot on a good day, "I am the eldest of this Society of…" His pause gave Annie hope, she needed to hear it again to correctly store it in her ample memory bank. "…whatever," he continued, dashing her hopes. "When I came on in '98, the rules were rigid and were enforced without prejudice." Ralph assumed '98 to be 1898, as 1998 didn't seem to fit either he or any of those gathered.

"The first violation, and some of you will remember this, was that of Hoffa. Not only did he make a name for himself—up there—he crossed state lines and flaunted every rule in the book. We had no choice but to silence him, and did so with swiftness and stealth that to this day frightens even me.

"Hoffa deserved what he got—every bit of it. The second violation was Edna the Woman. Her trespasses did not involve 'above,' but here below. She challenged the leadership and the Order of Things in such a way as to threaten our very existence. All of us live among the mortals, she proclaimed." This disgust in Ulysses' voice was evidence that he didn't agree with Edna the Woman. "Edna was dealt with, and now we have this breach."

For the first time he turned to the podium, had to bend his knees to straighten up to take in the full height of Mothman who looked like a man ready to be hanged, if he had a neck. His eyes were now without glow, nearly hollow clear shells where once burned fire.

"And now, we have this breach," Ulysses repeated. He looked to Taylor then turned back to face the amphitheater. "Let's face it. We have taken in Arnold like he was one of our own. We've embraced him.

He IS one of our own. And his infractions weren't serious. No loss of life." Ralph could have swore he heard Ulysses say, "That we know of," under his breath. "No breach of security, really." He turned to look up at Mothman who seemed to be standing taller now. The old man smiled a warm, friendly smile. Mothman's eyes began to glow again, faint at first, then brighter and brighter. Ulysses concluded with, "I say we forgive him and get on with the business of these three." The place erupted—mostly shouts of glee, a few were less supportive but went largely unheralded. Ulysses literally fell back in his seat and Ralph could tell by Taylor's demeanor he was concerned about the old man. The room finally grew quiet as Taylor turned to face the three trespassers. Mothman squared his shoulders up now toward Ralph, defiance in his stance.

"So," said Taylor, "what do we do with you three?" It wasn't a question, it came with a squint and just a hint of compassion, but not enough to make any of the three comfortable. After a long silence, Taylor seemed to hit on something.

"Tell you what, we conclude this annual meeting with a chamber session. At this session, you'll each have five minutes to convince this body of both your innocence and your honesty." Someone toward the back called out 'two' to which Taylor barked out 'ten,' effectively shutting up the dissenter. "You convince us, you're free to go—with certain conditions of course."

Ralph's stomach growled loud enough for the entire gathering to hear. The round cherub of a man who had called for them to be strung up cried out, "For heaven's sake Jimmy, get these people some food— they're starved to death."

40

The gathering at the Boyd Church of God was impressive. Nearly every able-bodied member was there and had brought with them other family members and friends. Howard estimated the crowd to be around 300. The minister gave him a nod and approached the podium.

"Good morning," he said with some enthusiasm in his voice. The congregation nearly in unison returned his Saturday morning greeting. With a smile the minister continued. "I hope we see some of you about this time tomorrow." Many in crowd smiled back, knowing their friend or loved one sitting beside them was not a regular attendee. Someone from the back called out a heartfelt 'amen.'

"I'll be brief this morning, you all know why we're here. Howard Moore, Annie's boss down at the paper, has organized this search party, convinced that she's still somewhere in the county being held probably against her will." He turned to the miked-up editor and said, "Howard?"

Unaccustomed to public speaking and having had a phobia that dated back to his high school days, he nervously approached the pulpit. He looked out at the gathered throng and part of him wanted to run, but the other part of him knew their cause was perhaps a matter of life and death. He took a sip of water the minister had kindly filled for him and began.

"My wife and I would like to thank all of you for coming out today. A small town like Beckley, a small county like Raleigh, even though we don't always see eye to eye, we're still family. And Annie was part of my family at work, and part of your family here at church. I don't know about you," he paused, seemingly about to lose it, "but I miss her. And it's my fault that she's missing in the first place—so I had to do something." He paused again, wiped a tear from his eye.

"I truly believe, from what I've learned about Ralphie Johnson these past few days, that he's a good boy at heart. He wouldn't hurt Annie." Aunt Minnie, who sat toward the back, nodded her head, also wiping a tear away. "Ralphie was also without a car, you've probably seen him thumbing and maybe even picked him up a time or two. I think he's still here, somewhere in the county. Perhaps a hunting lodge or cabin somewhere up in the woods. Maybe at a motel somewhere out in the county. He could be house-sitting for someone on vacation." Howard took another sip, somewhat calmed down now that the first words were out without his voice cracking.

"You know your part of the county better than most. Go back to your neighborhoods, hand out the flyers door to door. Trust your gut, if you feel this house or that abandoned mine might be his hideout, go with that feeling. However," he cautioned, his index finger pointed up, "our number one concern should be our own safety. Annie is already in harm's way, I'm afraid, so there's no sense in adding insult to injury. If you get in a situation where you're uncomfortable just..." He looked to the back where Chief Hall stood at the doorway. Hall took the cue and began walking up the center aisle.

"My men," he began, "along with the state's and the sheriff's boys are out in full force today. We're all in communication, we're all in earshot of 9-1-1. If you have cell phones and find yourself in ANY situation, and I mean ANY situation, that you're uncomfortable with, don't hesitate to call. We should have someone within no more than ten, fifteen minutes at most of your location. I agree with Howard, I think they're right here practically under our noses, but if we don't unite and start pounding the pavement we may never find them." About halfway up the aisle he turned completely around and eyed the faces that stared up at him. "As you leave, register with my men as to where you'll be. If there are any significant gaps in the county, we'll try to fill those with other volunteers. We start at ten this morning—that's fifteen minutes—and we gather back here a half hour after dark, compare notes, thoughts. And again, let me emphasize, don't get in harm's way. That's what got us here in the first place."

With that Hall made his way to the back and Howard again thanked them for coming and helping out. The congregation rose and began to filter out the three aisles to the back, pointing to a map or calling out a community in which their search would be centered. With yellow highlighters the map was nearly covered when the last of the group filed out. Hall looked at the finished product.

"We're good," he said, nodding his head as he looked down to the county map. "Matter of fact there'll be some overlapping in several areas." He looked up to Howard and his wife. "Why don't we head back out to the exhibition mine. My gut tells me something out there don't add up."

Howard looked to his wife who nodded. The three piled into the county vehicle, Chief Hall radioed all uniformed personnel as to his whereabouts, and up Harper Road and down Ewart Avenue they headed.

41

The feast that Ralph, Annie and Michael partook of was unbelievable. There was roast beef, ham, steaks. Different kinds of salads with every dressing known to man. The sweetest tasting juices, wines and teas washed down a literal cornucopia of food. The deserts, oddly enough, consisted of only pecan pie and cheesecake, both of which were delicious. Michael, being under-aged, drank a Pepsi that Taylor procured from a lit machine near the entrance—a machine that hadn't been there prior to the feast.

"Oh my God," Annie suddenly groaned, pushing the plate back away from her. Ralph, sitting across the table from her, and Michael, sitting next to her, both took in her pained look with concern.

"What?" said Michael, wondering if maybe the food had been poisoned. Annie's face took on a deeper expression of disgust as she glanced back down to her plate. Michael and Ralph both peered down onto the seemingly healthy portion of food still left.

"What is it?" Ralph pressed Annie.

She groaned again, nearly retching. Her finger pointed near the far edge of the plate, nearest Ralph. From the juice of her steak Ralph gingerly pulled out a hair that looked to be a couple of inches long. Annie turned her head in disgust.

"What?" said Ralph, looking to Annie then to Michael. "It's just a hair. It even looks clean."

At that pronouncement Annie nearly vomited, had to catch herself from doing so. Ralph leaned across the table and held the hair up next to Annie's face. "I think it's one of yours," he said as if the matter were settled.

"THAT," Annie glanced toward him with disgust in her demeanor, "is NOT one of mine."

Ralph leaned back and looked cross-eyed at the hair, then wiped it off on his pants underneath the table. His eyes moved back down to the half eaten steak still soaking in it's own juices.

"You not gonna finish that?" he asked of Annie. Her violent headshake seemed to indicate 'no,' so Ralph pulled the plate to him and began carving away. Annie had to completely turn away from the spectacle to keep from getting sicker. Ralph and Michael just shrugged their shoulders at each other.

Most were both feeling the effects of the heady meal and strong drinks, including the participants in this 'annual meeting.' Taylor— talking with a strange looking, tall fellow—was giggling like Santa Claus over a plate of cookies and milk. Occasionally Michael would whisper about making a break but both Ralph and Annie shook their heads, Ralph's cheeks swelled out with food. Whatever was to come, nothing was going to get between Ralph and this buffet unlike any he had seen before. He had managed his way into the pre-race meal at the Daytona 500 the year Dale Earnhardt was tragically killed and it didn't even compare to this.

With his feet propped up on the stone table Ralph loosened his belt as he felt a 'presence' coming nearer. He quickly took his feet off the table and sat up rigidly. It was Ulysses the Elder, shuffling along the bench and taking a seat across from Ralph.

Ulysses looked around the room then back to Ralph. He seemed to have something on his mind but he wasn't in any hurry to spit it out. Ralph nodded his head in respect to the old man.

"So, what do you make of all this?" Ulysses asked, his head tossed slightly to the mingling throng.

Ralph fished between his teeth with his tongue, trying extract a piece of steak lodged between them. "Strangest thing I've ever seen," he said matter-of-factly, "and I'm from West Virginia."

To this Ulysses laughed out loud, actually caught the attention of Jimmy Taylor who was quite inebriated. He smiled affectionately at Ralphie and said, "We're all West Virginian's son. Every last one of us."

Ralph's eyebrows knotted in confusion. "Even Mothman?"

Ulysses put his finger to his lips in a quieting manner and nodded. "Even Arnold the Younger."

Ralph leaned in closer and whispered. "What IS he anyway?"

Ulysses shrugged his sagging shoulders. "I don't have any idea. We were all pretty taken aback when he first showed up, but he's won us all over with his good heart and attention to detail." The Elder leaned in a little and asked quietly, "Did he kill anybody...up there?"

Ralph shook his head no, then countered with, "I don't think so, but the last time he was seen about fifty people died when that bridge collapsed in Point Pleasant."

Ulysses held Ralph's gaze for some time. "What do the people think?"

"They think he was trying to warn people that something like that was about to happen. There were a lot of Men in Black hanging around the area at that time too."

"Black men?" Ulysses asked.

"No, Men in Black. White guys dressed in black, government-like suits. Lot of weird stuff was going on then when the Silver Bridge collapsed it all seemed to end. The movie implied..."

Ulysses interrupted immediately. "Movie?"

"Yeah," Ralph nodded, "came out a few years ago. Maybe five."

"Who played Arnold?"

"Who?"

"Mothman," Ulysses replied, nodding his head in the direction of the creature.

"Oh, I can't get used to his real name. Nobody. You never once saw the Mothman, even though it was called The Mothman Prophecies. It was more about the Men in Black than it was Arnold there." This time it was Ralph pointing with a nod of his head.

Ulysses pushed out his bottom lip and nodded, seemingly lost in thought. Ralph finally broke the silence.

"Who are you people?"

Ulysses smiled and pulled a pack of Lucky Strikes out of his shirt pocket, tapped the pack into his palm then fingered a cigarette out. He offered one to Ralph who shook his head.

"Those things will kill you, you know that don't you."

"Not down here," Ulysses replied, lighting up and inhaling deeply. "One of the few pleasures we get."

"How do you get them? Surely you don't grow your own tobacco down here in the dark."

Ulysses smiled and shook his head no. "You asked who we are. You sure you wanna know?" The question made Ralph think of the ever-popular saying that 'if I told you I'd have to kill you.' He took his chances and said sure.

After a slight coughing spell Ulysses took in a deep breath and started. "Our agency started when this area broke away from Virginia and became a state."

Ralph's eyes widened. "You're telling me you're a state agency?"

"No, no," Ulysses hacked the words out around puffs of smoke, "not at all. Goes much deeper than that." Deeper? thought Ralph.

Ulysses stood and motioned for Ralph to follow. While the party went on, several noticed the ascent of Ulysses and Ralph up the stairs and through the hologram to the long hallway.

42

The Exhibition Coal mine's business had fallen off of late, given the controversy surrounding the abduction of the lady reporter and the possibility that she was being or had been held in the mine by her captor—a former employee of the mine. The non-local numbers were about the same, but nearly all local traffic and schools had stopped coming, pending the resolution of the disappearance. Hall, Howard and his wife donned the usual hardhats and, with an on-duty tour guide, headed back into the dimly lit, musty shaft.

Chief Hall led the way between the railroad tracks and took the left spur—usually the exit line of the exhibition route. It was about halfway back that the hieroglyphics had been found, on the left. They had marked the place with scratches on both the far wall and the railroad tracks themselves. Their mine lights, affixed to their hardhats, quickly found the indicators. Their mine lights did not find the hieroglyphics. They stood in awe as they peered at the now-blank wall.

"That is the most incredible thing," Howard said, pointing to about eye level so that his wife could see where the markings had been seen before. "They weren't there, then they were, now they're not. Hall, is there anyway those markings could be dated somehow, maybe carbon dating or something like that?"

Chief Hall snorted. "We can't even take a half decent finger print from time to time. No way does anybody in this county—maybe even the state—know how to carbon-date that I'm aware of. Maybe one of your college types at Marshall or WVU."

It was Betty that moved closer and rubbed her hand against the nearly smooth surface. "What did the original message say again?"

It was Chief Hall who had committed the lines to memory. "To all ye who enter these premises, to all ye who so desire, to all ye who regard life, be prepared for the fire."

Betty's eyes narrowed as she gazed hard at the equally hard surface. Something seemed to be drawing her in, pulling her mind into a place where it seemed she had been before. She finally shook her head as if awakening from a daydream.

"What is it, Betty?" Howard asked, concerned by her ashen appearance.

She seemed almost embarrassed. "Why, I…I don't know. It was like…"

After a momentary pause Chief Hall urged her on. "It was like what?"

She lightly chuckled and placed a hand to her forehead. "It was like…déjà vu, only the most intense version I've ever experienced in my life." She turned to look at her husband, tears welling up in each eye. "She's alive, and fine. Don't ask me how I know," she shook her head and turned away from her husband's intense stare, "but she's ok, really." With that said she began walking back out of the man-made cave with a certain unsteadiness. Chief Hall and Howard looked to each other curiously, back to the wall, then began following Betty out of the mineshaft.

43

Everyone was seated again after considerable persuasion on the part of Jimmy, and he announced it was time. Annie and Michael both looked to Ralph with concern on their faces, but he sat stoically without flinching.

"If the W's will lead the way," Jimmy said, looking up toward the hologram entrance. The entire top row stood and, beginning with the person nearest the entrance, began to file through the clever doorway. To Annie their gait reminded her of a funeral procession—albeit alphabetical—only fueling her trepidation. As the top row completely disappeared, the second row stood and made the semi-circular walk through the hologram, then the third, then the fourth, then the fifth. Finally the time came for the bottom level to walk up the stairs into the passageway and Annie felt a panic attack coming on quickly. Michael was anxious too, but Ralph stood, zombie-like, and followed Arnold the Younger who gingerly helped Ulysses the Elder slowly up the steps. Annie and Michael fell in line but were certain a firing squad or something equally horrendous waited for them on the other end. Jimmy Taylor, carrying the growling Matika, brought up the rear.

Through the hologram and into the corridor they passed. The shuffling of feet and kicking of stones could be heard well into the distance. Annie groaned as they passed the entryway to a path they had chosen earlier that led them, literally, nowhere. Michael's eyes darted to the left and the right as he was quietly planning his escape.

All three knew where the main artery led, and weren't surprised when they entered the giant catacomb with the winding path down from the feather-bottomed room. As Annie's eyes adjusted to the more intense light she could see that the 'W's' and all who had followed were now beginning to ascend up the Louvre-like staircase. Her fear of heights which had subsided with the physical exertion of walking now reared back up. Ralphie, even though he was in front of her, sensed—or presumed—her growing fear. She had not been a fan of coming down the narrow cliff-side path, and he knew she would be hesitant to go back up. He turned and took her hand.

"It's ok," he whispered above the din of shuffling feet.

His assurance did little to assuage her fear as they approached the lower end of the pathway. "What makes you think that?" she whispered back, some anger in her voice. "I'm just as scared of heights now as I was before."

Ralphie gave a quick shake of his head. "We're only going halfway up."

44

Howard sat in muted silence as he rode shotgun back to the church where everyone was to gather after the search of their stated portion of the county. Chief Hall hadn't said much either. Nor had Betty, who had put on her seat belt and stared out the window since Hall had started the powerful but quiet engine. Hall drove aimlessly around, knowing the groups wouldn't be back yet from the more distant parts of the county. On a lark, he turned up Concord Street, the turn jostling Howard out of his own stupor.

"Where are you going?"

Hall shrugged. "I've not personally interviewed Ralph's mom. Let's see," he turned, looking first to Howard then to Betty in the back seat, "if anything unusual develops." His slight emphasis on the word 'unusual' coupled with his glance to the back seat spoke volumes to Howard—some of which he resented. He muttered a curt 'fine' as Hall eased the car in the simple driveway of Minnie Johnson.

With less enthusiasm Howard opened his door then opened his wife's door. She stepped out dutifully, eyes straight ahead, head held high. Howard—for the first time since they had dated so long ago—couldn't read his wife. Hall was knocking at the door.

"Good afternoon, Mrs. Johnson," Hall said politely as the door opened to reveal a heavy-set, sixtyish woman. She knew of the Chief of Police and had seen him earlier in the day at the church. She said hi back to the editor and the chief of police, nodded to the one who she assumed was one of their wives. She was certain that the visit had to do with Ralphie. She was sure it was bad news.

Hall, sensing her fear, quickly put her at ease. "Everything's ok, Mrs. Johnson. We're still looking to talk to Ralphie, and the two citizens are still missing, but nothing's turned up that should concern you. We were just hoping to have a little talk."

Minnie pushed opened the screen door and sucked in her breath to allow a little more room for the three to pass. "Y'all want some herbal tea. I just got a new batch down at the health food store. One of your deputies loved it."

"That would be Eddy," Hall noted aloud, remembering his warning that, whatever else he did, don't drink the tea. Said it gave him diarrhea for two days. "No thanks, Mrs. Johnson, we can't stay very long. But we appreciate the offer. Won't you sit down?"

Minnie eased into her Lazyboy and clicked off the TV. She was going to miss Jerry Springer. Hall quickly introduced Howard as one of the editors down at the paper—Annie's boss to be precise—and his wife Betty. Everyone exchanged polite nods then Hall's expression turned serious.

"Mrs. Johnson, is there anything at all that you can tell us," Hall hesitated for a moment, brainstorming, "about Ralphie, his habits, his likes, his dislikes. Maybe some tidbit that might lead us to where he and the others are."

"First of all, Sheriff Hall," Minnie started, drawing a wince from the 'Chief' at being called sheriff, "my Ralphie ain't got nothing to do with them folks that are missing. Granted, he's a free spirit, but he'd never do anything like kidnap somebody. If you ask me," she said, lowering her voice and looking around, finally settling her gaze on Howard, "I believe he must have had a crush on your lady reporter."

"What makes you say that?" Howard questioned, cocking his head hoping that she was right.

Minnie shrugged her shoulders. "He had a crush on Delilah Eubanks in high school, he started a scrapbook on her. He had a crush on one of them NASCAR girls that kiss the drivers at the end of the races. He started a scrapbook on her. Now your lady friend is missing, and we find he's started a scrapbook." Minnie made eye contact with all three before continuing. "Did it ever occur to any of you that maybe they run off together—to get married, or whatever?"

The thought had NOT occurred to the three, but they were given some comfort from Minnie's analysis that maybe Ralph wasn't holding them hostage after all. Which elicited the Chief's follow up question.

"Any idea about the young boy? Had Ralph maybe befriended him the past few weeks?"

Minnie shook her head no, followed by a cough and drink of water. It was Betty who continued the query.

"How long did Ralph work at the Exhibition Coal Mine?"

At this Minnie looked up to the ceiling and seemed to be counting. "Near as I can recollect," she surmised, "he's worked on and off there for about three summers. He didn't work there this summer for some reason."

"Did he ever tell you anything strange or unusual about the mine?" Betty asked.

"Like what?"

Now it was Betty's turn to shrug. "I don't know—maybe he heard voices or saw passages that appeared and disappeared almost at will. Cryptic messages on the walls." Howard and the Chief gave each other quick, concerned glances. "Met people inside that weren't...from out here." Now the two men stared intently at the woman. If Minnie noticed their looks of concern, she didn't show it.

"No. Nothing like that."

"Well," Hall drawled, standing up, trying to shake off the weirdness Betty was causing within him, "I guess we've bothered you enough."

Betty continued as if she'd not noticed the Chief stand up. "Do you believe in ghosts, Mrs. Johnson, or 'other' worlds?" Hall looked down to Betty then gave a half-begging glance to Howard. Minnie said no and took another sip of water.

As Howard took his wife's hand and stood, Betty stood with him but not to leave. She released her husband's hand and slowly walked toward Minnie Johnson.

"Was Ralph ever in a coma?" At this Howard quietly said c'mon honey but she didn't hear. For once, Minnie answered in the affirmative.

"Yes. Car wreck, hit a bridge and fell down into the creek. If somebody hadn't come along, they tell me he would have drowned."

"Was he in a coma for four days?"

"Why yes, it was almost four days to the minute when he came out of it."

At this Betty turned and nodded to her husband. "No further questions, your honor." Howard looked to Hall and mouthed the words 'no further questions your honor' as Betty passed between them and went to the door. Hall tipped his hat to Minnie and said they'd let themselves out, no need for her to get up.

45

The walk up the narrow pathway was terrifying for Annie as her phobia of heights was only magnified. She kept her head turned to the wall with one hand gently touching it as Ralphie held her other. Jimmy Taylor brought up the rear with Matika firmly in hand.

They came to the small alcove where, earlier, Ralph had rubbed the stone that nearly drowned them in a spray of water that came from nowhere and went to nowhere. As if on cue the entire gathering stopped and turned toward the inside, facing each other across the abyss. Just ahead of him Ulysses the Elder leaned out from the wall and said, "Ralphie, will you do the honors."

Ralph smiled but shook his head no. "She's afraid of heights," he explained, motioning his head toward Annie. Ulysses nodded in tacit agreement and looked on down the line to Taylor.

"Jimmy?"

Taylor said fine and turned back into the alcove and placed his rough and callused thumb against the shiny stone and slowly began to rub up and down. Annie, with eyes closed, couldn't see the unbelievable swirl of colors that began to bathe the chamber. She could hear the first sounds of rushing water, immediately taking a deep breath and holding it.

"It's beautiful," Ralph said in a whisper, hypnotized by the swirl of colors and the rising tide of water. It sloshed and rose quickly and Annie could feel the spray now hitting her ankles, her pant legs, her blouse. Her scream was drowned out by the count—in unison by everyone but her—to three then the entire group, with Annie being pulled by Ralphie, jumped into the swirling vortex.

Annie knew she was drowning. Her mouth was full of water and she was completely submerged beneath the circling waters. She was reciting the Lord's Prayer when she realized Ralph was shaking her and calling her name.

Her eyes opened to the most stunning of sights, sounds, and sensations. First of all, she was completely dry as if she'd never been pulled into and completely submerged beneath the water. Second of all, there were sounds, normal sounds, in the distance—car horns blaring, a train whistle far off somewhere, a baby crying from a stroller nearby. And, most startling of all, right above Ralphie's head was the bronze bust of Abraham Lincoln, and above that the shining gold of the Capitol dome, and above that the most beautiful full moon that she'd thought she'd never ever see again as long as she lived. Her squeal of delight made even Ralph blush as she hugged him with all her might.

"Whoa there girl," he said, breathing in the scent of her hair as he tried to push her gently back. "Hold tight, we've still got a ways to go."

At this pronouncement Annie stepped back and looked at him, blinked once, then looked all around her. "Correct me if I'm wrong," she said with some condescension in her voice, "but we ARE at the state capitol are we not?"

Ralph nodded but said dolefully, "We're not free to go."

To this Annie snorted and said, "We'll see about that." Getting her bearings she decided to head west toward downtown, toward civilization—away from the madness that had consumed her since the ill-fated meeting with Ralphie in the Raleigh County Courthouse. She started walking.

"It won't work," Ralph informed her loud enough to get the attention of most of the group still milling around the statue and on the lower steps of the capitol. Eventually all eyes turned toward Annie who had just stepped off the sidewalk and onto the grass, only to find her legs in what felt like invisible quicksand. She raised her arms in a power-walking fashion, swinging them from side to side, trying to make progress. Her legs felt like they weighed a thousand pounds each. She finally stopped, no more than five feet off the sidewalk. She turned easily and found Ralph at the edge of the concrete. "Told you so," he said matter-of-factly.

Annie huffed and found her short journey back to the pavement as easy as simply walking. She turned and looked back toward downtown and took off again, only to find her personal quicksand consuming her once again. She turned, angrily, and stomped past Ralph and this time headed toward the east, toward Beckley, toward home. Her brisk walk was watched by every creature now seated on the capitol steps saw Annie cross from one side of the plaza to the other in ten quick steps, only to step again into a quicksand so thick that two steps was all she could muster. A few giggles could be heard from the audience that caused her head to snap quickly around. Silence was immediate as breathing was suspended. She walked back onto the plaza with a look of hatred so deep and so menacing that Ralph couldn't even make eye contact with her. Abruptly Annie turned on her heel and headed toward the boulevard. She would walk into the Kanawha River if needed to escape this maddening group.

"That won't work either," Ralph half-shouted, feeling sorry for his friend and realizing that every defiant step she took was a strike against them with the creatures. Annie came to the steps and her left leg reached down for the second step when the quicksand grabbed her again. Giggles welled up in the group and this time it was Ralphie who turned and, with his hard look, commanded and got silence. Annie's foot finally touched down on the second step but she was stuck—she couldn't get either leg to move. Ralph touched her shoulder and her upper body wheeled around on him like a cobra ready to strike.

"LEAVE ME ALONE!" she shouted, her tears beginning to flow in half anger, half sadness. To be so close to home, to be above ground, and to not be free was more than she could take. The gathered creatures slowly began to stand up, dust off the seat of their pants, and make their way on up the steps to the massive wooden doors that lead into the second floor of the rotunda area. Jimmy Taylor waited about half way up the steps, watching as Ralph pulled Annie to him and comforted her. Taylor's eye twinkled as Ralph began to lead her past the statue called Lincoln Walks at Midnight and to the stairs that led to the annual meeting.

46

Hall was startled awake by his wife's sudden movement in the bed. She had sat straight up, was looking around. Hall rubbed his eyes as he turned over.

"Doris, is there something the matter?"

He was met with silence, and the silence scared him. He attuned his hearing to the rest of the house, listening, as was Doris. Or at least she seemed to be. He could hear nothing, just his own heart now beating quickly deep within his barrel chest.

"It's started," she said.

Again Hall pricked his ears in the direction of the hallway and the stairs. Nothing. "What's started, Doris honey?"

She lay back down and was fast asleep. Hall was wide-awake, wondering if every wife in Raleigh County had gone as loopy as his and Howard's had in the last twenty-four hours.

47

The telephone startled Minnie out of a deep, sound sleep. She snored through ten rings before sitting up, finding her glasses, and checking the number on the caller ID. Out of area, the LCD readout indicated. Her heart skipped a beat as she took the call.

"Mom?"

She started crying. "Ralphie, are you ok son?"

"Of course I'm ok," he said assuredly, "sorry I hadn't called in a while. Something came up."

"Oh Ralph, something awful's happened and they think you did it..."

But Ralph talked over her. "Listen mom, I can't talk long, I've got to go into a meeting. I just wanted to let you know I was ok and not to worry. Talk to you again soon."

"But Ralph," Minnie said into an already dead line. She looked at the clock...1:24 in the morning. While Ralph had called from many places over the years, it usually wasn't after she went to bed at ten o'clock. She made a mental note to call Sheriff Hall in the morning and went into the kitchen to make some tea.

48

About every other seat was filled as Ralph, Annie and Taylor made their way down into the house chamber. Taylor indicated for them to take a seat to the left side, up front. Ralph stopped so suddenly that Annie walked into him.

"Where's Michael?" he asked, looking around the chamber.

Taylor shook his head as Matika gave a low growl. "He didn't make it." Annie's eyes widened at the thought that he drowned in the process of coming above ground. Taylor seemed to read her thoughts.

"No, he's fine. He just bailed on us in the corridor, went up the Harrison County hallway." Taylor gave a chuckle. "He should be sufficiently worn out when he makes it back. Those corridors are genetically specific. Wrong genetics, they lead you back to where you started." Ralph remembered the arduous round trip they had made in one of the side corridors, and didn't envy Michael one bit. Assuming the boy didn't end up in or under Clarksburg, twenty miles deep and a couple hundred miles from home.

Everyone was now seated as Taylor once again positioned himself behind a podium, this time in the House Chamber of the West Virginia legislature. With a somber expression he looked around and up at those gathered. He cleared his throat as he sat Matika on the podium.

"Anything?" he asked, scanning the seats, both filled and vacant.

It was then Ralph and Annie noticed that each person seated had one hand on top of the desk they were seated at and the other hand on a neighboring desk that was empty. They seemed to be in a trance, their chins held high and eyes closed. Ralph gave Annie a curious glance and she shrugged her shoulders.

"I'm getting something," said a high pitched voice at the seat marked 'Logan.' All eyes opened and moved in the direction of the voice. "Yes, yes," the thin man said, "definitely getting something." He was nodding, his eyes closed. His other hand left the vacant desk beside him and he placed both hands on the 'Logan' desk. "Curious," he said, cocking his head, "I never knew." The word 'knew' was extended for several seconds as the hush was reverent, church-like.

"Well?" questioned one at a nearby seat, "Get on with it."

"I never knew," then opened his eyes. "We've got some old wounds opened back up in the devil's home county," the waif of a man said with near glee. "It involves the sheriff's office, the assessor's office, AND the county commission. And as you recall, my county was clean this time last year."

A few circumspect ummmmm's and awwwwww's were muttered as each now seemed to focus more on their desks and what vibrations that might be gleaned from them. A rotund man in the back, sitting at Marion County but with a hand on Mason County's desk too, gave out an audible 'ooooooh.'

Again the room fell silent as every head turned in that direction. He too seemed to relish the 'feel' of corruption that passed through the wood grain in his desk and into his very being. "Ahhhhhh," he sighed, as voices called out 'what is it' and 'c'mon man tell us.' His eyes opened but did not focus on anyone, just looked above Taylor to the electronic vote board used during regular and special sessions.

"We've got a problem in Marion County boys," he announced, "and girl," he continued. He seemed to be recognizing his one female counterpart but excluding Annie's presence. Ralph could feel Annie stiffen as she counted the females in the room—two. "It would seem we have some shenanigans going on regarding the upcoming special election in BOTH parties." His emphasis on the word 'both' drew oooohs and aaaahs from nearly all gathered.

It was Taylor who guessed the nature of the problem. "Vote buying?"

The delegate from Marion shook his head no, but with a broad smile. "Worse than that, Jimmy. A candidate is being bought off and..." he paused seemingly for dramatic effect, "another is considering eliminating his opponent for sheriff." A wail of catcalls and whistles filled the chamber as the delegate nodded—seemingly pleased with his discovery of chicanery in his home county. If you could call the county twenty miles above you home, Ralph noted silently.

This went on for at least two hours as probably half of the delegates divined some offense of their elected leaders from their home counties. The smaller infractions –fixed parking tickets, little white lies and the sort—drew boos and spitballs from all around. But some of the infractions, Annie noted, were real scoops that—if proved—would be killer stories. And every time she raised an eyebrow it was like Taylor sensed it and his eye caught hers. She began to get nervous, thinking her very thoughts were subject to this homeless man from Beckley.

"What time is it?"

The question startled Annie out of her intense scrutiny of all the ethical and moral violations that were going on in the state right under her reporter's nose. She blinked, then said, "What?"

"What time is it?" Ralph repeated the question.

Annie looked to her watch. "Quarter of twelve," she responded, wondering why it made any difference at all what time it was.

"Now," Ralph began, "is that a quarter of twelve REAL time, or five after one, or twenty-five after eleven?"

Annie's jaw hardened as her lips pursed and her eyes narrowed. "You wanna know what time it is? YOU WANNA KNOW WHAT TIME IT IS?" She stood and began lecturing Ralph on what time it was. "It's time for your medicine Ralphie." With her index finger she poked him in the forehead. "It's time you woke up and looked at the REAL world Ralphie. It's time YOU started wearing a watch and setting it for whatever time YOU want it to be!" With that, Annie slid the watch off her left wrist and tossed it to Ralph's chest.

Ralph caught the falling watch about his belt buckle as his head nodded mockingly. "You darn right I need a watch little missy and let me tell you the first thing I intend to do with it." He was pulling out the stem as he talked and evidently had it ready to be adjusted. "Now WHAT TIME IS IT? IS IT A QUARTER OF TWELVE, FIVE AFTER ONE, OR TWENTY-FIVE AFTER ELEVEN?" His eyes were wide open and his face only inches from Annie's—close enough that she could detect he'd had the shrimp cocktail at dinner.

"Ah hem," Jimmy Taylor slightly feigned a cough on the podium as he looked over his glasses down at the bantering couple. "You two can take that outside if you don't mind, we've got a lot of work to do here."

Annie and Ralph looked around the room and noticed that it was totally quiet as every eye was on them. Ralph muttered sorry and Annie nodded her head in agreement as they both retook their seats. From the back of the room came a familiar voice.

"Motion!"

"So noted," Taylor responded softly.

"I say we take a break and deal with these two, then get back to the work at hand. They make me nervous. Reminds me of when I was married."

A few chuckles and chortles were carefully masked by coughs and hacks as Annie glanced up into the crowd with fire in her eyes. Taylor closed a large book that Annie hadn't noticed before and said very well. He removed his glasses and put them on top of his head, turned to face the two. Ralph asked for a point of clarification. "What about Michael?"

Taylor studied for a moment as he scratched his five o'clock shadow. "Whatever we decide to do with you two will apply with equal force to your young friend." With that Taylor stepped around the podium and out to the front of the dais. "Discussion?"

Nearly everyone piped up at once and the din grew louder and louder. From what Ralphie could decipher, the discussion wasn't going their way. His head dropped as he ran his hands through his already disheveled hair. Annie had drew a similar conclusion and also looked down. Taylor called for silence.

"I hear and understand your concern," he said forcefully, pacing from side to side, "we go a hundred years and receive no trespassers and in one fell swoop," he glanced over to Mothman seated near the front, "we get three." He paused, appearing to analyze what he had just said.

"Have any of you considered the implications of this?" Taylor looked up, took in every row, every face. It was Ulysses who finally answered.

"With two portals in every county, one in the courthouse and another in an undisclosed location, we risk inundation IF this was no accident." A few gasps were taken in as Ulysses stood to drive home his point. "IF this was an accident, our situation is vastly different," he said with some gravity to his posture, "but if this was no accident..." He could hardly even think of the consequences, much less say the words out loud.

"Then we," Taylor finished the sentence for him, "are doomed as a society." Shouts of 'no' and 'hang the prisoners' echoed throughout the halls of state government. For the first time since Ralph and Annie had been down under Taylor had trouble quieting the group.

49

Chief Hall called Howard with the news that Ralphie had called his mom sometime during the night. They met at Shoney's on Robert C Byrd Drive and mulled over the news over a cup of coffee.

"No clue as to his location?" Howard asked. After the Chief shook his head no, Howard asked if the phone call could be traced.

"Depends," the Chief answered. "I've got the phone company working on it. If he made the call from a cell phone we can obviously locate the phone but not the place where he made the call. If it was from a land-based telephone, such as a pay phone or a residential phone, we should be able to get a location."

The waitress filled their coffee cups as each mentally perused the new development. It was Howard who broke the silence.

"Have you mentioned this to Eddy? I personally take it as good news in that I don't think he'd have called his mom if he had," Howard struggled with how to put it, "done harm to Annie or the boy. Don't you think so?"

Chief Hall looked up to the ceiling in thought. "You may be right. I HOPE you're right. But here's what concerns me. Nobody really knows this boy real well. Ted Bundy called his mom a bunch of times over the years while he was whacking coeds all across the country. IF the boy has gone into the deep end of the pool, we can in no way predict what he has done or will do in the future. I just hope the phone records give us a location." His beeper went off and he recognized the number as the office. "Let me take this."

Howard chewed on a piece of bacon as Hall slid out of the seat and went outside to talk in private. From his body language he could sense Hall deemed the news to be good as he scribbled in a notepad he had extracted from his shirt pocket. He came in with a couple dollars in his hand, tossing them on the table.

"You're not gonna believe where that call came in from last night." Howard shrugged his shoulders, knowing Hall really didn't expect him to start guessing. In his mind he was thinking one of the several NASCAR tracks in the east. "Charleston, a pay phone inside the Capitol—AFTER hours when nobody but security should have been in the building. You wanna run up there with me?"

Howard said sure and they were off to the big city, pursuing the first real break they had had in the case since the hieroglyphics were found in the exhibition coal mine.

50

After several minutes Taylor finally restored order. Even he was now concerned for the safety and well being of his captive prisoners. As leader he could 'steer' the group considerably, but once the final vote was taken he had to carry out the wishes of the collective. Ralph and Annie both sensed things weren't going well either, as Ralph chewed on his fingernails with legs crossed.

"IF we decide to dispose..." a voice about midway up on the right drawled with a measured amount of glee, "how do you suppose we do it?" A rumble of comments followed while Taylor twirled his glasses in mock amusement.

"I'm not quite sure we're to that point in the discussion, Gummery," Taylor countered, drawing a few hisses and boos from the crowd. "IF we get to that point in the discussion, your concern is well taken."

"Sheesh," muttered Ralph to Annie, "I wonder if 'dispose' means what I think it means."

Annie nodded her head as if to say that's EXACTLY what it means. "We might have been better off bailing out with Michael when he did."

Ralph shook his head. "Nah, I guarantee you these people know exactly where he is at all times. They've got some sort of...what's the word I'm looking for..."

"Vocabulary?" Annie deadpanned.

Again Ralph shook his head, not getting her little attempt at sarcasm. "ESP or something. I wouldn't be surprised if they know what we're thinking and talking about at this very moment."

Annie mulled over that for a moment. "If they have that level of perception then they know that we mean them no harm in any way."

Ralph looked hard at her. "You're telling me you've not considered the journalistic prizes you'd win if you exposed this society for the prevention of whatever?" His question was rhetorical, and Annie gulped down the answer in silence. They turned as they realized Taylor was addressing them.

"Well?" Taylor asked.

Ralph and Annie looked to each other, then back to Taylor. "Pardon?" said Ralph, "I didn't catch the question."

Taylor sighed heavily at the thought of recounting the entire conversation that had just occurred. He summarized it considerably. "Gummery wondered if, as your sentence, you'd accept exile to Siberia?"

Ralph turned to Annie and asked where Siberia was. Annie, her face considerably flushed, said out loud to all who would hear, "I AM NOT going to Siberia or anywhere else for that matter."

Taylor looked up to Gummery who nodded his head in comprehension. Ralphie again asked Annie where the place was as every voice in the chamber was talking again.

"I'm not sure she whispered, but I think the Russians used to send their dissidents there to never return. Seems like it's really cold. I can hardly stand Beckley during the winter, much less someplace colder."

Ralph nodded his head in agreement as the din grew louder. "Jeez Louise," he said in frustration, "this is all my fault." The dejection in his voice touched Annie. She placed her hand on his.

"Hey, it's ok. Beckley's a dead town, this is the most excitement I've had in a long, long time." Then she tempered her persuasion with a muttered, "If we get out of this alive."

The touch was not lost on Ralph, nor was her concern that they might not make it out alive. He stood abruptly and approached Taylor at the podium. Taylor eyed him suspiciously as the chatter dissipated. You could hear a pin drop as Ralph stepped up next to Taylor.

"May I address this body?"

51

It was just after ten when Hall pulled the cruiser into visitors parking 'on official business' as he told the guard at the gate. Ignoring the meter, he and Howard walked up the slightly winding wheelchair entrance and pulled open the massive outside doors that led into the west wing of the state capitol building.

The phone company had verified the call had originated in the capitol and had provided the exact phone from which the call was made. Hall had called in his tech support group for fingerprint analysis but they wouldn't be there for another half hour or so. They went straight to the police detachment located in the basement—the group that was responsible for the governor's safety and capitol security.

Marshall Williamson had been waiting for the Beckley Chief of Police since he had received the call around nine. He wasn't certain of all the details, but he was aware that a suspected kidnapper had made a call from the building sometime during the night—a time when the building should have been empty—and locked—save a couple of nightshift guards. He stood and greeted the two men who entered his paneled office.

Chief Hall quickly introduced Howard and his association to the case and the missing reporter. Williamson nodded his approval then asked what he could do for them.

"Well, first and foremost we'd like to take a look at that payphone that the call allegedly came in from. Maybe check for fingerprints. We have Ralphie's prints from the time he applied for a job with the department, and we'd like to possibly confirm his usage of the phone if he did use it."

"We've quarantined that phone. Go on," Marshall nodded, making notes on a formerly blank yellow legal pad.

"We'd like to speak with your personnel that was on duty last night," Hall continued, "see if they saw anything. Maintenance, janitorial, security, anybody who might have been in the building or on the grounds and seen something."

With the pause Howard broke in. "We're particularly interested in if the fugitive was alone or with others. We're missing two people—a kid and one of my reporters—and, obviously, we're concerned for their safety."

Marshall looked up from his notepad. "I've been following the case in the Gazette. Is this boy a bad seed or what?"

Howard and Chief Hall glanced toward each other. Hall took the lead. "That's just it. Nobody believes Ralph is capable of what it appears he's done. Nobody. But there's no doubt that he had something of a crush on the lady reporter. We're not sure how the young boy fits in."

"Crush on her, huh?" Marshall asked, half mumbling. "Had she in any way reciprocated, or maybe rebuffed him?

Howard shook his head no. "Not that we know of." The intercom came to life on Marshall's phone. It was his secretary.

"Sir, we have a report of graffiti on the walls of the House chamber." Her pause indicated she was looking for some direction.

"Content?" asked Marshall efficiently.

Papers could be heard moved around on his secretary's desk. "Something about toll house cookies, I think."

Marshall's eyebrows raised. "You sure it's not about the TOLLS," he said, placing considerable emphasis on the final word.

"Yes, here it is. The tolls must go dot dot dot now. You want me to send up the lab guys?"

Marshall was already moving around his desk as he barked back to the phone, "Yes, I'm headed that direction." To Howard and Chief Hall he asked them to come with him. "The phone in question is just outside the house chamber. You can take a look at it while I inspect this graffiti."

The three fairly large men dominated one stairwell and all three were huffing and puffing when they reached the rotunda area of the second floor. Marshall led the way into the house chamber, forgetting for the moment the phone booth that the other two men came to see.

Marshall began to walk slowly on the thick, red carpet that began to slant down toward the main podium, his head turning from side to side as he scanned the room for the alleged graffiti. Howard and Chief Hall, several steps behind, were mimicking his actions. Three state guys entered from the back of the room carrying equipment to check for fingerprints and to collect a sample of the substance used in generating the graffiti. Now six full grown adults were scanning a room as pristine as the day it was finished nearly a century ago.

52

Taylor yielded the podium to the determined young man. Ralph turned to face the crowd, grasping both sides of the podium in a white-knuckle fashion. Fear of public speaking is the number one phobia of humans, and Ralph was no exception. However, he had a message that he had to get out.

"Now listen here you people," he began, his voice cracking and somewhat wavy, "I don't know who you are nor do I know why we're down here, but we didn't come to hurt you. Annie and I," Ralph turned to nod toward the lady, "and Michael, wherever he is, want nothing more than to get back up to the top—here, where we're at now—and get on with our lives. And let you people be and continue doing whatever it is you do."

Ralph scanned the crowd, noticing the general look of disdain and distrust that the gathering held for him. "Is that all?" Jimmy Taylor asked from the side.

"No that's not all!" Ralph nearly exploded around the podium, pointing at Annie. "You got the little lady here scared plumb to death." He stepped down a step and continued his tirade. "Is this what you do? Threaten innocent people, women and children? Is this the best you've got to offer?" Ralph was visibly trembling, more with anger than fear, when he stopped dead and gasped.

Taylor, who had retaken the podium and was about to call for order, noticed Ralph's sudden change in posture and sharpened his senses, trying to detect any change in the field surrounding them. Everyone was now silently twisting and turning in their chairs, looking for danger. It was Ralph who broke the silence.

"Shhhhhhhh" he shushed to an already silent group, pointing toward the slowly walking figures, "they're right there, don't you see them?" His voice was near pleading, as he watched their heads turning to the left and to the right but not focusing on the two uniformed and one casually dressed men that had entered the chamber from the back. It was then he looked up over their heads above the portal into the hall. There, in large black letters, were the words that looked very carefully spray-painted—The Tolls Must Go...Now!

53

"Who called in the graffiti report?" Marshall asked into his walkie-talkie as he continued to scan the room. His secretary reported back that it was the doorkeeper of the House Chamber.

"But it wasn't him who seen it," she continued, "according to the report it was one of the House members, Smith from Mercer. Over."

Marshall continued to slowly turn, looking high and low, finding nothing. He wasn't surprised that he found nothing, nor was he surprised at the message that Smith had seen. It fit the pattern that had been going on since the tolls were constructed on what used to be called the Turnpike but now was simply a small part of interstates 64 and 77 through the southeastern part of the state. He was surprised however that it had occurred at a time when the House wasn't in session. That had never happened before. The two gentlemen from Beckley were still with him.

"I'm sorry fellows," he apologized, "that payphone is just out that door there to the right—at the top of the stairs. Just duck under the tape." As Marshall began to speak with his tech guys Chief Hall and Howard moseyed down to the front and toward the left exit that, it would appear, only the House members would normally use.

54

Jimmy Taylor had now crept up quietly beside Ralph and gazed intently at him from the side. His eyes tried desperately to see what Ralph was seeing, but there was nothing. Ralph shushed again and whispered, "Two of them are coming this way."

Annie was now standing beside Ralph too, also sensing the dread that had gripped the room so suddenly. She whispered back, "Two of who?"

Ralph momentarily tore his eyes away to glance at Annie. "You don't see them?"

"See WHO Ralphie?"

Ralph looked back at the men who slowly sauntered down the carpeted aisle. They were getting closer and closer and showed no clue that the room was filled to overflowing with creatures the likes of Mothman. Ralph watched in wide-eyed wonderment as the men came closer and closer then literally passed through Annie as they made their way to the door.

"They just passed through you," he whispered in astonishment.

Jimmy Taylor now moved around Ralph so that he could clearly see Annie. "Ralph, you don't have to whisper, they can't see or hear us. But who are you seeing?"

Ralph turned to Taylor. "You can't see them?" Taylor shook his head, looking past Annie but in the precise direction of the two men now passing through the open door. "It was two guys, one I'm pretty sure is the Chief of Police of Beckley, and the other I think is your boss, Annie."

"Howard?" she said, her eyes widening as she turned to peer after them. She then bolted, crying his name over and over in the hopes he could hear her. "Howard! Howard! I'm here Howard, I'm here!"

Taylor now stepped into Ralphie's line of sight. His expression was hard to read, but it had a seriousness to it that Taylor had not yet revealed. The next words chilled Ralphie to the bone.

"This," he said, "changes everything."

55

After scouring the entire House Chamber, including the use of magnifying glasses over the doorway as you enter the chamber where the graffiti was seen, his men concluded that the incident was a hoax. Marshall, of course, knew it wasn't, but was in no position to reveal the nature of the messages that had been conveyed in a similar fashion over the years, since the inception of the toll practices on the Turnpike. He made a mental note to record the activity in the secret file, then went looking for the two gentlemen from Beckley.

He found them leaning against a wall across a small hallway from the only pay telephone within some distance of another. He nodded to them that they had indeed located the phone from which the call had been made.

"My guys should be here any minute for fingerprint and fiber analysis," Hall informed his counterpart of the state capitol complex. Marshall stood before the phone and peered through his bifocals at it close up.

"Do you reckon," he asked, "there's a Chinaman's chance that that lady reporter was with him?"

Howard gave out a large sigh. "We're hoping. But the phone records only indicate the one call was made in the last 24 hours on this phone." He turned to Chief Hall. "Do we have Annie's fingerprints on record?"

Hall shook his head. "No, but it wouldn't be hard to get them from a glass at her house, or maybe a Coke can at the office. I'll put in an order and we'll see if any we find here match."

Voices came up the stairwell followed by two uniformed officers wearing Beckley police badges. Chief Hall greeted them and pointed to the phone, asking that in addition they dust the doorjambs local to the payphone for clear prints. With his cell phone he put in the order back at the office to procure Annie's fingerprints, preferably from her home where the likelihood of those being her prints were far greater. He turned to find Marshall gone, but Howard had his head cocked as if he were listening to some faraway event.

"What's up?" he asked, straining his own hearing.

Howard's face contorted into a look of deep concern. "I don't know," he mumbled, "it was like I could hear someone calling my name. But... it was a long way off."

Both men, and the techies from Beckley, stood silent and listened intently. Finally Howard shook his head and motioned for the men to go on with their work. Hall touched his shoulder with a look of concern. Howard turned from the men dusting the phone and lowered his voice.

"I'm not one to hear voices, Chief, but I could have sworn it was Annie's voice. I could just barely hear it—she kept calling out Howard, I'm here, over and over." He wiped his brow and gave out a sigh. "I'm telling you, I think I'm having a nervous breakdown."

Hall patted him on the back. "Can I ask you a question? A very frank question?"

Howard turned to the Chief, knowing exactly what the question was going to be. "No, I'm not having an affair with her. I care deeply for her, as I do all my employees, but that's it. I swear to God." His sincerity was clear and Chief Hall finally put that notion to rest. They returned into the House Chamber to find it empty.

56

Annie's voice was hoarse as she reentered the chamber to the stares of everyone. Her eyes were reddened with tears. She turned from the collective stare and bit her lip, unwilling to appear weak to those who wished to see just that.

"He's coming back in," Ralph said in a whispered voice, mostly to Annie, but all could hear. She didn't react, didn't turn, didn't seek out the direction that Ralph would surely indicate. She stood with her back to all, her eyes welling up with tears again, as Howard passed right through her and into the center aisle where he and Chief Hall slowly made their exit beneath the still-visible graffiti.

"We have a situation here," Jimmy Taylor said as gravely as he had ever spoken. All eyes shifted from the weeping Annie to their leader now firmly ensconced behind the podium. All eyes except Ralph's. He continued to stare at Annie, never more sorry for the trouble he had brought into her life. It was the second intonation of his name that drew his attention away from her.

He turned to see Taylor looking at him somberly. His words echoed in Ralphie's ears—this changes everything he had said. Ralph turned his body so that his posture said bring it on, whatever you're going to do to me, do it now. He raised his head slightly and hardened his jaw. His silent defiance was apparent, his readiness to face the consequences etched in his face and his eyes. Taylor nodded as if to say, so be it, and stepped around the podium to the youth before him.

Ralph's chest expanded ever so slightly as Taylor approached. Annie turned, sensing the moment they had come to dread was now upon them. Her tears were gone, she too was ready to fight until the bitter end. Her fists were clenched in rage as she took her first step forward. But Taylor's sudden smile seemed out of place, disarmed her as quickly as she had loaded her missiles to strike. His smile was wide, full of cheer and warmth. She stopped only having taken a couple of steps. He wasn't smiling at her—he was smiling at Ralph.

Taylor stopped within an arm's length of Ralphie—a head shorter than the young man—and looked him up and down. "I would have never guessed it," he said with incredulity in his voice and mannerisms. "Never in a million years."

Ralph stood his ground, but was also disarmed by Taylor's sudden lightheartedness. "Guessed what?" he asked dryly, his voice almost a whisper. Annie tip-toed around to the side so that she could see Ralph and Taylor's facial expressions in this duel of heads harder than the copious marble that surrounded the palace-like structure in which they stood. Taylor's smile broadened even farther.

"Did you ever see the movie Willie Wonka and the Chocolate Factory?" Taylor cocked his head to the side to allow Ralph a moment of reflection. It was Annie who stepped in closer.

"I saw it," she joined in, still apprehensive but less so than a minute ago, "years ago, when I was a kid."

Taylor looked to her then back to Ralph. "You never saw it?" Ralph shook his head no and Taylor turned back to Annie. "Do you remember in the end when Charley returned the Everlasting Gobstopper to Wonka?"

Annie said, "Of course I remember, that was the climax of the story."

Taylor smiled and nodded, then looked back to Ralph but continued to speak to Annie. "And what happened then, Miss Wolf?"

Annie shrugged her shoulders. "He gave him the factory."

Taylor nodded again. His gaze turned to Annie, eyebrows raised, seemingly trying to draw some obvious conclusion out of her.

"You're giving Ralph the factory?" she deadpanned.

Taylor sighed and looked up to the ceiling as catcalls erupted from those gathered. "We don't have a factory, per se, Miss Wolf," which further elicited shouts and whistles from those around them. "What we do have," he said, looking back to Ralph, "is a clear indication from the Overfather that there's an opening in our society that only you can fill."

The room erupted with shouts and hoots and whistles. But, unlike the earlier instances that were filled with hatred and ridicule, these expressions were more celebratory, almost loving in their delivery and prose. Taylor took Ralph by the left arm and turned him toward the gathering as if introducing him as the newly elected king or president. Annie stood behind, dumbfounded by the sudden, inexplicable turn of events.

57

"The Overfather has spoken," Howard's wife said as she sat up from a sound sleep. Her husband grunted 'huh' and turned over, punching his pillow to firm it up to meet the curve of his spine. He immediately returned to a peaceful slumber.

Then, with a voice barely audible, she said, "I wonder if the Undermother agrees..." With that, she too wrestled her pillow into a comfortableness that seemed to suffice as she was out like a light—a cool refrigerator light that never came on.

58

As Ralph was being patted on the back and his hand shook by every single freak in the chamber, Annie stood in stunned silence. Taylor had both identified the exiting member of the so-called 'Order'—the ancient Ulysses the Elder, clearly in failing health—and his replacement, one Ralphie Johnson.

What Annie couldn't read was Ralph's reaction to being doomed to the rest of his natural—and perhaps beyond—life miles below the surface, the only life heretofore he had known. Ralph smiled politely and nodded with each pat on the back and offer of congratulations. For people, and creatures, that seemed to really dislike them just moments ago, now the group was huddled around Ralph as if he were the new messiah. She felt a touch on her elbow.

"Michael!" she gasped, wheeling around and hugging the youth to her bosom. "Where have you been? How did you get here?"

He gave his characteristic, nonplussed shrug. "I snuck out as everybody was headed out of the chamber. I WAS exploring, when all of sudden I turned down one cavern and came into that door."

Annie's eyes widened. "You're telling me you came here from down there on your own?"

"Where are we?"

Annie looked at him surprised. "We're in the house chambers, at the state Capitol—Charleston."

"No way," he said emphatically, "we fell miles and miles down there. I didn't go up a quarter of mile in all my wanderings." His eyes widened. "Can we leave?"

Annie shook her head no. "Sorry, it's like quicksand trying to leave these people."

He looked around the room. "What's going on?"

Now it was Annie's time to shrug. "They just gave Ralph the chocolate factory."

59

Howard and Chief Hall sat in Marshall's office, disappointed at what little they had discovered. Fingerprints only revealed Ralph's on the phone, not a single print—even though the phone was used often—was of someone else. It was like they had been wiped down. The doorjambs, table tops, trash cans, nothing yielded the slightest hint of Annie's presence.

"What came of the graffiti report?" asked the chief, remembering the call had come in right as they were heading down to check out the phone.

"Nothing," the state officer replied dolefully. "Crank report evidently." Williamson gave a lot of thought to whether he should proceed, and decided to give it a shot. "The graffiti allegedly"—he put emphasis on the word—"said 'the tolls must go...now! Your boy ain't got anything against the tolls between here and Beckley does he?"

Hall shrugged. "Nobody likes 'em, but I don't see nobody spray painting any signs or overpasses. Ralph don't drive, he hitchhikes everywhere he goes. And he's been to every NASCAR race on this side of the country."

"Maybe," intoned Howard, "you know he's gotta get a ride with a lot of truckers. Maybe they hate the tolls bad enough to spray some graffiti. Ralph seems pretty impressionable, maybe they encouraged him to do it."

Marshall shrugged. "Ralph's what, 27, 28 years old? These graffiti 'sightings' have been going on since the tolls were put on." Marshall didn't mention that only the governors and members of the legislature in the counties along the route saw them, or that they weren't visible to anyone else, or that they always said some variation of 'the tolls must go.' He kept that close to the vest as it both seemed crazy and probably didn't involve this case.

"You think maybe there's a secret society that has down through the years orchestrated these sightings, as you called them? Sounds like Elvis sightings to me." Hall chuckled as he rolled the toothpick in his mouth.

Howard jumped in. "Maybe so—like in the Da Vinci code—I think it was the Priory of Scion that has protected the Holy Grail down through the years."

Marshall Williamson looked at the journalist with disdain. He had just seen a special on TV about the book and all the controversy that it had raised since it became a best seller. "You ain't buying into that crap that Jesus was married to Mary Magdalene and had kids are you?"

Howard could tell that the senior officer wasn't, so he dropped it. "Oh no, of course not. Just the secret society thing reminded me of that."

As Chief Hall and Howard exited the building through the west wing and toward the parking lot, Hall asked, "Jesus had kids?"

Howard chuckled. "Your fellow officer in there certainly don't buy it."

"I never heard of such a thing," said Hall, "and I've gone to church off and on all my life."

"I hadn't either until I read the book—The Da Vinci Code by...can't remember his name. It paints a pretty compelling picture that Jesus was indeed married and fathered at least one kid by Mary, and that SHE, instead of Paul, may have been who Jesus left the keys to the church." Howard glanced at his friend who was now unlocking the door to their vehicle. "We get free books all the time down at the paper and, the author hopes, we'll give it some space with a glowing review. That book was one of the few that we did just that. Sunday section, it was spring as I recall."

Hall fired up the police SUV and headed east on 64/77. As they passed through the first tollbooth at Sharon, Howard muttered aloud, "The tolls must go—when donkeys fly."

Hall nodded. "Secret society. Man, there's a conspiracy if somebody farts in this screwed up world we live in today. You wanna get some coffee when we get in to Beckley?"

60

Jimmy Taylor finally called the meeting to order and everybody took their seats—or somebody's seats—and the room grew quiet. Jimmy's round face was beaming as he looked out and up to the representatives he'd known for so long.

"Let's take a moment to welcome back Michael." With that he turned toward Annie and Michael who were whispering about the movie both had seen. Sheepishly Annie looked up to Taylor and muttered a polite 'huh?', indicating that they weren't listening. "We were just wanting to welcome Michael back into the fold."

What fold, Annie though to herself, certain that Ralphie now had it made, but equally uncertain that she and Michael would get a free pass out of jail. Michael sat quietly as he—and Annie—seemed to be the only two that didn't know how he got here. After an uncomfortable period of silence, Taylor moved on.

"Is there any other order of business that we need to cover before we conclude this years' session?"

To the left, very near where Annie and Michael sat, someone pointed at them and said, "What about these two?" Taylor, and Ralph standing behind him as if he were the speaker of the house, turned again to look at them. Taylor nodded his head.

"These will be dealt with in executive session after we return but before the great feast. I have a feeling considerable debate will precede their ultimate outcome."

Annie groaned at the mention of the great feast. She was starved, number one, but number two, she remembered Ralph's concern that they might be cannibals. Even though the meal they had had earlier didn't seem to involve them, she still couldn't help but wonder where all the food came from.

"Anything else?" Taylor queried. After a long pause, he said words that were complete pig Latin to Annie and Michael and asked Ulysses the Elder to give the benediction. Unlike spiritual services above ground, as Ulysses began what appeared to be a fervent, closed-eyes prayer, everybody got up and began filing out the back, shaking hands and patting each other on the back. Annie and Michael had already decided to hold back, maybe get lost in the shuffle and sneak down some hidden corridor, but an unseen force gently moved them in step with the group. The two looked at each other and glanced behind them to see no one, nothing, yet they were in-step with the exiting 'Order.' They even passed Ulysses whose heartfelt prayer was largely drowned out.

Annie did pick up a couple of words as they passed the old man— something about our precious Overfather and our loving Undermother. What the heck, thought Annie, as she looked to Michael who now had to turn a good bit to see the elder statesman.

"Is he not going?" Michael whispered to Annie.

She shrugged. "Maybe he's not. He's the one Ralphie's replacing."

Outside the group squinted in the brilliant sunlight. Maybe it was a particularly sunny day, or maybe it was their living deep in the bowels of the earth, but few could see and had to feel along and gingerly descend the steps down the front of the capital. Even Annie and Michael, overlanders as they were called, were nearly blinded by the suns' golden radiance. Eventually everyone had gathered around the statue 'Lincoln Walks at Midnight,' and Taylor got everyone's attention.

"Now remember, we meet again tomorrow night in the chamber to discuss unfinished business. I'll work up an agenda so that we won't be all day deciding what to talk about. Everybody ready?"

At this, Annie raised her hand. "Yes Miss Wolf?"

She nodded her head back toward the east wing. "Ulysses hasn't come out yet."

At that, Taylor smiled a knowing smile. "Thanks for pointing that out. Anything else?" he asked of the gathering as a whole. As he began to gently rub one corner of the marble base of the statue, he said, "Let's all tighten up just a bit now."

Wind came out of nowhere and swirled around the group. Annie noticed passerbyers were suddenly slowed to a stop, in mid-step, as were the cars. Even a plane overhead was slowed to just a crawl as the ground began to gently quake beneath their feet. Annie and Michael held onto each other as the skies darkened and lightning struck and thunder clapped in their ears. Big raindrops began pelting their faces as they ducked down to avoid the unbelievably quick storm. In doing so, they missed the whirlpool that rose from the mighty Kanawha—just across the boulevard—that bent over when it reached fifty-five feet in the air and cascaded over the statue and the cowering crowd around it.

Immediately the whirlpool disappeared, the skies brightened, and the humanity in and around the Capitol building resumed their daily activities. And the one-armed Door Keeper of the House Chambers resigned that very day. One Ulysses Grant Hawkshaw was appointed his replacement on, as with all state employees, a six-month probationary period.

61

Minnie Johnson hadn't driven in years. Maybe decades. Aside from being loaned out to neighbors and family from time, neither had her car. She had to shoo the cats out of both the front and back seats. The engine ground and ground and ground before finally turning over and roaring to life. Remembering what used to be a daily routine, she let the car warm up for ten minutes before finally easing the seventy-seven Olds Cutlass out of the narrow garage and out into the street. Neighbors stared agape at the sight of both the car and the woman driving it. Cell phones signaled ahead warning relatives and friends to stay off the roads this late July morning.

After several turns Minnie eased right on Harper Road, then made a left down Ewart. She eased between two cars parked headlong and turned off the engine. She sat for several minutes staring at the keys in her trembling hands. Entering the gift shop, she found the cash register and said, "One please."

"That'll be $7.50," the young girl behind the counter smiled, and Minnie pulled her change purse out of her handbag and counted out eight one dollar bills. "The next train is already boarding, they leave in about five minutes."

Minnie nodded her approval and shuffled back out the door and to the right. While her Carl had spent his entire life inside the mines, Minnie had been in this mine a few times with Carl as a tourist. She took a seat on the back, half-filled shuttle, wringing a handkerchief between her stubby fingers.

A large, elderly black man emerged from a shack-like building where the railroad tracks seemed to end. He wore a hardhat with a light and carried a lunch bucket very much like the one she used to pack for Carl at the start of every shift. She could remember the feel of the aluminum alloy, how the different parts nested into each other, how she'd put ice in the bottom tray to keep his coldcuts cold. And most times his thermos carried coffee, but on occasion she'd make a batch of homemade vegetable beef soup or chili and he'd take that instead. Her nostalgia was broken by their guide who began giving his usual spiel about safety and claustrophobia and such. She was struck by how much the black man resembled her Carl—but only AFTER he came out of the mines. He went into the mines—or left the house anyway—as a very handsome Caucasian. When he came out of the mines, he looked like this man—still handsome, but in black-face from the coal dust that eventually riddled his lungs and took his life at the young age of fifty-seven. Most times he got a shower at the bathhouse, but on occasion, when there was problems with the water or they were repainting the interior, he'd come home and all you could see was the white of his eyes. Like this man, thought Minnie as he powered up the man-trip and began pulling the two cars behind him. The flat cars rumbled along the steel rails and turned gently to the right, approaching the yawning entrance to a life that few humans knew intimately.

One-hundred watt bulbs dangled above the track from the top of the mine—seven feet high in most places along what was the Beckley seam of coal—mined at the turn of the previous century. The first stop was a widened out area where the seam had been mined perpendicular to the main track. Here the guide pointed out some old equipment and explained the wage rates a hundred years ago when this seam was mined. He talked of 'black damp' and the canaries that signaled the loss of oxygen. He then informed the two dozen or so paying customers that he was going to turn out the lights—was everybody ok with that. Nobody said anything so he reached for the switch.

The moment the lights went out the single word erupted from Minnie's lips. "Carl!" There he stood, as if backlit and taller than she remembered him being. Beside him stood their son Ralphie, also seeming to be a bigger man than he'd turned out to be. The lights came on almost as soon as they went off as everyone stared at the now standing little old lady.

"Turn them back off!" she demanded, turning toward the old guide who had never felt spooked before while giving these tours five times a day, six days a week.

"Pardon me, ma'am?"

"Turn the lights back off," she now pleaded, "it was my Carl." The guide looked at the remainder of his paying customers and saw the fear and concern in their eyes too. He tried to reason with Minnie.

"If you don't mind ma'am, we need to continue our tour…"

"Please," she said, cutting him off, tears welling up in her ancient eyes. "Please, it's my Carl. I've not seen him for fifteen years."

The guide nodded his head as if he understood. He gave the rest of the group a quick glance and said, "Let's turn them out again for just a couple of minutes." With that he flipped the switch again, plunging one of the few tourist mines in the country into total blackness again.

And there they stood, her Carl and Ralph, smiling at her. "It's ok, Mom," Ralph said. "You're not seeing things, it's us."

"I know it's you," she said, her voice choking from emotion. The guide and the other customers could hear Minnie's side of the conversation, as each felt the hairs rise on the back of their necks. Minnie reached out and Carl took her hand.

"How have you been Minnie?" he said, his face full of love and remembrance.

Minnie almost had to sit down at the sound of his voice, so clear yet from such a long distance in time. The tears rolled down each cheek and onto her neatly ironed blouse. "I've been missing you Carl, that's how I've been." The guide wanted desperately to turn the lights back on, but knew he'd probably need assistance to help control the old lady who had seemingly lost her mind. He resisted the urge, and instead stood in silence.

"I've come to tell you, Minnie," Carl said with a smile, his head nodding toward their son, "Ralphie's got a new job."

A slight cry escaped Minnie's lips as she looked to her good-natured son. She knew without a doubt that he hadn't kidnapped that woman or boy, and now her dead Carl was confirming that. "Where you working at boy?"

Ralph smiled again. "It's underground," he nodded, not having the heart to explain that he wouldn't be back up again for a long, long time. And he knew she'd take it to mean in the mines, some twenty miles higher than where he would actually be working.

Minnie nodded, knowing that to get a good job around these parts—without an education—it had to be in the mines. She had always regretted not saving up enough money to help send Ralph to one of the local community colleges. "When will you be coming back?"

Ralph shrugged. "It's pretty far away from here, I'm not sure when I'll be back. You doing ok without me?"

She nodded. "It's pretty lonely. But I'm doing ok." She turned to Carl. "Are you ok?"

Carl smiled and nodded. "I'm fine Minnie. Aside from missing you real bad, I'm doing really well." A long silence followed and the guide was almost ready to turn on the light switch but felt fingers on his, keeping the light off. His eyes widened in fear but he didn't dare panic and cause twenty-some paying customers to go running off in different directions.

"Can I come back and see you?"

Carl's head slowly moved left and right. "No, at least not here. When you get 'home' we can spend the rest of time together."

Minnie touched her heart and smiled back at her husband of so many years. "I love you Carl," she said, seeing his image begin to fade into the rock that was behind him. He mouthed the words 'I love you too' as he and Ralph completely faded from view. Minnie sat back down, causing the metal car to creak, staring into the crust of the earth that contained her husband's spirit. Just as she said in a strong, clear voice, "You can turn the lights back on," the guide felt the fingers leave his and he did just that. While every other eye was trained on the now-composed Minnie, the guide looked up to his fingers, alone, around the simple switch. He climbed back into the shuttle and didn't make another stop, although three were scheduled, until they were back out and at the station.

The black man almost appeared ghostly white as he passed the mechanics sitting in the maintenance shed. He dropped his hardhat and identification badge on the desk as he told the on-duty manager that he quit. The woman sputtered and tried to talk him out of it, but the retired miner just shook his head as he walked away. He'd worked with a man named Carl, twenty odd years ago, and his wife looked a lot like that lady on the tram—just older. He didn't really need the money, he just wanted something to do. He decided he'd try to find something else—maybe be a greeter at Wal-Mart.

62

Hall and his men entered the courthouse through the basement doors and fanned out in all directions. The anonymous call had said there was a secret passageway out of the courthouse, but the caller didn't know where it was or where it went. After assigning a desk clerk to attempt to trace the brief call, the chief rounded up most of his on-duty officers and made the short walk to the courthouse.

The janitor followed the sheriff and opened lock doors as needed. One of the maintenance crew followed another group of men and did the same. For three hours the men searched, prodded, poked, pulled and pushed trying to find the entrance to a hidden exit. Finally they gathered back in the basement, all shaking their heads.

"Nothing on level three, Chief."

"Ditto level two."

"Ground was clear."

And the Chief himself had inspected the basement and found nothing. "You men," Chief Hall said, carving about half of his men out with the sweep of his arm, "check the perimeter of the building, again looking for exits or hidden or trap doors. Then work your way out to the surrounding streets, look in the alleys, down in the gutters. Report back in an hour."

The chosen men exited the building and circled it, searching for any sign of a possible exit route from the courthouse. Inside, Hall assigned two men per floor—insisting they inspect a floor different from the one they had just inspected.

"I know for a fact," he said, ready to send them out, "that someone was in this building the night Miss Wolf disappeared. And we never found nothing. Give it one more look-see, ask the employees if they've ever encountered anything suspicious in the building. Dismissed."

With that his men hit the stairs and began to comb the building again—going into locked rooms that had been unlocked earlier. It was a full thirty minutes when a young deputy called out on his walkie-talkie.

"Chief, I've got something here you may want to look at. Basement, south exit corridor."

The Chief hustled down from the first floor and found his two deputies standing in the narrow exit. "What's up, Bub?"

The deputy pointed to the wall. "Rub your hand over that stone," he pointed to a stone in the wall about belly high. The Chief did so.

It was solid stone with a heavy coat of off-white paint, as were all the stones. "Yeah?"

The deputy pointed to the right. "Now rub your hand over that stone."

The Chief did and raised his eyebrows, looking back to his young protégé. "It feels rubbery, almost like rubber Styrofoam."

The deputy nodded. "Feel all the stones around it." The sheriff did. This unusual, rubbery fake stone, covered with the same thick coat of paint, was surrounded by real, legitimate stones.

"Well I'll be darned," the Chief muttered, beginning to poke at the soft substance. "Beats anything I've ever seen." After sending someone to get the head of maintenance, he got on his portable radio and called in to the station. "Rachel, patch me through to the state police, homeland security division down at Princeton. Pronto." Rachel responded in the affirmative and in less than a minute a male voiced crackled on the line.

"This is Radford."

The Chief blinked. "William H. Radford the Third?" the sheriff asked, mirth seeping into his voice.

"That would be me," the voice said fairly dryly.

With a broad smile the sheriff nearly sang into the radio. "Well this is Beckley Chief of Police Lester Hall on the line. How the heck have you been Billy?"

Radford chuckled into the phone. "Lester the Molester. How in the Hades did you become Chief of Police?"

"Contacts, boy, contacts. You vote right things get done around here. Where have you been the past twenty years? Ain't nobody heard nothing from you since we graduated. Last we knew you were off to Europe."

Radford sighed. "I was in Europe for only six months, I came back and landed in DC, been there ever since. Just got assigned to this region for Homeland Security."

"You been with the CIA or the FBI?" Hall asked, winking at one of his deputies.

"Now if I told you that," Radford deadpanned, "I'd have to kill you." After both men laughed Radford asked what he could do for his former classmate.

"We've uncovered what we think may be some sort of device that triggers a trap door in the courthouse. Hold on." He covered the receiver as the head of maintenance entered the small passageway. "Your people insert a false stone in the wall for any reason?" He almost touched the phone to the stone in question.

The thirty-year county courthouse employee rubbed his hand over the stone in question, then the surrounding stones. "Nope."

"Check with your other people, we need to know ASAP if this is supposed to be here for any reason." The fellow nodded and headed back to this work area. The Chief returned his attention to his high school classmate. "Sorry. You ever hear about that good looking lady reporter here in Beckley that disappeared over a week ago?"

"Yeah. Wasn't that a domestic situation?"

"Possibly. Probably. And we don't know if what we've found relates to her disappearance or not, but she was last seen in this vicinity. We'd sure like to x-ray this thing before we go setting off some explosive device. Maintenance just said it wasn't anything that they knew of to do with the building. You got any of that equipment laying around."

"As a matter of fact I do," Radford said. "Want to schedule it for two this afternoon?"

"That'll be fine," the Chief said appreciatively, "it ain't going anywhere. And oh, Trey," he called him by his nickname in high school, "sorry about that time we pulled your pants down during assembly..." A dial tone greeted the Chief before he could finish his sentence. He was kind of a bully back in those days, and Radford was one of the many who had suffered at his hands. He hoped he wasn't the sort to hold grudges.

63

Annie broke through the surface, gasping for air. She thought she'd die one of the two ways she dreaded—drowning and fire. Having nearly drowned, she was certain that, for all the panic, she'd now choose drowning over fire. The movie Titanic had pretty much convinced her anyway.

She looked around, dog-paddling, for Ralphie or Michael. But then she felt the water level dropping quickly and her concern now was that she was being sucked back into the vortex. Instead, her feet touched a solid bottom and the water swirled around her until it was all gone. She looked over and saw Michael on his hands and knees.

"You ok?" she asked running to him, helping him up.

"I think so," he said, digging the water out of his ear. "That was some ride."

Annie muttered 'it sure was' as she looked around, dripping wet. They were in the huge catacomb of a room, the one from which they had left to go to the 'meeting.' Oddly, they were alone. "Where is everybody?" she asked, looking up toward the domed ceiling a good football field up. Michael shrugged, looking at two very wet dollar bills that had been in his pocket.

"Know where I can get a happy meal?" he asked facetiously. Now Annie shrugged her shoulders.

"I don't think that's going to do you much good down here."

"Hey!" the voice called across the chamber, "there you are." It was Ralph, strolling across the stone floor like he owned it, dry as a bone.

Annie glared at him. "Why didn't you get wet?"

Ralph smiled an impish smile. "If you believe, you don't get wet."

"Sheesh," Michael muttered, "first he gets the keys to the factory and now he's freakin' Peter Pan." Annie laughed out loud, the first time in a long while, as Ralph blushed. Evidently he had seen Peter Pan.

"Come on, they's a place down here that can dry those clothes in a heartbeat." Annie and Michael followed their turncoat companion, lacking any other options. They turned down the long corridor with which they were already familiar. About halfway down Ralph pointed to a entrance to the right. "Go in there, hold your arms over your heads, and say King Ralph five times."

Annie and Michael looked at each other, deciding whether or not they'd prefer to just dry naturally.

"Just kidding," he said with a smile, "you don't have to hold your arms up." Tentatively they walked into the dark passageway and immediately exited from another several doors down. They looked in amazement at their clothes—they were dry, pressed, and clean. Ralph said come on and led them down the corridor to the meeting room where they first had encountered Taylor and his little dog Matika.

Taylor sat on the top row across the way and continued working until the three were all the way down to the podium. He looked over bifocals and gave a broad grin.

"The feast," Taylor explained, as if they were in mid-conversation, "won't be until tonight." He stood. "But oh, lassie, a feast it is."

"How," Annie asked, "can you tell night from day down here?"

The empty chamber echoed with their voices, much like it did when Ralph and Annie first found it. Taylor slowly made his way down the stone steps, looking older than before. He climbed onto the podium and smiled at the three.

"It gets much lighter during the daytime. Any questions before dinner?"

Annie blinked the look of surprise at him. "Questions?" she asked, "of course we've got questions, a million of them. But why ask if we're not going to make it out of here alive..."

Taylor shrugged. "Professional courtesy? Personal curiosity? Inquiring minds want to know?"

Ralph threw him a softball. "How many hours until dinner?" Annie huffed and turned, disgusted at his ascension, or 'de'scension, into their good graces. And now he was taking the lead in questioning their kidnapper.

"Who are you people really and why won't you let us go back home?" Her glare at Taylor indicated this was a more personal, rather than professional, query.

"I think we indicated some time back that we are the Society for the Prevention of the Proliferation of Corruption of Elected Officials Above. We've been such a society since the birth of this great state, and we'll be a society long after your newspaper no longer survives." He took a deep breath after saying all that. "And as to you returning to the surface, it is the very continuation of this society that seems to be at stake with your intrusion."

There was a knock at a door that didn't exist. It echoed around the chamber and Taylor politely said, "Yes, who is it?"

A door opened, but to the overlanders' surprise it opened in the ceiling. A wiry scrap of a man stuck his head through, upside down with a hat on that showed no sign of slipping off. "Sorry to bother you mate," he said in a decidedly Australian accent, "but we've got a potential breech of security in 41A." He tipped his cap directly at Annie. "Hello, sorry to bother."

"You on top of it Merriweather?"

"Got it covered, Bobby, should have a report back down at 1800 hours if that's ok."

Taylor nodded and waved him away. The one called Merriweather tipped his cap again, gave a very suggestive wink to Annie, and disappeared as fast UP into the hole as he might have were it a downward facing hole. The door, the moment it was shut, was no longer visible.

Almost immediately Taylor shouted up toward the hole, "1800 hours is during the feast! Don't interrupt us!" No reply was evident as his monitions bounced from wall to wall and surrounded the four. "Now where were we?" Taylor asked once the echoed died down.

"You were about to tell us how three," Annie corrected herself, "two people of six billion plus were going to threaten you're little sanctuary down here."

Taylor gave her a hard stare. "You know how many people read your piece on mountain top removal and flooding?" Annie had no idea. "Seven-thousand, two-hundred and fifty-eight people. And one really bright kid at Prosperity Grade school. Granted," he said, taking his glasses off and blowing a spec of dust from the left lens, "it wasn't that well written and anti-coal pieces aren't everyone's cup of tea..."

Annie's face grew hot at the less-than-constructive criticism.

"And that story wasn't picked up by the wire services," Taylor continued. "How many people do you think would read THIS story, Miss Wolf?"

He had her there. If she were to win a Pulitzer, every writer's dream, the story had to go national, international. And it would, no matter how poorly written, just because of the story itself.

"What if it did go national, even global?" asked Annie. "Your security people couldn't handle it?"

"My security people," Taylor said haggardly, "can handle a mild breech of security as we're experiencing right now in 41A, but they couldn't handle literally millions of your people with shovels and mallets trying to find us."

"Where's 41A?" Ralph asked.

He looked to the innocent young man, then to Annie. "It's the portal you two came through." He looked at Michael. "The young lad there came through 41B."

"41C?" Ralph queried.

Taylor shook his head. "Only two portals to every county, one in the courthouse and another nearby." He looked to Annie and pointed his finger. "You didn't hear that."

64

William H. Radford III and two of his men were setting up shop, running extension cords and such while Chief Hall evacuated the building. It was only a couple of hours until closing time anyway, and he knew the people would appreciate the time off. Give them a chance to get dinner on early, pick up a prescription at Rite-Aid, or just relax and catch up on their favorite soap operas.

It was 2:30 when the equipment was finally set up and the building was largely empty. A couple of elected officials insisted on continuing their work as deadlines approached, and Hall nodded his acquiescence. In the basement Radford and his people were ready to go, but waited patiently for Hall to return, knowing that he wanted to be in on this procedure. Another man, who Radford did not recognize, turned the corner, huffing, and apologized for being late.

"Sorry," Radford said, "but this isn't..." He then looked hard at the smiling man who had a vaguely familiar crooked smile.

"Billy H. Radford the Third," Howard said beaming, "how the heck have you been buddy?" Radford took the extended hand in his then finally made the connection.

"Howard—I can't believe it's you! I'd have never recognized you out on the street." Radford stood and the two men embraced quickly. He introduced yet another old school chum—this one he liked—to his men, then asked, "Where the devil is that Molester?"

Howard cackled at the nickname that he'd heard no one use since high school. And even then, you didn't call Lester that to his face. He knew of the nickname, but pummeled anyone who used it generally.

At that moment Hall too turned the corner and the small corridor was now filled to capacity with Radford and his two men, Hall and three of his, and now Howard.

"First of all," Radford spoke with authority, "from what you've told me and our initial analysis, this is not—and you'll pardon the pun—an explosive situation. We've never encountered an explosive device actually embedded in a wall, and it would actually diminish the damage as the walls surrounding it would contain the outward force. Unless it were a load-bearing wall, which this one is not."

He turned and pointed to one of his men seated on the floor. "John here will monitor the readings while Mike," he pointed to the man beside him, "will actually work the equipment. First thing we'll do is xray the wall to see if it is indeed hollow—and that might give us the structure of the release mechanism if this is indeed some sort of trap door." He turned to Hall. "Now which stone is it that was false?"

Hall leaned around him and pointed. "That one right there."

"Ok," said Radford, nodding to Mike. The middle-aged gentleman put on a headset and inserted his hands into two oversized gloves. "This is the latest equipment," Radford explained, "it's kind of a cross between doing an ultrasound on a pregnant woman and working with high levels of radiation."

Everyone nodded as if they understood completely the latest technology built by the most brilliant minds on earth. Radford squeezed out a soft gel onto one glove, then Mike rubbed the palms of the two gloves together.

"This one?" he asked without turning.

Hall replied, "That one," and Mike gently placed his hands on the stone and began methodically scanning it with both hands. He looked for all the world like a proud soon-to-be-papa massaging his wife's very pregnant stomach. Only this stone wasn't pregnant, nor was it hollow.

"Nothing," Mike said after only a couple of minutes, and John suggested his readings didn't show anything either. Hall looked dumbstruck.

"Well here," he said, pointing again at the stone, "just feel the thing, you can clearly tell it's not a stone."

Radford himself moved forward while Mike removed the gloves and placed them on the floor at his feet. He touched the stone with his index finger. "Feels like stone to me, Lester."

Hall looked down at the smaller man as if he were nuts. "It doesn't," he insisted, demonstrating himself that the stone wasn't stone at all. "You touch these," and he did, "that surround it, and they feel exactly like stone should feel. But you touch this one, it's got kind of a rubbery..." His jaw dropped as that stone felt exactly as did the other stones surrounding it. He looked to the left and right.

"Bubba, this was the stone we identified isn't it?"

"Yes sir," said the young deputy half-heartedly. Hall continued to poke and rub the wall up and down, left and right. It was John who broke the awkward silence.

"Got something. Mike put your gloves back on and scan the floor where you laid your gloves." Mike bent down and picked up the gloves, sliding them back on. He knelt to the floor and began massaging the floor as he had done with the wall. All eyes watched either Mike or John for some reaction.

"Gone," said John, disbelieving.

"What's gone?" asked Radford.

"It WAS hollow beneath this floor panel," he said, shaking his head. "Now it's not."

Hall broke in. "I think you've got a problem with your equipment, Trey. You bring a backup?"

"There's not a problem with my equipment," Radford snapped, bending down to John. "Show me."

John turned the small monitor around so that both men could see it. "See, this is where Mike was scanning the wall, then he laid his gloves down on the floor. From that time until he picked up the gloves, this was showing hollow. After the gloves went on, it's no longer hollow."

"And thus a problem with your equipment!" enjoined Hall.

Radford stood and pushed the Beckley Chief of Police with both hands back against the wall. "It's not the equipment!" he said venomously. Hall followed with a left jab right into the man's bespectacled face, sending him the short distance back into the other wall. Radford's men jumped in the middle while Hall's men came crashing in and before you knew it you had a Yankees-Red Sox game in mid-swing. Punches were being thrown, kicks, one deputy got bit, all the while Howard was reaching in from the edge of the melee trying to break it up.

"Whoa boys whoa!" he called out time and time again as the fight spilled out into the wider hallway and pairs of two each fell to the floor wrestling and punching. One of the six law officer's guns fell to the floor and Howard dashed to get it. He released the safety and fired three times into the ceiling. Every man scrambled to his feet and pulled out his own weapon, with the exception of Radford. Howard had his.

"What in the world are you doing?" he cried out, now with his hands in the air as five guns were trained on him. He handed the half-spent weapon to Radford and now had six guns leveled on him. Hall recognized his friend's peacekeeping efforts first and told everyone to lower their weapons. His men did, but Radford's men didn't.

"For heaven's sake, Trey, you and your men want to put your guns away, he was just breaking up the fight."

"Which you started!" Radford barked at his old schoolmate.

"You want another piece of me," Hall said growling, starting forward toward the armed federal agent. Radford backed up two steps and told him to back away. Howard stepped in between the two, placing his big hands on Hall's chest.

"Come on, Lester, let it go," he said softly, pushing his friend back. He turned to face Radford. "If you don't put that gun down Trey I'll personally kick your behind back to Princeton."

Reluctantly Trey lowered his weapon and told his men to do the same. "Get your equipment," he said sharply, "let's get out of this two-bit popsicle joint." His men did just that as Hall turned around, staring at the ceiling. He was half embarrassed that the fight had started, half wishing he'd gotten another lick or two in on the little weasel. The men came out of the corridor carrying their equipment.

"I'm filing a complaint the moment I get back," Radford said, turning all the way around while walking.

"You file a complaint," Hall shouted back at him, "and I'll knock your head into next Thursday!"

Merriweather watched it all in glee as he nearly finished replacing 41A across the hall.

65

At Shoney's Hall snapped at the waitress, one of the twins no less, and said, "Just bring the coffee, ok?"

Howard apologized to the attractive waitress and explained it had been a long day. "You've got to let it go, Les," he said as the waitress returned to the kitchen. "Your and Trey's problems were twenty years ago, forget about it."

The Chief of Police of the city of Beckley huffed. "Son of a federal gun thinks he can come into MY turf and call the shots." The waitress was back with a carafe of coffee and just left it without a word as Hall bit his lip.

"Let's focus, Lester, on WHY he was here, not what happened. Let's not forget it's Annie's life that's at stake here, not yours or mine or Trey's."

Hall looked at his friend with disdain, then softened a bit. "You're right. But man, does that guy get on my nerves. Always did, lucky I didn't kill him back when I was a lot dumber."

Howard chuckled at the honesty in his friend's statement. Lester Hall was no rocket scientist—coupled with a big, strong body—he was a danger to himself and mankind in general. And Radford was indeed a studious nerd who could get on anybody's nerves. He hadn't seemed to have changed much since their high school days.

"Look at the bright side—there is no trap door in the courthouse. That could have revealed maybe a LOT of skeletons in the proverbial closet."

Hall nodded. "Closet, courthouse—would have been full." He paused while he sipped the still-too-hot coffee. "But I'm telling you, that stone was fake this morning. I touched it myself."

Howard nodded. "It's like the 'writing on the wall' in the mines. One minute it's there, one minute it's not."

A long silence passed between them before Hall muttered, "The tolls must go," with a chuckle. It was Howard who tried to put two and two together.

"Hey, think about it." The reporter in the editor was kicking in. "Here we've got stones turning from fake to real, words materializing then disappearing on a mine wall, and graffiti on Capitol granite that says the tolls must go. Let's face it, either two perfectly rational people are losing their minds simultaneously, or there's something going on here beyond the pale."

Hall mulled that for a minute. "Sure does seem strange. You take any one of those events, I'd say you're crazy. Put them all together, and considering who's witnessed them," he said, pointing to the editor and himself, "I think we've got something bigger than us going on here." The waitress brought back their bill and laid it on the table between them.

On the drive back to the office, Chief Hall put in a call to Marshall at the Capitol Complex. He got his voice mail, briefly explained their theory, and asked him to call him back at his earliest convenience.

66

The feast lasted for what seemed to be half a day or more. There were speeches—which few seemed to listen to—an award for the representative of the year—which the Logan County delegate won for his work on voter fraud—and shouting matches and near fisticuffs as everything from politics to religion to the World Series to the Sports Illustrated Swimsuit issue was discussed.

The first to leave was two delegates from the eastern panhandle— said they had 'a long ways to go.' At that quite a number of delegates began to get up, stretch, hug each other, and make their way up the stone steps disappearing into holographic doors all along the upper chamber. Michael even followed one older fellow up to his passageway and watched in awe as the man simply disappeared into the rock. He was startled when just the hand emerged back out of the rock and waved softly to him. Shaking his head he returned back to the encircled podium and took a seat beside Annie.

"What I wouldn't give for a cigarette," the young boy muttered loud enough for Annie to hear. She looked at him in dismay.

"You don't smoke, do you?"

The boy shrugged his shoulders. "Every now and then. A couple of the older guys downtown will sometimes give me one."

Annie looked back to the podium where Taylor seemed to be holding court with a few of the remaining delegates in whispered tones.

"That's a nasty habit," Annie said.

Michael shrugged. "We're gonna die anyway down here. What's one more cigarette going to do?"

A pall hung over the two as both contemplated his gloomy assessment. Then, through the handful of men on the podium, Annie saw Ralph sitting on the other side on the front row by himself.

"If I get us out of here, will you promise to never smoke another cigarette as long as you live?"

Michael smiled a crooked smile. "Sure," he said, "why not."

Annie stood and circled the podium, sitting beside Ralph who was looking the other way. He seemed to be deep in thought until she touched his hand resting on the bench.

"Oh, hey, I didn't see you come over."

"It's ok," Annie said in a soft voice, "can I talk to you?"

"Sure. What's up?"

Annie looked incredulous at the innocent young man. "What's up?" she said, trying to control the pitch of her voice, "what's up is that YOU seem to have a new job. Michael and I are facing a firing squad."

"Aw," Ralph drawled, "they ain't gonna shoot you." Annie waited for a moment but Ralph didn't continue the thought.

"Then what are they going to do to us?"

Ralph shrugged his shoulders. "It hasn't been decided. They've voted to have a special session."

Annie rolled her eyes. This group had been watching the West Virginia legislature way too long. "Just over Michael and I?"

Ralph shook his head. "No, there's some other stuff on the agenda, but you two are at the top of it."

Annie sized Ralph up, wondering if he was in full control of his mental facilities. None of these...people...seemed totally right. But then again, she realized, Ralph wasn't the sharpest knife in the drawer to begin with. "What do you think they'll do to us?"

Ralph shrugged his shoulders again. "I have no idea."

"Will you get to vote?" He nodded. Annie blinked—hoping for some show that he would support them. "And?"

"And what?" Ralph asked, clearly clueless as to what she was meaning.

"And what?" Annie repeated. "You're going to tell them that it was YOU who breached their precious security. If it wasn't for you these meetings wouldn't be necessary."

"That's not true," Ralph informed her, "the annual meeting and feast occurs, well, every year. And as for special sessions, seventy-eight percent of the time…"

"Cut it out, Ralphie," Annie hissed, not wanting to draw attention to her efforts to sway his vote. "Listen," she softened, for the first time since meeting him trying to appeal to his inner man, "I'm not so worried about me as I am Michael, he's young, he's got his entire life ahead of him. It would be a shame…"

"They won't kill you," Ralph said matter-of-factly, interrupting her discourse.

Again Annie blinked, waiting for additional information. When none was forthcoming, she asked, "What will they do with us then?"

Ralph crossed his arms. "Do me a favor. Find out from Michael the precise time that he got in. I've got an idea." With that he stood and left her company, whether she was done or not. She too stood and returned to Michael's side.

"Well?" said the young boy hopefully.

Annie shook her head. "I'm not sure." She chewed on her bottom lip, thinking. "He wanted to know what time you got in."

Michael raised his eyebrows. "I'm not sure if I know the precise time. Even if I did, should we tell him?"

Annie was thinking the same thing. "Tell me, then we'll decide if he should know or not. He could either help us get out of here, or he could seal us in for the rest of our lives."

"Assuming we have the REST of our lives," Michael muttered.

"Oh," Annie remembered, "he said they wouldn't kill us. But he didn't say what they would do."

"So," Michael said, pulling a cigarette from behind his back, taking a deep, satisfying drag, "I can still smoke?"

Annie's eyes widened. "Where did you get that?"

Michael smiled. "The really ugly dude over there. He motioned for me to come over and handed it to me, already lit. Like he could read my mind."

"Uh oh," said Annie.

"What?"

"What if they can read our minds?" The two began to look around the room suspiciously, seeing if anyone was watching them. A few casual glances were cast their way, but were followed up by conversations that didn't seem to involve them.

67

William H. Radford III walked confidently down the granite corridor, his superior—and second highest in command in the newly created Homeland Security force—matching him stride for stride. At the desk they announced their presence and their appointment, and the secretary nodded.

"The president will see you now." With that the two armed marines stepped aside while the two civilians passed between them. Radford's confidence was beginning to wane as his boss opened the doors to the Oval Office.

"Bobby!" the president gushed, pushing his chair back and walking around the desk, leading with his right hand. "How the heck have you been?"

"Good Mr. President," Robert Valey nodded with a smile, shaking the hand back vigorously. "I'd like you to meet one of my right hand men, William Radford."

"Pleasure to meet you Mr. Radford," the president said, a surprisingly strong grip in his handshake.

"The pleasure is all mine," Trey Radford replied politely. While he had voted for this man's opponent, he was appreciative of the opportunity his administration had presented to him—even if it wasn't under the best of circumstances.

"How's the family, Bob?" the president asked of Valey, seemingly sincere.

"They're fine, Connie sends her best wishes, and," Valey reached into his breast pocket of his navy suit and pulled a letter from within, "your good friend Lorna sends her best wishes."

The president smiled a knowing smile as he took the letter and slid it into his breast pocket. He then shed the coat and laid it across a small table near his desk.

"Have a seat gentlemen. I've been briefed, of course, but I'd like to hear your report straight from the horse's mouth if you don't mind."

As the three gentlemen sat down on a sofa and chair—Trey with the president—he knew his moment of truth had come. The confidence that he had carried all morning with him was now all but gone, the majesty of the moment crushing him in self-doubt.

"I gotta be honest with you Mr. President, I'd not be here today were it not for the tireless and creative efforts of Trey here." The president turned his gaze toward Trey, who looked to his boss but peripherally was well aware that the president of the United States, the president of the world—for all practical intents and purposes—was staring at him from less than two feet away. "The same kind of intelligence failures that led to 9/11 was imbedded in the new culture of Homeland Security. The proverbial left hand didn't know what the right hand was doing."

Trey could see the president nodding his head as Valey continued.

"After several months of frustration the West Coast office made something of a breakthrough—an indexing if you will of every questionable action and activity recorded by our agents throughout the world. It took a while before the programming was both in place and secure—and routed through the Pentagon, CIA and FBI." Valey chuckled slightly. "This government that you're the head of is one bear of an animal to get your arms around."

The president chuckled too. "You ain't telling me nothing I don't already know."

Valey continued, knowing their allotted time was fifteen minutes. He also knew the president didn't have another meeting for a half hour after their meeting, but wasn't sure if the president needed any preparation for that meeting. "A programming group in our Midwest office made the secure connections with all the agencies. It took a month and a half, but every test and attempt to breech the security since has been thwarted. It was then that we began to upload the data from the many platforms on which it was stored. That was another three months of data conversion, but we're finally on one platform speaking one language that's impossible to read if you're outside the infrastructure."

The president leaned back and crossed his legs. "You're speaking a lot of Greek but it sounds like we're making good progress. So where does the Mothman come in?"

Valey smiled and looked over to Trey, who was now about to hyperventilate. "Trey here began running some queries—anybody could have done it but it was Trey who took the initiative—looking for patterns of thought, locations, distress. He was a good three weeks building and improving the queries, but finally the fog began to lift. It was late last week when he made his startling discovery." Nodding toward Radford, Valey concluded with, "I'll let Trey fill you in from there."

The president uncrossed his legs and turned more directly toward Trey, who smiled wanly as he prepared to deliver his well-practiced oratory. Upon seeing the president's concerned look, close enough to smell his cologne, see the pore spaces in his face, Trey wanted to loosen his tie which, at the moment, felt more like a noose than an article of clothing. The slight quiver detectable in his voice did nothing to put him at ease.

"Mr. President," he started, paused, then started again, speaking too fast. "Mr. President, after running a series of initial inquiries, all of which were probative of, shall we say, the unusual, the off-the-wall, I was finally struck by the commonality of what appeared to be fancy rather than fact. I was about to dismiss the latest query when I noticed the sequence of the actual events." Trey paused to take in air, giving the president an opportunity to ask a question.

"Sequence of actual events?" He asked the question slowly, trying to slow the fellow down.

Trey nodded. "Yes sir, Mr. President. I noticed in the Point Pleasant area of West Virginia increased inexplicable activity was becoming more common since December 11th of 2002. Did you know anything about the so-called Mothman?"

The president nodded. "Read the book and saw the movie. That's about it."

Trey was impressed that the president of the free world was somewhat versed in Mothman lore. "He was last seen just before the Silver Bridge collapse. For over thirty years he remained a name in legend only. Wherever he/it came from, he seemingly went back."

"I don't follow you," the president said honestly, "has there been new sightings?" The president looked to Valey. "I've not seen anything in the papers—not been briefed of late."

"Of course you wouldn't Mr. President," Trey continued, "because the government has had a taskforce in the area since the sightings first began in the sixties—Men in Black—who deliberately add a layer of confusion and disbelief to the situation."

"I know that son, I'm the president."

Trey nodded, glad—and not surprised—that the president had been briefed upon taking office of the numerous UFO/alien situations. "Here's the deal. Every Thursday a different movie quote unquote disappears from the Movie Store in Point Pleasant."

"Could be anybody," the president interjected.

"Right," said Trey, "but not in this instance. The Movie Store recently renovated. And one of the improvements made on the property was a surveillance camera. Now here's the funny thing: even though a movie is taken every Thursday, it's always—always—returned, even rewound if it's VHS, the following Monday, in the dropbox in the front of the store."

"Where the surveillance camera is," the president guessed.

"You've got it," Trey responded, finally calming down to the point that he could think clearer. "We've got a link set up to my office if you could activate your TV here." The president lifted the arm on his end of the couch to reveal a panel of buttons and knobs. He pressed one and across the room a wall panel opened up to reveal a flatscreen TV of enormous size. It blipped on to life as Trey still stared at the control panel.

"Glad one of these ain't the nukes," the president joked. "Whoa," he said in mock surprise, "there goes Russia. There goes Iraq!" Valey laughed out loud. He'd heard the president make the same joke during several of his visits, but knew that it would be new to Trey. On screen from above a door the well-lit parking lot and front door could be seen. About five seconds passed when Trey asked the president if he saw it.

"Saw what?" the president asked, thinking that Radford was joking.

"Part of the surveillance provides a computer readout for whenever the dropbox door is opened, it records the precise time. The missing movie—and how they know it's missing is that it wasn't rented—was deposited at precisely 12:03am. So they reviewed the tape for that time—watch the screen readout in the bottom right-hand corner—it gives the day and time."

All three men sat and watched the five seconds tick off as nothing, visually, happened on-screen. The president turned to Trey, puzzled.

Trey smiled. "Fortunately, the Movie Store bought a really nice, fairly expensive video monitoring system. It takes 220 shots per second. So when we took this same five second film, slowed it down to show each picture, watch what happens between frames 187 and 192." Trey fast-forwarded the frame-by-frame viewing to frame number 180. "Watch closely," he said, his eyes fixed on the screen.

"What the..." the president exclaimed. "Run that back."

Trey did just that, and the president whistled through his teeth. "No other sightings?" he asked.

"Nope," Trey responded, "not a single one. But it would appear as though Mothman has been renting, or rather borrowing, movies for a year and a half at the Movie Store in Point Pleasant."

"And this is the best part, Mr. President. Tell him what he likes to watch," said Bob.

Trey smiled. "He prefers science fiction—has seen the entire Alien series a dozen times each. He likes the X-Files, sci-fi comedies—Galaxy Quest and the like—but his favorite movie of all time..."

"The Mothman Prophecies," interjected the president.

Both subordinates nodded. "Thirty-eight times," Trey said in amazement, "and he's not in the movie one single time."

"Did Richard Gere vote for me?" asked the president who stood, looking at his watch.

Bob shrugged his shoulders and took the not-so-subtle hint. "I wouldn't count on it Mr. President." Laughing, he stood to take his exit, with Trey following.

"Gentlemen," the president said, shaking their hands, "I really appreciate your coming by, and I like the idea of inserting a subliminal message into the tape. If we could get him working for us, we might not need armed forces anymore," the president chuckled. As he circled back around behind his desk, he followed with, "Make sure you run that message by me before you deliver the package. I want to see exactly what we're asking him to do before we ask him to do it." And as an afterthought, "Get me a copy of Mothman, Bob, I'd like to watch it again."

After the two had left the president called in his National Security Advisor, who had been listening remotely from another room in the White House.

"What do you think, Cal?" asked the leader of the free world.

Calvin chewed his bottom lip. "Certainly interesting, Mr. President, but we've got a dossier that thick," he said, separating his flattened hands about a foot apart, "on the Mothman."

"Get out of here," the president said astounded. "Did he come from Area 51?"

"THAT," Calvin replied with raised eyebrows, "we don't know."

68

Howard had just settled in at his desk when his buzzer went off. He hit the intercom button and said, "Yes?"

"A Mrs. Johnson is on line four, said you'd know who she was."

Howard raised his eyebrows as he thanked the receptionist and punched line four. "Mrs. Johnson, how are you today?"

The old lady was slow to respond, but finally said, "Fine. I was wondering if you had a minute or two?"

Howard both nodded his head and said of course. He asked if she wanted him to stop by.

"No, I can just tell you on the phone. I had a dream last night."

At this pronouncement Howard let out a sigh and rolled his eyes. Her lengthy pause seemed to be waiting for him to give her the go ahead. He did so as he slouched down in his seat.

"It was the most real dream I've ever had, and I've dreamt a lot in my time. I think maybe it's the caffeine, but sometimes if I get pizza too late in the evening I'll dream a lot." This time it seemed she heard his sigh and continued. "At first I was here at the house when the ground began to shake. Why I was scared to death—as you can imagine—when the next thing I know I'm on one of the trains out at the Exhibition Coal Mine."

Howard sat up, changing ears with the phone. "And?"

"I've been through that mine a few times with Carl before he died and once just a couple of weeks ago so I know the mine reasonably well. Anyway, this time instead of going up the right-hand side track we went up the left-hand side—the return side."

Licking his lips, Howard's heart was beating rapidly. "Go on, Mrs. Johnson, take your time."

"You know I've been through there every single time I've been in that mine, but always came OUT thataway, never went in."

Good point, thought Howard. But then he remembered the officers that had walked both sides of that track in their search for Annie last week. On top of that, he remembered that he was hearing the dream of an elderly, somewhat ditzy old lady.

"You still there?" the ditzy old lady asked, seeming to sense his mind wandering off.

"Yeah, yeah," he said, taking in a deep breath, "go on, what happened next."

"There was this man—he had a British accent near as I could tell—digging into the face of the mine. Our train—tram if you will—stopped and I noticed there was no driver, it just seemed to stop on its own. I asked the young man what he was doing, and he told me, plain as day, that he was digging another entrance into the Netherworld. That's what he called it, the Netherworld."

Howard tried his best but could not keep Michael Jackson and his Neverland Ranch from flooding his mind. "Then what?" he asked, his enthusiasm nearly gone.

"I asked him about my Ralphie." Howard wanted to cry. "He said he was fine, doing quite well, and that your lady reporter was with him and doing fine too." Now it was Mrs. Johnson who did cry, and Howard cooed into the phone platitudes that it was just a dream and he was sure they were indeed fine.

After a full minute the old lady seemed to regain her composure. "And the funny thing was, right there where he was digging, there was this writing on the wall." Howard sat up. "It was Greek to me, but the man noticed me looking at it and he said whatever you do don't tell Howard."

Howard's bottom jaw dropped. Of all the lunatic dreams he had heard in his lifetime, this one was the most bizarre. A man with a British accent warns an old lady not to reveal hieroglyphics that she had no reason to know were there in the first place to a man heavily involved in a missing person investigation.

"Are you still there?"

"Uh, yeah," Howard stammered, half in shock at the exotic dream. "Was that it?"

"That's all I can remember of it. There might have been more, I don't know. But what I remember it's like it really happened."

"I believe you Mrs. Johnson," Howard said, only half lying. "Let me ask you this—if we took some deputies down there and went through the mine looking for…clues and such, would you be willing to ride in with us?"

There was no hesitation on the other end of the phone. "Why sure Howard, you just say when."

69

Annie was dreaming that she was driving her truck around Beckley, the window down, the wind in her hair. She threw her hand up at everybody on the street, and a few waved back. She recognized no one, until Ralphie was suddenly in her windshield and calling out to her.

"Annie," he seemed to be whispering, "Annie, wake up."

Annie sat up and realized she had indeed been dreaming, and the gentle glow of the underworld now replaced the brilliant sun in which she had basked in her dream. Ralph had sat back on his haunches and waited for her to come fully awake.

"You've got to see this," he continued to whisper, taking her hand and pulling her up to her feet. He led her out of the main hall where she had fallen asleep and back up the passageway that they had originally taken into the great hall. About halfway through he stopped with openings on both the left and the right.

"Up or down," he now said in a quiet voice, somewhat above a whisper. She looked in both directions, and noticed how dark and scary the down side appeared to be. Up, on the other hand, seemed better lit.

"Let's go up," she said flatly, sensing a return to the normal, light-hearted Ralphie, but not willing to play along in case it was a trick. He immediately bounded up the stairs. While Annie followed as closely as she could, she was soon a landing behind him and could just see his heels as he turned the corner and headed up another flight. Rounding probably the fifth landing she bumped into the wiry lad who had stopped. The light had nearly vanished and, after a slight tilt of her head, she was sure she heard the distant sound of...thunder?

Ralph was grinning at her. "You ain't going to believe this," he said, taking her hand and leading her into the vanishing light. They were half running on stone that was originally dry but was now becoming wetter and wetter as they progressed. To the left was darkness, but to the right was the cave wall onto which the little bit of light that had come up the stairway was bouncing off of. With her fear equaling her enthusiasm, Annie was growing tired quicker than Ralphie and asked if they could stop for a rest.

"Right around the corner," he said.

They turned a corner to the right and stopped and Annie literally gasped for breath. Ralph let go of her hand and watched her reaction from the side.

"Oh my God," Annie said. She put her hands on her knees trying to catch her breath, but never took her eyes off of the most surreal landscape she had ever seen. There, not thirty yards away, was an ocean. Smallish waves were crashing to what appeared to be a sandy beach—this ocean as restless and churning as the oceans on the surface. But it was like being at the beach at night with just a sliver of moon above. It was just as scary as it was beautiful.

"How did you find this place?" she asked, finally turning to Ralph who was beaming at her.

"You're not going to believe this," he said, looking back out to the underground ocean, "but there's more just like it."

Annie's gaze carried back out to the white, frothing waves as her feet began to take her in that direction. In no time the waves gently pushed water up around her tennis shoes. Without unlacing her shoes she forced each shoe off with the other foot, gasped as the cold water encircled her now socked feet.

"What did you expect," Ralphie asked laughing, "Myrtle Beach?" He had to talk loud because, acoustically, the waves didn't just crash once but over and over in the huge echo chamber that was this beach, this underground shoreline.

Dipping her cupped hands into the water she raised a handful to her face and breathed. With eyes wide open she proclaimed, "It's fresh water!"

Ralphie nodded and did the same. "Taste it," he said, supping a bit from his own hands.

Annie did the same and was stunned at how clean it tasted. The sound, while deafening, had a calming effect deep down to her very soul. In the entire time that she had spent beneath the Raleigh County Courthouse she had never felt this peaceful, including when she slept.

"What's that direction, Europe?" she asked, pointing into the darkness beyond the cresting waves.

Ralph smiled his biggest smile. "Nothing. This is just the border of West Virginia. This entire underground state has the same shape as the one on the surface, it's just not as big. And every border county is coastal." Ralph looked to the left and right, then said, "I think we're somewhere in Mason County."

"Wow," said Annie, also looking left and right with no clue as to how Ralphie divined this to be Mason County. Had there been a power plant up river, or a recognizable bridge, or a city limit sign she might have. It finally dawned on her. "Wait a minute, Mason County is bordered by the Ohio River. This is the Ohio River, you idiot."

Ralph laughed. "When did you ever see the Ohio River with waves?"

At that Annie had to sit back and think. Her feet were pretty used to the cold water now, but it was way too cold to go in any deeper. The few times a larger wave washed water up above her ankles reaffirmed her comfort at being only ankle deep.

"Well what about the Mason/Dixon Line? Or for that matter the eastern border, where the tops of mountains form the boundaries?"

"THAT," Ralphie said in earnest, "they say is something to see." He looked out into the darkness and Annie followed his gaze. The cool, night breeze lightly blew back the hair from their faces. From the corner of her eye Ralph looked taller, wiser, older. She only hoped his wisdom included she and Michael rowing his boat to shore, hallelujah.

70

Pango Babaturd was walking serenely along a meandering stream and contemplating the nature of life when a head popped out of the ground right in front of him and exclaimed in a loud, shrill voice boo!

He nearly fell backing up until he recognized his practical joker friend Ennead Pribble from neighboring Pocahontas County. "Holy mother of Overfather!" he exclaimed, clutching at his chest with his left hand, "you nearly gave me the fright of my life!"

Ennead pulled himself completely out of the ground and dusted himself off before taking Pango's hand in his and giving it a vigorous shake.

"Wasn't the meeting this year kinda quiet?" he asked, catching his elder's eye. They walked slowly among the rocks and gravel.

"I don't know," Pango looked up as if reliving the event, "the three visitors were a welcome change for once."

Ennead nodded his head in agreement. "True, true. And Wowfie, him turning out to be our next member, that was quite a shocker."

"RALphie," Pango corrected the younger man's pronunciation, "starts with an R, not a W."

"Oh." He turned to Pango. "So who's he gonna replace?"

Pango's eyes widened in amazement. "You didn't know? The old man stayed behind to take his place as Sergeant at Arms in the House Chamber. You didn't notice that he wasn't with us at the feast?"

"Ulysses is gone?" Ennead asked in disbelief. He shook his head as if to clear his thoughts. "He was our elder statesman, our Rock of Gibraltar, our rudder in the stormy seas. Who becomes Elder now?"

Pango shrugged. "Why naturally it would fall to the eldest. I just can't recall if the eldest refers to physical age or time of service."

Ennead patted his old friend on the shoulder and laughed. "You gotta be one of those two I would imagine old friend."

Pango sighed. "I am the oldest," he said with a sly grin. His slow gait and chiseled face gave away his advancing year. "I'll be 132 the month of the great disappointment."

"Ah, no," said Ennead with a full measure of compassion. "You were born in THE month?" Pango sighed and nodded his head. "At least the serpent doesn't pass through either of our counties."

"Yes, we have that." Pango eased down on a bench and Ennead joined him. "I honestly believe if it had, you know, that I could have defeated the basilisk. I've always said you cut off the head," and with that Pango made a slashing motion with his quivering hand, "the rest of the body dies."

Ennead stared ahead. "Keep that in mind comrade, in case it does refer to physical age." After a pause he continued. "Is...how do you say...Rrrrrralphie...up to the task of handling Ulysses' county, do you think?"

With this Pango stood. "I don't know. We've never had one this young or inexperienced before, but if the Overfather chooses, who am I to question his judgment."

Ennead nodded his head thoughtfully. "Well," he said suddenly, "I must be off." And with that pronouncement, he headed back to and dived into the hole he'd come out of as if he were a groundhog or Olympic diver.

71

Another candlelight service was held at the Boyd Church of God. The church, which usually had crowds averaging seventy-five or so, saw double that on this one week anniversary of the disappearance. It was as much a social outpouring as it was a religious service, despite the best attempts of the reverend to direct the focus onto God and his eternal wisdom.

Howard and Chief Hall chose not to attend this gathering of the faithful and instead met at Tamarack for a bite to eat and a cup of coffee. At this time of the evening the milling people were largely finishing up their browsing and getting back on the highway for destinations unknown.

"Lucky people," Hall said to no one, watching the parents gather up their children to get back on the highway. Between the second and third major tolls, the pay-as-you-go turnpike saw literally millions of tourists pass through its antiquated turnstiles.

"Who?" Howard asked, taking a bite of a bagel slathered with cream cheese.

Hall exhaled in near exhaustion. "People who don't have anyone missing, that's who." He looked his friend directly in the eye. "I'm telling you, this has taken a toll on me old buddy like you'd never believe. Sometimes I wish we lived in a bigger city where this kind of crap happens all the time. You'd get hardened to it. As it is," he looked away and fell silent.

His beeper went off and he removed the device from his belt. Hall dialed the number and was in contact with the night desk.

"Is that a fact?" he said, some enthusiasm in his voice. "Give me their address." He scribbled something that appeared to Howard to be entirely illegible, said thanks and hung up. A smile crossed his big, round face.

"That Justice boy that disappeared over around the Exhibition

Mine—his best friend has confessed that he told him he was jumping off the train and heading back."

"We already know that," Howard interjected.

Hall nodded. "But now he says he thinks he saw Michael on the trip back out, crouched down in one of the passageways." Howard raised his eyebrows. "Was afraid he'd get into trouble if he told us earlier. He's a good boy."

Howard spoke up. "Did I tell you about the dream that Ralphie's mother had night before last?" Hall shook his head no. "We've got to go back in there and I think we need to focus on the left side, the return trip. That's where the boy had to have seen Michael, that's where we saw the hieroglyphics, and that's where Mrs. Johnson's dream really got weird. Think you can arrange something tomorrow?"

It was a brilliantly sunny day the following morning as Howard arrived at the Beckley Exhibition Coal Mine escorting Mrs. Johnson. At about the same time five city cars pulled in the parking lot with Hall in the lead, escorting Gary Burchett, his little sister Kendra and his parents. Before turning off the engine Hall patted Gary, who got to ride in the front seat with the Chief, and said again for the umpteenth time that he was a real good boy and a good citizen for coming forth with additional information.

"I've seen cases blown wide open with much less information," he drawled, now opening his door. The family piled out of the car and headed to the shelter where the tram sat waiting patiently. Howard and Minnie stood waiting.

"You made arrangements inside?" Howard asked, pointing his thumb toward the gift shop. Hall said yeah but excused himself anyway and made his way through his men into the shop. He was gone about five minutes and came out barking orders.

"Listen up ladies and gentlemen." Everyone grew quiet as he stepped into one of the waiting trams to use as a bully pulpit. "We've been in this mine before with pretty much a fine-toothed comb and found nothing." He consciously chose not to go into the hieroglyphics to see if they were visible on this day. "But young Gary was in this mine with his friend Michael the day he disappeared and he thinks he may have seen the boy on the return trip. If he did, he was the last to see him since the field trip. I guess," and he looked down to Gary standing before him, "you were the last to see him regardless." Gary nodded his head.

"Pay attention to detail in here," Hall said, his index finger pointing to the dark entrance to the underworld. "Both of the engineers— retired miners both of them—are going in with us. As they're in these mines more than anybody, I'd ask them," and he turned and nodded to the already hard-hatted men, "to pay even more attention to detail, as if there are changes you would probably notice them quicker than anybody."

He completed his opening remarks and began dividing his men in half, sending an engineer with one group to the right when the intersection came, and leading another group that included Howard, Gary and his family, and Mrs. Johnson to the left. Everybody donned hard-hats and slowly started walking toward the hundred-year-old driftmouth.

The entire group walked the football field-length to where the tracks separated, and the first group headed off to the right. Hall led his group to the left, thankful that the lights were on in addition to the lights provided on his and the engineer's hard-hats. After the two groups had gotten out of earshot of each other, Hall turned and addressed his group.

"Gary, you look for that spur where you say you think you saw Michael."

Gary shook his head. "Spur?"

"Uh…" Hall stammered, "passageway, opening, cave." He turned to Mrs. Johnson. "Minnie, I understand you had a pretty real dream about this place the other night."

Minnie Johnson nodded. "'Deed I did, sheriff." Howard smiled at her constant use of the word sheriff to describe the Chief of Police of the city of Beckley. Chief Hall, however, didn't share the joy and turned to carry on.

Without turning he said loud enough for all to hear, "Gary, how far back in here was it you think you saw Michael?" People became conscious of the sound they were making by walking between or outside the graveled tracks and tried to walk quieter as Gary offered his answer.

"It's kinda hard to tell," he tried to speak loudly, "I was coming the other direction."

"Understood," the Chief boomed, "but keep looking, you may see something you recognize in here." The group continued to walk until they were almost to the area where they had found the hieroglyphics a week earlier. Hall slowed his gait and everyone followed his lead. When he was just past where the ancient looking writings had been, he turned and addressed the gathering.

"Nobody seen anything yet?" There was a collective shake of heads and a few murmured 'no's. Hall made a sweeping gesture with his arm and suggested that at least two of the people they were looking for had connections to this place. "Michael of course disappeared here, and Ralphie," he cast a sympathetic look toward Mrs. Johnson, "worked in here a few summers." While he was talking he'd made no direct eye contact with the wall to his right where the cryptic warning had been, hoping someone else would see it and he'd reward them with praise at such fine detective work. But nobody said anything, and he soon began casting an occasional glance to the right rib of the mine. Nothing. Eye contact and a shake of Howard's head confirmed what he already knew, the writing was gone again.

"Let's move on then," Hall said, disappointment in his voice. He wasn't sure what exactly they hoped to find this time around, and he hoped they would have found it by now—at least something of a sign where the writings had been before.

The group came to a spur to the right, but this spur was within sight of daylight at the back of the mine where the tram circled around outside and came back in. It was in this spur where Howard and his photographer had hid and later found the writings had materialized again on the very spot where Hall and his people couldn't find it. And, both Howard and Hall knew, this spur went all the way through to the other side and did not in any way fit the description that Gary had provided of where he thought he saw Michael crouched low on the ground. As instructed, two deputies carrying flashlights were coming through the spur from the other side, reporting that they had seen nothing. Soon they exited the mine out the backside and stood in a fiery hot and brighter than usual sun. Both groups of law enforcement converged.

Howard moseyed over to Hall and made a suggestion. "We've got enough people—particularly on our side—to station one person about every 200 feet or so. Let's space everybody out, except the little girl of course, and cut the lights for a minute or two. Have everybody listen, look."

Hall nodded his head. "And let's position the boy there where we saw the writing before, see if the stuff materializes again."

"Good idea," encouraged Howard.

The Chief laid out the plan and when everybody had nodded that they understood their assigned task, the two groups headed back in the same side they had come out. Officers stopped first as Hall motioned for them to do, then Howard, Gary was next right at the former 'writing on the wall,' then Minnie, Gary's dad, Howard, and Gary's mom and sister stopped within the gentle glow of daylight from the main entrance so that the little girl wouldn't be frightened from complete darkness. Hall sent a message back the way they had came which looped around the spur and down to the main switch on the other side. The lights went as two of the five senses normally enjoyed by humans was squelched—sight and sound. Hall said to fire back up the lights on his mark, and he waited as long as he felt everyone was still ok before sending the word up the tracks to turn them on. You could hear the relay from man to man until finally the sound disappeared. A minute passed and still no lights.

72

Taylor and Ralphie were climbing a set of stairs that Ralphie had never been on while Taylor droned on and on about his Harley and the difficulty they had getting spare parts for it thirty miles below ground. Ralph knew they were down deep but had thought they were closer to twenty miles than thirty. And, of course, he wasn't entirely sure that Taylor had it right, but he was in no position to question the data.

"And gasoline," Taylor continued, "if the DEP knew how we keep that stored down here we'd but shut down in a heartbeat." With that said he gave out a sharp laugh then passed through a very normal looking door—the most normal looking thing Ralph had seen since he'd been down under.

The door, however seemed to have no function. It didn't divide one room from another, it didn't seem to be a fire door, it was just a meaningless door along an undetermined corridor.

"You should have seen us bringing that bike down the chute—it wasn't made for Fat Boys you know." Ralph muttered 'I bet' and wanted desperately to ask where they were going. "Lost both side mirrors, nearly lost my head a couple times when the bike rolled."

Quickly Ralph jumped in. "How'd you get it in the courthouse?"

Taylor stopped, turned, and eyed Ralph. "Didn't," he huffed, "brought it in through the coal mine." He turned and started walking again, this time a little faster. "Anyway, it's the same chute, both feed into the same tube."

"Where are we going?" Ralph cut in again, having a hard time keeping up with the man he knew to be at least twice his age. Again Taylor turned and eyed Ralph suspiciously. "Just wondering," Ralph said.

"Need to inspect the closure of 41-B and its replacement. You got anywhere else to be?"

Ralph shrugged his shoulders and Taylor continued his brisk walk for another maybe fifty feet and stopped dead, with Ralph nearly bowling him over.

"Here we are," he said, seemingly at a dead end. "Merriweather!" he called out really loud. Less than five seconds passed when Taylor groused, "Now where is that rapscallion?" He had just taken a deep breath to shout again, even louder Ralph guessed, when a head popped through the wall in front of them.

"Oh there you are boss," the distinctly Australian voice accompanied just by a head said. Taylor was about to speak when Merriweather shushed him. "We've got company," he informed in a half whisper.

Taylor's eyes widened as he turned and shushed Ralph who was saying nothing. The head of Merriweather disappeared back through the hologram and Taylor stepped through and disappeared right behind him. Ralph stepped through into another passageway and was staring into what appeared to be a two-way mirror at a city deputy that looked vaguely familiar. The deputy was standing between the tracks of some train, looking up and down the tracks at regular intervals.

"Where are we?" Ralph whispered.

Merriweather turned to Ralph and whispered, "41-B."

73

In the total darkness and complete silence both Howard and Chief Hall had the sinking feeling that this revisit to the mine wasn't going to turn out well. Hall wasn't even listening anymore, his mind was churning the improbable events that had happened since he'd gotten that phone call from Ernest T. Bass—or was it Ralph Johnson.

"I said fire the lights back up!" he barked to his left, with each deputy repeating 'fire the lights back up' on up the line until the sound coursed around the spur and into the other side. Another half minute passed when the word came back, echo-like, that the lights wouldn't turn back on.

"Holy smokes," Hall muttered to himself, then to everyone within earshot, "turn your flashlights on." He reached to the switch on his belt that activated the battery-charged light on his hard hat and found his light too was dead.

"What the..." he said as now several reported into the darkness that their lights weren't working. He heard Howard's voice a hundred yards or so down the track toward the entrance.

"This may be it, Chief, this may be what were looking for."

The Chief blinked in the darkness, wondering what in the heck his editor friend was talking about.

74

"The mine?" Ralph asked, thinking he recognized the area where the deputy was standing.

Taylor nodded his head. "Come 'round this way." Their pathway seemed to parallel the tracks, and soon another deputy was standing sentinel.

"What's going on?" Ralph asked, concerned that HIS mine had been the target of vandals or, even worse, a cave-in. But nobody said anything, only shushed as they continued walking. Ralph now recognized the police chief, Hall as Ralph recalled. They passed right in front of him. Next came a young boy that Ralph didn't recognize. Then his mom, looking as small and as frightened as the young boy.

"Mom!" Ralph said in a half whisper before he could catch himself. Taylor grabbed his arm and Merriweather stopped in his tracks in mid-step.

"Ralphie, is that you?" Minnie said in their direction just as Hall told his men to hold their positions. Being the person next to Mrs. Johnson toward the mine entrance, Howard thought he heard her speaking but couldn't be sure for Hall's dominant voice.

"Everybody ok?" Hall called out in both directions as Ralph turned to Taylor with a pleading look. Taylor shrugged.

"Go ahead, but keep it down." As Ralph walked toward his aging mother Taylor murmured, "I sold her some hair brushes, she's a nice lady."

Ralph took his mom's hand as shouts went up and down the corridor and came back in the form of echoes that everybody was ok. Everybody but Howard, who was desperately trying to listen to see if Mrs. Johnson was in trouble or just talking to herself.

"Ralphie, is that you?" she said softly, tears welling up in each eye.

"It's me," said Ralph, pulling his mom into a warm embrace. Her tears flowed from both relief and happiness.

"Oh my boy," she cried into his chest, "you ok?" She held on for dear life, not wanting to let go of her baby boy.

"I'm fine, mom. You doing ok?"

Hall was barking orders up and down the dark track and Howard's straining ears was definitely picking up something of a conversation from up the tracks. Softly he took a step toward the old lady, then another, and another. He wished to God that Hall would shut up for a minute.

"I miss you so much Ralphie," his mom said into his wet shirt. "When you coming home boy?"

Ralph held her tight and patted her back. "I don't know mom, I've got a new job and it keeps me pretty busy most of the time. But I won't be far away, when I get a chance I'll come and visit, ok?" He could feel the small, white head nod against his chest as she snuffed loudly.

"You ok, Mrs. Johnson?" Howard called out.

Merriweather was in Ralph's face behind his mother. "Ix-nay on the alking-tay." Ralph nodded his head and pulled his mother's face up to him.

"I gotta run, mom," he said into her ear, "but know that I'm ok and love you very much."

Her tear-strewn face nodded up at him. Even though she couldn't see him in the darkness, she could feel his breath and smell his Dale Earnhardt cologne. "Ok boy, you call me, ok?"

Merriweather was dancing around, as would a child about to pee. "We need to be going," he said sing-songy, pointing down the tracks at the tiptoeing editor getting nearer and nearer.

Ralph whispered 'I love you,' touched his mom's face and drew back. The three sojourners from below melted into the wall as Howard touched Mrs. Johnson's arm.

"You ok?"

Minnie Johnson fell into his arms, her heaving sobs he mistook for sorrow. The overhead lights came on just as did the flashlights and the hard-hats. Although the light wasn't overly bright, it was still an adjustment to those who had been in complete darkness.

75

An hour later in Shoney's over coffee Chief Hall was shaking his head. "There's no way Ralphie was in that coal mine, Howard." Before the editor could speak Hall continued. "I've got half a mind to lock that old lady up, I think she's been leading us on wild goose chases from the start of this thing." Before Howard could interrupt, Hall let forth another volley. "And to tell you the truth, I can't blame her none. If it was my boy I'd probably be protecting him too. But he ain't my boy and he's kidnapped two people in my community and he's darn well gonna pay. I just hope he ain't hurt one of them."

With that said he rested, knowing that the newspaper guy had opinions of his own and just as strong.

"I hear what you're saying, and some of it makes sense." Howard took a sip of some really hot coffee. "But I think you're giving way too much credit to Mrs. Johnson. If she'd been doing what you claim she's been doing we'd have seen through her in a heartbeat. I just don't buy it."

Hall nodded as the waitress brought their orders. The two men removed their elbows from the table and smiled and said no as the young girl asked if they needed anything else. "Oh wait, ketchup," Howard said as she was walking away.

"You know we gotta start eating better or we ain't going to live to see fifty, neither one of us," Hall said, sprinkling salt on his country fried steak.

"Tell me about it," Howard agreed, sipping the sweetest tea he'd ever had in public. "But here's the thing, Lester, everybody—and I mean everybody—says Ralphie isn't capable of doing this kind of thing."

"I know that," chimed in Hall, "but look at the facts, Howard— forget what you feel inside. You think Ted Bundy's family and friends ever thought he was capable of doing what he was doing?"

"Ralph is no Ted Bundy," Howard said, fingering a French fry as Hall's pager went off. He pulled the digital readout up closer to his bifocals and read the number out loud.

"Never heard of it, think it's a Virginia exchange." He pulled his cell phone out of his pocket and dialed in the number. The look of surprise on his face was quickly subdued.

"Trey, how the heck are you?" he asked, rolling his eyes toward Howard. "Fine, doing fine, just getting a bite to eat at Shoney's." Then for a good two minutes Hall listened, his face reddening while his jaw dropped. "You're telling me..." but he was cut off his former high school classmate. "If you think..." but he was cut off again as he started squirming in his seat. He made a horrible face at Howard and pointed to the phone. "I..." Silence. "I..." More silence. "When monkeys fly out of my butt!" he finally exclaimed and clamped the flip phone shut.

"What," Howard asked, "was THAT all about?"

Hall ran his fingers through his thinning hair, shaking his head. "Said he wasn't going to bring me up on charges for the altercation the other day. Said he had permission from his boss to take over this case. Said any and all evidence was to be handed over to him. Said it was a matter of national security. Said if I cooperated he'd try to keep me from losing my job." With that said Chief Hall dropped his cell phone into his glass of water. "Hate the thing anyway."

Howard whistled through his teeth. "Did he say the words 'matter of national security?'"

Hall chewed on the inside of his lip and tried to recall. "Yeah, matter of national security. You think your boy's innocent now?"

"First of all," Howard pointed out, "he's not my boy. Second of all, I see no connection whatsoever to these three disappearances and national security. What in the world has Trey uncovered?"

"I don't know," said Hall, fishing his cell phone out of his water with a spoon. As he dialed he winked and said, "Time to call in a few favors, if this thing will work."

76

The young boy lay on the floor, his tasseled hair hanging down in his face, his nose in the next-to-last installment of Harry Potter, the boy wizard who had survived the attacks of Lord Valdemort time and time again. His mother, a tear running down her cheek, peered in from the kitchen while dinner was slowly being prepared on the stove.

"Mom!" the boy called, not knowing that his mother was discreetly watching him. She wiped the tear from her eye with her apron and went into the living room with a smile on her face.

"Yes dear," she replied, seeing that he was about a third of the way through the fairly large tome.

"Mom," he said, sitting up and pulling the large book to his lap, "you think Michael can be like Harry Potter and come back to us?"

The mother of two felt tears welling up in both eyes. "I hope so, Alex." She had to be brave and not show the pain and fear that gripped her heart. Since the boys' father had left them alone seven years ago, it had been a hard row to hoe for the 35-year-old legal secretary. She had done everything she could to be both mother and father, but the absence of a strong male role model she knew was taking its toll on her two little men. And having lost Michael on a school outing was more than she could take.

"What do you think he's doing right now?"

Mary Ann Justice bit her lip but could not keep a solitary tear from running down her cheek and falling to her breast. "I think he's missing us right now. What do you think?"

The boy smiled and nodded. "And he's missing this," he said, holding up the book.

"Yes," the mother smiled through her tears, "he is missing a wonderful adventure with Harry Potter." She looked out the window at the summer landscape. "You'll have to tell him all about it when he comes back."

"I think it's Dudley," the young boy said with a smile.

"The half prince?" the mother asked.

The boy nodded and buried his nose back into the week-old book.

77

Utauka Lazareth looked to the book she was holding in her hand then down to the paper on which she wrote. Carefully she tried to duplicate the writing in her own free hand.

"Shoot," she said, the black India ink smudging on the page. She stood, carrying the book and the parchment on which she was writing with the pen precariously perched in the same hand, and walked through the rock wall into a neighboring room.

"RALPHIE!" she called, her ample voice echoing throughout the mid-sized chamber. "RALHPIE!" she called again, this time even louder. Through what appeared to be solid rock the young man emerged, his eyebrows raised.

"You called for me?" he asked tentatively, not advancing on the large, elderly woman.

"Come over here boy, don't be shy, I won't bite you," she said with a toothy grin. She patted a seat next to her and Ralph gingerly sat down with some space between them. "Now then," she offered him the book, "which of these do you think will work the best?"

Ralph studied the book for a moment then peered over it at the woman who had called for him. "Where are we?"

"We're in sitting room C," she said matter-of-factly, sweeping her arm to indicate the entire cavern. "It's one of our many meeting rooms where we sometimes get together and map out strategies." She again thrust the book back toward Ralph's face and asked, "Which one, love?"

Ralph again studied the two pages open to him. It just looked like letters, with minor adjustments in their shape and hue. He shrugged. "I don't know, they all look fine to me."

Utauka sighed. "Ralphie," she said softly, half purring, "this is one of your many jobs now. You're the font master—didn't you know?"

Ralph looked at her curiously. "What's a font?"

"Font," she said, holding the book back up in front of his face, "these...different styles of letters."

Again Ralph looked over the book to his queer hostess. "I cain't tell much difference in them to be honest with you."

With heavy lidded eyes, Utauka asked, "Do you know what one of your 'other' jobs is?"

Ralph swallowed, shaking his head no.

"You get to escort me to the November 8th dirge." With that the woman's eyes fluttered so rapidly Ralph thought she might be trying to take flight, were it not for her tremendous bulk beneath her.

"What's the November 8th dirge?"

Utauka's eyes stopped fluttering at once as she sat up straight. "The November 8th dirge," she said in the haughty voice of a schoolmarm, "is the day we sing songs lamenting the day that free travel died. There's been no worse assault on the citizens of this great state—why this great country—as those outhouses with bandits in them."

Ralph studied her to see if she was joking, but clearly she wasn't. "Are you talking about the tollbooths?" he asked.

"Of course I'm talking about the tollbooths!" she snapped and stood up. She began to pace back and forth, running her right hand through her thinning hair while studying the page of different lettering. "How are we ever going to rid ourselves of them if we can't find the proper font?" She looked back to Ralph as she stopped her pacing, her eyes beseeching him to take another look, which he did.

"I like that one," Ralph said as convincingly as he could, pointing to the letter 'E' in a font labeled 'Perpetua.' Utauka's considerable frown immediately turned into a ray of sunshine.

"Well why didn't you say so," she said, gushing. "I like that one too, and we've not tried it yet." She leaned over his sitting form and kissed his forehead. "Thank you so much, I can take it from here." With that she turned and walked through a portion of the rock cave and immediately disappeared.

Ralph looked around the room, uncertain of where he had come in. Several hours later he finally found the passage back and into the great hall.

78

Annie and Michael sat crouched in a small alcove not too far out of the main hall. At least twenty-four hours had passed since the great feast, and both were getting pretty hungry again. Michael leaned out of the alcove and peered in both directions before continuing to whisper.

"Here's the way I see it. We find us some rope, a couple of knives, forks, whatever we can get our hands on, and we come out the way we came in. It's just rock climbing. It can't be that hard."

Annie was shaking her head no vigorously. "There's no way I'm going back up that path to the top. I can't stand heights. It was all I could do to come down it." She paused for a moment, reflecting. "Were it not for Ralph I'd have never made it." After a moment of clarity, her voice took on an edge. "Were it not for Ralph, I wouldn't be down here in the first place."

Michael nodded his head, having heard the story of how Ralph was merely drumming up business by breaking windows for the lady reporter that he'd found attractive.

"But you gotta admit, this is pretty neat."

Annie was loathe to admit that being down here was 'pretty neat,' but she knew that she was witness to—literally—an underground society that the six billion plus people above were clueless about. Certainly if she could get out of her present predicament with her life and her memories intact, a Pulitzer would be hers.

"Wish I hadn't left my notebook up at the top of that room," she said wistfully.

Michael raised his eyebrows. "Spiral, attached at the top?"

"Yeah," Annie replied, "you see it?"

Michael again peered out the alcove in both directions. "I picked it up and hid it," he said smiling. "Want me to go get it?"

This was the happiest Annie had been in quite a while and her broad smile showed it. "I'll go with you."

Michael stepped out from the alcove and headed to the left with Annie closely behind. He turned quickly, shaking his head. "It had to have gotten wet the other day when water filled the chamber. It went halfway up you know."

It made sense to Annie, but something else didn't. "How did you keep from drowning?"

The young boy shrugged his shoulders. "I don't know. It was like I was in a bubble, could see everything. I saw you guys swirling around and around until you just vanished, then the water subsided. I was wet but not like you'd expect. More damp than wet."

He turned and continued walking. Just before they got to the water room he turned to the right and, on tip-toes, reached up to a flat ledge and pulled out the notebook that he had put up there the day he had entered the exhibition mine.

"Dry as a bone," he noted, handing it to Annie.

She fished in her pocket for her pen and drew it out. "Let's go back to the alcove," she now whispered, not really knowing why.

"Hey guys!" the voice came from behind them, the direction they had come. It was Ralph, his pleasure at seeing them genuine. "Whatcha doin'?"

Annie subconsciously slid the notebook behind her. Ralph couldn't help but notice. "You found your notebook," he said flatly, glancing to her hip that hid the small notebook.

Annie blushed. "Yeah, well, actually, Michael found it and brought it down." On a lark she said, "I thought maybe we'd try to get a note up to the top and try to get some help."

Ralph studied her for some time before speaking. "I don't think that would be wise." After a pause he continued with, "Even possible."

"What do you mean?" Annie asked, holding his gaze.

Ralph shrugged. "We're thirty miles under, for one thing."

Annie cut him off. "You said twenty earlier."

"It was just a guess. And the other thing is, you get a note up, more people are going to be coming down. We can't have that. It wouldn't do at all."

Annie huffed. "What wouldn't do, Ralph? Saving Michael and I? I think you're right," she said mockingly, "we can't jeopardize these goofballs down here to save a couple of normal people, now can we?" Her tone was more than condescending.

"These goofballs," Ralph explained, his patience seemingly strained, "are doing everything they can to help up above."

"How?" Annie exploded, "by holding innocent people hostage? Whether you want to admit it or not you're being held hostage too!"

Ralph mulled over that for a moment. "Perhaps," he said. In a sudden change of subject he asked, "Don't y'all work with a lot of different fonts at the newspaper?"

Annie blinked through her anger and tried to understand the question. Flustered, she finally said, "Yes."

"Come with me," Ralph said, turning his back on them and walking back the way he came. Annie and Michael looked at each other, shrugged and, with little else to do, followed.

They came to a mid-sized, rather square-shaped cavern of a room and Ralph motioned for them to sit down. Whispering, he said, "This might get you two out of here if you can help."

Annie and Michael's eyes grew wide as Ralph yelled to the top of his lungs for—phonetically—it sounded like 'you talka.' In less than a heartbeat the thick head poked out from a sidewall, eyelids fluttering madly. Annie and Michael recognized her as the only female representative that they had seen since they'd been below.

"Yes love," her voice dripped with passion, her ample body covered in a large muumuu, "you rang my dear?" It was then she saw Annie and Michael and her demeanor quickly changed from syrupy to harsh. "Oh," she said with a voice that sounded more like a man's than a woman's, "it's you two." She looked at Ralphie contentiously. "Why did you bring them here?" Annie couldn't help but notice how much she sounded like one of the fun girls from Mt. Pilot from the Andy Griffith show, the 'hello doll' girl—which made her recall Ernest T. Bass—which made her recall why she was here in the first place.

Ralph pointed to Annie. "She works at the newspaper."

Utauka stared at Ralph, then looked to Annie. "So?"

"So," said Ralph in a syrupy voice of his own, "she knows fonts better than anybody."

"Ohhhhhhhhhhh," said Utauka, her demeanor changing again as fast as it had earlier. She said she'd be right back and disappeared through the rock from which she'd emerged. Ralph turned to Annie and Michael and winked.

"Yes, let me see," she said, reemerging through the gray stone thumbing through her big book of fonts. "Ralph and I thought this one was just darling," she said, looking up to her new inamorata and batted her eyes some more. "It's called Perpetua," she explained instructively, "I like that, don't you Ralphie?"

Ralphie smiled and nodded, still not telling much difference in any of the fonts on the page. Annie quickly scanned the two pages and started thumbing back through the book which immediately caught Utauka's attention.

"No, no, no," she said, taking the book from Annie, "we've done all those. We're up to here," and she handed the book back to Annie and turned her attention back to Ralph. "She doesn't seem very smart," she said in a low voice, raising her eyebrows.

Annie heard the remark but maintained enough calm to speak. If she had to eat camel dung to get out of this place alive, she would. "What, may I ask, are we trying to do with these fonts?"

Before turning Utauka whispered to Ralph, "I told you so," then put on a big fake smile and turned back to Annie. "These fonts," she said as though she had all the patience in the world, "are how we communicate our wishes on occasion to those in power above." With that said she gave a curt nod and turned back to Ralph and winked.

Annie's brain kicked into overdrive as she considered the possibility of hijacking whatever method these people used to 'communicate' with the powers-that-be and getting a message out regarding their predicament. She hmmmmmmed thoughtfully and worded her question such that her intentions weren't obvious.

"How are these fonts presented to the powers-that-be?" Quickly she added, "It makes a huge difference whether the fonts are all capital, on paper or video, whether color or black and white is used." With a nod of her head in Ralph's direction he spoke up in total agreement.

"It's true, Utauka, and they ain't nobody down here knows fonts any better than Annie."

Utauka surveyed Ralph for a moment then turned back to Annie with the same careful perusal. Finally she spoke. "To be honest with you, I don't know. I work up the message, which always says 'The tolls must go,' then I get it to Pribble Mermidon in Mercer and he actually sends the communiqué at a time and place of the subcommittee's choosing."

Lately, if Annie had any luck, it had all been bad. She studied this turn of events for a moment in her mind and finally asked, "This... Pribble fellow, maybe if I talked to him. I would think the time and the place would be more important than the," as she was saying this Ralph was waving his arms and shaking his head no behind Utauka who, as Annie came to realize, was about to explode, "font," she finished in a small voice.

"Time and place," Utauka said in a loud voice, turning back to Ralphie who looked up to the cave ceiling, "time and place...more important than font? Did I hear her right, Ralphie? Did she say time and place was more important than font!?!"

Annie stood quickly and spoke in a loud voice. "Did you say Perpetua?" she asked, her eyes focusing on the page before her. "Was it Perpetua, Utauka?"

Utauka had turned and eyed the lady reporter suspiciously. "Yes, Perpetua."

Annie gushed. "I LOVE it, I really do." She turned to Michael and pointed on the page for him to see. "Isn't it lovely?" she asked, her eyes pleading with the young boy to not only agree but to agree with enthusiasm. He took the cue and ran with it.

"That is one beautiful font," he said a little too enthusiastic, "I can't believe they've got those other fonts on the same page with that one."

Utauka's hard gaze continued until Ralph gently put his arm around the old lady. "See, I told you she knew her fonts."

The warm embrace was not lost upon the woman as she melted into his arms, sending her own arms around his slight waist. Both Michael and Annie noticed that, while a foot shorter than Ralph, Utauka's head was twice as large. Her square and jutting jaw, enhanced by a sizeable under-bite, made an already manly appearance even less attractive.

Her eyes began to bat again as she looked up to her young, less than willing suitor. "They do like it don't they," she gushed, on the verge of tears. "Our first font together, I'll never forget it Ralphie."

"Neither will I," Michael muttered under his breath. Annie nudged him in the ribs and kept her broad smile on the time bomb named Utauka.

"Where in the world does she get all that make-up?" Annie whispered.

79

Annie and Michael were walking back to the main hall in silence, their steps quick but their hearts were heavy. Ralph hadn't managed to get away from the woman who had clearly chosen him as her new beau for the moment. He wanted to leave, he tried to leave, but Utauka was having none of that. The one-thousand page book of fonts was laying across their laps and Ralph rolled his eyes and pointed toward the exit for the two fortunate ones.

"If I could somehow hook up with that Mercer County fellow," Annie said, trying to muster some enthusiasm. "I think he's the key to getting us out of here. That bat," Annie nodded her head in the direction they had come, "couldn't get out of a public toilet if she had to."

Michael smiled just as his stomach growled. "You know I once had a cat named Charley."

Annie raised her eyebrows. "So?"

"Know what I named his litter box?" Annie shook her head no. "The chocolate factory."

"Now THAT is funny," said Annie, turning a corner and trying to get her bearings as to exactly where they were in time and space. She stopped and turned completely around. "Any idea where the heck we are?"

Michael too spun 360 degrees and shrugged. "It can't be far, we didn't walk maybe ten or fifteen minutes getting to the dingbat room."

Annie chuckled and continued walking.

80

Howard was doodling on a notepad in his office when his phone buzzed. "Chief Hall's on line one," said the female voice.

He cradled the receiver under his ear and continued doodling. "This is Howard."

"Of course it's Howard," said the seemingly jovial voice on the other end of the receiver. "After all, I did call your number didn't I?"

Howard took the phone in his left hand, heaved a heavy sigh into it. His mood was not up for fun and games. "What can I do for you, Hall?"

The Chief sensed the editor's malaise and reigned in his slight enthusiasm. But his idea was, in his mind, brilliant.

"You much of a camper?" he asked.

Howard let out a slight chuckle. "Yeah, last time I camped I was in the Boy Scouts—fourth grade as I recall." After a slight pause, he added, "I think you were there. Didn't you catch your pants on fire roasting marshmallows?"

Hall laughed back. "Yeah I did. But after years of therapy I had forgotten about that. Thanks for reminding me." Both shared the memory in silence for a moment before Hall returned to the present. "How about me and you camping out in the exhibition mine?" Howard was about to interject but Hall cut him off. "One night, that's all I'm asking. I'm telling you that mine holds the key—or at least part of the puzzle—to this whole dad-blamed thing. We can smoke 'em out."

Howard had leaned back in his chair as he pinched his bottom lip. He was deep in thought when Hall prodded him further. "C'mon, it'd be fun, unless you've got a better idea."

Certain that he didn't have a better idea, Howard said ok and asked when. Before Hall could answer, the editor thought of a potential problem. "Didn't Trey tell you to back off and he was taking over the investigation?" Howard knew the answer was yes, and plodded on. "Wouldn't you be in contempt or something if you continued to investigate when you've been told to cease and desist?"

At this Hall chuckled. "Trey? That little weasel? I could still whip him with one hand tied behind my back. Besides, we ain't making a public spectacle of it. We just go in, they lock the gates behind us, and two old friends spend a night under the...mountain, as it were." Again Howard asked when, and Hall suggested this very night. "I honestly believe that there's something in that mine that wants us to find it—like a ghost or something in one of those haunted houses."

Howard said fine and began to wonder if he even owned a sleeping bag anymore. Maybe one of his kids left one behind after they went to college.

81

There had not been an emergency meeting of the council since the early part of the Moore administration's third go at state leadership a couple of decades earlier. The call to order was somber. Everyone wore black. Everyone, that is, except for Annie and Michael. They both wondered where Ralph had gotten a change of clothes that fit him - nicely.

"What in the devil has happened?" Annie quietly asked of no one.

Michael was equally quiet in his response. "I hope it's nothing we've done. You think butthead over there," his head motioning toward Ralph, "told them we were trying to get a message up?"

Annie stared at Ralph wondering the same thing herself. As much as she loathed him at times, she didn't think he was capable of this. Only about a third of the seats were filled, but those in attendance had the look of funeral attendees. Jimmy Taylor's voice silenced the murmurs that echoed throughout the great hall.

"Dearly beloved," he began somberly. Michael whispered someone must have died. Annie shushed him. "We are gathered here—those of us on the Confiscatory Highway Council Subcommittee," there were a few grumbles and a 'hear hear,' "on one of our darkest days in a long, long while." He lowered his head and appeared to be looking over notes.

"I hope it's that painted desert that died," Annie whispered, not seeing Utauka in attendance, but not surprised since only a third had showed up. The way the woman fawned on Ralph, she figured she had probably played up to nearly every one of the others.

"We have long fought the battle against unfair government taxation in any and all forms, but none has so troubled us as the blight on our beloved highway from our state's glorious capital to the east and our neighboring state of Virginia." A chorus of boos followed, sounding like some sort of athletic rivalry—which was common thirty miles up. "Jeer if you must, but remember Virginia's extension of our highway has no toll," Taylor seemed to be welling up, "but our state in the year of our Overfather ninety-one..." Curses flew up to the domed ceiling, echoing back, as paper and confetti rained down on the dais nearly obliterating the speaking leader.

"In the year of our Overfather ninety-one," he spoke now over the din that had become enormous, "this state that claims to be free—montani semper liberi—shackled its citizens and those citizens who choose to go through our state with armed bandits stationed every forty or so miles—robbing the populace of money while smiling and saying 'y'all have a nice day." Taylor quickly backed up a couple of steps from the podium as more paper and spitballs rained down on the dais. It looked like it was being covered in snow.

Annie looked to Michael who shook his head. "What are they talking about?" he asked.

She too shook her head. "Could it be something has gone wrong with the tolls?"

Michael's eyes widened. "God I hope it's not that Perpetua font that's gone wrong. We're goners for sure if that's what it is."

Taylor finally got the half-full room quieted down and resumed his oratory. "Well, y'all have a nice day is now going to cost the good citizens of this state and this country TWO DOLLARS PER TOLL my friends!" He quickly slapped the dais and backed away. The catcalls and shouts of NO and general mayhem that erupted was overwhelming. Annie couldn't imagine the reaction being any greater or more negative had the room been full. Taylor was now ankle deep in confetti and spitballs.

Then Annie noticed Ralph. While everyone of the regular members of whatever this group claimed to be was standing and yelling and throwing things—sometimes at each other—the newest member just sat there, legs crossed, chewing on a fingernail. The rest of the throng didn't seem to notice the less-than-lively reaction by their recent addition—only Annie, and now Michael who followed her gaze to the lonely figure.

"What's up with Ralph?" Michael asked above the din.

Annie shrugged her shoulders. "Maybe he's having second thoughts about all this," she whispered back. Indeed, he seemed too young to give up a life above for this semi-madness below. On the other hand, Annie speculated, he didn't have much of a life above—near as she could tell.

It was then that Ralph raised his hand—like a schoolboy. The noise hadn't abated one iota since Taylor announced the tolls were going up to two bucks a pop. Yet, in the maddening mayhem Taylor saw Ralph's raised hand and pointed the young man out.

The crowd grew silent quickly. Strange, given their usual hesitance to come back to order. In a near-dead silence Taylor nodded his head and said, "Yes, Ralphie?"

Ralphie stood and turned just as slowly, seeming to awake from a dream and wondering where he was. Not a word was said as he finally turned to face their leader.

"Exactly how do we combat the tolls? How have we gone about it in the past?"

Mouths around the room gaped open as if the dumbest question ever had been asked. Jimmy Taylor raised his hands to silence the group before they got started. "We have, since the year of our Overfather zero-one, communicated our wishes to the powers that be, from the sitting governor to those in the legislature who come from counties along the toll road." Taylor seemed to have to swallow hard to get out the last two words. "This communiqué is always private and always says some variance of 'the tolls must go.' Why do you ask?"

Again Taylor threw up his hands to quell the comments from the regular membership. Now it was Ralph's turn to swallow hard.

"So you've been posting messages...in different fonts," he looked to make sure Utauka wasn't around, "since the tolls were put up, and not only are they still up but they're being raised?"

Jimmy's best efforts to keep the crowd silent went for naught as the melee reached epic proportions. Where they got the paper to throw was a mystery, but their willingness to throw it wasn't. By the time Taylor got the crowd to settle down Ralph's head and shoulders were covered in white, giving the appearance he'd just come in from a winter storm. "That is correct," he said, still holding hands up commanding silence.

Ralph chewed on his bottom lip, seemingly considering his next statement carefully before saying it. "Since it's been over 50 years since the tolls were put on and they're still there, have we thought of changing tactics? Maybe trying something else for a while?"

A collective 'ooooooooh' went up through the crowd as every eye was now on Jimmy Taylor. Jimmy's hands now gripped the podium, and from the quiver in his forearms it appeared as though he was livid. Michael whispered to Annie, "Be prepared to make a run for it."

A full minute passed in total silence. Ralph continued standing, looking up to Taylor somewhat sheepishly, and Taylor continued gripping the stone podium, looking down to Ralph. Annie began to wonder if the standoff would ever end when Taylor finally, through clenched teeth, spoke.

"I'm open to suggestion."

Another collective 'ooooooooh'—though lower in timbre—vibrated from the gathering.

Ralph, sensing he was treading on thin ice but unwilling to back down, pulled out a small writing pad from his shirt pocket and flipped it open. "Uh...anytime I suggest something that goes beyond our capabilities or that we've tried before, feel free to speak up." As he glanced around the room confetti fell from his head and shoulders. Finding no support in any corner, he looked down to his notepad.

Annie could tell he was on the verge of abandoning his discussion when Taylor himself said, "Go on."

Ralph gave a half-smile then plunged ahead. "Have we tried the newspapers? Almost every daily newspaper now has a place where you can call in and they'll print it, like a reader's voice or a ventline—except for the cuss words. We could call in daily and say the tolls must go, or we could even say why we believe they must go. And I was thinking we could encourage the traveling public to—as they approached the toll plazas—begin to honk their horns in protest. My God those good people who are toll collectors could be retrained to do practically anything else."

Neither Annie nor Michael had ever heard this room so silent. Ralph's echoing words finally died down and not a foot shuffled, not a hand stirred. Another very awkward moment passed before Taylor again said, "Go on."

Ralph seemed stunned at Taylor's permission to carry on. He licked his lips and looked down at his notepad. "I think we can even use our two guests to our advantage," he said, looking over to Annie and Michael.

Michael could sense Annie was about to erupt in anger. He took her arm and squeezed it. "A chance to get out," he whispered.

Taylor looked to the two then back to Ralphie. He nodded his head as if to continue.

"The kind lady," Ralph said, nodding his head toward Annie, "is already in command of ink by the barrel. We could ask, in return for her freedom, two things." Every eye was now on Ralph, who himself was looking over to Annie. "First, we'd ask for her silence. About this group, about this place."

Annie's eyes smoldered as Michael squeezed her arm again. "Hear him out," he whispered in measured tones.

"And second, we'd ask that she dedicate her professional career, or at least that portion of it that would allow her to remain employed, on the removal of the tolls."

In any other situation, the words 'removal of the tolls' would have brought down the house. But this time not a creature was stirring, not even the mouse from Hancock County.

"As for Michael," Ralph said, turning his gaze to the young boy, "we train him up to be a great leader. We see that he's educated in the finest schools, nurture him through the murky waters of politics, and see him to the governor's mansion in about 30 years. We've waited this long, if all else fails we can wait another 30 years."

You could have heard a pin drop. Every pair of eyes shifted from Ralph to Taylor and back. Annie watched the elder man's forearms—they looked liked rocks, clutching onto the stone that was the podium. After an interminable silence she saw the forearms begin to relax, noticed the white knuckles clutching the podium begin to show signs of circulation again.

Michael broke the silence with the lowest whisper Annie had ever heard. "Can you imagine me being governor?"

82

The first lady padded out of the bathroom in her silk pajamas as the president, with a remote control, turned off a TV across the room.

"What are you watching, honey?" she asked.

The leader of the free world shrugged. "Just a security video."

His wife slid under the sheets in the king—or in this case presidential—sized bed. "Anything interesting?"

He chuckled. "Yeah, but if I told you I'd have to kill you."

The first lady smirked and replied, "Now where have I heard that before."

The president smiled and leaned over and kissed his wife's cheek. "You promise not to tell?"

"Of course," she demurred sweetly.

"Ok, but you are NOT going to believe what you see." He clicked the 'on' button on the remote and a black and white image of what looked like a storefront came into view. "Watch closely," he whispered, pointing toward the screen. Then it happened. Something big and dark and menacing—in slow motion—approached the door, slid something into what must have been a drop box—turned to look in both directions to see if it was seen, then was out of the sight of the camera from one frame to the next.

The first lady's mouth hung open in disbelief. "What was that?" she gasped, putting a hand to her heart. "Tell me it's not real."

"Oh it's real alright, and if we can get him on our side I think we can get a lot done—covertly—in a lot of areas. The possibilities are endless."

83

Howard got home after work and asked his beloved if she had seen their sleeping bag. He wasn't even sure if they had a sleeping bag, but he remembered their boys going to church and Boy Scout camps and surely they had sleeping bags for those trips.

"What on earth would you need a sleeping bag for?" she asked.

Howard let out a small sigh. He knew the question was coming but didn't want to get into Hall's whole theory about the exhibition coal mine somehow being a key to the investigation. So he told a little white lie.

"Hall's idea," he said nodding his head slightly, "he's wanting to, as best we can, drive the back roads tonight and see if we can see anything."

His wife stopped cooking and turned to look him dead in the eye. "It'll get cold in that mine tonight." Howard's jaw dropped as his wife turned and began stirring the spaghetti sauce again. "I'm not sure if the UnderMother would approve."

Howard blinked away the foreign word he had heard, now, for the second time come out of his wife's mouth.

"Honey," he said in a near pleading tone, "who do you mean when you say the word 'undermother?'"

His wife turned to him again. "Pardon?"

"Undermother," Howard repeated. "You just said it, and you said it about a week ago in the middle of the night."

Howard's wife looked at her husband with a good measure of pity. "My poor baby," she said in a cooing tone, "you have just been working way too hard. You need to have a drink and relax and let me finish dinner." With a small wave of her hand she attempted to dismiss him as she moved to the refrigerator.

"I'm not overworked," he said in a voice that was too high-pitched. "But you just said 'undermother' and I just want to know what the heck you're talking about."

Betty stopped what she was doing and gave her husband a hard look. "Howard, I've got a lot to do to get dinner on, I'm not in the mood to play games."

Howard exhaled loudly in frustration. "Betty, you just said 'undermother,' you did, I heard you. You said..." he struggled recalling her exact words, "something like I wonder if the 'undermother' will be alright with it." She looked back at him with a blank expression. "You did," he said, his voice softer and less certain.

84

Annie sat doodling in her notebook, alone, in the main hallway. She drew a sketch of Howard. Wasn't very good. She outlined her home that she loved and missed dearly. It was better. She could draw inanimate objects a lot better than she could draw living things she learned at a very early age. She could draw stickmen with the best of them, but she never quite got the hang...

Whoosh!!! Something went by so rapidly that she neither heard its approach nor saw it go by. And it was completely out of sight before her hair blew across her face and in the direction of the meeting room.

She stood and carefully leaned out of the alcove where she'd been sitting to see if anything were coming like a bat out of...well...where she found herself. Nothing she could see, but she hadn't seen what had just went by either. She looked back toward the meeting room and saw a couple of men emerge from different passageways and head away from her. They seemed to be in a hurry. As they disappeared around the corner she began to hear for the first time...she couldn't tell if it were wails of sorrow or shouts of joy. Dare she go see what was going on?

Michael popped out of another passageway not far from where Annie stood. He nodded to her and approached, but kept looking behind him as he too could hear the cacophony of sound.

"What's going on?" he asked.

Annie shrugged her shoulders. "I'm half afraid to find out." They stood in silence as another couple of gents popped out of passageways and hurried away from them.

"C'mon," Michael said, grabbing her hand. "What's the worst that could happen to us?"

"For one thing," Annie said, "we could die if whatever has gone wrong involves us."

"I could be wrong," Michael whispered, "but I don't think Ralph would let them do anything to us. Particularly after the last meeting. He had them eating out of his hands."

Annie was loathe to give Ralph any credit, but his suggestions—after considerable discussion—were well received. "But this may be bigger. Ralph may not be able to control whatever's going on now."

Michael appeared to give that some thought but continued walking anyway, with Annie not providing any resistance. The din grew louder and louder as they headed down the final stretch—ending at what they now knew to be a holographic wall of the meeting room. Just before the entrance Michael stopped, having lost some of his nerve.

"What do you think?" he turned to whisper to Annie.

Again she shrugged her shoulders. "We've come this far, let's see what's up."

Still holding hands they passed through the hologram into the party of the century. Paper planes where flying around as Mothman batted them down. Rolls of toilet paper—Annie wished she knew where to find them—flew across the room and unrolled as they went. More than half the crowd, which seemed like nearly all the 'representatives,' wore party hats like you might see at a child's birthday party. And not a single word was intelligible as everyone seemed to be trying to shout down another. A roll of toilet paper hit Michael in the chest and fell to his feet. He picked it up and gave it a fling at the circling Mothman who batted it down onto the head of Utauka, who looked up in disdain then back at the two standing near the portal. It was like she could trace the contrail of the toilet paper back to Michael's right hand. After a long stare Michael finally just shrugged his shoulders. Utauka turned back to the party at hand. Her celebratory technique was to grab each and every member and give them a big kiss on the lips, regardless of their looks or willingness to celebrate in that fashion. Annie almost felt sorry for the old bag.

"Good shot Arnold!" Michael called out next time the Mothman swirled by. Arnold reversed his course, looked down at the young boy, and winked one of his great big red eyes and took off again.

Annie had to raise her voice for Michael to hear her. "I'd forgotten his name was Arnold. I always knew him as Mothman." Michael nodded in understanding. They stood and watched the revelers for another ten minutes before moving to the right along the top row and sitting on a couple of stone benches. They still had no idea what the celebration was for, but was certain that their lives were temporarily in no danger. Michael finally spoke up.

"I'm guessing they took the tolls off."

Annie laughed out loud. "Don't hold your breath. Those are cash cows and the governor and the legislature know it. Believe me, it's not that."

Michael chewed on his bottom lip for a moment. "Well miss smarty pants, what do you think they're celebrating?"

Annie shook her head. "If dingbat wasn't down there it'd be my guess that she died." It was Michael's turn to laugh out loud as he watched Utauka pinch the butt of a delegate he couldn't remember seeing before. "And," Annie added, lowering her voice, "I'd be down there celebrating too if that were what happened."

Michael was about to agree when Utauka turned and looked directly at them, as if another toilet paper roll had whapped her in the head. The two stared down at the beehive hairdo, their mouths agape, remembering independently that there was an outside possibility that these people, or some of them, could read minds. They both heaved a sigh of relief when the heavyset lady turned back to the revelry.

"Think she heard us?" Michael asked quietly. Annie shook her head, coaxing him into silence in the event the old dingbat did have exceptional hearing or telepathic powers. Another few minutes of silence passed when Michael asked, "Have you seen Ralphie?"

Annie's eyebrows rose at the realization that no, she hadn't seen the newest member of the whatever club. They both began to scan the room as would a couple of five-year-olds searching for Waldo in a kid's book. He was nowhere to be seen.

"Uh oh," Annie whispered loud enough for Michael to hear.

"What?"

Annie pursed her lips, continuing to scan the makeshift party. "What if they're celebrating HIS demise?"

85

The dark parking lot was empty at the Beckley Exhibition Coal Mine save for that of the recently shined car of the Chief of Police. Hall sucked on a mint as he waited for his journalist friend to show up. He wanted a cigarette bad, thankful that he didn't have any.

The late-model sedan pulled into the lot just before ten and eased into a parking spot beside the police cruiser. Howard nodded to the Chief as he opened his door, popping his trunk lid as he got out.

"Can we even get in there?" Howard asked, seeing the black, metal gate closed to the entrance of the mine.

Hall held up the key and let it dangle from his index finger as he too retrieved gear from the trunk of his car. "We can lock it from the inside so we'll be undisturbed by any pranksters who might be lurking about."

Howard nodded his head as both closed their trunks and started walking toward the yawning entrance to a life many West Virginia men had lived, and died, by. Hall fiddled with the lock until it finally popped open and the chain holding it to a post dropped free. A metal-on-metal grind sounded as the heavy gate swung open, outward. Both men turned their flashlights into the mine—their lights not strong enough to make the first bend.

"You ready to do this?" Hall asked, motioning his head for Howard to enter.

"Yeah, sure," the journalist mumbled, passing beyond the gate but still not under the hill rising before them. The chief of police slipped in beyond the gate and pulled it to, wrapping the chain back around the post anchored deep in the ground. The padlock clicked resoundingly shut, and Hall turned to face his life-long acquaintance.

"You got a plan?" Howard asked tentatively.

Hall chuckled. "No, but I got a gun and enough bullets to last us hopefully all night." The two men started walking and soon came to the fork in the passageway. They stopped. Howard looked to the chief, whose big idea it was to be here in the first place.

"Well?" Howard droned.

Chief Hall was nodding his head as if the wheels were turning. Howard was hoping they were, and it wasn't just a mannerism the chief exhibited when he was stumped. After a long silence he was pretty sure it was the latter when Hall spoke up.

"First thing we've got to do is make sure this mine is empty. You go to the right all the way to the back gate, make sure it's locked, then switchback through the passage where you hid that evening when Trey was here. I'll do the same thing thisaway and we should meet somewhere along that connector."

Howard nodded his head but neither men moved. "Think we should turn the lights on?"

Hall shook his head. "No, not that our lights aren't going to alert somebody in here, but we might sneak up on them a little better with just our flashlights. But I don't think anybody's in here, so we should be safe."

Howard then asked the obvious. "Well if there's nobody in here, then why are we here?"

After a long silence Hall spoke. "I'm certain that this mine has something to do with what's going on. I have no idea how, call it gut feelings. But the boy disappeared while in here, Ralphie used to work in here, and I talked at length with Jim Bowman the other day..."

Howard interrupted him. "Jimbo? All-state in football for Shady?"

Hall nodded. "He was a tour guide here for about six years, up and quit one day last week. Said he was scared to death."

Again, to himself, Howard questioned the wisdom of two men with one gun camping out in a possibly haunted exhibition coal mine. "Scared of what?"

"Said Ralphie's momma was in here 'on a tour' with about twenty others—just the other day. Said the lights went out, Minnie talked to somebody for about five minutes, then the lights came back on. Said he had his hand on the light switch, something kept him from turning the lights on sooner, until her conversation with whoever was over. Walked out and will never come back in this mine as long as he lives he said."

86

William H. Radford the Third sat on top of the very hill that Chief Hall and the journalist now walked under. He and several of his men were discussing the current state of baseball and steroids when one of his scouts came hustling up the hill.

"Trey, we have a situation."

The G-man stood up and dropped the bag of chips he was so enjoying. "Go on."

"Your buddy the local yokel and that newspaper fellow just went in—flashlights, sleeping bags, the works it looks like."

Billy Radford's slight smile and nod of the head indicated the wheels were turning. With a lowered voice he began giving orders as the group moved down the hill toward the entrance to the mine. Five years of cowering to a bully in school was about to be reversed in one glorious moment in time.

87

The mother of all parties showed no sign of winding down a half hour later as Michael and Annie had got up the nerve to mingle on the fringes of the underworld hoedown. It was like they were invisible. The revelers continued to toast each other and toss wads of paper with enthusiasm. Another hour into the gathering Jimmy Taylor finally mounted the paper-covered pulpit and tried to bring the mass to order.

His pounded gavel was considerably muffled by the inch-thick paper on the podium, but after he swept it off with his hand the stone-on-stone kinetic energy began to get people's attention. Even Mothman swirled to a stop and took his seat in the middle row. Annie and Michael took their usual place behind the pulpit on benches that seemed to have been carved out for guests such as themselves. Which made Annie wonder what guests might have visited since this body was established.

She made a note to ask Ralphie in her notebook.

"Lady," Taylor nodded to Utauka who sat in her mid-level row, "and gentlemen, we have gathered here this evening on a truly momentous occasion." A chorus of 'hear hears' erupted but quickly died down. Annie could sense the elderly gathering was losing steam quickly.

"I don't know when we've had as much to celebrate in recent memory, but this certainly ranks up there with the convictions of the elders Moore and Barron. And while this involves only the southeastern counties of the state, it is a victory in which we can all celebrate." Another cacophony of sound burst forth from the group and died down quickly. Taylor seemingly eyed each one of those gathered before speaking again.

"For the second time in a decade the tolls have been lowered from two dollars back to a dollar and a quarter!" With that pronouncement he slapped the dais and backed away as the group in unison stood and cheered and clapped and threw stuff. Annie and Michael were, as was Taylor, as was most in the first couple of rows, covered in confetti and toilet paper. Annie grabbed what toilet paper she could and stuffed it in her back pants pocket. Michael noticed and began collecting his own allotment.

The ages of the revelers, combined with the intensity of the party that just ended, was evident as the combined group practically fell back into their chairs. Taylor scooted back up to the dais and continued his oratory.

"Our work on the tolls is far from done, and I ask that you remain seated and quiet during this next pronouncement." Annie and Michael looked to each other, and immediately thought of Ralph, and his uncharacteristic absence. "There is movement in both houses of the legislature to remove the tolls completely."

Some couldn't contain their enthusiasm, but the interruption was brief. Taylor continued. "Of course the 'toll authority' is suggesting that the roads will suffer and tourism and..." his voice drowned out, mockingly, as his head bobbed up and down and around and around. "Have you ever known, can you imagine, a government agency or program that isn't going to look for further funding and work to continue their existence?" His rhetorical question was answered by a handful of 'no's.' "Can you believe the arrogance of this group sitting in their air conditioned offices a FULL HALF CENTURY after the tolls were put on?"

Another chorus of 'no's' wafted up while Annie was certain she was beginning to hear snoring from several directions within the great hall.

88

"Why here?" asked Howard, laying his sleeping bag down beside the tracks. He could tell that his thin sleeping bag was going to provide little comfort or warmth.

"Hieroglyphics were right there on that wall," Hall said, pointing up as he pulled his sleeping bag up around him. "And the boy thought he saw Michael right down there," he pointed toward the entrance and the left rib of the mine. "And you got all weirded out right down there when the lights were turned out when we had Minnie in." Howard had to nod in agreement. "So I think this is as good a place as any to bed down for the night."

Howard sighed and remembered his wife's reference to the 'undermother.' His chuckle made the chief ask 'what.' Howard debated whether to even bring it up, finally decided that they needed to talk about something.

"Twice now my wife has referred to an 'undermother' regarding this whole thing, but when I pressed her on it earlier this evening she denied saying it. It was like she couldn't even remember saying it, and she had just said it."

Hall lay quietly, seeming to chew on the information a bit. "Who the heck is the 'undermother'?"

Howard shrugged. "Be darned if I know, but I'm sure it has something to do with this situation." After a long pause he asked, "Do you think they're still alive?"

Hall said an emphatic yes then began coughing. After pounding his chest with his dominant right hand he laid his head back down. "I do Howard. I can't explain it—again call it a gut feeling, lawman's intuition—but I truly believe they're ok. Maybe that 'undermother' is looking out for them," the chief said with a chuckle that grew into a hacking cough.

"What's up buddy? The humidity getting to you?"

Hall shook his head, his cough subsiding. "All that crap in my lungs after years of smoking is breaking lose. God if I survive this I'm going to become an advocate against smoking."

"I tried to talk you out of those things when you started back in the tenth grade."

"I know," Hall replied, his breath raspy. "Now that I got a couple of grandkids I want to live more than ever."

Howard smiled. His two boys were both married but so far no word on grandchildren. A noise toward the back of the mine drew each man's head up and looking in that direction. After a long pause both eased their heads back to the ground.

"Probably just a rib popping," the chief suggested.

"One of yours?" the journalist asked with a grin. Hall was about to respond when they heard another noise, this time toward the front of the mine. Both men eased up on their elbows, looking both up and down the tracks. Hall fully sat up and Howard did the same. The journalist pushed the button on his watch and saw the time—10:15. It looked like it was going to be a long night under Mother Earth.

89

The FBI agents were gathered at both ends of the exhibition mine and in radio communication with each other. Whispering to each other and those at the other end of the mine, Trey Radford had goose bumps in anticipation of what was to come.

"You make the call?" he asked for the fourth time in fifteen minutes. For the fourth time in fifteen minutes his assistant said yes. Trey squeezed the light on his wristwatch on and viewed the time, it was now 10:30. "Come on, come on," he muttered, looking back toward the parking lot for headlights. There were none.

"Listen up guys," he whispered, both to those around him and those on the other end of the walkie-talkies, "on my mark you guys in the back breach the gate and move in—slowly. Make a lot of noise. Two of you break off down the left side and hustle it up to the Y here close to us, make some more noise to keep them from turning back down that passageway and hiding. We want them coming through this front gate. Everybody clear on that?"

"Roger that," came softly through the walkie-talkie, nods were given by those standing around him. A crackle came through the walkie-talkie and a voice said tentatively, "And when do we expect that directive, sir?"

"ON MY MARK," Trey enunciated clearly into the mike, and one more time for effect, "ON MY MARK."

After a short silence the voice on the other end said, "Roger that."

Trey looked with disdain down at his walkie-talkie, hoping that his raised voice hadn't echoed through the mine to his prey.

90

Taylor could tell those gathered were worn down so he began to wrap up his comments. Annie for the first time felt some measure of compassion for this group—seeing them for the first time as old and withered creatures whose days seemed numbered.

"We do have a report," Taylor continued, "that both sides of the legislature are considering measures to remove the turnpike authority and turn the care and maintenance over to the federal government, into the Overfather's jurisdiction. THAT would be the beginning of the end, in my opinion, of the tolls on our beloved highway." Taylor slapped the podium and backed away, but only a slight chorus of 'hear hear' and 'praise be to the Overfather' emerged. Smiling slightly, Taylor pulled himself back up to the podium.

"But tonight, lady and gentlemen," Annie looked over and Utauka's head was back and her mouth gaped open, sound asleep, "we've celebrated enough. Let's take our revelry back..."

The metallic sound of a door bursting open and hitting a wall was as clear as could be and echoed throughout the chamber. Taylor stopped and several sleeping heads snapped up. Every head turned in the direction from which the sound came and stared, hearing running feet rapidly approaching. Michael grabbed Annie's arm and once again whispered that they should be ready to make a run for it. Annie uncrossed her legs and put both feet on the solid floor.

It was then that Ralphie burst through another portion of the holographic wall, his face flushed from running, his hair and eyes wild. Taylor moved around the podium and called to him. "What is it boy?"

Ralph bent over, struggling to catch his breath. "Trouble," he gasped, almost unintelligible.

He finally stood and pointed the direction from which he had come. "Possible breach..." he said, followed by deep, lung-filling gasps, "of 41B."

91

Trey Radford was looking at his watch when he saw a couple sets of headlights pulling into the parking lot of the exhibition coal mine. There was urgency to the sound of the tires as they clutched the dark pavement. Several people spilled out of the two vehicles, one a white van, the other a dark, mid-sized automobile.

"They're here," Trey's assistant said clearly, making sure that his stranger-than-usual boss was 'fully informed.' The assistant was quite disappointed with his boss' attitude since they had been assigned the case.

Trey nodded, lifted his head with confidence, and walked to meet the crew from Channel 11 News.

92

Howard, on the verge of his first snatches of sleep, awoke to the sound of Chief Hall rising to his feet, and the gravel beneath him groaning under his considerable weight. "What's up, Hall?"

"Shhhhhhhh," the chief whispered, facing the direction of the main entrance to the mine. "I heard something that wasn't natural," he said in a low whisper.

"Not natural in a ghostly kind of way?" Howard asked, now fully awake again.

Hall shook his head no, but Howard couldn't see the gesture in the complete darkness. "Voices," Hall muttered, unsnapping the safety harness holstering his gun. "You stay here, listen for anything behind us. I'll be right back."

Now Howard was clambering to his feet. "Will do," he said to dead space. Chief Hall had already moved several feet down the tracks—surprisingly quiet for such a big man. Howard nervously rubbed his hands up and down the front of his jeans, as if cleaning them might make the situation less tense. He suddenly got a chill, and for some reason remembered the old saying that it felt like 'someone walked over his mother's grave.'

He occasionally heard what he assumed to be slight missteps by the chief. They grew more and more distant, and Howard now assumed the lawman had turned the bend and was within sight of the front gate. Then he heard the footsteps reverse and come back much quicker, noisier. In the total darkness he was certain the chief was going to run over him.

"Hall, what is it?" he whispered in the direction of the footsteps growing nearer and nearer.

"Men," Hall whispered back, pulling up near the journalist in the pitch-black darkness. "Quite a few of them. Let's see if we can get out the back."

The two men had shuffled quietly for maybe fifty feet when Howard asked, "Who are they, what do they want?"

Hall again shook his head to the darkness. "I don't know, but I could clearly see six and maybe more." The big man stopped dead in his tracks and Howard bumped into him.

"Shhhhhhh," the officer shushed, holding dead still. Howard could now see what the chief was seeing. The back entrance was also covered by several ominous looking men, one or two of them smoking. "Back up slowly," the chief whispered and the two men began making their way back to their make-shift beds. They finally felt their sleeping bags beneath their feet. Both bent down and began rolling the bags up. They felt for their flashlights but knew better than to turn them on.

"What do we do?" Howard asked, his heart racing.

Hall was quiet for a long time as he continued listening for some evidence that the men were entering the mine. "I don't know," he finally confessed. "If I knew who they were, I might have a plan. But I don't have a clue who they are or what they're doing here." After a slight pause he made another confession. "I don't think they're my men," followed by yet another thought, "I think they may be Trey's."

93

Ralph, Taylor and all who could cram into the narrow passageway looked into the coal mine at two men who looked like trapped rats at a cat convention. The two men, and those close enough to the passageway, looked up and down the tracks for some sign of life. Those inside the cave wall looked with less trepidation than those inside the mine.

Taylor glanced over to Ralph. "Know them?"

Ralphie nodded. "The one on the right is the Beckley Chief of Police. Guy on the left is Annie's boss."

Taylor raised his eyebrows. "They good guys?" Ralph nodded.

"Who's at the gates?" Taylor asked of Merriweather, who had just joined the group.

"Feds," Merriweather replied ominously. "About a dozen of them." After a short silence he added, in his out-of-place Australian accent, "Oddly, sir, it looks a trap—not for us, but for those men." He pointed to the two adults just on the other side of the wall.

Without another word Taylor moved to the cave wall and, backward, spelled out the words 'Come in.' He lightly tapped on the wall then spread his arms, telling everybody to back up and make room. With no visible effort from Taylor another holographic wall appeared between the group and the original cave wall. It did nothing to deaden the sound within the mine.

"Did you hear that?" Howard whispered, his eyes looking toward where he hoped Hall was still standing, and the wall that had just made a tapping noise.

The chief was staring at the same spot. "Yeah I did." He quickly dug his shirt out of his pants and slid his flashlight up under the garment to reduce the visible light. "I'm going to shine this light at the wall and see if the hieroglyphics are back."

"We can't read them," Howard said as the softened light came on and the words 'Come in' were as plain as the nose on your face. "Holy smokes," Howard muttered a little louder than he intended.

To their right, toward the back of the mine, they heard bolt cutters sever the medium-link chain that kept the gate closed. The heavy metal gate groaned as it was forced open at an uncharacteristic hour. Flashlight beams lit up the corridor around the bend and the elongated shadows of walking men filled the chamber. Hall grabbed Howard's arm.

"Let's accept the kind offer." His light now off, Hall nodded toward the open invitation and walked the short distance to what appeared to be solid wall—until his extended arm passed through what he now realized was some elaborate magic trick. He completely disappeared, and Howard quickly joined him.

They found themselves in, basically, a stone closet. The ambient light of the approaching men also lit up their tiny hiding place. Hall placed his hands on the three walls that surrounded them to the back and found the magic had ended. He turned back and saw a sleeping bag between the tracks.

Howard too saw his sleeping bag, remembered it dropping out of his hands as he was shocked to see the writing on the wall. Quickly he jumped out, grabbed the bundle of fabric, and jumped back into their hiding place.

The lights were now visible as what appeared to be four men walked slowly in their direction. Hall whispered to Howard, "Two of them must have gone around the other way." Howard nodded in understanding, his breath held in the hopes that the wall they just passed through appeared solid to the G-men that were approaching. Howard could see the suited men and recognized one that was with Trey the afternoon at the courthouse.

The chief tapped Howard on the left arm and pointed out the now-backward words, 'Come in.' "Wish we could get rid of that."

Taylor too, standing right behind the large lawman, peered around and saw the invitation was still very much evident. With a wave of his hand he wiped clean the slate. Then, on a whim, he quickly wrote—

backward—Trey R. loves Becky M. Howard and Hall had to cover their mouths to keep from laughing out loud. Becky Mullens, a rather homely girl a year behind them, had had a crush on Trey their junior and senior years. And she was aggressive. More than once Trey beat a path around the school on the outside of the building because he knew Becky was waiting for him at or near his locker. The two men stood dumbfounded, hands clapped over their mouths, as they realized more than ever that they were in the presence of—to quote C.S. Lewis—deeper magic before the dawn of time.

Taylor looked over to Ralph. "You and Merriweather go move their cars. Hide them about a half mile away." Ralph and Merriweather passed back into the hallway, closing the metal door quietly.

94

"This is Sheila Jameson with Channel 11 News. I'm standing here with special FBI agent William H. Radford III whose men have now entered our own Beckley Exhibition Coal Mine. Mr. Radford, can you tell us what your men are looking for inside the mine at this late hour of the night?"

Alex Fourchase stood in the control room of Channel 11 News watching the events unfold right at the start of the eleven o'clock news. The rumor that came to the office in the form of an anonymous call was that something involving the missing newspaper reporter was going down at the Exhibition Mine. Sheila Jameson and a camera crew were immediately dispatched to the scene. He wore a slight smile, sensing this was the break that law enforcement—and his station—was looking for.

"Miss Jameson," Trey began, looking directly into the camera, hoping his nervousness didn't show through before his hometown crowd, "we have reason to believe that there is activity at this moment that directly affects the missing person cases of Wolf, Johnson, and Justice. We're not sure if the activity inside the mine will further the investigation," he paused for effect, "or hinder it. What my men will find should be evident real soon. I'd keep that camera rolling." With a nod to the pretty lady, Trey stepped out of the spotlight and moved back toward the entrance. He expected his plan to come to fruition at any moment.

95

At 11:15 Alex Fourchase tapped his foot nervously as he watched the regular portion of the news drone on about the recently ended legislative session. He had hoped that, by now, the Feds at the Exhibition Coal Mine had uncovered whatever it was they were looking for. He grabbed the headset of his production assistant.

"Sheila, what's going on out there? We're running out of time here."

Sheila Jameson walked away from her chatting camera crew so that she could hear. "What's that Alex?"

"What are we waiting for? The newscast is halfway over!"

"Keep your pants on chief. I can hear the phones ringing now," she said excitedly, "around the county of people calling their friends telling them to tune into our station as there's about to be a break in the case."

Alex gave that a moment's thought. "Hey," he said, thinking aloud, "Letterman's a rerun tonight, we could even preempt the first few minutes—IF we have some hard news."

Pushing the earpiece into her ear farther, Sheila agreed. "I think this is the real thing. The Feds don't usually cooperate unless there's a break in a case, and this Radford guy is pretty swelled up with...hold on chief, there's some activity. Get ready to go live."

Alex tossed the headset back to his assistant and, knowing they were on a commercial break, said loudly, "Alright people, I think we're about ready to go live out to the mine. Be sharp." People scurried across the set and the anchor adjusted his tie—more of a nervous mannerism than need.

"Three...two...one..."

"Welcome back," said the sharp-dressed news anchor. "We're going to go back live to the Beckley Exhibition Coal Mine where our own Sheila Jameson is monitoring events that could lead to a breakthrough in the missing persons cases of three of this community's residents. Sheila," he said, glancing down as if straining to hear his headset, "what have we found out so far?"

Television sets all over Beckley and the Channel 11 market switched from the newsroom to Sheila Jameson, who had moved much closer to the entrance of the mine. Her profile greeted the camera, her left index finger holding her earpiece, well aware that she was now live and on-air. She turned to face the camera, a nervous smile on her face.

"Brad, I'm standing here at the Beckley Exhibition Coal Mine where

FBI agents are scouring the scene. It would appear..." As she spoke arguing voices spilled out of the mine. "Brad let's listen in for a minute and see what we can find out."

Sheila backed out of the camera and the lens focused another dozen feet or so to the very entrance to the yawning, man-made cavern. A heated discussion was occurring, but who the players were the newscaster, and the general public, didn't know. The expensive camera and sound equipment were picking up the heated exchange, word for word.

"You said they were there," a smallish man seemed to be accusing a taller man.

"They WERE there," the taller man shouted back, I saw them go in.

The shorter man threw his arms out wide. "Well then where are they?" he asked mockingly, "Huh? Where the Hades are they?"

"I don't know Trey," the taller man said, now peripherally aware that there was a possibility that they were on camera. "Let's go back in the mine and discuss this."

"We're not going ANYWHERE!" Trey Radford shouted, shoving a finger into the face of his subordinate. "Now those men have to be in there because their cars are out here!" Trey was now pointing toward the parking lot and, ironically, directly toward the camera. He too was now aware that Channel 11 News was still present, and from the light that was on in front of the camera, they were still rolling.

The taller man delivered more bad news. "Their cars are gone, Trey."

"Get that camera out of here!" Radford screamed, rushing toward the camera. As his reddened face filled the television sets of 54% of the market area, Alex Fourchase called 'cut' and instructed his crew to go to commercial.

96

As the news returned from an unusually long commercial break, Sheila Jameson's face now looked stern as she stared into the spotlight.

"Brad, what we assumed was a break in the three missing person cases here in the Beckley area seems to have devolved into a shouting match between Federal agents who are now holed up back inside the Exhibition Mine. As you can see," she half turned so that the camera could pick up the area behind her, "we've been moved a good fifty feet from the front entrance of the mine and, unfortunately, out of earshot of what might be revealing details regarding the disappearances." Turning back to face the camera, she continued. "What we did hear before we were pushed back was certainly strange, Brad. One of the Federal agents revealed some graffiti on one wall inside the mine that said—and I'm repeating here—Trey R. loves Becky M. It was at that moment that the apparent leader of this FBI sting effort, William Radford, went literally ballistic, Brad, and withdrew his men back into the mine—after pushing us back to this point."

"Sheila," Brad interjected, their images now splitting the screen, "do we have any idea of who they were talking about before we went to break—he kept saying 'they' and 'their cars'—any ideas?"

Sheila shook her auburn mane. "Sorry Brad. Nothing to this point reveals who, or what, the federal agents thought they were going to find in this mine tonight. But one thing is clear; what they thought they were going to find, evidently they didn't. Back to you, Brad."

Brad smiled into the camera as his face now filled the screen. "We'll keep Sheila there at the Beckley Exhibition Coal Mine for a while in case there are further developments. We thank you for watching tonight, and now let's join the Late Show with David Letterman already in progress."

"Hey Paul," David Letterman said, adjusting his glasses while sitting at his desk, "did you see today where the governor of West Virginia proposed giving everybody in the state a one-thousand dollar across the board increase?"

"No, Dave, I didn't see that," Paul replied in his usually nasal voice.

"Yeah, evidently he told them to move to Ohio." The audience roared as Letterman stared out at them through his narrow glasses.

97

"You know who I hate?" Michael asked of Annie. When the passageway to 41B became a bottleneck and they could neither see nor hear what was going on, they made their way back to the meeting chamber and sat alone.

"No," Annie replied, "who?"

"I can't stand Jay Leno. He has never one time made me laugh out loud."

Annie smiled. Being an early bird, she didn't catch much late night TV, but had over the years seen enough of Leno that she had to agree. "You know who gives me the willies?" she asked of Michael. He shook his head no. "Paul Shafer, the band leader on David Letterman."

"Oh yeah," Michael said, "he gives me the creeps too."

Annie looked at her watch. "Hey look, IF it's 11:45 at night, Letterman should be on right now."

"And Leno," Michael replied dryly. Then he grabbed her wrist and looked at the reporter's watch again. "It's not 11:45. It's 12:05. Who taught you to read time?" Annie sighed.

As the two grew silent again they began hearing the faint stirrings of footsteps coming back down the ramp to 41B. The faint stirrings built to quite a crescendo as the entire group spilled back into the meeting chamber. Taylor mounted the podium and quickly went to work.

"Security council, meet in alternate chamber and prepare to reconvene in fifteen. Ralph, remain here. Everyone else is dismissed." There was a chorus of grumblings as everyone stood and made their way out of the chamber. Annie and Michael stood to go but Taylor caught their eyes and shook his head no.

"Prepare to make a run for it," Michael whispered to Annie.

Annie turned to face him. "Would you tell me one thing—where would we run to?"

Michael shrugged his shoulders and said uneasily, "41B?"

Annie's eyebrows rose, her lips pursed in thought. "That's not a bad idea, young Michael the braveheart."

98

The lawman and the editor sat on their haunches, their backs against the stone wall and listened to the intense arguing near the mine entrance. Their moods swung from near cackles to some measure of compassion for their old buddy Trey Radford. It was becoming quite clear that the trap had been set for them—Chief Hall in particular—and now he had considerable egg on his face not only in front of his men but, if they were hearing right, the entire viewership of one of the local news stations.

"Wonder what happened to our cars?" Howard whispered.

Hall shook his head. "You got me. I hate the thought of walking all the way home." He checked his phone for signal again, knowing full well that there would be none under the heart of the mountain.

"You'll have signal as soon as we get out of this mine," Howard advised his buddy.

"I know," Hall responded, "I just don't know when it'll be safe to leave this mine. Knowing Trey, and knowing how bad he hates me, he'll probably post a couple of men to watch both exits the rest of the night."

Howard looked up to the low ceiling, giving that some thought. "You're probably right," he said, "you should have let up on ol' Trey some back in high school."

Hall chuckled. "Who would have thought he'd hold a grudge this long. Heck, I ain't thought of the old boy three times since we graduated. Listen."

The squabbling died down as the men exited the front entrance to the mine. They could still be heard, but it was much fainter now. The heavy gate was closed, a chain rattled and clinked. Car doors, very distantly, were shut.

"You still got that key?" Howard whispered. Hall nodded and leaned forward.

"They didn't lock the back gate," he said, looking left and right.

"Could be another trap," Howard intoned.

Hall nodded again, leaning back. "Let's stay here another hour, see if we hear anything, then make our way out." He chewed his bottom lip as his mind raced with the possibilities. "Even if they catch us, I don't think the TV station will be here to record it."

99

Sheila Jameson and the camera crew waited a full half hour before finally packing up and heading back into the station. She knew that the story hadn't panned out as well as they would have liked it to, but it had the appearance of the first real break since Annie Wolf had disappeared. Being in the same business—video versus print—she felt a certain empathy for the lady reporter that had disappeared so completely. It could have been her, she thought, and she wondered what story, if any, had driven the abductor to such an action.

Trey and his men piled out of their cars at the Holiday Inn on Harper Road, shoulders slumped, moods foul. Several headed straight to the bar, others to their rooms to go to bed. Trey Radford went to the front desk and asked for a phone book. Knowing he had probably lost the support of his men this dismal night, he didn't have the nerve to ask them to continue to help. He thumbed through the white pages until he came across the Halls, then Lester. He penciled the number down in a matchbook. He did the same with the editor's home number, and went up to his room.

He tossed the matchbook onto the nightstand between the two double beds, pulled his shirt out of his pants and began unbuttoning it. He plopped down hard on the bed, scooting up to the headboard. Grabbing the remote, he hit the power button and found an infomercial in full swing. While he wasn't interested, it was the outside noise he needed to drown out the roar in his head. He stared blankly as the familiar guy chided, with the audience, set it and forget it.

His eyes were closed as he relived portions of the previous debacle at the mine. He wondered what he looked like shoving the camera back while he screamed incoherently. He wondered if the audio picked up on the inexplicable graffiti they found spray painted on one rib of the mine. He wondered if they had put two and two together yet—that the Federal agent, William Radford the Third—was the same Trey Radford that had grown up in the Beckley area and had once been questioned regarding the disappearance of one Rebecca Mullens. Fortunately she was later found with a guy in Boca Raton.

He picked up the matchbook and stared down at the two phone numbers. Without thinking he picked up the phone, dialed the outside access code, and pushed in the number for Lester Hall. It began to ring.

100

Taylor and Ralph sat on the back of the dais, facing and quite close to Annie and Michael. Annie glanced toward the hologram that led to 41B, sure that she could find it again, but not sure that she could outrun Ralph if she took off. Plus she'd have to get by him, as they were sitting precisely in the way.

"We've got a situation here," Taylor began, the thumbnail of his right hand digging beneath the nail on his ring finger on his left. Annie watched Ralph's body language, trying to see if this was a good situation or a bad situation. Ralph never moved, just stared off to his left as if in another world.

"Go on," she finally said.

Taylor sighed. "It would seem your disappearance—the both of you—has caused quite a stir 'on top' and it would also seem that Ralphie here is being blamed for it." He paused while Annie thought that, at least in her case, that was entirely correct. As if reading her mind, Taylor went on.

"We all know that it was a one in a gazillion chance that Ralph's anger would have led him—and you Annie—down 41A. It was equally unbelievable—and discouraging—when young Michael found 41B within two days of our first guests in over half a century." He looked up to Annie and Michael, seeming to invite comments. None were offered.

"So," he continued, looking down to the ground, "we as a group have wrestled with your…disposition, in every sense of the word." He looked to Ralph, as if for support, but the youngest member of the group continued to stare off into space. "There was a time I thought your fate was sealed, early on, and it wasn't good. And, to be quite frank, were it not for Ralph's implication in your disappearance, your fate would still be sealed."

At this, Ralph turned and looked at Annie for the first time. He seemed changed. He was no longer the bull in the china shop that she had first met. He seemed to have grown in stature, maturity. And his eyes, they held her with a measure of compassion and tenderness that another twenty years above would not have provided.

"I'm sorry," he said to Annie, his voice a whisper, choked.

A long pause followed that gave Annie ample time to wonder what Ralph's show of emotion might mean. She had almost convinced herself that she, and Michael, were about to die.

Taylor stood abruptly and approached the podium. He swept additional confetti and paper off the dais until he found bound copies of what looked to be legal documents. He returned and sat down, his feet dangling over the raised platform. He handed the yellow-bound copy to Annie, the blue-bound copy to Michael.

"In short," he said quickly as Annie opened her folder to the first page, "these are agreements that will provide your freedom."

Annie looked up at the man she knew to be homeless on the streets of Beckley. "In exchange for what?" Michael wanted to whisper to her to be cool but would have clearly been heard by Ralph and Taylor.

Taylor nodded his head toward her document. "You'll be free to go this Saturday evening. In exchange," he said, taking a deep breath, "we ask for two things, and you've already heard these." He looked to Ralph, who had suddenly found his voice.

"Your silence about this group, this location. And your dedication to using your position as a journalist to help us remove the tolls."

"What about me?" Michael asked, willing to sweep cattle dung for the chance at a Wendy's junior bacon cheeseburger.

Taylor fielded Michael's question. "You, young man, must do several things. Number one, you must attend school regularly and maintain a 3.25 average through high school, a 3.5 throughout college."

"Better than a B?" Michael asked astounded. "You've got to be kidding!"

Taylor smiled at the young lad. "You're very bright Michael. But the loss of your father has set you back both academically and emotionally. We've made arrangements—it's all in there," he said, pointing toward his folder, "to provide tutoring in any subject at any time at any location."

Michael's eyebrows rose. "Any location?" Taylor nodded. "Here?"

Taylor nodded again. "Even here. For your silence of course. Some of the best and brightest minds are in these halls, and I suspect the company would do us good from time to time."

"What else do I gotta do?"

"Aside from using proper grammar," Taylor smiled, "you 'gotta' go to law school. You gotta keep your nose clean. And you gotta take an interest in politics. We have you penciled in for the gubernatorial race in the year 2036. You'll still be a young man, hopefully have a couple of house or senate victories under your belt. And you may not win your first time around running for governor. But you will have help, and you will eventually win. IF the tolls have been removed by that time, you'll have free reign to govern as you see fit in the times you find yourself in. Cleanly of course."

"And if the tolls are still on?" Annie asked for Michael.

Taylor looked at her. "Then you, my dear, have not done a very good job. But we would ask for Michael's unfettered assistance in getting the tolls removed. He would be free to govern, with honesty, in all other aspects of his position, but we would expect—demand—his cooperation in removing the tolls."

"My mom can hardly afford breakfast for me and my brother. How's she going to send us to college?"

"It's all in there," Taylor nodded again at the portfolio he held in his hands. "I'd ask that you both read those documents completely and quickly. Our situation," he looked to Ralph and Ralph nodded, "is still upon us. We need an answer yesterday."

Annie had no doubt that she was going to sign her agreement and get the heck out of dodge. But one thing worried her. "What happens if I—either of us—break our agreements?"

Taylor held Michael's eyes while Ralph stared into Annie's. It was Taylor who spoke. "I'm afraid we'll have no other recourse but to have you terminated."

"Killed?" Michael asked incredulously.

Taylor shrugged. "Not my choice of words, but yes." He turned to Ralph. "Let's get back up topside and see that our guests get home safely."

101

The two men were both getting stiff sitting with their backs resting against the cold stone behind them. It hadn't been quite forty-five minutes since they had decided to wait it out, but Hall was willing to wait out another fifteen minutes before attempting an escape. He was 99% sure that Trey or his men would be waiting at one end or the other of the two mine exits, but was equally sure that the TV people had probably already left. Worst case scenario, there might be a mug shot of he and the editor on the six o'clock news.

Hall's cell phone began to ring. He looked to Howard who looked equally baffled. There was no way cell phone reception was possible several hundred feet underground, but there was no denying the phone was ringing.

Hall looked at the lighted display. "Huh," he said, "Holiday Inn. Should I take this?"

Howard shrugged his shoulders. "You know anybody at the Holiday Inn?"

The chief shook his head then punched the accept button on the sixth ring. "Hello?" There was silence on the other end, and Hall again said, "Hello?"

"Lester!" the voice said with a forced excitement. "Listen, didn't mean to call you so late. Was wondering if any of your people might have been out at the Exhibition Mine tonight?"

Hall covered the cell phone with his oversized paw and whispered to Howard, who was now on full alert, "It's Trey." He uncovered the cell and put it back up to his ear. "Trey, no problem. What's that you ask?"

Trey had to bite his lower lip. "I was wondering if maybe you had stationed any of your men out at the mine tonight? We had a report..."

Chief Hall winked at Howard with a big grin on his face. "No, none of my men. Maybe it was the state's."

"Might have been," Trey said agreeably, wondering how he had been played like a fool this most disagreeable evening. "Well, sorry to have bothered you. I'll let you get back to sleep."

"Trey," Hall quickly spoke before the federal agent could hang up, "how did you get this number?"

Trey huffed into the phone. "You're in the book, Lester." He hung up the phone, not slamming it down into its cradle like he wanted.

Hall slapped the editor's leg as he closed his cell phone and slid it back into his pocket. "He called the house. Somehow the call got forwarded out to here!"

"Y'all have call-forwarding?" Howard asked.

"Not that I know of. But I'm pretty sure we can get out of here now. He thinks we're at home."

The two men's knees cracked and popped as they wearily pushed themselves up to standing positions. Howard placed his hands against his haunches and leaned backward, trying to get the kinks out. "How do you suggest we leave, front door or back?"

Hall poked his head outside their hiding place and looked high and low. He pulled it back inside. "They didn't lock the back gate. Let's give that a try." He and Howard grabbed their flashlights and gear and stepped out of the alcove, stopping dead in their tracks.

"Ralphie!" Hall said, his right hand instinctively flexing as it neared his holster.

102

Annie stood up and ran her fingers through her unkempt hair, having read her agreement in its entirety. She blew out a good deal of air and looked over at Michael who was lying down with his document covering his face. She lifted one corner and caught his eye.

"Fascinating reading, huh."

Michael sat up. "I couldn't get through it. Too tough. My little brother can sit down and read an entire Harry Potter book in a week's time. I've never read much." He looked down to the multiple-page agreement in his hands. "The one book I did read—Tom Sawyer—got me down here. Thought it would be an adventure to hop off the tram in my umpteenth visit to the coalmine. Maybe next time I'd better read how to become a millionaire."

Annie lifted his agreement and found him to be on page two—of twenty-six. Hers was only fifteen pages—she felt a little slighted. But, after all, Michael was chosen by this group of misfits to be the future of governor of the great state of West Virginia. Still, twenty-six pages seemed like a lot for a bribe of silence and complicity.

"Want me to give it a once over?"

Michael shrugged. "If you want to. I'm going to sign it. I want to go home. I know mom and Alex must be worried." Annie sat down and began scanning the agreement. "What did yours say?"

Annie shook her head. "It told me one of these yahoos down here is a lawyer. I've never seen so much legalese since I covered the legislature for three days when Mannix was sick. But, all in all, it said basically what Taylor said, just much more wordy." She paused and then remembered a key point. "And it does use the word terminate."

Michael's smile was a sad one. "I'll never make it. But you will, you're already doing what they want you to do, you just gotta put some effort in getting rid of the tolls. And keep your mouth shut."

Annie nodded. "That last part is going to be hardest. You and I are going to be like the kids who went to Narnia and couldn't tell anybody about it. Only this is real life, not fiction."

"Went where?"

Annie was about to respond when Taylor entered the meeting chamber from the direction of 41B. She continued to scan Michael's agreement while Taylor straightened up the papers—and trash—on his podium.

103

Ralph held up his hands, palms toward the Beckley Chief of Police, in a demonstration that he had no weapons. The Chief relaxed his dominant right hand but remained on high alert.

"Ralph," he said tentatively, "you doing ok?"

The younger man squinted into the lights and nodded. "I'm doing fine, thanks. So are Annie Wolf and Michael Justice." At this pronouncement Howard tensed and started to move forward to throttle the guy. Hall laid his left hand on the journalist's forearm.

"So you did have something to do with their disappearance?" Howard asked.

"No," Ralph replied confidently. "We all three lost our way, we just happened to be on the same path when it happened."

An awkward silence passed between the three men as Hall weighed his responsibility to the community-at-large versus his desire to retrieve Annie and Michael unharmed. "You said they're doing ok?"

Ralph nodded. "Quite well."

It was Howard who spoke up. "Can we see them, talk to them?"

"Yes," Ralph said, "but not right now. Arrangements are being negotiated as we speak for their release."

"Release?" the chief intoned. "You're holding them hostage?"

"No, we were all being held—somewhat against our will."

Howard's patience was wearing thin. "Aw c'mon Ralph, we don't buy that. You're here, they're not." He half-turned to the chief, throwing his left arm toward Ralph. "Arrest him, Lester."

"Hold on," the chief replied. "If you're not involved in their abduction, then who is? We have the entire law enforcement community at our disposal. Even the FBI."

At that Ralph smiled. "Doesn't sound like Trey Radford is exactly on your side."

Hall blushed, wondering how he knew that. He dropped his guard entirely, took his gun out of its holster and tossed it behind him, toward the front entrance of the mine. "C'mon Ralph, level with us. What the devil is going on? We'll do everything in our power to help but we've got to know what we're up against."

Howard's jaw was slack as he watched the chief of police toss their only weapon twenty feet away. He wanted desperately to run and get the gun, but looked back to Ralph to gauge his response.

"You're not up against anything, Lester," Ralph said, his own defenses lowered considerably. "Honest, we got lost, and ran into some trouble. Not trouble that the law needs to deal with," he quickly added.

"When will they be released?" Howard asked, his jaw still set for fight.

Ralph looked to the alcove, could see through both layers of holograph, and saw Taylor quietly closing the metal door. Their eyes met, he raised the two documents in his left hand and gave Ralph the thumbs up sign with his right hand. His face was beaming. Ralph looked back to the two men.

"Saturday at four, here at the mine. I'd plan a party if I were y'all. Don't be inside the mine. We can find our way out. You two can meet them at the front gate."

Hall wanted desperately to believe the young man, but was torn between letting a suspect go and granting that trust. He voiced his part of the bargain. "Ralph, if it goes down like you said, you'll be a legend in this community the rest of your life." After a slight pause he added, "If it doesn't, I will personally hunt you down like a dog and see that you get the death sentence."

Ralph gave a slight smile. "There's no death penalty in West Virginia, but I appreciate your concern for its citizenry. Saturday at four." Ralph turned toward the alcove but stopped abruptly.

"Chief, could you do me a favor?"

Hall nodded. "Whatever it takes to get Annie and Michael back."

Ralph looked him hard in the eye. "Invite Trey to the party."

104

The Feast of the Solstice was an odd celebration, Annie thought, for a people who rarely, if ever, saw the sun. But the meeting chamber was decorated like a kid's birthday party, complete with balloons, pin the tail on the donkey, and even a piñata. Annie and Michael, with nothing else to do, were the first to arrive, finding the hall completely decorated but empty of life.

"What a goofy bunch of people," Michael said to Annie, his voice lowered.

Annie nodded. "I am so looking forward to a nice bubble bath—and commode—when I get back. But I think I'm going to miss this goofiness after I get back."

Michael chuckled. "I'll bet I'll have to write a report 'what I did on my summer vacation.' Should be a riot."

Annie looked at him curiously. "Why was there a school field trip to the mine in the middle of summer vacation?"

Michael blushed. "Summer school. I usually end up there to get promoted to the next grade. Plus it helps mom—she just has to get a babysitter for Alex."

Several representatives began filing in from the upper level, laughing and talking and paying no attention to Michael and Annie down on the floor. They took their seats and each put on their party hat, pulling the strap beneath their chin. Annie and Michael looked at each other and rolled their eyes. Then Michael donned his cap.

"You're as goofy as they are," Annie said laughing, putting her own cap on.

In thirty minutes the room was full of delegates from every corner of the state. Utauka's outfit resembled a clown's suit, with every color of the rainbow. The sky blue eye shadow seemed to be an attempt to pull it all together. She hadn't been in the hall fifteen minutes and Annie counted twenty kisses—on the lips—that she had gathered. Annie was beginning to wonder if it were too late to apply for a position.

The din slowly began to quiet down as another sound began to replace it. Annie's pained glance to Michael said it all. "Bagpipes."

The shrill sound filled the hall a good five minutes before Smokey stepped through the main entrance and made his way down the stone staircase—his cheeks red and full as he played what Annie took to be an Irish version of Dixie. He'd gotten better since they last heard him.

Behind Smokey was Jimmy Taylor. Michael and Annie's jaws dropped at how nicely he cleaned up in full tuxedo with tails, hair slicked back. He looked downright impressive—almost princely—as he followed Smokey down to the dais. He hit the floor nodding and making eye contact with many, then began ascending the few steps up the podium. He looked at Annie and winked, did the same with Michael. On the raised platform he turned and took his position before the gathered throng. The chorus of cheers and boos filled the hall many times as Smokey's song built to a crescendo.

Annie looked across the room to discover that Ralph was looking at her. He too had cleaned up nicely, but was casually dressed in khakis and a golf shirt. He smiled a sad smile then turned his attention to Taylor who was pounding his gavel like a madman.

The room finally grew silent. Taylor surveyed those in attendance. In a voice louder than Annie had ever heard, he called one name; "ARNOLD!"

With that said he pounded his gavel once, twice, three times. Those gathered began stomping their feet in unison with the slow beat Taylor had established. Michael raised his legs and joined in the call for the winged wonder. Annie finally relented and joined in the silly ritual.

This went on for a good five minutes. It reminded Annie of concerts she had been to when the lights went down and the main act was about to take the stage. It had been so long, though, that Annie began to think 'Mothman' was indisposed and unavailable—until a rush of wind took the breath of all those gathered in the hall.

The cacophony rose in decibel several levels as the winged creature was nothing more than a blur, circling the room in a clockwise direction. His speed was so great that anything loose on the desks was pulled up into his contrail. In no time the domed ceiling looked like a giant kaleidoscope, full of swirling colors led by two red streaks that had to be the beasts' eyes. The stuff directly in Mothman's contrail was a colorful blur. The detritus that had migrated toward the middle of the room swirled more slowly, twisting and turning and dancing to the beat that Taylor had established. Annie whispered to Michael that she had never seen anything as beautiful.

Mothman began to slow his flight and papers and party hats began to descend, settling on the desks where they had been located originally. The shouts and screams continued, along with the bagpipes, until Arnold settled down in his own seat along the middle row to Annie's left. Taylor began banging on the dais with his gavel again but the silence was harder to reign in this time than before.

"Lady and gentlemen," Taylor called out several times, finally getting the throng to settle down. "We meet on this, the summer solstice, as required by our original charter in section 4.2.3a. Welcome one and all, and a special welcome to our newest member, Ralphie Johnson." Taylor nodded his head toward Ralph and, with his extended palm, indicated to Ralph to rise and take a bow. Shyly the young man stood quickly, gave a nod, and sat back down. The smattering of applause was less than enthusiastic but, Annie sensed, came with some measure of respect—given Ralph's adopted suggestions for she and Michael's conditional release.

"And," Taylor continued, "we're here to say goodbye to two guests who have promised full cooperation regarding our continued attempt to remove the tolls." His raised hand seemed to be coaxing Annie and Michael to stand, but both just sat and nodded to Taylor in an embarrassed manner. The only clapping came from Ralph, with a smattering of boos emanating from around the room. Annie noticed Utauka was the most vocal of the boo-birds.

"Let's eat!" someone shouted from the back in a deep tone that sounded very much like Mothman. It must have been because Taylor reprimanded him directly.

"Arnold, we'll eat in a minute. But first we have a little business, as required by our charter, to take care of first." A few more boos followed as Taylor spread out what must have been a one-page agenda.

He recounted the recent dark days regarding the toll increase with such malaise that you'd have thought his own mother had died. But his voice lifted in joy as he recounted the increases being rolled back by the legislature—the second such increases attempted by the 'authority' in the last half-decade. He honored their most recently departed member, Ulysses, and said he was doing well in his new roll with the legislature and promised to visit before the November dirge.

He asked for new business and, hearing none, said, "Let the feast begin!" A series of whoops were let out by the Logan County delegate as the center platform filled with a meal fit for a king and his court. Annie and Michael filled two plates, remembering how good the food was the last time and how long it felt between meals since they had landed in this netherworld. Evidently all were more than hungry when these occasional feasts occurred given the ravenous, almost animal-like manner in which most ate.

105

The feast lasted three hours and featured Mothman playing badminton with a turkey leg as a racquet and anything anybody decided to throw as a shuttlecock. His backhand was as accurate as his forehand, as evidenced by the amount of foodstuff that had found its way to Utauka's recently coifed hair. And she wasn't the least bit happy with it either.

After the platform was cleared Taylor bounded up and took his place behind the dais, asking everyone to take his or her seats. It was a fifteen-minute affair but finally everyone was seated, although not all in their usual assigned places.

"We are nearing not only the end of our feast but also the end of our visit from our esteemed guests." He turned toward Annie and Michael and bowed deeply. Not a word was said—no jeers, no cheers. Taylor looked above the two, as if at a clock. "The hour approaches when we enter a new phase of our existence as an association. For the first time," he looked back down to Annie and Michael, "we'll have associates on the outside, assisting us in one of our most important issues."

He turned to look at the other side of the room. "No longer will our contact only be through cryptic communication. Annie, with the power of her pen, will make every effort to rid the southern counties of the serpentine banditry. And Michael, dear Michael," he turned and smiled at the boy warmly. "Michael will someday be governor of this great state and, among his many duties," Taylor's voice was now low and respectful, "will encourage legislation to remove the tolls once and forever from our southern route." A smattering of applause was followed by a suggestion—in a decidedly feminine voice—that they go ahead and kill 'the girl.'

Taylor winked to Annie as he looked back up to the larger group. "No, we'll kill no one this time around. We've only done that when we've had to, and fortunately this isn't one of those times. Now, if everyone will return to their home counties," Taylor looked around the great hall, "Ralph and I will escort our guests home."

Annie and Michael could feel the hair rise on the back of their necks. They suddenly felt cold, the room seemed to dim considerably. Soon it was empty, save for Ralph, Taylor, Michael and Annie.

"If you'll excuse young Michael and I for just a moment," Taylor explained, turning the boy toward the entrance to 41B, "we need to talk about a couple of things." The two made their way up the staircase and disappeared into the shortcut to the second entrance to the underworld.

106

The lot to the Beckley Exhibition Coal Mine had been full since nine o'clock this Saturday morning and the overflow spilled in every direction. The mine had an occasional capacity crowd on weekends, but usually involved multiple tour busses pulling into the lot. This was all private and government cars, with news vans from all over the tri-state area and CNN. Chief Hall used the mayor's office to make the announcement that a major break was about to occur at the exhibition mine. Channel 11, burned once before and alone in their quest for a major breakthrough, called the chief and demanded to know if this time the story was legitimate. He assured them, with fingers crossed, that it was.

There were probably a thousand people or more mingling around the cars in the parking lot. Those that could fit in the small gift shop and picked up mementos from a day that—by all accounts—promised to be collectible. Another five hundred or so spread out picnic blankets on the grassy knoll above the mine entrance with kids running up and down the gentle slopes. A hotdog vendor that usually sold around the courthouse during the weekdays had wheeled his cart into the throng around lunchtime. He was completely sold out in an hour and wishing he had brought more supplies. The summer was still sweltering.

The several television news stations jockeyed for position as near as allowed before the front entrance to the exhibition mine. Each had several dry runs testing their equipment and a few live feeds in anticipation of what was to come. No one knew anything specific, it was all speculation at this point. The local TV people eyed the CNN folks with envy and suspicion. About the only time the national news came to West Virginia was covering, ironically, coal mine disasters. This familiar scene, however, seemed to promise a better ending than most coverages of coal mines in the state.

Chief Hall and several of his deputies stood with Howard and several of his reporters and photographers behind the roped off area near the front gate. The board of directors for the exhibition mine were nearby, nervously hoping for a favorable outcome for the sake of tourism. And they were concerned with the missing citizens of the community of course. Hall and Howard had moseyed to one corner at Hall's insistence.

"What's the chance we're being played like Trey was the other night?" Hall asked his friend and former schoolmate.

"Well," Howard drawled, surveying the largest crowd he could remember seeing for a while in Beckley that wasn't inside the armory, "the main difference is that it was you and me that lured Trey into his fiasco—and we got caught up in the," he seemed to be struggling for the right word, "middle some how. We, or rather, you have invited these people here upon the recommendation of our prime suspect. I'd say the odds are not in our favor."

Hall nodded his head while sucking on a mint. He knew he was taking potentially a career ending risk, but police work was—or used to be—about instincts, gut feelings at times. He had thought maybe real estate was the way to go if this didn't work out and he lost the next election, which he probably would. He'd even talked to his wife about it.

"You realize," Howard continued, "that every news media in the surrounding area, including mine, is going to skewer you if this doesn't pan out." Again Hall nodded without speaking. "I just think we should have cuffed the guy while we had him."

Hall looked at his accuser. "What did the Undermother have to say about it?"

The journalist's face flushed. His wife had had another session of... channeling...Howard called it, and the Undermother thought they were doing the right thing. He wondered if his wife should go to counseling after this nightmare was over, IF it was ever going to be over. "Did you invite Trey?" he asked, changing the subject.

"As a matter of fact I did. Offered to share whatever results comes of this with him and his staff." Hall paused for a second. "Said he'd think about it. I'm guessing he's afraid of getting burned again. Want a mint?"

In the distance a faint noise could be heard. It was one that Howard recognized immediately. "Is that the high school band?"

The chief nodded, a smile crossing his face. "Nice touch, huh." Howard shook his head as the marching band began making their way up the driveway and the crowd began to part. The seventy-five-plus member band drove people into the back of pickup trucks, onto car hoods, and kids on top of their daddy's shoulders. Hall heard his chief deputy, Eddy, calling out to him from the direction of the gift shop. He was pointing to a small woman with a little boy in tow.

"It's the boy's mother," the deputy mouthed, continuing to point down at the young lady. Hall nodded and waved for the mother and boy to come and join him. They ducked under the crime scene tape and made their way to the chief of police.

"Glad you could come, Miss Justice," the chief said sincerely. He pulled her to the side, out of earshot of everybody else. "As I told you over the phone I've been led to believe that your boy is ok, he's not been harmed in anyway, and he might be coming home," he looked at his watch, "in about a half an hour." He nodded to the smaller boy. "His brother doing ok?"

She nodded. "He's missed his bubby a lot, but he's been stronger than me through most of this." She looked around then back up to the lawman. "Will whoever is responsible for Michael's abduction be put in jail?"

Hall nearly swallowed the half eaten mint and choked. "Of course we'll seek justice—no pun intended ma'am—with whoever is responsible. What we have to determine first is precisely that—AFTER we get your boy back safely. We'll give y'all some time together but pretty quickly we'll need to sit down with Michael while it's still all fresh in his mind."

The woman seemed satisfied with the answer and returned to her younger son's side. Howard eased over to the chief. "She ok?"

Hall unwrapped another mint and popped it in his mouth. "I picked a bad week to give up cigarettes," he said, borrowing a line from the movie Airplane. "What worries me most is that the community is going to demand a culprit. I'm not sure—yet—if we even have one."

"I'm not sure," Howard suggested, "that we even have the hostages back. Hey look, here comes Trey." Howard backed away to give the chief and the G-man an opportunity to talk, assuming they wanted to.

"Hello Trey," the chief bellowed a little too loud, "glad you could come." He thrust out his hand in a show of solidarity as he and his men ducked under the tape.

The federal agent, with many in the crowd whispering, looked down to the big paw that once—a long time ago—threw a dodgeball so hard at him that it knocked him out when his head hit the floor. His mind raced with the events that humiliated him at this very location just two nights ago. He was still certain—from post-interviews with his staff—that the Beckley Chief of Police had been there that night, as had the editor of the local paper. He was just as uncertain as to what went wrong as the events unfolded, largely on local TV. But he was grateful that his nemesis had called, offered him at least a partial chance at redemption. He extended his hand and accepted the greeting.

"Quite a crowd, Lester."

The chief nodded. "Case of the century—so far—in a sleepy little town."

Trey nodded. "How are we going to handle this?" Both men were looking out at the TV stations that had made a semi-circle around the group at the mine entrance.

"Like I said on the phone," the big man said, "we honestly don't know much. When it comes time for a statement, I'll suggest—honestly—that our office, in conjunction with that of the FBI, yada yada yada. We'll make it up as we go along. I'll turn it over to you after my yada's are done and you yada all you want to."

Trey stood silent for several minutes. Without looking up to his old schoolmate, he asked, "How did you manage to get out of the mine undetected the other night?"

Hall said nothing. Howard, standing close enough to hear the question, wondered how the big man might answer. He said nothing. Silence was his story, and he was sticking to it. The editor looked at his watch. It was five 'til four. He touched the chief on the shoulder and showed him his watch.

Oscar Davitz got his editor's attention. Howard turned to face him.

"Mark my words," said the older man, "it'll be Alfred E. Newman that will come walking out of that mine. You mark my words."

Howard smiled at the old badger and patted his shoulder. "If it is, Oscar, I'm buying you dinner tonight."

107

Ralph and Annie stood beside the platform in an awkward silence, not unlike the one at the courthouse the very first day they met. They started to speak at the same time and smiled. Ralph nodded for Annie to go first.

"Listen," she said, "I know I've been rough on you since all this happened and, now that it's almost over, I'm sorry. I really am."

Ralph blushed, shaking his head. "It's ok. I got us all into this mess. I'm not sorry it happened, I'm just sorry that I got you involved."

It was Annie's turn to blush. The Ralphie that she met at the courthouse, the Ralphie that was rocking the windows of downtown buildings, that Ralphie was gone. The man who stood before her now was taller, more confident, mature.

"I hated it here," she said, "but now that I'm about to go back, I'm pretty sure I'm going to miss it."

Ralph dropped his head and scraped the ground with his left foot. "I've talked with Jimmy, he said you can come back whenever you want to."

Annie blinked. "Utauka agreed to that?"

Ralph smiled. "Well no, we didn't exactly run it by her. We might have to keep that our little secret." After a momentary pause he asked, "Would you want to?"

Annie gave it some thought. "Yeah, yeah I'd like that. IF you can promise me that I can get back up when I'm ready to leave." Ralph nodded his head. "And you've got to install at least one working toilet somewhere—with toilet paper."

"You never found the bathrooms?" Ralph asked incredulously.

"THERE ARE BATHROOMS?" Annie asked, equally incredulously.

Jimmy Taylor poked his head through the hologram. "Almost time folks. We need to be getting up topside."

Ralph waved him away and gently took Annie's arm, leading her up the steps. "This is hard," he confessed, his legs weak.

Annie was sure she knew the answer, but asked anyway. "Why?"

Ralph swallowed hard. "Remember that first day we met, July 4th, there in the courtyard?"

Annie smiled. "How could I forget?"

He stopped, but didn't look at her. "I fell so far in love with you that day that it hurts. And now I'm letting you go again. Who knows if I'll ever see you." The tears that welled up in his eyes were matched by those in Annie's.

She took his arm and turned him to face her. "I said I'd be back," she said assertively. "And I mean it." She leaned in and kissed the tear running down his left cheek. Then she moved over to his lips.

Taylor stuck his head back through the hologram, got an eyeful and quickly covered young Michael's. He ducked back into the corridor. "They're almost ready," he said nervously.

"I never in a million years thought I'd be saying this," Annie said, "but I do love you Ralphie." The younger man smiled down at her with tears streaming down both cheeks. "I kinda envy that old bat that's going to be all over you," she said, wiping his tears away.

When he finally regained his composure, he asked the only question that he could think of. "What time do you have?"

Annie laughed out loud and looked at her watch. "It's 4:10."

Ralph smiled back. "Now is that 4:10, 4:30, or 3:50, Miss Wolf?"

Annie pulled the stem out and turned back the minute hand precisely twenty minutes. "That's 4:10, Mr. Johnson."

108

Inside the alcove in the exhibition mine Taylor made sure everybody had their stories straight. They had covered every contingency they could think of and then some. Annie and Ralph gave each other furtive glances while Michael stood as bored as he was the day he'd jumped off the tram and got into this mess in the first place. After he had spent some time with his mom and little brother, the first thing he wanted to do was to go skateboarding again. He was seriously out of practice and feared his buddies had gotten better than he.

"Ok," Taylor said with the same level of trepidation as would a parent sending their kid off to college. "It's showtime." He handed them each a pair of sunglasses.

Michael smirked. "What, do you think we're going to be celebrities or something?"

Taylor licked his fingers and combed the boy's bangs to the side. "In about thirty years you will be. But for now, you've not seen sunlight for quite some time. You'll be blind without these." He looked to Annie. "Run by when you get a chance and pay Rite Aid if you don't mind." He handed her the three price tags.

Michael put the sunglasses on but quickly took them off as they rendered the mine completely dark. They held their sunglasses to their sides as Jimmy nudged them out of the alcove.

"Off you go," he said, as might a mother bird to her flock if they had vocal chords and a command of the English language. "No, no, to the right," he said, and the three made their way down the tracks as the light got brighter and brighter. Within a hundred feet of the entrance each had their sunglasses on and thankful that they had them.

109

Hall nudged Howard and said, "Here they come." Howard had already hit the panic button and was begging the chief to send in the armed forces. Hall had asked for his patience, but was nervous too as the minutes beyond four passed.

Howard let out a sigh of relief. Tears filled his eyes as he saw a paler but healthy version of the Annie Wolf he'd come to know and appreciate for the past year and a half. Hall was motioning to the TV people to get ready—the 'unknown' event was about to happen. The three slowly emerged from the mine and shouts of 'they're back' and 'they're ok' filled the air. A roll of applause started slowly then filled the sunny day that was nearly blinding the three. Those on the hill above the entrance crowded to see, as did those in the parking lot. People stood on top of cars, trucks, even news vans. Flowers were tossed and fell at the feet of those nearest the lost souls.

Howard could no longer contain his emotions and burst into tears, pulling Annie to him and hugging her tightly. "I missed you so much," he said, "I am so sorry I put you in harm's way that night."

Annie kissed his cheek and smiled. "It's ok, Howard. I'm fine, I'm back, and a better reporter for it."

Michael's mother and brother rushed the boy and hugged him tighter than he'd ever been hugged. The book Alex was holding was pressing into his back uncomfortably. "What do you have here?" he asked, pulling the book out of his back.

"It's Harry Potter," Alex said excitedly. "You ain't going to believe what happens!" Michael looked over to Annie with a 'see, I told you so' look.

Annie smiled at her companion of late then to his mother. "He's a good boy," she said over the din that now included My West Virginia Home by the marching band. Through tears the mother nodded her head then buried her face in her son's hair, breathing him in like she had so many times over the years.

Michael pulled back and looked at Annie with a knowing look. "You kissed him didn't you?" he asked with a smile. Annie blushed and turned away from her accuser.

Howard looked to Ralph who had slunk back from the pressing throng and rested against the concrete wall that led into the mine. He eased away from the crowd and approached the grown boy.

"Ralph," he said, extending his hand, "I want to apologize."

Ralph took the hand and shook it. "For what?"

The journalist looked away momentarily, then back. "I had you guilty as sin. I would have locked you up two days ago and thrown away the key. I just want to tell you I was wrong, and I appreciate so much you seeing them back here safe and sound."

"No problem," Ralph replied, looking at Annie and envying the hugs she was getting, "it was my pleasure."

Howard touched his arm and turned to go. "Are you coming to the party tonight?"

"Where's it going to be?"

"Downtown," Howard replied, "big block party slash chili cook-off."

Ralph continued to look at Annie, who was now up to the TV reporters and almost out of sight. "I just might do that. Thanks."

110

Alex Fourchase, as with all local stations and CNN, led with the safe return of three of Beckley's citizens missing for several weeks. "Three, two and go," he called out as the anchorman smiled into the camera.

"The missing persons cases involving local reporter Annie Wolf, student Michael Justice, and Ralph Johnson came to a miraculous end today as the three walked, under their own power, out of the Beckley Exhibition Coal Mine today at about 4:15. Sheila Jameson is standing by at the mine to file this report. Sheila?"

The camera focused on the lighted image of the lovely, dark-haired reporter while the rest of the visual was under the cover of darkness. "Thanks, Brad. As you can see from these images," Alex nodded to his director to roll the tape and the screen filled with scenes of the three emerging from the mine, "Annie, Michael and Ralph walked out of the Exhibition Coal Mine without a scratch on them. At one time this man," the camera zoomed in to capture Ralph's face, "was the primary suspect in the disappearance of the other two, but as it turns out it was a case of being in the wrong place at the wrong time. The three entered the mine on their own and Ralph, who used to work summers at the mine as a helper, said he found a spur in the mine that he had been unaware of when he worked here. Brad, it would seem that the three got turned around and somehow ended up getting lost in what we assume must be abandoned portions of the one-hundred-year-old mine. How they survived with little food or water all this time is still a mystery."

The camera returned to the anchorman at the news station. "Sheila, what about the mine itself? Have steps been taken to prevent this from happening again? After all, the mine is quite a tourist attraction for not only Beckley and West Virginia residents but also for those who travel through our state."

Sheila nodded as she listened to the lengthy questions. "Yes, Brad, according to my sources the mine has been completely inspected and the spur that nearly cost these three their lives has been sealed off. As a matter of fact Brad, when those officials most knowledgeable about the mine returned inside, they couldn't even find the spur that these three wound up being lost in for all this time."

"Sheila," Brad asked, "you'd mentioned that at one time Ralph

Johnson had been the prime suspect in the disappearance of Miss Wolf and young Mr. Justice. I take it no charges will be filed now that it appears to be a case of Tom Sawyer and Becky being in the wrong place at the wrong time?"

"That's right, Brad, no charges will be filed. Both the Beckley Chief of Police and the FBI confirmed that their investigations would wrap up as soon as they completed the necessary paperwork."

"One more question," the anchorman pressed on, milking the story for nearly half the newscast, "I'll bet the families were ecstatic to see their loved ones returned home safely."

Sheila nodded. "They were, Brad. Miss Justice, Michael's mom, could hardly talk to us for the tears of joy. Michael's little brother peppered his 'bubby' with what happened in the sixth book of Harry Potter. One local bookstore promised little Alex the final book.

"As for Miss Wolf, as we all know she's never been married but her parents were here from Princeton and a couple of sisters and I can tell you for a fact the tears that flowed were tears of joy.

"Oddly, Brad, Ralph Johnson—who is by all accounts something of a loner—disappeared again amidst all the hoopla. A phone call to his mother who lives here in town was answered by a man claiming to be a Fuller Brush salesman. We took that to be Ralph simply trying to avoid us and the spotlight that he found himself in today."

The anchorman nodded. "Thanks, Sheila. Any final words on this amazing story?"

"Brad," Sheila concluded, "how many times does the national and local press converge on mine sites in West Virginia with a happy ending?" Then she answered her own question with a shake of the head. "Not very often. Back to you, Brad."

111

At work the next morning Annie could feel the curious, compassionate stares of her coworkers. She had become a reluctant celebrity—and the recipient of three cups of coffee and four pastries from coworkers who thought she needed the extra boost to get back into the swing of things. Oscar Davitz said thanks when she offered him his choice of pastry.

"It's good to have you back, Annie," he said in his gravelly, hobbit-like voice.

"Believe me," she replied, "it's good to be back. Glad I've still got a job."

Oscar winked at her then nodded toward the editor's door. "You wouldn't believe how hard the boss took it when you disappeared. We all thought he was going to lose his mind."

Annie looked in at her editor who was on the phone. She smiled to Oscar, got up and approached the windowed door. Without knocking, she entered.

Howard motioned for her to sit down as he finished his call and cradled the receiver. "That was CNN," he said. "They want some stills to add to their broadcasts today. Looks like your fifteen minutes of fame is going to last the entire twenty-four hour news cycle."

Annie blushed. "This is NOT my fifteen minutes of fame. There's more to come, believe me."

Howard nodded. "How does it feel to be back?"

"It feels great," Annie flushed, "I missed this place. You don't know how bad I missed my job while I was stuck inside that mine."

"Was it life-changing?" Howard asked perceptively.

Annie looked above Howard to the award he had won regarding mine safety a couple of decades earlier. "Yes it was, Howard. I spent a lot of time alone inside that mine—for several reasons. And I have two missions in life now."

Howard raised his eyebrows. "And they are?"

"Eventually," she said, "I intend to write a book. A book about the human spirit, and how strong it not only is, but could be when faced with adversity."

"Oprah will love it," Howard deadpanned. "And second?"

Annie smiled. "I'm going to win one of those awards, Howard. And do you know what I'm going to win it with?"

Howard shrugged. "I'm all ears."

"It's not right," she said. "You can travel from Charleston north, west, and south without a penny to your name. But you can't come east to Beckley without $2.50, one-way. That's not right, Howard, it costs this part of the state dearly."

Howard was remembering conversations that occurred inside the state capitol building with the head of security. "Are you telling me, Annie, that...the tolls must go?"

Annie held his gaze. "That's precisely what I'm telling you, Howard, the tolls must go. And I'm going to do everything in my power to get them removed."

Howard's smile was something of a smirk. "Good luck with that, young lady," wondering if by chance she had something to do with the graffiti at the capitol. "I personally don't see it happening."

Annie stood to go. "I personally don't see it NOT happening."

About the Author

Mark Scott Burgess was born in Logan County and raised in the small community of Blair. His educational background was forged in the halls of Spruce Grade School, Sharples High School and Marshall University where he received his Master's degree in geography in 1980. His entire professional career has swirled around the halls of state government and the field of property tax. He's currently employed by the state tax department as a tax manager appraising public utility properties and natural resources.

A divorced father of two beautiful girls, Burgess is an avid golfer and an adjunct professor for Marshall University. He lives in Charleston.